Praise for
THE GREAT TRANSITION

Best Science Fiction and Fantasy of the Year, *The Washington Post*
Best Science Fiction nominee, Goodreads Choice Awards

"*The Great Transition* sets itself apart through its visionary scope and possibility for change . . . Urgent but hopeful . . . an important read for those ready to advocate for future generations."
— *Chicago Review of Books*

"Emotionally compelling and humane."
— *The Washington Post*

"A page-turner chock full of optimistic ideas for how we can reimagine our collective future, *The Great Transition* is a necessary antidote to climate doom and nihilism."
— *Literary Hub*

"A magnificent debut novel that's both an important cautionary tale and a deeply compelling family story . . . I can't remember ever being more impressed with a first novel."
— William Kent Krueger, *New York Times* bestselling author of *This Tender Land*

"Hopeful, bold, imaginative, and heartbreaking, *The Great Transition* lucidly shows the incredible capacity of utopian thinking to inspire and change lives, while addressing the devastating costs of climate inaction. I can't stop thinking about this visionary novel and its singular characters."
— Michelle Min Ste̶███████████████d author
███████p Zero

"I was moved by the enormous moral conviction at the heart of *The Great Transition* and its vision of the future, one that is full of human folly but ultimately offers hope. This is a profound work of great wisdom."

—Alice Elliott Dark, author of *Fellowship Point* and *In the Gloaming*

"Nick Fuller Googins demonstrates exactly the kind of clear-eyed utopian thinking we'll need more of as we work together to solve our climate crisis, wrapping a call to action, accountability, and mutual aid in a story that's as thrilling as it is moving. Every worthwhile novel sets out to change its reader—this one sets out to change the world. I hope it does."

—Matt Bell, author of *Appleseed*

"*The Great Transition* asks what it means to start over—as a society and as individuals—and then answers with visionary scope. Offering readers thrilling glimpses into utopian possibilities born from collective mobilization, as well as an unflinching assessment of our climate crisis, Nick Fuller Googins brilliantly renders the personal political and the political personal. A must-read debut that kept me enthralled and left me inspired."

—Allegra Hyde, author of *Eleutheria*

"This book melds the huge and the intimate, the imperatives of our global climate crisis with the more compact narrative of a family trying to do right by one another when the world goes sideways. Fuller-Googins stares down some of today's biggest societal issues with abundant imagination and endless empathy."

—Emily Nemens, author of *The Cactus League*

THE GREAT
TRANSITION

A NOVEL

NICK FULLER GOOGINS

ATRIA PAPERBACK

NEW YORK   LONDON   TORONTO   SYDNEY   NEW DELHI

An Imprint of Simon & Schuster, LLC
1230 Avenue of the Americas
New York, NY 10020

First Atria Paperback edition August 2024

ATRIA PAPERBACK and colophon are trademarks of Simon & Schuster, LLC

Simon & Schuster: Celebrating 100 Years of Publishing in 2024

For information about special discounts for bulk purchases, please contact Simon & Schuster Special Sales at 1-866-506-1949 or business@simonandschuster.com.

The Simon & Schuster Speakers Bureau can bring authors to your live event. For more information or to book an event, contact the Simon & Schuster Speakers Bureau at 1-866-248-3049 or visit our website at www.simonspeakers.com.

Interior design by Kyoko Watanabe

Manufactured in the United States of America

1 3 5 7 9 10 8 6 4 2

Library of Congress Cataloging-in-Publication Data
Names: Fuller Googins, Nick, author.
Title: The great transition : a novel / Nick Fuller Googins.
Description: First Atria Books hardcover edition. | New York : Atria Books, 2023. | Summary: "A hopeful climate crisis novel exploring the possibilities of our near future and humanity's capacity for change, about one family trying to protect each other and the place we all call home"—Provided by publisher.
Identifiers: LCCN 2023026219 (print) | LCCN 2023026220 (ebook) | ISBN 9781668010754 (hardcover) | ISBN 9781668010778 (ebook)
Subjects: LCGFT: Apocalyptic fiction. | Ecofiction. | Novels.
Classification: LCC PS3606.U5585 G74 2023 (print) | LCC PS3606.U5585 (ebook) | DDC 813/.6—dc23/eng/20230607
LC record available at https://lccn.loc.gov/2023026219
LC ebook record available at https://lccn.loc.gov/2023026220

ISBN 978-1-6680-1075-4
ISBN- 978-1-6680-1076-1 (pbk)
ISBN 978-1-6680-1077-8 (ebook)

For Ella, Adela, Dario, Henry, Athena, Noah, Willow, Nirona, Hunter, Felix, Leon, Blair, Samaya, Isaiah, Solomon, Eli, Liam, Kleio, Sydney, Sabine, and all the other bright futures to come

For your friends beneath the earth,
for your friends above, prefer
a brutal rage to joy. Perform
the scarlet stroke; erase the cause
of criminal and crime.

—AESCHYLUS

THE LIBATION BEARERS (458 BC)

We are not expecting Utopia here on this earth. But
God meant things to be much easier than we have
made them.

—DOROTHY DAY

ON PILGRIMAGE (1948)

In order to rise
From its own ashes
A phoenix
First
Must
Burn.

—OCTAVIA BUTLER

PARABLE OF THE SOWER (1993)

EMI

There was this big throwback craze at school that started on Cooperative Day with a band called U2. Cooperative Day is when all the major cooperatives make presentations in the auditorium to convince you to apply. PepsiCo was there, and the Alibaba Cooperative, and CareCorps (Juniors and Seniors), and Uniqlo and Public Safety and DisneyCo and MemeFeed and tons more. The day isn't so awful except it's on a Sunday and mandatory. It got me out of garden hours with my mom, but still, who wants to be at school on a weekend? But then Maddie Choi somehow got on the network during the very first presentation—the Carbon Capture Cooperative was onstage—and she cast a song, "Sunday Bloody Sunday," through the auditorium. It was hilarious. Maddie Choi was a hero—for the prank and for introducing us all to U2. I remember sitting in the auditorium, laughing, and then suddenly quiet with everyone as we were like, *How come we've never heard anything this good before?*

Overnight everyone became U2 obsessed. Lunch was a battle zone: either you ate on this side of the cafeteria because *The Joshua Tree* was the greatest album ever, or you ate over there because *Unforgettable Fire* was best. My basketball team warmed up to "Beautiful Day." The only oldies I knew before then were Dolly Parton and Taylor Swift and Valerie June, because my dad said his mom used to listen to them. But now I became obsessed along with everyone else. The difference, however, was that to everyone else the oldies were a fad that ended like all fads end. For me though, the fad just keeps going and going.

I can pick almost any year before the Crisis and name the top hits around the world. I have them all memorized. I love oldies. Music recorded pre-Crisis sounds different. Better. More real. There were still huge problems back then. Obviously. Like the band U2 was from Ireland, which had been colonized by England for basically five hundred years. There was poverty and pandemics and like a thousand people owned everything on the planet. But nobody had any idea what was coming. Not really. It's hard to imagine what it must have felt like. I try. I pretend it's 1980 or 2010 or 1960 and we think everything is great and will continue being great forever. Not even thinking it—just assuming it. Maybe that's why their music was so good. And why I love it so much. I can slip on my headphones and turn up Madonna or Beyoncé or Prince and pretend that nothing bad is ever going to happen again.

PART ONE

CHAPTER ONE

The day before my mom leaves for extraction duty, she's not herself. She doesn't wake me early. She doesn't force us to jog upcity together. Instead, she makes breakfast. I smell it before I see it: egg tacos, sweet potato hash, warm cinnamon milk with honey. She has her screen on the counter streaming something upbeat and bland, and she's smiling—practically singing good morning—as she pulls out chairs for us to sit.

My dad and I throw each other looks like, *Who is this woman?*

My dad's always the one who makes breakfast. Also lunch and dinner. It's always been this way. He's a team nutritionist for the Tundra and he's really good at his job, even if I don't always eat what he cooks. When I don't eat, my mom will say I'm spoiled, or picky or ungrateful, or accuse me of being difficult on purpose. But I'm not. Sometimes I just don't want to eat. Sometimes I can't. Even when she tells me I have to eat so many bites, like I'm a little kid. She'll ask if I have any idea how lucky I am not to know real hunger. She'll lose her temper. She'll ignite. She's most predictable in this way.

Other ways to ignite my mom:

Tell her you want a cat.
Tell her you want your own screen.

5

Tell her you hate getting up early.
Tell her you wish you lived somewhere less crowded than
   Nuuk.
Tell her school is stressful.
Tell her Sundays aren't meant for sifting compost in the
   plaza garden.
Tell her you're scared of choking on your food.
Tell her that you're scared of anything at all.

But the day before she leaves for extraction duty, the sparks bounce off her. She won't ignite. When I take one sip of milk and push back my plate, she just smiles and says, Maybe later.

I look at my dad while she scrapes my tacos into the compost.

He shrugs like: *I'm not complaining.*

My mom's strange mood doesn't end at breakfast: usually my dad and I walk the compost to the garden and then he drops me at school, but today she insists on taking me. Except instead of walking to school—after we dump the compost—she stops in the middle of Norsaq Plaza under the shadow of the maglev tracks and touches my arm so that I stop too. Morning sun is glowing over the tallest landscrapers like an aura. People stream around us. A group of workers is unloading tools from crates. They have been building a Day Zero stage for our plaza. Next to the stage, the McDonald's Cooperative is putting up this huge food hall. Hanging on the landscraper behind their hall is a banner that curls in the breeze, the fabric rippling upward from REBUILDING TOGETHER! at the bottom to 16 YEARS AND ONWARD! at the top. I'm one thousand percent ready for my mom to make fun of the slogans, as she loves to do, and remind me of all the reasons the holiday is a chance for grown adults to play dress-up, eat junk, and get drunk, but this isn't why she stopped us. She doesn't mention Day Zero at all. She nods to the upcity rambla and suggests we go on a walk.

A walk where? I ask.

Oh I don't know. Summit Park?

I can't skip school, Mom.

Who's skipping? You'll only be late. It's the day before vacation. I leave tomorrow. Your teachers will understand. We'll make it a picnic. We'll grab lunch.

I just had breakfast.

You didn't eat a thing.

I'm not hungry.

You can get a smoothie.

I said I'm not hungry.

Well fine, we don't have to eat, Emiliana. We can just walk and talk.

———

It's not until I'm in North American History, and Mrs. Helmandi is reminding us that completed drafts of our Great Transition projects are due after break, that I realize why I didn't go picnicking with my mom.

One, what would we have talked about?

Two, I know what's going on: she hates the holiday but feels bad leaving us.

She and my dad have been arguing about it for days. Their arguing isn't unusual, only their volume. I don't care. She's always leaving for extraction duty. Nine or ten times a year. And our family doesn't even celebrate Day Zero. My mom doesn't allow it.

Yes, we slowed the warming, she'll say. Avoided annihilation. But everything we lost? We should be throwing a funeral, not a party. We should be mourning. Organizing. Working twice as hard to ensure it never happens again.

So for the holiday week, that's what we do. Literally. We work. Every year my mom volunteers us at the geothermal farms, which sounds worse than it is. You have to fly east to get there, and Greenland from a blimp is insanely pretty. The farms are by the sea with tons of hot springs and saunas. After work, you soak and watch the waves. Last year we saw orcas. But this year's different. This year we're splitting up. She's leaving for extraction duty and my dad's staying home and I'm going skiing with my basketball team.

Or I'm supposed to go skiing. The problem is this: I keep seeing myself at the ski lodge getting hungry and there are no soups, no smoothies, nothing easy to swallow. And instead of helping me, like teammates should, the other girls laugh as my throat closes up while I'm stranded hundreds of miles from home. So I've decided I won't go skiing. I haven't told my mom. She will one thousand percent ignite. I guess I'm saving the spark. Which brings up one last reason I couldn't skip school to walk and talk with her, even though a part of me really did want to: sometimes it just feels good to tell her no.

CHAPTER TWO

The day before Kristina leaves for New York it is like we have woken up as a family ten years in the past. You cannot go back. Not overnight. I know this. Still.

The first thing that is different is she does not shake Emi out of bed to jog with her. Their morning argument is my usual alarm. Today Kristina jogs solo, returns, showers off. Then there's no sound of the front door. She does not leave for the windfields or the energy docks. She pops her head in and tells me not to step one damn foot out of bed until I can smell the coffee. After breakfast she insists on walking Emi to school. She puts a hand on my chest. Kisses me goodbye. Gestures that may not sound terribly exciting. But. Her hand over my heart. Her lips. I am washing the dishes when she returns.

Hey you, she says.

Hey yourself.

She swings the compost bucket under the sink. Leans against the counter. Smiles.

You look happy, I say.

I have news.

Do you now?

9

I hold my breath. Praying she has not decided to run again for Leadership Council.

You're going to skip work, she says.

I am.

Yes. You're going to skip work to stay home with me.

It's the day before vacation, I say, turning off the water. Staying home won't look great.

I'm doing it.

Easy for you, shipping out tomorrow.

She slides behind me. Wraps her arms around my waist.

Please?

I examine the sponge in my hands. The soapy suds. Her hands.

Convince me, I say.

We'll catch up, she says. Have fun. Celebrate us.

I continue scrubbing the spatula. Kristina rests her head against my back. Her breath is hot through the threads of my shirt. I try to relax as if this is a common marital scene for us. It is not common. I could remind her of this. I could unclasp her hands and say it is not fair to turn a page backward right before she leaves. Not fair to me. Not fair to Emi.

But then again if you are dreaming a soft warm dream why risk waking up?

All right, I say, rinsing and racking the spatula. Let's celebrate us.

CHAPTER THREE

After school comes basketball. After basketball comes CareCorps. CareCorps is where I fulfill my hours by feeding kids, playing with kids, soothing kids to sleep for naptime. Today I introduce them to a band called ABBA and a game called zombie tag. After we dance and eat each other's brains and the last of their parents have picked them up, Maru walks me home. Maru's my neighbor. She lives below us. She's a CareCorps lead attendant, and even though I'm taking a class at school—Early Education and Child Development—everything I've really learned about kids is all from her.

How was basketball today? she asks as we turn off the lights.

Okay. We scrimmaged.

Scrimmage means you play against your friends?

I wouldn't technically call them my friends.

Their loss.

Yeah.

We walk outside and onto the upcity rambla, then Maru asks: Before a game, if you could run onto the court to any song, what song would you choose?

Nirvana? I say. Smells Like Teen Spirit.

Do I know that one? she says.

I synch my headphones. She slips them over her ears. Frowns.

11

Smiles. Hands them back and says the fantastic thing about music is that there's something for absolutely everyone.

I laugh.

Maru takes care of kids but has none of her own. Just her cat, Alice. You might think living alone with a cat would make someone shy. Not Maru. I interviewed her for my Great Transition project. She did seven deployments with Deconstruction Corps, which my dad says was the worst because of the bodies you came across. Maru was easier to interview than my parents. She talks to me like I'm an adult. She asks interesting questions. About school. About music. About life. If Maru had asked me to skip school to walk upcity with her this morning, I think I would've definitely said yes.

We've almost reached Norsaq Plaza when she asks about my ski trip: All packed for the North Pole?

Actually, I'm not going.

What happened?

Don't feel like it.

She opens her mouth like she's about to say something. Then she smiles: Smart girl. Freeze your butt off some other time. Z-Day only comes once a year. You'll love it.

We step into Norsaq Plaza. The holiday is still days away, but the neighborhood is so busy it feels like Day Zero could start any minute. Workers are setting up speaker systems, bolting together dance floors. Maru and I step over extension cords, cables, strings of glass bulbs that clink as they snake along the tiles to be hoisted onto lampposts. Two artists are finishing a mural: Wind Corps workers swinging a turbine into place. A famous image but the muralists are painting it with these unexpected colors and lines.

I heard it's so crowded on Day Zero that you can't even move, I say.

This is Nuuk, girl—find me one place that isn't crowded.

And doesn't everyone just get super drunk?

Wrong. We get super drunk and we dance. It's the best day of the year, girl. People thought last year was big, but this year's supposed to be even bigger. I'm glad you'll be around. About time you get to experience it.

Then we're inside our building and outside my door. For a moment I think we've accidently entered the wrong floor; the door has the correct number, but from the other side comes music and laughter.

Sounds like you got a party of your own, says Maru, and kisses my cheek goodbye.

My mom and dad don't hear me open the door. They're dancing. My mom's wearing a dark blue dress I've never seen. My dad has a black tie. The air's warm and heavy like the Tundra training room. Like they've been here all day.

Hi? I say, hanging my keys on the hook.

Emi! they cheer like I've been gone for years.

Thank God! shouts my mom over the music. Cut in. Please. Your father's a terrible lead.

It's hard! laughs my dad.

It's the rumba, she says. You just follow the steps. It's no different from a recipe.

It's *so* different from a recipe!

You'd think I'd be happy to see them laughing instead of fighting— and I am happy—but I also feel this pressure behind my eyes, even though nothing remotely sad is happening. I notice my mom's lipstick, the color of beets. I notice the same beety color on my dad's neck. I notice wine on the table, the bottle empty, and dishes piled in the sink. I notice that my mom isn't wearing her hair up like usual, but down, hiding her bad ear and cheek. I can't remember ever seeing her so pretty.

Come, Emiliana. Dance with me.

All yours, says my dad with a bow. Good luck.

I stare at him, waiting for a wink—some clue like he sent me over breakfast to let me know we're still playing along with her. But he sends no clues. Just his dopey smile, which makes me feel like he and my mom are the ones in on the secret together, without me.

I'm gross, I say, picking at my clothes. I smell like kids and basket-ball. I have to shower.

Wait! says my mom. I made you a smoothie! It's in the fridge.

I'm not hungry.

It's blueberry and peanut butter. Your favorite.

You drink it. I have to get started on homework.

Homework over break? says my dad. What's wrong with these teachers?

My Great Transition project, I say, heading to my room. I told you. It's half my grade.

They argue for me to stay and dance but—trust me—I've heard them argue a million times louder and harder.

CHAPTER FOUR

LARCH

Kristina and I are cooling off in bed. My finger traces the valleys and hills of her vertebrae in the dim cityglow that fills our window. The bed belongs to both of us in name but does not always enjoy us as a unit. Many nights one of us takes it solo. Alternating with the futon. I know we are not the only couple that fights and makes up and fights and makes up. But we have been stuck for so long on fight that making up now feels like an unexpected gift that must be returned. I do not want to return it. I want to keep tracing the topography of my wife's body. Run my hands down her strong legs. Take in her warmth. Fall asleep together. Wake up. Repeat and repeat until we are old and soft and our memories a little crumbly so only the happy bits are left.

What are you going to do by yourself all week, Mister Bachelor? she whispers.

Miss you and Em.

Liar.

We are trying to keep quiet, for Emi's sake, but when Kristina accidently knees my butt as she climbs on me we cannot help laughing.

Seriously, she says, sweeping her hair from my face.

Seriously. And while I'm missing you I might sleep in. Sleep in and cook big disgusting breakfasts.

Breakfast nachos?

You know it.

Mmm. What else?

Organize the clubhouse kitchen. Sharpen the knives. Season the cast iron. Do inventory for the rest of the season. Thrilling stuff.

What about Day Zero? she asks, not missing a beat.

Probably get a beer with Lucas.

Probably?

Most likely.

Just one?

Possibly more than one.

But upcity, right?

Upcity, I repeat.

You won't go to the Esplanade. Even if Lucas wants to.

I take a calming breath. It is one thing for Kristina to volunteer for extraction duty over the holiday and another for her to tell me how I can celebrate with my friends in her absence. But she has been adamant: Making me promise that I will not join the big parade by the seaport. Making me promise—in her words—that I will not be a sheep among sheep.

Larch, she says, not whispering. You won't go down there, right? Let me hear you say it.

I'll try my best to resist, I say. But you know Lucas. He can be convincing.

She withdraws her arms and legs. All her warmth slips away with her. She pulls on a shirt. Gathers her hair. Begins pulling it back violently. Turning her head. Giving me her face. Her ear. She would never admit that she uses her scars like armor when she is upset but I know. Her way of telling me we are waking up from the dream of today. She is done acting like we have traveled back ten years as a family. And so am I.

What's wrong? I say.

Nothing's wrong.

You're the one who told me to call out. You said we'd catch up.

We did, she says.

We had lunch. We got drunk and danced. We fucked.

Well what do you call that? she says, stepping into sweatpants.

Just say whatever it is you want to say, I sigh, exhausted at the idea of another round. But the bell has rung. The fight is on. I tell her that this feels very much like some political stunt—volunteering over the holiday while everyone else celebrates. I ask her bluntly: Is she running again for office?

She laughs. No. That ship has sailed.

Then don't leave tomorrow. Go next week.

I can't.

Says who? The world won't fall apart without you loading batteries for two weeks.

It would if everybody said that.

Everybody is not saying that! Stay. Emi will be skiing. We'll get the week together. Think about today. How great was today? We could have a week of todays. We won't do any holiday stuff. We can just work. If that's how you want to celebrate. At the garden. The docks. Wherever. But we should be together.

I'm sorry, Larch. I can't.

What if I come with you? I say, sitting up, my back against the cool wall that separates our room from Emi's. We could go to New York together.

She shakes her head: I need to go alone. I told you.

I could just show up at Gowanus and work with you. I don't need your permission.

She laughs. You're going to volunteer for extraction duty? Over the holiday?

Sure. Why not?

She raises an eyebrow, then shakes her head. No, she says, pulling on a sweatshirt. The answer is no.

Sixteen fucking years, I say.

Keep your voice down. Emi's sleeping.

Sixteen fucking years, I whisper. Everything isn't perfect. I know that. But there's still a lot worth celebrating.

Not for everyone, she says.

For us, I say. So celebrate it. With me.

I can't.

You *could*.

I won't.

I blurt the obvious and not for the first time: Are you seeing someone else?

She looks at me through the dim half-light for a long moment, then puts a knee on the bed. Another knee. Crawls over in that way that gets me every time. Takes my face in her hands.

Larch. Listen to me. Seeing someone else is the last thing on my mind.

Then what is? What's on your mind?

Even in the dim I catch a shine to her eyes. Like she wants to cry. Like she wants me to tell her she is allowed to cry. Allowed to lower her armor.

Instead it is me who opens up. As always.

She catches my tears with the back of her hand. She wipes her hand on my chest. You're right about today, she whispers. Today was so wonderful. My love. Let's not ruin it.

CHAPTER FIVE

EMI

With my headphones on, and Nirvana playing as loud as I can make them, I can't hear my mom or dad through the wall. But I can still imagine I can hear them, which is somehow worse. Each time I take off my headphones to check, they're trying to be quiet, and failing. The moaning is the worst. So I keep my music loud. Lie in the dark. Feel my heartbeat in my fingernails and ride the wave of my hunger.

I can't say if hunger is the same for everyone, but for me it starts small—a little wave in my belly, which swells without warning into something large and panicky that begs me to fill it. With focus, I can ride the crest of the wave and glide down the other side. Then the wave will close out neatly into a flat, still surface that sparks with a kind of giddy light-headedness that melts everything away. Even when the world is spinning so fast—everything that's wrong or could go wrong—if I ride the wave just right, I can control the spinning. Like magic, the spinning stops, and I disappear into something clean and calm and completely mine.

That's one outcome of riding the wave. The other outcome is I fall. Falling off the wave is like the ocean opens up and wants me and everything else. Then the world comes rushing back—school, grades, kids at school, my parents' fighting, my mom yelling at me about the Crisis and how it could happen again—spinning faster than before.

Falling happens most easily after basketball practice. Or in the school cafeteria. Also late night such as now when there's a blueberry peanut butter smoothie in the fridge. Times like these demand the highest discipline. Your hands shake. Your heart hammers. But the reward's worth it. Because it's important to know hunger. My mom grew up in a border camp. Once as a girl she went four days without food. She says it made her stronger. She isn't right about everything, but she's right about this: not only to know hunger, but to feel it in your core. How else can you control it?

I switch from Nirvana and lower the volume. Finally it's silent through the wall. Quiet at last. But no.

Emiliana?

My door is a pale rhombus of light. I close my eyes. Slow my breath. Twitch a little. Pretending to sleep. I want her to leave me alone. At the same time, I don't want her to leave me alone. I don't want to want both of these things at once, but with my mom, it's often the case.

She sits on the edge of my bed. If she's brought my smoothie, I'll tell her I don't want it. She puts a hand on my forearm. She rocks my shoulder.

Hi Mom, I say, sliding my headphones off one ear, leaving the other guarded.

Hi sweetie, she says. What are you listening to?

Music.

What music?

You wouldn't know. It's old.

So am I. Try me.

Britney Spears.

She laughs lightly: I remember Britney.

Okay.

She sits there holding my arm. Her hair's no longer down. She smells warm. Sweet. She doesn't have my smoothie. She crosses and uncrosses her legs. Like she's waiting for me to say something. But that's her job. She's the mom. Not me.

Did you finish your project? she asks.

It's not the whole project, I remind her for the millionth time, it's just a draft.

Did you finish your draft?

No. It's huge. I'll be lucky to finish it by the end of break.

I'm one thousand percent ready for her to say how lucky I am to be worried about school instead of refugee camps or wildfires. But tonight's like this morning. She won't ignite. She squeezes my arm and says I'm a good student.

Thanks, I say.

You try so hard at school, Emiliana. I'm glad you asked me to help with your project. I wish I could've interviewed my mother like that.

Yeah, I say.

There's a long pause that just keeps on pausing. I'm grateful for Britney even if she's just singing in one ear.

Then my mom asks, Are you excited to go skiing with your friends?

This would be the time to tell her the girls aren't my friends—just my teammates who invited me because our coach probably made them—and no, I'm not going. But my mom's been nice today. She hasn't made me feel guilty for anything. She made me a smoothie. She's trying.

Yeah, Mom. I'm super excited.

You'll have fun, she says, then whispers my name again: Emiliana?

Yeah?

She lowers her voice and switches to Spanish: Everything I do, I do for you. For your future. You know that.

Thanks, I say in English.

But do you? Do you know that?

Yes, Mom.

Never forget what happened. How close they came to destroying everything. And how lucky we are. You can't understand. You're fifteen. That's why I tell you. We're so fortunate. We fought so hard for this. But it's not over. Don't let the holiday celebrations make you forget.

Okay.

And remember that you are strong.

Thanks.

You're so strong when you want to be.

Okay, Mom.

She kisses me on the forehead and leaves, closing the door to seal off the light. I stare at the ceiling in the darkness and promise myself—if I'm a mom one day—never to make my kid feel guilty for things she can't control. Like being born after the Crisis. Like going to high school instead of saving the world. Like having a room of her own and food whenever she wants it. I promise my future self to remember that if you tell your kid how lucky she is, it never makes her feel lucky. It makes her feel terrible. Like it's her fault for being lucky, and her fault for needing to be told all the time how lucky she is, and how everyone has sacrificed everything so she can continue being so lucky without knowing how lucky she is.

I fold my pillow and face the wall, my stomach clenching, the world spinning. This is how you fall off your wave. I rebalance. Refocus. I'm glad she didn't bring my smoothie. At the same time I wish she had.

Then my door opens. My mom's back. She remembered the smoothie after all.

But no. Wrong again. Four quick steps across the room.

Scooch, Em. Make room.

She slides under my blankets. Puts an arm over me. Folds her legs behind my legs. All my body is tense. This isn't something we do. Not since I was young. But as the seconds go by, she begins breathing deeply, and I relax. Muscle by muscle. Even my stomach. Like melting. Like the best sort of melting. Something has changed. Between her and my dad. Between us. Maybe she's made the same decision as me not to leave this week. In the morning she'll be here, bags unpacked, shaking me awake to jog with her, and I'm saying, Okay Mom, and we're running to the very top of Nuuk and she's wearing her hair down and me too and our hair's blowing behind us like one long scarf one banner one cape.

But, of course, we're not. As suddenly as I've fallen asleep, I'm awake.

I'm awake and she's gone. Not gone from my bed. Not gone jogging. Just gone.

I pull on a sweatshirt and drag myself to the kitchen where it smells like coffee and toast. My dad's streaming a sportscast. The table is set for two, not three.

Morning, Em! What can I get you?

The smoothie that Mom made.

How about something warm? Oatmeal? Eggs? Tapioca?

Just the smoothie, thanks.

You sure? I'll make anything you want.

Yes, Dad. I'm sure.

Emi Vargas Brinkman
North American History
Mrs. Helmandi
Great Transition Project (First Draft)

Introduction

Imagine your home is on fire, but instead of getting the fire department, you just watch the flames and live life like everything is fine. That was the Climate Crisis. It's hard for people now to imagine, but during the Crisis, everyone knew what was happening and did basically nothing to stop the criminals causing it. When my parents were my age, to take one example, the destroying classes were still extracting oil and producing gas-powered cars and airplanes while getting richer and richer. Some people like Mama Greta tried to stop them but failed. Then the West Antarctic Ice Sheet collapsed and the Great Transition started.

The Great Transition led to everything good that people take for granted now, including the Southwest Solar Authority, the Half Earth Accords, the San Francisco BayGate, the Big U, the Great Green Wall, plus carbon and methane capture, and new cities like Nuuk, as well as recycled old cities like Miami, where life was impossible because of heat waves and flooding and mosquito diseases like West Nile and dengue, which we thankfully have vaccines for now.

All of these combined efforts helped get us to Day Zero. Day Zero was the day the world reached net-zero emissions. This year is the sixteenth anniversary. Most people treat Day Zero as a major holiday but not everyone. Some people (my mom, for example) say celebrating Day Zero would be like my basketball team celebrating a win after losing a thousand games in a row while destroying our own court and all getting injured. Other people (my dad, for example)

Maybe a more neutral term? "private corporations" or "extractive industries"?

Wow, this is a long sentence! Fantastic supporting details but try to avoid run-ons.

Strong claim! Could this be your thesis?

say that's exactly when a win is needed most. In conclusion, the Great Transition was essential for our survival, but should have started decades, or even a century, earlier. Then kids now would be able to see animals like koalas, giraffes, and elephants. To add on, we would have white sandy beaches and coral reefs with neon fish. Lastly, billions of people wouldn't have been forced to flee their homes or die. For example, my grandparents, who never got to hear about the Great Transition, or celebrate Day Zero, or meet me.

Emi: Biographical details about you and your family were PERFECT for our Personal Narrative unit of study, but they aren't as appropriate for informative historical writing. Please reread the assignment and keep this in mind. I'm excited to see what you come up with. I can feel your passion on the page!   – Mrs. H

PART TWO

CHAPTER SIX

LARCH

Fireworks before dawn. Bass thumping our walls. Neighbors laughing loudly getting a big jump on their day drinking. Today is the day. I roll over and turn on my screen. Parades in Wellington. Moscow. Johannesburg. Minsk. Upsala. Holiday inching our way with the sun.

Dad?

Emi in the doorway.

I pat the bed: Holiday watch party, want in?

No thanks. Want to run?

I flip on the light. Emi is dressed in basketball shorts and a sweatshirt. Her sneakers in one hand. My sneakers in the other.

Seriously? I say, yawning. Okay. All right. I'm awake. Let's roll.

Our jogging loop is a zipper—straight upcity and straight back down—a route that sends us through each of the six plazas above ours. If Kristina were here she would be clocking Emi. Pushing her to lift her legs higher. Beat her best time. Emi and I keep an easier pace as we pass beneath the streetlamps and the hanging gardens and the last wisps of northern lights. Two mornings since Kristina has left and two mornings Emi has woken me early to jog: her way of saying she is happy to do anything that her mother does not force her to do. I don't mind. Except today. Today I mind a little. It is extremely early.

We are not alone in the first glow of dawn. Workers in headlamps putting final touches on food booths. Unloading portable toilets. On Sorlaat Plaza three older women in beach chairs and blankets have arrived early to stake a spot. They wave sparklers as we run by.

At Summit Park—when Kristina jogs with Emi—they do push-ups and squats and lunges. On our own Emi and I high-five and throw in a few half-assed hamstring stretches. We catch our breath as morning turns the horizon into a thin pink ribbon. Still too dark to see the bay or the fjords. Little cotton balls of fireworks burst silently below, lighting up columns of geothermal steam from the plants. Strains of music reach us from downcity. Horns and bells. One loud drum thumping quarter notes. I squeeze Emi's shoulder: Happy Z-Day, Em.

Happy Z-Day, Dad.

Emi should not be here this morning. She should be skiing with her teammates. Am I disappointed she backed out of her trip? A little. She worries so much. I want her to be a carefree kid having fun with friends. But she is growing up. I must accept that. She is making choices for herself. And this week she chose me. I squeeze her again.

I love you lots, Em.

Love you too, Dad.

We watch fireworks. Enjoy the quiet. Then she asks, Are you glad Mom left?

Glad? No. I'm not glad.

But it's more fun without her. You have to admit.

I don't like to hear that. Your mother loves you.

I know, but she always—

Emiliana. She just wants the best for you.

Hey party people! Happy Day Zero at the top of the world!

Five young men stagger over the lip of the park. Draped over each other laughing and weighed down with bottles. Either the end of a long night or an early start to a long day.

Emi steps behind me.

Happy Z-Day fellas, I say.

They totter over. One hugs me. Another pushes a shot glass into my hand. I toss the liquor over my shoulder when they cheers and throw their heads back.

─── ──

Emi and I return downcity juking through the growing crowds. Norsaq Plaza sounds as though every speaker wall has been assembled and every DJ is playing a test set. The music stops Emi. She bobs her head. Shuffles her feet. Dawn has chased away the last of the northern lights. Emi asks if we can stay.

Let's go home and eat first, I say.

I'm not hungry.

You will be. We have a long fun day ahead of us.

Then we'll come right back?

Her excitement is contagious. I feel the spark in our kitchen standing at the sink: Emi chugs a glass of water then wipes her mouth and asks—practically yells—out of nowhere if we can go downcity to the Esplanade? Please?

I hear Kristina's voice in my head and I almost say no. But I do not say no. I entertain the idea. Emi must be the only kid in Nuuk to miss last year's big anniversary celebration. And this year is estimated to be even more spectacular. She does not love crowds but she will be okay by my side. And how special to experience her first time with her? Especially from the Tundra viewing box with Lucas and the team. Plus if Emi is volunteering—begging—to step outside her comfort zone then I have to encourage her. Although she is not merely stepping outside her comfort zone. She is also rebelling against her mother. Like the early-morning jogging. But a little rebellion is a good thing. Kristina of all people would agree. Kristina who has not been in touch once since leaving for New York. So maybe—if I am being honest—I want to rebel a little bit too.

Sure, Em. We can go downcity.

Really?

Why not? I laugh. We'll go straight to the Tundra box, watch the parade, then come straight back. Deal?

Deal, she says, bouncing over to hug me.

Deal, I say again. But first breakfast.

———

Meals have become difficult for Emi. She prefers soft foods. I try to accommodate. Breakfast this morning is a gazpacho of cantaloupe and peach. Applesauce. A single hen egg slow-poached. I crack the shell for Emi as she sits. The egg is warm and creamy and perfect. I nudge over the saltshaker. I pour a glass of watermelon juice for her. Coffee for me.

I watch her examine her food. I say nothing. I eat.

I was genuinely excited for her to go skiing this week. I want her to stay up late with other girls eating junk. Laughing, slaphappy. Kristina agrees she needs to spend more time with kids her age. Emi seemed excited too—bags packed—but then two nights ago she backed out.

What if something happens? she wanted to know.

Something will definitely happen, I told her. You'll have fun with your friends.

What if I fall off the ski lift?

They have safety bars.

What if there's an avalanche?

The resorts are very safe, Em.

What if I choke?

You won't choke.

I could.

Then do this, I said, and demonstrated how to perform a solo Heimlich using the back of my chair. A skill everyone should have—especially Emi who was never an anxious child but fifteen now and she suddenly is. Anxious of crowds. Anxious of choking on food. Kristina and I have different theories of what is happening. What we should do.

Lately Emi has been gagging on her food. She says she can't help it. I say the problem is anxiety. Anxiety from what, Kristina wants to know. She says Emi has it too easy: without anything to challenge her, her mind is inventing challenges. When Emi declared she could eat only smoothies, Kristina all but gave away our blender. Today it's smoothies, tomorrow it's something else, Kristina says. We cannot give in so easily.

But this week, without Kristina, I decide I will. Give in. Give my girl whatever she wants.

———

I change into my old Forest Corps jumpsuit and return to the kitchen and sneak a peek at Emi's plate. She has not eaten a thing—just redecorated her food like a pro.

Well, how do I look?

Fat? she says. Old?

Wrong, I laugh. I look like a hero.

That is the message they push in the lead-up every year. Plastered on the maglevs and windbelts and banners on farms. The old episodes of *Corps Power* they love to recast on a loop.

Correction, Emi says. You look like a fat old hero.

I suck in my stomach and say that most veterans cannot even fit into their uniforms and Emi points out I'm not exactly fitting into mine and we laugh and the laughter feels so good—like a vitamin that has been missing from the diet of our family for too long.

Can we go now? she asks.

Try to eat something first. Have a bite of egg.

I did.

Doesn't look like it.

I mean I tried.

Can you try again?

Emi has the same wavy hair as Kristina. Same thin upper lip. Same skin that freckles and browns at the mere mention of sunshine. The likenesses end there. Kristina is not tall but she is solid. Emi on the other hand is all length: already taller than her mother. But too thin. She has a calcium deficiency, her doctor tells us. She needs more calories. More protein. She had a difficult start to life. Born premature. In and out of newborn intensive care. Infections and IV drips and catheters. I worry that she might never catch up.

We'll be on our feet all day, I say. You need energy. Just a few bites. Please, Em?

She will not look up from her plate. We are no longer laughing.

Her teachers have had her studying the Crisis all fall. Big research projects to honor the Transition. She has interviewed me. Kristina. Our neighbor Maru. I think it was too much too soon. Kristina disagrees. She thinks research projects are too little. It's unnatural for a fifteen-year-old girl to begin and end each day in luxury, she says. The human body is not built to sustain endless comfort. She must face challenges—and no, the basketball court doesn't count. She must have something to overcome. Something real.

I watch Emi mash her egg into paste. She has never gone hungry. Never worried for water. Never inhaled a burning forest or waded through a drowning city or buried friends. She missed the collapse of the ice sheets. The extinctions. The evacuations and migrations. I like to believe this is a positive development. I like to believe we should not worship the past. Instead start over. A blank happy slate.

Yet we must remember. Like Kristina always says. To avoid our mistakes and such. And our children must face some adversity. I know this. As a father. As someone with common sense. But does knowing make it easier? It does not. The other night for example, watching Emi practice the Heimlich on the back of her chair to rehearse for a time when she has nobody to save her—not Kristina, not me—it turned my vision narrowblack. I told her to stop. Maybe yelled at her to stop. Maybe knocked the chair away and hugged her thin body to mine and told her she didn't have to go skiing if she didn't want to. She could shadow me at the Tundra arena all week. Hang out in the clubhouse. Help with inventory. Meal prep. We'd have fun. I promised.

Dad? she says now at the kitchen table.

Em?

She looks up. Her eyes are glassy.

I can't eat, she says.

That's okay.

Can I make a smoothie?

No, I tell her. Let me.

———

Norsaq Plaza is a solid mass of people dancing and singing and swaying and sweating. So many bodies that they block the view—no fjords or bay. Just a panorama of celebration. We shoulder through. Emi's hand hot in mine. You're doing great, I tell her. Broken glass pops underfoot. A slight tang of vomit in the air.

Larch my man! Emi! Happy Z-Day! Have a nip!

Maru hugs me. Kisses Emi. Knights us with beaded necklaces from the collection around her neck. She is so intensely happy and red-eyed from whatever liquid is in her jar that Emi cannot help flashing her gums like she does when smiling her radiant unguarded smile.

Hi Maru.

Hey there girl.

We are fortunate to have Maru as a neighbor. She mentors Emi at CareCorps. Walks Emi home. Trusts Emi with feeding her cat when she is gone on extraction duty. Today she is wearing her Deconstruction Corps uniform. A patch on her sleeve: Miami Company. Meaning Maru has earned the right to celebrate as hard as she wants.

Make it a party, Larch baby, just toss it on back.

I take her jar. It is cold fire behind my eyes one instant then a heavy blanket the next. My pulse drops. The music wobbles.

And you girl?

Emi looks at me.

Special occasion, I shrug. Don't tell your mother.

Where is wonder woman? Maru asks as Emi sips and coughs.

Brooklyn, I answer. Extraction duty.

Maru raises an eyebrow: Storm season. Tough draw.

She volunteered.

Course she did.

We're going downcity! Emi blurts. To the Esplanade.

Just for the parade, I add.

Can you get me in that VIP box with your Tundra girls? Maru asks.

I tell her where to meet us. Assuming she can still walk by noon.

She eyeballs her jar and estimates her chances at twenty-eighty.

We laugh. She kisses Emi. Shimmies off.

Emi and I bump into a few more neighbors as we weave our way to the maglev platform. Waiting for the next downcity train is a dance troupe in face paint and headdresses. A youth group in red uniforms. More people surge onto the platform. Emi holds my arm.

One of Maru's jobs during the Transition was to find people who drowned, she says.

Deconstruction was not fun, I say.

You did some.

Not like Maru. South Florida was a very challenging deployment.

I know, Emi says. People drowned in their attics. Maru had to chop through the roofs. That's why you should never go to the attic when it floods. Maru says always get on the roof.

She's right. But you don't have to worry about that here, Em.

Some people had been in their attics for months. Their bodies were rotten.

It wasn't a fun time, I say, wondering what else Maru has shared with my daughter.

Maru's parents died too, Emi says.

Em, I say, pushing against the crowd to better face her. We don't have to worry about those things anymore. Nuuk's a safe city. The safest. The ocean is hundreds of feet below. Look. We have seawalls. Raingardens. Barrier islands. We are so fortunate. That's why we're celebrating. Don't you want to celebrate? Don't you want to have some fun?

She seems to think on this. Then she tells me that it could happen again. A second Crisis.

I tell her she is wrong. It can't. It won't.

She tells me that we shouldn't have waited so long to begin the Transition. You should've acted sooner, she says.

I say I agree. Which I do.

She wants to know why we waited so long.

I say it was complicated. Which it was.

She wants to know how exactly it was complicated and although it is clearly my daughter speaking, I am hearing her mother. And perhaps some of the cold fire from Maru's jar.

I remove my beads and slide them over her head.

Look at Maru, I say. Her life's been tough. She's witnessed horrible things. But you saw her just now. She isn't scared. She isn't worried. She's happy!

She's drunk, says Emi, leaning into me as the maglev whispers up to the platform.

―――――

When the maglev tilts downcity you get the famous Nuuk view: a sparkling flow of hexagonal metal and mass timber and photovoltaic glass that cascades from plaza to rambla to plaza to rambla—the whole city hugging the cliffs above the ocean which has nearly finished rising, the scientists say. As a little girl standing in Norsaq Plaza, Emi learned to count the clipper ships sailing north with batteries from New York. Cargo blimps like ribbons of seabirds returning home to nest. Geothermal plants pushing their towers of steam skyward. The living rooftops and hanging gardens that sway and ripple in the breeze to make the city appear as though it is breathing which Emi—as a girl—believed it was. People from away like to call us elitists. I hear it every game. We act as though Nuuk's the center of the world, they say. All I can say is come live it for yourself. We are the new New York. But safer. Younger. Greener. Twenty-one glorious daylight hours midsummer. Northern lights. An international hub of public finance. A bedrock of the precious metals industry. And home to the Tundra: defending world champs.

Do I miss the forest? The morning dew drip? The hiss of waves on sand? We all miss something. But unlike Kristina I am not stuck in the past. I am thankful for the now. The security we have built. Our rescued planet. Our new economy. The view from the maglev. Emi. All of it.

———

Three stops from the seaport a man with puffy eyes and a red nose shuffles onto the maglev. He nods at my jumpsuit and thanks me for my service.

It was a team effort, I say.

I wasn't old enough to enlist, he says. Sold T-bonds instead.

His breath is sour with alcohol. Trying not to slur. Doing so-so. He eyes the patch on my sleeve and asks if I fought fires or reforested.

Both, says Emi on my behalf. He was a smokejumper. He did controlled burns with the tribes. And deconstruction in New York. He was on *Corps Power*. Season three.

The man squints as if trying to place my face.

Only a few episodes, I say.

They ever send you to Jersey? he says.

I shake my head.

So where'd they send you?

Kansas, Dakotas, Montana, Idaho, Washington, California, Mexicali, Nevada—Emi rattles off my deployments. Her pride makes me proud.

Hell of a lot of tours, says the man.

My mom did even more, Emi says.

Not *that* many more, I say, mostly joking.

My people were from Jersey, says the man. Held out till the end. Still be there if they built us a damn seawall. Instead they sent you to Mexico. We need our borders back if you ask me. You ask me, it's time for some goddamn housekeeping.

I feel Emi tense. If Kristina were here she would be reminding this man—and the maglev—that the Crisis didn't give a shit about borders and why not pack his racist ass south if he misses it so much and good luck surviving down there and while he's at it go ahead and fuck the fuck off.

Kristina's public lectures in such situations are locally famous. A few have been upvoted to the top of MemeFeed. A big reason she nearly won a council seat. An equally big reason she lost. And a small reason I am glad she is in New York: one thing I do not want to do on Emi's first Day Zero is relitigate the politics of the Great Transition.

The maglev glides to a stop. We are two plazas upcity from the Esplanade but I whisper to Emi that we could walk and she gets the message. We stand.

My dad wasn't old enough either, Emi says as we step onto the platform.

Huh? says the man.

My dad wasn't old enough to enlist either. Neither was my mom. But they did anyway. It's called courage. And sacrifice for the common good. Asshole.

She flashes him a thin middle finger as the doors hiss and close.

Emiliana! I say as the maglev pulls away. You can't do that!

Mom would.

You aren't your mother. That is one hundred percent not okay.

Then why are you smiling?

I'm not smiling.

Dad. You one hundred percent are.

———

We hear the Esplanade before we see it: a tangled chorus of competing basslines and drums. The hightide roar of the crowd. The crackle of fireworks. The sounds grow louder until suddenly the rambla delivers us into the hot supernova of the holiday. Emi stops walking. She chews on her beaded necklace.

We can turn back, I say. No pressure. We can watch from home.

She frowns like I have offended her and yanks me ahead by the hand.

The Esplanade hugs the seawall along the curve of the bay. Sitting along the main causeway are the bleachers and viewing boxes where people are claiming spots. On the landward side are the mutual aid associations and Transition veteran clubs and unions and cooperatives. Each with their own flowing tent with banquet tables and induction grills and dance floors jumping to music from speaker towers ten feet tall. There are rides for kids. Games and prizes. Paper lanterns and flowers strung through the birch trees turning the Esplanade into a fluttering canyon of color.

Emi and I are theoretically making our way to the Tundra viewing box. In practice however it is stop-and-go and stop again. Stop to make way for a Teamsters' marching band. Stop to watch a drum corps on stilts. Stop so I can eat a salmon kebob. Stop for a beer. At one tent run by Carbon Capture they play a song I have heard from Emi's room a million times and she is hooked—she lets go of my hand to run over and leap in with the other kids. All of them dancing in synch like they know the same moves which they clearly do.

I watch from the bar. A group of CCCers are swaying arm in arm singing their anthem. One waves me over: Happy Z-Day brother!

She pours me a dark beer the color of tar and one for herself.

Happy Z-Day, I say back.

We cheers.

Keeping an eye on Emi I sing along with the CCC crew knowing maybe half the words. They laugh and clap me on the back. Big bear hugs that lift me off my feet. We always had a friendly rivalry—Forest Corps and Carbon Capture. Same end different means. But today it is all love all around. Like when the Tundra won the championship— everyone in Nuuk suddenly best friends. Strangers hugging strangers. High fives in every plaza.

Kristina would enjoy this. The solidarity.

I take out my screen and ping her. No response. I try again. I aim

my screen at Emi to record her dancing and laughing. Her joy is a fil-
ament from her heart directly to mine. It tugs on me. Pulls tears into
the back of my eyes. Threatens to yank me off my stool. So real I can
practically reach out and pluck it.

That's my girl! I shout to the woman refilling my mug.

Girl's got moves, she says, smiling back.

I will never see this woman again but I am thrilled she can experience a flash of my Emi. The real Emi. How she used to be. Unafraid.
Unabashedly joyful.

I send Kristina the recording. She will not be happy to see us
downcity but I am feeling expansive. She will be happy to see Emi so
happy. She has to be.

Em's having a blast. We're thinking of you. Love you so much.
Happy Z-Day.

Emi runs over, out of breath. She wants to stay for one more song.

Have at it, I say with a wave.

I tell myself that Emi has loosened her knots of worry because of
the music. The holiday atmosphere. The taste of Maru's liquor. But I
know it is really her mother's absence. Kristina puts so much pressure
on the girl. She wants Emi to be resilient. Strong. Prepared for any
future. I want these things too. Of course. What father would not?

The CCC woman goes to pour me another beer.

Better make it water, I say. Long day ahead.

Right it is, she says, and refills my mug all the same.

———

We take our time enjoying the Esplanade. When we finally arrive at
the Tundra box Lucas has a necklace of beads over his Forest Corps
uniform and sure enough there is Maru.

See you found your sober legs, I say.

Same place you lost yours, she says, throwing Emi a wink.

Maru is not so interested in basketball as she is in women in ath-
letic uniform. To her grave disappointment however the players are
dressed as civilians. Lucas introduces her to Dani Te, our star rookie

point guard. Maru must be twice Dani's age but she has Dani blush-
ing and getting her a drink and all we can say is Go, Maru, go.

Lucas pounds me on the back. Hugs Emi. Brings us to a spot he
saved up front where Emi can see. The parade is already underway.
Huge decorated floats with multiple levels, some as long as a maglev.
Musicians and dancers. When the Forest Corps float rolls by Emi
whistles and cheers. Lucas and I take our bows.

After the floats come balloons and bands and jugglers followed by
the largest floats from the Leadership Council and the Nuuk Mining
Cooperative and the Nuuk Financial Cooperative. Amid the cheering
there is some light jeering. Some good-natured. Some not-so-good-
natured. It grows louder and less kind as the floats inch by.

Why are they booing? Emi asks.

You know why, I say.

Because people can't live without a villain, Lucas says.

Because they profited from the Crisis, Emi says.

Not all of them, I say.

And right then—as if Kristina can sense she is missing a chance to
shame the Council and big cooperatives with Emi—my screen pings
and after two days of silence here she is.

I open my mouth to greet her but she beats me to it.

Why isn't Emi on her ski trip? Why would you bring her downcity
of all places? You promised, Larch! You promised not to go to the
Esplanade!

Mom? asks Emi.

I nod and turn a shoulder so she won't overhear every word.

Lucas flashes me a sympathy grimace.

Calm down, I say. Emi's fine. You saw her dancing. She's having a
blast.

Leave, she says. Take Emi and go home. Right now. You have to.

No we don't, I say, my voice rising. We're allowed to celebrate.
Today of all days. Give her a break, Kristina. Let her have some fun.
Let her be a damn kid.

Larch! Shut up. Stop talking. Listen to me! If you love our daughter, you need to get her away from there. Go upcity! Now! Please, my love. Please. Go!

A switch flips in me: *My love.*

Is something wrong? I ask.

Just go! Take Emiliana and run!

My arms prickle. A slug of nausea in my gut. I look at Emi.

Okay, I tell Kristina. We'll go. We're leaving right now.

You are? says Lucas.

We are? says Emi.

We are, I say, and grab her hand. Lucas follows as we start pushing through the crowd. I nod for him to tap Maru so she can join us but we are too late.

They sound like fireworks. Two sharp bangs. They are not fireworks.

A board member collapses on the Finance float.

Another from the Leadership Council loses his head in a red mist. Shock ripples through the crowd. Then a swell of panic.

The Esplanade heaves. People jumping off floats. The sky fills with drones. Everyone screaming and scrambling and trying to escape— but from what and from where?

I hold Emi. She is suddenly so small in my arms. She clings to me. People stampede. The fence around the Tundra box splinters and falls. Emi yells as she and I are crushed together. The breath from my chest is squeezed out. My ribs strain. Lucas helps lift Emi onto my shoulders.

She screams: Maru!

Not ten feet away we watch Maru go down. The crowd closes around her. Over her. Emi screams Maru's name again and I try to push against the rush of panicked people but they are a wave crashing into us and you can never save everyone—believe me—you can at best save some.

Lucas and I turn with the crowd and push like we are back in the Sierras knocking over a beetle-killed pine. Together we break through. Arrive at the seawall. Nuuk Bay twenty feet below. The water maybe four degrees above freezing. The crowd is crushing us against the seawall which was built to keep us safe, yet this is the nature of walls—they work both ways.

I raise Emi above my head so she can can climb up and straddle the wall. Then I claw and scramble to join her, using Lucas for leverage. Once secure, I reach to give him a lift. All down the Esplanade people are following our lead.

We have to jump, Lucas says.

I nod. He's right.

The music from the Esplanade suddenly cuts. The silence makes the screaming and crying that much louder. Emi can't look away. I touch her chin. Turn her face. Lock eyes.

Em. It's going to be cold. Just keep breathing. You'll feel like you can't, but you can. Keep breathing. Start swimming for shore. I'll be there with you. Lucas too. You can do this. Got it?

Got it, she says, her eyes huge like she knows I mean it and because there is no other option I do.

Her mother would be proud of her. Will be. I tell her this.

I kiss the side of her head. Take her hand. Lucas takes her other hand.

We jump.

CHAPTER SEVEN

LARCH

I was fifteen—same age as Emi—when the ocean saved me for the first time.

My father and I were harvesting kelp. Working the granite ledge at dawn. Wetsuits and goggles and knives. Plastic laundry baskets on the boat to collect the slick ribbons that we would dry and cut and package and ship. The early-morning sky was veiled in haze from faraway fires that had been raging all summer. This was the heart of the Crisis but hardly anybody called it that. It was just the world I had grown up in. Which is the only world that any of us know.

When I was eight Acadia burned shore to shore. We lived well north of the park but all summer the sun shone sickly through the haze. No stars. The blackberries my mother grew on a trellis by the drying huts turned sour. My parents and I were eating breakfast when the sky finally cleared. We had just sat down for oatmeal by the big kitchen window when it happened: a shock of blue so sudden we all stopped eating.

The winter I was nine we had record snowfall.

The winter I was ten it did not snow an inch.

When I was eleven there was a fish die-off in the Penobscot. Nobody knew why.

When I was thirteen the lobster disappeared.

When I was fourteen the puffins disappeared.

When I was fifteen the hemlocks disappeared. They had been fighting the invasive woolly adelgid as long as I had been alive. You could spend a whole morning crushing the tiny insects between your thumb and index finger and not clear one branch of one tree. I had to walk deep into the woods to find a healthy hemlock. One such walk I came across an emaciated moose calf on the ground covered in thousands of ticks. Some big as grapes. Moose were extremely rare then. This was partially why. The calf opened an eye like it was pleading with me: *Do something*. So I ran home and got our rifle and I did.

Ever since her school project Emi has been asking why we did not act sooner. Her mother has an easier answer. She grew up protesting with her family. Blocking oil trains. As for me, what can I say? My parents were loving people. Resourceful. Intelligent. They knew what was happening. My mother pointed out how the goldenthread blossomed months before the pollinators arrived. And the loons that used to winter on our shores—how long since we'd heard their ghostly calls? My father knew the tide pools better than anyone. He'd watched the Irish moss march south. Alaria gone north. He'd watched *Laminaria longicruris*—a kelp that prefers cold water—disappear in favor of sugar kelp, which likes slightly warmer shallows. He'd seen the last of the eelgrass.

So yes they knew. We knew. But I am asking for Emi—and not in a rhetorical sense—what more could we have done?

My family—like most families—was busy adapting. My father's father had built our home with upcycled materials at the turn of the century. The house was a patchwork castle rising three stories out of the hemlock and pine. Each floor had its own woodstove. I remember that warmth. My mother reaching into cast iron with bare hands to turn logs and encourage embers. The glow on her face. Steam on the windows. The windows were not true windows but used glass patio doors my grandfather had sealed horizontally in place. For ventilation he had built a system of flaps into the walls to cycle out the damp maritime climate. But that climate had long since passed away with him—by the time I was fifteen our woodstoves were cold ten months a year. Instead of chopping wood we were assembling cisterns to collect rainwater. Installing solar. Digging a deeper well. Constructing tent platforms for the migrants coming north from the Gulf. We gave up on corn. Planted peaches. Dug two-tiered paddies for rice. We continued the family business: Wild Maine Seaweed.

My father and I foraged and harvested. My mother prepared. Her kitchen was her laboratory. Mortars and pestles and hanging scales. Little glass jars by the dozens. She had formulated seaweed blends that she packed in capsules to treat everything. Hypothyroidism. Weight gain. Heart disease. Gut health. Clients across the globe as far as Japan. She'd authored a cookbook. Seaweed soups. Dulse salads. Kelp noodles. Irish moss custard. Kimchi. Dashi. She kept a ball cap on a peg above the sink. She'd flip it backward for a hairnet as she worked and turn up the kitchen speakers and sing along to Dolly Parton and Valerie June and Taylor Swift. Everything about sharpening knives and seasoning cast iron and pickling and canning and caring for sourdough starter—all I know about food and cooking I learned from her. She was a resourceful, fun woman. Emi would have loved her.

The Crisis was economic ruin for our neighbors who knew nothing but lobstering. Lots turned to drugs. Some to suicide. For my parents however it was a boon because kelp contains iodine 127, which prevents the thyroid from absorbing radioactive iodine 131. This was important because the Turkey Point nuclear plant outside Miami had gone underwater. And the ocean had almost completely eroded the cliffs beneath the Diablo Canyon plant in California. And the San Onofre nuclear depository was leaking north of San Diego. And sunny-day waves were cresting the seawall of a plant near Houston. My parents had more demand than they could meet. And then my mother came down with a new strain of Lyme.

She spent all her kitchen time trying for a cure. Alaria-kelp reductions. Tinctures. Salves. When not experimenting she was in pain. Joints. Back. Head. Everything hurt. It was not a fun time. She slept a lot. Sleep was her great peace.

She was sleeping that morning when my father and I were harvesting kelp. Dawn slipping over the horizon. The ocean beginning its lazy tilt from low tide to high. Later with the Forest Corps I would learn more about wildfire than I ever wanted to know. At fifteen I never could have imagined the speed.

I was underwater cutting kelp. When I surfaced the sky had turned a glowing red and my father was gone. Just like that. I heard the whine of the gasoline outboard motor that was only used in emergencies.

The dead hemlock forest. It had gone off like a bomb.

The sky was flickering. Towering fingers of smoke and embers like an angry blizzard. And my father speeding right toward it. I watched him ground the boat. Run for the house. The smoke took him whole as the fire jumped to the shore in one rush. The fire made its own wind. And the sound: a roar like a freight train. Three hundred yards offshore and I could feel the heat on my face.

The fire announced its entrance to our house by shattering the windows my grandfather had sealed in place so many decades earlier—clear crystalline pops that met me as I stood waist-deep on the ledge. Embers and burning shingles sailed out on the fire wind to hiss and die in the cold water around me. I held a twist of sugar kelp in one hand. My knife in the other. I remember that. And the tide coming in. Like it always does.

Emi Vargas Brinkman
North American History
Mrs. Helmandi
Great Transition Project (First Draft)

Title is a bit broad

Half Earth, Polar Circles, and Sister Cities

Before the Transition almost nobody lived near the poles except Indigenous peoples like the Aleuts, and obviously the Inuit, who lived here in Greenland for thousands of years before us. Everyone else lived between the poles. My dad lived in Maine, for example. My mom lived in Mexico. My neighbor Maru Badia lived in Florida.

Now it's like the world is a shirt that got turned inside out. Everyone lives near the poles. The rest is for Half Earth biomes and rewilding and carbon sequestration and scientists and Indigenous, who can live there if they want. Some people say the Half Earth Accords aren't fair because they keep so much land (half) off limits, but other people say how can nature heal if we don't give it time? Animals and trees didn't cause the Crisis. No matter how many biomes we reserve, you can't undo extinction. Plus, even if you could move to a Half Earth biome, it would mean living in floods, drought, hurricanes or wildfires, or surviving in heat over 95 degrees plus humidity, which is how all my mom's grandparents died.

Ordinary people can still experience Half Earth. To take one example, if you fly from Nuuk to the geothermal farms on the east coast, you get nonstop views of wild meadow and trees and caribou herds so big they look like a long brown river.

Sister cities are also in Half Earth, technically, but you only visit sister cities for extraction duty. In Nuuk, once you turn eighteen, you do two weeks of extraction duty in New York per year. Some people volunteer for more

Try to vary your sources

because you can bank hours, especially during storm season or holidays. Other people, such as my mom, volunteer to keep the spirit of the Transition alive. Before the Transition, lots of people spent their entire lives doing the same jobs, like packing boxes or sweeping floors or delivering supplies, while other people did almost no hard work at all. Extraction duty helps even things out, according to my mom, while also reminding people that the Transition is still alive and we're all part of it. According to my mom, extraction duty reminds us not to get too comfortable, which is important because people are already forgetting how close we came to extinction. Everyone back then knew the Crisis was happening and did basically nothing to stop the corporations and destroying classes that caused it. So who's to say people might not get lazy and let it happen again?

But the primary reason we have extraction duty is for resources we need to survive. Sister cities give us mass timber, carbon fiber, plant medicine that can't grow near the poles, and, most important, energy. Every city has at least one sister city. Moscow has two. No sister cities are in the polar circles except for Johannesburg's sister city, Ross Island, which is in Antarctica. Nuuk's sister city is New York. We go to New York next year for the overnight trip. According to everyone, the trip is a highlight of junior year. There are ruins to explore, water buses and the hyperloop to ride, plus the Tenement Museum and the Penthouse Museum, where actors reenact how the super poor and super rich used to live. Also, Central Park and the Statue of Liberty and the Big U and the Met, which people come to visit from all over. The number one reason New York is considered the greatest sister city is because it's the number one hurricane hot spot in the western hemisphere. [According to MemeFeed] New York captured 1.2 quads of storm energy last year. The energy gets shipped to us in

*Reputable sources only for this project, please.
MemeFeed not allowed.*

the batteries we use for basically everything. Inside every battery is a piece of a storm, if you think about it.

The only sister city that captures more storm energy than New York is Manila. New York's top three exports are batteries, carbon fiber, and tidal turbines. If I could visit any sister city I would choose Cleveland, for the Rock & Roll Hall of Fame. My last choice would be Phoenix, because of the heat. My mom's first deployment was in Phoenix with the Forest Corps. She says human beings can get used to anything. Her sister (my aunt) died in a wildfire. Given the choice between heat or cold, I would choose cold. You can always put on another layer.

In conclusion, if we continue extracting carbon from the ocean and the atmosphere at current rates while concurrently moving ahead with our robust sequestration and reforestation efforts, people may likely repopulate Half Earth biomes again in a century. We will all be dead by then, obviously. But that is no reason to stop trying.

Remember to go light on personal detail for informative assignments.

Nice transition, but are these your words? Remember to cite sources.

Nice effort Emi. Your big challenge, however, continues to be avoiding personal details and opinions. Maybe we can find a different type of project for you that would include oral histories? I have a few ideas. Let's chat.

— Mrs. H

CHAPTER EIGHT

LARCH

In the later years of the Transition—once emissions were really dropping and you were not embarrassed to hope—they sent counselors into the field to help us process some of what we had seen. What we had lost. There was a therapy for everyone. What worked for me was shaking. If you have ever seen a dog after an accident—or during a lightning storm or a visit to the vet—you know what I mean. Animals shake to release trauma and we are animals too we sometimes forget. To start the shakes you follow a series of specific poses to tire your legs. Once the shaking begins the goal is to keep it going. You shake and you shake. You feel better. A full body reset. This is how I explain the process to Emi after Public Safety has fished us from the bay and bandaged her arms and we are back home dry and warm and safe. We shake it out.

———

Emi falls asleep on the futon. I cover her with a blanket. Put a hand on her chest to be a part of her breathing. She saw people shot. Trampled. She nearly drowned. But she did not. She scaled the seawall. She jumped. She kept her head above water. She swam. My girl.

Replaying it all in my mind brings me close to falling apart so I stop replaying it. I shake. I set my screen to demoisturize. I shake some more.

When my screen finally beeps I ping Kristina straight away. No answer. I roll over to MemeFeed. Not since the Transition has there been violence like this—not in Nuuk—and Nuuk was not alone: Wellington. Rovaniemi. Reykjavik. Sault Ste. Marie.

Some big names. A former head of the Scandinavian Sovereign Transition Fund. A prince with Saudi Solar. A retired American secretary of state. People are already blaming the Russians as we so love to do. But others are pointing out that Moscow and Tynda were targeted too—and also this is MemeFeed—so let's downvote the rumors and upvote the facts.

Two facts as they stand upvoted now:

1. Day Zero celebrations hit globally. Parades and rallies. Some celebrations as large as Nuuk. Others as small as senior living facilities. Targeted assassinations. Sniper drones.
2. Many people injured in resulting stampedes. Numbers still coming in.

I close my eyes and see Maru going down—the crowd closing around her. I ping her. A woman answers. Not Maru. A nurse at Seaport General.

She's here, the nurse says when I ask for Maru.

I hear machines beeping in the background. People yelling. Intercoms blaring.

Is she okay?

Are you family? the nurse asks.

Sure. I'm family. Is she okay?

She's stable.

Can I talk to her?

She's not that stable.

The nurse takes my name. Promises to leave Maru a message. I thank her then ping Kristina again. She does not pick up. I reach out to Lucas. Really needing him to answer and he does.

Talk to me, man. How's Emi?

Fine. Resting, I say. You?

Dealing with some crisis management.

Lucas had gone straight to the Tundra medical facility after Public Safety pulled us out of Nuuk Bay. Now he tells me that everyone is freaking out because Dani Te broke a finger while escaping the stampede.

Shooting hand? I ask.

Of course, he says.

Physical therapist and massage therapist and team therapist—everyone is hovering and waiting for X-rays and panicking about playoffs, he explains.

Glad we have our priorities straight, I say.

He laughs.

You check the Feed? I ask.

Yeah. What else am I gonna do?

I got something for you.

What's that?

My neighbor who was with us in the box?

Miami Company, he says.

Maru. She got beat up pretty bad. She's at Seaport General. Sounds like a madhouse over there. Can you put in a request to transfer her to the team facility?

And take care away from Te's finger?

Good point, forget I asked.

Lucas laughs. Says he's on it. Says he has a question.

Shoot, I say.

Kristina pinged you.

That's not a question, I say, keeping my voice steady. I lean against the kitchen counter and rub my eyes.

What did she say, Larch?

Nothing. You know Kristina. She was upset we were there.

Right, Lucas says, after what feels like a long pause.

We say our goodbyes. I roll back to MemeFeed. What has happened today? Nobody knows.

But of course that is not true.

I hear Kristina begging me to grab Emi and run.

My love.

I ping her again. I ping Gowanus Outpost where she does her extraction duty. I cannot reach her. Cannot reach anyone. Only an infuriating AI operator wishing me a happy Day Zero and informing me that all transfer requests for Gowanus duty must be made in person due to overwhelming demand. I ping Kristina again.

My love. We are safe. Where are you?

Then I lie down with Emi. I shake.

———

Emi surprises me later in the kitchen. Walks in barefoot with a blanket over her shoulders and her headphones around her neck and announces as if it is nothing: Smells good, can I have some?

I have been softening and dicing dulse for a miso soup. Slicing scallions to sauté with leeks. Marinating cubed tofu. Scraping spaghetti squash for a side. More food than anyone could possibly eat alone but kitchen therapy is real.

I set a bowl in front of Emi before she can change her mind. Try not to stare as she lifts a spoon. I almost say something encouraging but she is fifteen and I have learned better. Instead I act casual as she slurps. I explain that Maru is in the hospital recovering. I tell her all the news. She will find out anyway. Best coming from me.

She swallows then asks in a flat voice: Is Mom dead?

I choke on a leek and repeat the facts. There were no attacks in New York. Mom is fine.

Then why hasn't she pinged us?

She will.

Emi puts down her spoon. She ate only broth. She stares at the remaining tofu and vegetables as if they are to blame for what is happening.

So Mom could be dead, she says.

Emiliana. Stop saying that.

You don't know for a fact that she isn't.

Em—

She lunges for my screen. Knocks over my tea. I grab a cloth to wipe the table as she tries for her mother. And tries. And tries again.

She warned us, Emi says. She told us to run.

Emi is thinking the same thought as me and Lucas but unlike us grown men she doesn't glance at the matter. She stabs directly for the heart.

She knew what was going to happen, she says.

We don't know that.

Why else would she warn us at that exact moment?

Intuition?

What do you mean intuition?

Like a gut feeling.

Emi looks at me from across the table like she cannot decide if I am bullshitting her or bullshitting myself. To be honest I could not say. Maybe some of both.

Then her eyes go distant like she is seeing everything from earlier today. She runs to the bathroom. Sounds of vomiting. I walk over to press my forehead against the cool door. Inhale. Exhale. Knock.

Em? You okay?

The toilet flushes. The sink runs.

She comes out with her hair pulled back tight. Brushes by me and slips on her shoes by the front door. I have to check on Alice, she says.

Alice?

Maru's cat. Someone has to feed her.

Emi has developed the ability in the past year to flash from girl to woman in a blink. It is the age. I should be used to it by now but I am not.

Do you need help? I ask.

You can come if you want.

I stare at this young woman with my daughter's face.

Dad? she says. If you're coming, let's go.

Maru's unit is eight levels below ours but she has a helio system to funnel daylight. I am so rarely underground anymore that I forget how well the fiber optics work: when Emi lets us in with her spare key the place is blinding—completely flooded with light.

I blink and squint as Emi scoops up Alice. The cat will not stop meowing. Emi nuzzles her. Murmurs into her fur. Opens a bag of dry food. Refreshes her water. Strokes her back and tail.

Maru's level is sparse and ordered as if she never left the Corps which in her mind—I am beginning to think—she has not. Framed medals and certificates. Screenshots lauding Miami Company. A go bag by the door. Five-gallon jug of water. Jumbo box of rice. So many who lived through the Crisis have never felt safe again. Not even here in Nuuk. Maru could not be more different from Kristina but maybe they both share this worry: that the worst is not over. And after today? Maybe they are right.

Next to Maru's go bag is a bookcase crammed with romance novels. I pry one out. The cover art is not pornography but about as close as you can get.

Had no idea that Maru was such a reader.

Emi tells me I shouldn't snoop. She empties the litter box then runs Alice around with a feathery toy on a string.

I watch while making a heroic effort not to check my screen.

You're good at taking care of her, I say.

It's easy.

Not for everyone. You're a naturally caring person, Em. Caring and responsible.

Thanks.

Well it's true. You're just amazing. You know that? Right?

Then I am tearing up. Usually Emi and Kristina are there to tease me when I get suddenly emotional like this. But now it is only Emi. She sees me bring a knuckle to my eye.

What's wrong? Did you hear from Mom?

I shake my head and sit on Maru's couch.

Then what's the matter?

I cannot say it out loud.

Are you mad at her? Emi asks.

Mad? I'm not mad.

I wish she'd ping us.

She will. We just have to be patient.

Emi sits on the couch and leans against me. Head on my shoulder. Hand on my arm. Alice jumps onto her lap. Meaning Emi is taking care of two creatures at once. Which is unfair to put on her but she is good at it. And this is another type of therapy—caring for something besides yourself. So she and I are sort of helping each other.

We could visit Maru while we wait, Emi says. Let's bring her dinner.

See? I say, throwing my hands in the air and losing it all over again.

See what?

You! Everything!

———

Once Alice is fed we head home to pack food for Maru. Emi thinks miso soup would be best. But as we step off the elevator and turn the corner I stop. A man and woman are outside our unit. The woman knocking. Testing the handle. Calling through our door.

Mrs. Vargas?

I touch Emi's arm to stop her but the man has seen us. He touches the woman's arm like he is mirroring me. She looks up.

Mr. Brinkman! She smiles.

A voice in my head says to tell the woman I'm not who she thinks I am, and keep walking. My actual voice however says, Can I help you?

Case Manager Rachel Min, says the woman.

Byron Rich, says the man. He reaches into his jacket and flashes a Public Safety badge. He is my height but thicker. Barrel-chested. Shaved head. Min comes to his shoulders. Half his width. Her hair in a sharp bob. Both are dressed in suits.

You must be Emiliana, says Min.

Emi nods. I reach for her hand.

Everything okay? I say.

Depends on who you ask, says Rich, pocketing his badge. It's been a day, hasn't it?

We're hoping to speak to Mrs. Vargas, says Min. Kristina. Is she home?

On one hand I experience a high tide of relief because they are not here to report Kristina injured or worse. But just as quickly the high tide recedes because why are they here?

Speak to her about?

Is she home? Min asks.

She's working.

Working on Day Zero, says Rich.

Someone has to, I tell him—word for word what Kristina would say.

She has the most volunteer hours on Norsaq Plaza, Emi adds.

So she's volunteering, says Rich. Not working.

Volunteering is work, says Emi—again Kristina's words.

Where's she volunteering? asks Min.

A farm, I say, squeezing Emi's hand hard before she can jump in with anything about New York. I have made a decision so quickly that it is not really a decision but instinct: Instinctively I do not care what Kristina knows or what Public Safety thinks she knows. I only care about her. And how my instinct swings her way when it matters—I care about that too. Because it means we are still on the same team. Which of course we are. But it also makes me nauseous with regret for these last wasted years. All I want is to start over. And disaster—for all its ruin—can offer that. Like wildfire. A blank slate. I squeeze Emi's hand harder.

Which farm? says Rich, pulling out his screen.

I don't know.

You don't know where your wife is on Day Zero.

Nope. Why's this important?

Did she serve with Phoenix Company throughout the entire Transition? asks Min.

Twenty-three deployments, Emi says.

Wow. Did she ever serve abroad?

South America, Emi says, looking to me. Right?

Why is this important? I say again.

You know what happened today, says Min.

We were there. What does it have to do with my wife?

How long has she been involved with the Furies? asks Rich.

The what?

When did you last speak to her? Min asks.

Is she okay or not?

That's what we're trying to find out, says Min. Please. We want to help.

How often does she travel abroad? says Rich.

To New York?

No, not New York, says Rich. Johannesburg. Puerto Montt. Yellowstone. Abroad.

The question genuinely catches me off guard. I answer honestly: Never.

Tell us about her extraction duty, Rich says. Does she always go through Gowanus?

Yes, Emi says.

No, I say. Sometimes. Why?

Are you experiencing marital problems? Min asks.

The thing about that, I say slowly, is that it's actually none of your fucking business.

A moment of cool settles in the hallway between us. Sounds of a newscast come from a few doors down. A blender. Laughter. Someone practicing what sounds like the cello. At times I can feel a little claustrophobic living in proximity to so many people. Right now is not one of those times. I'm glad for my neighbors. I squeeze Emi's hand and ask the case managers if that's it: Are we done here?

Min tucks a lock of hair behind an ear and apologizes. We don't mean to be insensitive, Mr. Brinkman. We're exhausted.

You and me both, I say.

What happened to your arms, love? she asks Emi.

Emi looks at her bandages. She looks to me.

She climbed the seawall, I say. We had to jump.

Was your mom with you? Min asks.

I already told you, I say. She's working.

Volunteering, corrects Rich. At an unknown farm.

Yep, I say.

Love, have you spoken to your mom today? Min says.

Stop talking to her, I say. You direct the questions to me. Got it?

Rich clasps his hands in front of him and tilts his head: You seem upset. Everything okay?

We saw people get shot today. We almost died. Of course I'm not okay.

Larch, we got off on the wrong foot, Min says. We aren't here to get anyone in trouble. We just want to keep everyone safe. Your wife included. That's our job. That's why we're here.

All the power to you, I say.

The four of us stand still. They look at each other again. The elevator dings and the doors slide open to a delivery worker. We all smile and nod as she passes by pushing a dolly stacked with packages. She turns the corner. Min gives Rich a shrug. He digs into his pocket for a business card. Tells me to contact them as soon as Kristina returns. From the farm.

I take the card. Willing my hand to be steady.

You work for the Tundra, Rich says.

I nod.

Think we'll pull it off again this season?

I'm optimistic, I say.

Not me, says Rich. I always assume the worst.

———

You lied to them! Emi hisses when we are inside. You lied to Public Safety!

She is shocked but within that shock I detect a volt of glee.

No I didn't. Mom could be working at a farm. We don't know for a fact that she isn't.

If Public Safety's looking for her, she must be in trouble.

That isn't true, Em. It doesn't work like that. They're just asking questions.

This is crazy, she says, lifting a glass on the counter. Putting it back down. This is crazy.

Her getting so worked up gets me worked up. Autopilot kicks in. I set the kettle to 194 degrees. Crush a handful of dried chamomile in my pestle with some magnesium carbonate. Divide the mixture evenly between two mugs. Halve a lemon with one clean stroke. Squeeze the lemon halves and then hot water when the kettle clicks ready.

I have to check the news, Emi says, can I use your screen?

Drink this first, I say, giving her the calming tea and my screen. She takes both to her room. I am pouring a jar of miso soup to bring Maru when I hear another knock. A high voice.

Mrs. Brinkman?

Who's there? I say quietly through the door. Not wanting Emi to hear.

Case Manager Willis. Public Safety.

I crack the door.

A woman with straight bleached hair holds up a badge: NUUK PUBLIC SAFETY.

You all were just here, I say.

She blinks. Who was just here?

Public Safety, I say. Min and Rich. Case managers.

I fish into my pocket for the business card. She gives it a puzzled look.

Captain Rich? Captain Rich was up here? You're sure?

Huge white guy?

That's him. Huh. Who was he with?

Min, I say. Rachel Min. Asian woman. Shorter. Thin.

Willis shrugs: Never heard of her. She shakes her head. Mutters something.

What? I ask. What's wrong?

Nothing's wrong. Just irritating. Rich's precinct is way downcity, by the Kalaallit Quarter. Leadership is running around ragged, after today. Sending people all over. I don't care. Just wish someone had told me. Waste of my time, doubling up doors like this. No offense.

None taken, I say.

She passes back the business card. I drop it into my pocket and keep my hand there so she will not see it shaking. I want to believe that Captain Rich was at my door because of some bureaucratic mix-up. I want to believe that Case Manager Willis has never heard of Case Manager Min because the Nuuk Public Safety force is so large. But the other possibilities rise in my mind, and as soon as they break the surface, I know they are closer to the truth.

Well, sighs Willis, pulling out her screen, let's get this over with.

She runs me through similar questions to what Min and Rich asked. But no mention of Gowanus. Nothing about Emi. She keeps calling Kristina *Mrs. Brinkman*—as if Kristina took my name. She does not know half as much about us as Min and Rich.

Before she leaves I ask: Hey do you people always do that?

Do what?

Flash your badge when you knock?

Of course, she says. How else would you know we are who we say we are?

———

The first thing I do after shutting the door is wipe my palms on my pants. Then I inspect the business card. CAPTAIN BYRON RICH. NUUK PUBLIC SAFETY. Emi has my screen in her room, so I use the wall screen to ping Public Safety—not the number on the card but a general nonemergency number. I ask for Captain Byron Rich. One moment, the operator says, connecting me. I disconnect and try again. This time asking for Case Manager Rachel Min.

The operator informs me there is no such personnel.

I open Emi's door. She is sitting cross-legged on her bed with my screen in her lap. Tea on her nightstand untouched. I tell her to pack a bag. Just for tonight.

Dad.

We'll stay at Maru's, I say. So we can take care of Alice. It'll be fun.

I try to sound as calm and collected as possible. I could be doing better.

Dad, she says again.

Move it. Come on. Hurry up.

I run into the kitchen to fill my leather knife roll with as many knives as there are pockets along with my favorite spatula and best whisk. Roll it up. Fasten the straps. I grab a canvas tote from a drawer and drop in a vacuum bag of nori and another of alaria and a matchbox of saffron that Kristina gifted me a million years ago. I reach into the back of the fridge for my sourdough and yogurt starters. Then remember my backups in the Tundra kitchen and decide against it. What else? I look around. Inhale. Exhale. I like to believe that I am the type of man who thinks and acts rationally during an emergency. But right now I have this one kernel that keeps popping in my mind: Min and Rich know where we live. Where I work. Kristina's extraction duty routine. Emi's name. And Rich should not have been at our door. And Min was not who she said she was. They might very well be with Public Safety. Also they might be with someone else.

Dad, Emi says from the doorway.

Where's your bag? Emiliana! Put down the damn screen and start packing.

I'm trying to show you something.

Not now.

But look!

She is holding my screen. I take it.

We all know loss.

We all know what happened.

We all know loved ones that should be with us but are not.

We all know that none of this needed to happen.

We all know who caused it.

We all know who had the power to stop it.

We all know who did nothing.

We all know who did worse than nothing.

We all know who delayed and deceived.

We all know who did so for profit.

We all know this was the most wicked crime in history.

We all know who should have been held responsible.

We all know who was not.

We all know who they are.

We all know that Earth is our one and only home.

We all know there is nowhere else to hide.

Today, in consideration of their personal and premeditated
    responsibility for the Climate Crisis, thirteen condemned
    criminals have been executed.

Tomorrow we continue the work.

We are the Furies.

We are a voice for those who will never forget.

Mom wrote this! Emi blurts.

Quiet! I say, glancing at the front door. Don't say that! This is MemeFeed. This could be literally anyone.

It is true that Emi and I have heard variations of these words spoken at our table over dinners. Yelled through bullhorns at marches. Argued during debates for Nuuk Leadership Council. Which doesn't prove a thing, I remind Emi. People have been saying this stuff since the Transition. Even long before. Even I talk like this when I'm upset.

What are the Furies? Emi says, refreshing the screen.

I don't know.

The case managers said Mom was with them.

Wrong. They asked. And the answer is no. Of course she's not.

How can you say she's not with them if you don't even know who they are?

All I know, Em, is that we need to get packed and go. Right now.

She chooses not to hear me. She refreshes the screen and reads aloud from subthreads branching off the original manifesto. Did I know the assassinated secretary of state was CEO of a public relations firm for the American Petroleum Institute? Or that the head of the Scandinavian Sovereign Transition Fund also captained Norway's state oil company? Or the Saudi prince ran the kingdom's oil empire before they went solar?

Don't believe everything on MemeFeed, I remind her. Anyone can post anything. Also—you do know that doesn't make murder okay. No matter who they are. Right, Em?

Well it's better them than regular people, she says with a shrug.

I put my face in my hands. Inhale. Exhale. The Saudis must now go on the list of possible groups that Rich and Min could be working for. The thought warps my mind with panic. I am back at the Esplanade— fear switching off all sectors of the brain except for that reptilian nub that screams at you to grab the people you love most and run.

New plan, I say. Pack for a few days. Right now.

Okay, Emi says, absorbed in the screen.

Now! I yell. I rip the screen from her hands and push her into her bedroom and order her to pack. I slam her door and walk into the kitchen to ping Lucas. He answers right away.

Man, are you on the Feed? he says. You catching all this? Sounds awful close to home.

Lucas has sat with us at our kitchen table. He knows Kristina's opinions as well as anyone. I tell him case managers came by looking for her.

Public Safety? he says.

It's a misunderstanding, I say. She's volunteering at a farm. You know her. She's passionate. But she wouldn't get involved in something like this. Not Kristina.

I space my words carefully as if reading a script so that Lucas knows he might not be the only one listening. A few beats pass. I want his take on Rich and especially Min. But not now. Not over screens. Right now I need his help. For three decades I have watched my father speeding away from me. Heard the high scream of the outboard motor on his final trip to shore. For thirty years he has rushed to my mother. Chosen her and left me. But now I feel it differently. I feel it in the bodily way he must have—not a calculated decision that sent him into the fire but something more primal running hot through his veins. He had to go. Could not have stayed on the granite ledge and watched as his wife burned alone. I understand that. Because I sense that Kristina is also in danger. My daughter's mother. *My love.* I must go to her. Not a choice. The only difference is that I will not abandon my child. Emi is not strong enough to survive alone on the ledge. The ledge is not safe. Safe is being together. As a family. As in all three of us.

You there? Lucas says.

Here, I say.

They dropped off your neighbor. She's sleeping like a queen.

Thanks, I say and then get to the point: Is our plane in the hangar?

Our plane?

The Tundra plane. Is it there?

Let me check.

He goes dark for a moment, then returns: It's here.

Great. Don't you have a scouting trip this week? A point guard you've been dying to see?

She's next week.

No, I think she's this week. And I think Emi and I should tag along. For fun.

I can't just take the plane, man.

Sure we can. It's our plane. We're a cooperative.

A cooperative with bylaws and a managing council and an auditing committee.

And last I checked you were vice president of scouting and player development with a seat on that managing council.

Larch.

Please Lucas. For Emi.

Lucas is quiet. Then says, Damn—you're right. Not often I forget the date of a big scouting trip. Totally blanked. It is this week. You're right.

Thanks. Thank you. When can we leave? Tonight?

The plane's charging.

Morning then. First thing.

You getting me in trouble Larch?

We're not doing anything wrong.

That's all I needed to hear.

Where are we going? Emi asks when I put down my screen. She is standing in the kitchen doorway with a bag slung over her shoulder. Headphones around her neck. Jacket in the crook of her arm.

On a trip.

To the geofarms?

No. Other direction. We're going to find Mom.

CHAPTER NINE

LARCH

A common misconception about wildfire is that it burns everything in its path. Untrue. A wildfire—even a large one—is no perfect lawn mower. More like a weed whacker that cannot make up its mind. The flame front moves too quickly to consume all the fuel it encounters. The real threat is from the embers thrown ahead like so many vengeful scouts—firebrands we call them—but even these are not exhaustive. Inevitably they miss a spot:

Two peach trees behind the packing shed.

The packing shed.

The Honda in the driveway.

You can pour all sorts of meaning into what is spared. But it is exhausting. Believe me. Better to take each pardon for what it is: some small chance to start over.

———

After the fire I stayed on the granite jut of coast that had been my home. Drank stale rainwater from the cistern. Ate myself sick on peaches. Filled buckets from the ocean to douse the tiny blue flames that kept sprouting from charred tree trunks and roots. The fire had spared our packing shed with the season's inventory. The customer manifest was right there on the wall where my father had tacked it. I didn't know what else to do. So I got back to work.

The zip of packing tape. Brittle snap of dried kelp. Careful zeroing of the scale. These were my days. The smell of seaweed and cardboard and toner—enough to mask the creosote tang hanging outside. I scrubbed the ash off the shed's solar array and replaced a melted PV lead. This provided power for music and the label printer and the charger for the chainsaw which I needed to clear the driveway of treefall. When the sky hinted dusk I washed in the ocean. Then shut myself in the shed before the mosquitoes came hunting. Nights were for sharpening the chainsaw's teeth. Eating peaches. Falling asleep as Taylor Swift and Valerie June ran the PV batteries dry.

The fire had entered the home that my grandfather had built and collapsed it into a two-dimensional slag. There was no avoiding it. Did not matter how hard I worked. The roof was now the floor. A mat of melted asphalt shingles. My parents somewhere underneath. The only surviving relic was the chimney. Rising out of the rubble like a tombstone. Walking from the driveway to the packing shed I would stop sometimes at the foot of the ruins. Let my vision blur in the patterns of destruction. I never dug around. Excavation would change nothing. And did I want to see what I might uncover? I did not. Plus I had work to do.

But then the day arrived when the work was done. No more orders needed boxing. The driveway was cleared of treefall. The peach trees were picked clean and the cistern was dry. We had two vehicles: an old Land Rover and a Honda EV. The Land Rover was torched— tires melted, leaving wreaths of fine metal tread—but the Honda was unscathed and one-quarter charged. Key fob in the cup holder where my mother always kept it.

I filled the Honda with boxes of seaweed and headed for the Jonesboro post office. Then turned back for the chainsaw. The road was bad. Treefall at every bend. Three houses shared the long gravel road that hugged our cove. Not one driveway had been cleared. Struck me that the only sounds these past days had been waves and gulls and my mother's oldies. No chipmunks. No neighbors. No rescue crews.

Meaning the fire had reached into homes beyond my own.

Which made sense. But also felt impossible.

And this is what I tried explaining to Emi about fire and disaster and the Crisis: our brains are not made to process the scope of mass loss. Like when Emi asks why we didn't save animals if we knew they were going extinct. Why didn't we retreat cities inland if we knew the ice sheets were about to collapse?

What can I say? The ocean was not the only problem. The problem was everywhere and everything. Not even one million years of evolution have prepared our brains to deal with something so encompassing as that.

What our brains are very good at is focusing on the chaos immediately at hand.

For my brain that meant getting our seaweed orders to the Jonesboro post office. Which meant ignoring how I was driving barefoot in my wetsuit because my wetsuit was all the clothing I had. Or what to do when the Honda's battery died. What to eat when I got hungry. How to survive without family. My entire world was narrowed to keeping the car on the road. I could do that.

———

The following months were not fun months. Driving around pirating an EV charge whenever possible. Churches and schools had set up food pantries and clothing drives all over. The fire was still going— spawning across New England. Spot fires continued to burn well into the fall. It was underground. Spreading among tree roots. The anthem of the season was the blare of sirens. Fire engines. Ambulances. Volunteer firefighters in pickups. A general wailing at all times.

I stuck to the coast where the breeze scattered the smoke and it was easier to find a charge.

Why did I need a charge? To keep driving.

Where was I driving? To find a charge.

This was no great road trip adventure. I remember exhaustion. Boredom. Twice on I-95 I nodded off at the wheel. Rumble strips caught me both times. I felt indifferent about crashing. All I wanted was sleep and the peace that came with it. Peace like my mother had found. My mother. My father. A dizziness fogged me. I found it difficult to focus. Impossible to think more than an hour into the future. I listened to the radio but the music always cut out for bad news or very bad news. Hurricanes and drought. Fire and tornadoes. Central America migrating into Mexico and Mexico into the Gulf states and the Gulf states north toward us. The other side of the globe even worse. Australia one big fire. Spain one big heat wave. Bangladesh one big mudslide. Everyone trying to flee but only one planet. The world scattered and on the move. Unable to rest. Like me.

The news felt especially real because I saw it daily. License plates from Texas and Alabama. So many from Florida. Makeshift camps in highway rest stops and beachside parking lots. I kept my distance. I was a child of the woods. Homeschooled. Unaccustomed to crowds. My mother and I had together read *The Grapes of Wrath*. She loved Steinbeck. Now I was living the novel—all these migrants with life's belongings strapped to RVs and trucks—headed off to the promised land only to arrive and learn no such place exists. People would eye my Maine plates and ask where to find work. Southerners were especially talkative. They thought nothing of walking up to my car and standing there smiling like a lunatic until I cracked the window so they could share their life story. Which was more or less how I met Lucas.

I was at the Kennebunk rest stop in line for a charge. The Honda's battery had nearly died. I was pushing in neutral. Lucas ran over to help push without asking if I needed help. A very Lucas thing to do.

He was from Florida. Like everyone. His basketball scholarship to the University of Miami had fallen through with the flooding and radiation, he said. He asked if I wanted to play catch. He ran to get two gloves and a ball before I could answer.

We threw a baseball in the parking lot until dusk. His family called to him. He asked if I was hungry—they were grilling—and bytheway did I know anywhere hiring?

His family waved me over. Their camp was two RVs playing music and draped with flags: USA and Miami Hurricanes and Puerto Rico. Their grill smelled good. I felt the tug. But I thought of the questions they would have for me, and did I want to answer even one? I did not.

I told Lucas I had to go. Before leaving I gave him a bottle of digitata pills from my trunk.

Digitata?

Kelp. Seaweed. For fighting radiation. In case you all got exposed.

Right on, he said. Thanks.

———

The fires finally burned themselves out. But then we faced a new problem which was always the case then. The new problem was the cold. Previous winters had been so mild. This winter was not. All I had for shelter was the Honda. The Honda had great battery life as long as I didn't abuse the heater. Striking a balance required loads of blankets and a plastic bottle so I could pee in the car without inviting in the cold.

One morning I woke up earlier—around dawn—to an older man knocking on my window. I was parked on the Mid-Coast by the Rockland pier where the police bothered you less. I cracked the window. Cold poured in.

The man asked from behind a million scarves and hats if I needed somewhere to stay. He asked if I had a home. His breath steamed the window. He called me son.

I put up my seat and told him I had a home. Which—in my mind—I did. I had a home waiting for me whenever I decided to go back. So why hadn't I? The packing shed was uninsulated, for one. Also I might get stranded out there. No way to charge the Honda. Other reasons too.

Well, son, we have a warming center right here in town. People are freezing in their cars. Would be a real shame. Why don't you come in from the cold? Try it for a night.

I asked him about the warming center. I liked how he called me son. I wanted to hear if he might say it again.

We'll set you up with a hot meal and a bed, he said. No California king but it'll beat your bunk here. And, of course, there's the arena in Bangor if you want something more permanent.

He gave me a flyer and a muffin and wished me luck and I just have to point out that this was one story I was excited to share with Emi for her project. Because many people during the Crisis hoarded guns and toilet paper and built fences—true—but many more people did not. Emergencies bring out the best in us. I have seen it over and over. Like that morning I showed up at the warming center. They gave me a paper plate of pancakes. Chili for lunch. Pasta for dinner. A bed. Everyone was friendly. The volunteers. The families. So much warmth. Like the man said.

Two days later I drove to Bangor. The Great Northern Greens Arena by the Penobscot River had been converted into a shelter. I parked. Stamped my boots in line waiting to register. Warm air billowing from the arena entrance. Warm air and music. And laughter. Which is not the sort of thing you realize has been missing until suddenly you do.

At the front of the line a woman asked for identification.

I had none, I explained. I had lost everything in a fire.

She asked if anyone could vouch for my age. My identity. Or was it just me?

I nodded my head: just me.

I guess she saw something in my face. Oh baby, come here, she said. We got you now.

———

The Great Northern Greens Arena became my home for the next fourteen months. I got my own cot. I hung bedsheets for privacy which was vital as I had three thousand roommates and more coming in from the cold every day. Earplugs were key too. When people flee their homes they apparently never forget their musical instruments. Some guitar circle was always strumming. We had a brass band that played oldies. Lots of Beyoncé. They were good—good enough to trick you for a few beats into thinking things were normal—but the human mind can take "Crazy in Love" only so many times.

The arena had an attached convention center for families. They put me there because I was under eighteen. Someone from the state was supposed to check on me. Nobody did. We later learned it was like this all over: the government so busy saving property and the stock market—as the saying went—that it forgot about the people. So the people took care of themselves.

In the Great Northern Greens Arena this meant everyone over the age of thirteen was asked to do one cleaning or security or cooking shift per day. But you didn't have to. It was my first experience with the concept of mutual aid and I loved it. I could sleep all day. I could watch the big screen in the club lounge. I could find a seat high up in the nosebleed section and pop in my earplugs and zone out. Some adults might throw me a little side-eye but nobody made me lift a finger. And if anyone did order me around? I had my Honda outside. I could leave whenever.

But I did not leave. April tipped into May into June. It was summer. I was sixteen. I was two inches taller. I was as bored as ever.

Boredom was a serious problem. Some people coped with drugs. Others fought. One girl threw herself off the arena scaffolding. After that came a big effort to build structure into our days. People started leading yoga. Chorus. Painting. There were trombone lessons. Contra dances. Baking contests. I joined a book club reading *War and Peace*. It was good. But I missed Steinbeck. I missed the ocean. My home. My head felt so foggy. I ate. I slept. I grew.

Six foot one.

Six foot two.

Since moving into the arena I had hit a growth spurt that kept on going. Like my body was trying to stretch itself as far from the past as possible. Growing pains. Stretch marks. I was uncomfortable in my own skin. What felt best was not feeling at all. Not feeling was easiest when asleep. But I could not sleep forever. Waking hours I spent in front of the screen. I followed a reality streamcast—*Buggin' Out*—about a family of survivalists in South Dakota. Life there seemed worse than in Maine. That was some relief.

Then a psychologist moved into the arena.

Dr. Alex. He set up shop in one of the luxury suites and offered free therapy. At first nobody went. By the next week the line snaked around the concourse. Then someone recognized Dr. Alex from the Portland Fish Pier and it surfaced that he was no psychologist but had worked on a lobster smack where he was a lowly deckhand, not even a captain. At first people felt duped but then the line to see him was just as long. He had no medical training but he was good. I found out for myself one afternoon way up in the nosebleeds.

Seat taken?

I shrugged: Free country.

He sat a few seats to my left. Then he jumped up and moved over so our elbows were almost touching. His closeness among all the empty seats was a little uncomfortable but then he started talking and because we had both worked the ocean we had lots to say. Mostly how we missed it. How it put everything in perspective—his words but I knew what he meant. The expanse. The horizon. The cradlerock. How it made you feel small but in a good way. Then he slapped his thigh. He let out a big sigh and pointed and said, Wouldja look at all those losers down there?

I laughed a nervous laugh. Kids were shooting hoops on a patch of court far below. Their sneakers squeaking in that nice warm way.

No. It's true, he said. Not a single person in this place who hasn't lost something. So many holes, my dude. Holes inside holes. All of us. The world's ending and we're all losers in it together.

I was quiet. I had not thought hard on the idea that others were experiencing loss like mine. Considering something so obvious so late made me feel small, but not in a good way. Someone across the arena was playing the trumpet—a scale that went up and down.

So what'd you lose? he asked.

I shook my head. Not going there.

Lobsters molt, he said. You know that. You've seen it. They crawl out of their old shells. It's how they grow. By losing. So I say okay—I can build up my armor till it's so thick I can't move. That's one way. Or I shed my old skin. Drop my armor. Make some breathing room. Free myself to grow.

I shrugged. He didn't know me. I had grown. I had enough stretch marks for a lifetime.

You angry? he said.

I shrugged again.

You got every right to be. Me I'm wicked pissed off. Whatever you lost, my dude, it shouldn't have happened. Wasn't your fault. Was it the fires? Your folks? Your family?

I shook my head. Said I was fine. But I was blinking back tears which undercut my case.

Dr. Alex said, Well, you knew this question was coming, so here it is: The world's ending but it's not over yet. What're you planning to do with the freedom you still got?

The trumpet across the arena kept playing the scales. Working for those highest notes.

I don't know, I mumbled.

Time to start figuring it out, he said. Because you got a future. A good one. I can see that. Anyone can see that. But you got to work for it. That's why you need to help out. Not for me. Not for those other losers down there. For you. I'm telling you, my dude. Helping—it's the only thing that helps. Be part of something. Join a team. It's the most human thing we can do. It's in our DNA. It's how we shed our skins. Might not be the only way, but it's a good way. Trust me.

I will not pretend I had an epiphany in the bleachers and told Dr. Alex he was right—nobody does that and certainly not at sixteen—but looking in the rearview that small push from him certainly moved me.

A couple days later I signed up for a cooking shift. To nobody's surprise but my own it was a million times better than sitting solo in the bleachers or watching *Buggin' Out* till my eyes felt like bleeding. Working the kitchen was fun. And I had skills. I did not realize the full extent of these skills until I pointed out how the knives were dull and watched everyone blink vacantly—as if dull blades were an unavoidable force of nature. Nobody knew the first thing about sharpening. I ransacked the kitchen. There had to be a set of sharpening stones and sure enough. I taught the kitchen regulars how to start with coarse grain and finish with a polisher. I taught them how to rinse and salt and soak cabbage for kimchi. An elderly lady arrived one day with a tin of sourdough starter—the most important item she'd grabbed before fleeing her home, she told us. She stood at my hip for one probationary day to ensure I knew what I was doing. I did. I sanitized a trash can. I kept the can at room temperature. Fed the starter religiously three times each twenty-four-hour cycle. Mornings I would use twentyish pounds for loaves and save two pounds to restart the whole process with fresh flour and water. Enough to keep the arena in the warm scent of sourdough. A small miracle that I helped make happen. It felt good. To help. To be useful. I became a kitchen regular. I got friendly with the other regulars. One of those regulars was Osman.

Osman and I did not appear on the surface to have much in common. He was older—early twenties—and Somali American. His great-grandparents had come to Maine as refugees in the late twentieth century. His family's building had lost power last winter like so many. Pipes had burst. They had joined the crowds squatting in the renovated paper mills along the Androscoggin. Diesel space heaters for warmth. Someone had closed all the windows against the cold. Osman had happened to be out for a night walk. He couldn't sleep. By the time he got back his family had died from carbon monoxide poisoning. So we had something in common.

We became quick kitchen friends. He was clueless because his mother had done all the cooking. But he was happy to learn. He soaked cabbage and diced scallions and measured flour. He was calm. Easy to talk to. He assisted me when I got to captain my first lunch. We grabbed the boxes from the Honda that I had never shipped and made my mother's favorite recipe—potato-leek seaweed soup. I had to settle for defrosted spinach instead of leeks and flat industrial soy butter. But lunch was a hit. They called me Seaweed Guy. I liked the nickname. I liked feeding people. I liked watching them enjoy my mother's food. Osman and I were washing dishes one afternoon when a voice hollered from the counter: Seaweed Guy! Knew that had to be you!

It was the kid from the rest stop. Lucas.

Just got in, he said. What're you doing? Who are you?

I'm Osman.

Right on, Osman. I'm Lucas. Now both of you shove on over. Let me squeeze in there. Never met a pan I couldn't make sing.

Huh? we said, laughing.

I said let's do this! he hollered, rolling up his sleeves.

———

Lucas had an uncle and two aunts. Three young cousins, all girls. A mother. A father. They invited me and Osman to move our cots near theirs. We did not wait to be asked twice.

Lucas's parents had left Puerto Rico for Miami during one of the big storms that flattened the island. Then they had moved from Miami to the Panhandle when the Miami Beach crowd bought up the inland neighborhoods. And now Maine. Refugees three times over. At this rate they'd be in the North Pole soon, his uncle said. Joking but not by much as it would turn out.

Growing up I had homeschool friends I saw maybe twice a month. It was different with Lucas and Osman. We were like brothers. To-gether all the time. We worked the same kitchen shifts. We wandered paths to the banks of the Penobscot to skip rocks and look for turtles. We worked out. Lucas made a barbell from two five-gallon buckets and a mop handle. He was hopeful Miami would honor his scholarship when things returned to normal. Osman and I exercised with him. Push-ups. Squats. Planks. He was surprised we could keep up considering we had never set foot in a gym. I had been carrying seaweed buckets since I could walk, I explained. Chopping wood. Framing sheds. And Osman had worked construction. Swinging a pry bar. Pushing wheelbarrows of cement. Lugging solar panels up ladders.

Functional fitness, Lucas called it. Natural movement. He said we were lucky.

Osman and I looked at each other. We did not feel lucky.

Lucas slapped us on the back. Pulled us in for a group hug. Said we three were going to stick together and everything would be all right.

———

Where was I when it happened?

People always want to know. Emi's first question when she interviewed me for her Great Transition project. I was in the kitchen of the Great Northern Greens Arena. Washing dishes with Lucas and Osman after serving breakfast. We heard shouts from the arena. Everything got eerily quiet. We rushed out. They had it on the jumbotron. The West Antarctic Ice Sheet. Drones streamcasting live. So much ice. Ice the size of Pennsylvania, they told us. Glaciers ten thousand feet thick. An avalanche that continually slid into the ocean for days on days. Scientists had been warning for years but the collapse was still a shock. The seas were going to rise. There was nothing anyone could do about it.

Emi asked if I cried. She knows how easily I tear up. But I do not remember crying. Nobody did. The news was too big to absorb. And for me: What could the Crisis take that it had not taken already? I was a dry well. And I had work to do. Everyone in the arena was digesting breakfast. Soon they would be hungry for lunch. Someone had to get on meal prep.

———

Things moved quickly after that. Not as quickly as we should have, Emi points out, but still. Partly it was luck: It happened to be an election year. People were desperate. Fed up. The old parties had so spectacularly failed. People who had never had a reason to vote were lining up to throw the bums out. To cast a ballot for something new. Anything. Like most I had never heard of the People's Party. Apparently they had been around for years earning a steady two to three percent of the vote. This time they won up and down.

The People's Party made promises like all parties do. The difference was that they delivered. They established a new Department of Emergency Transition. Less than two months later the first recruiter arrived at the Great Northern Greens Arena to make his pitch: They needed twenty million volunteers to save the world. The Great Transition, they were calling it. The largest mobilization in human history. He promised we would be legends. They would tell stories about us for generations to come.

He was pacing a makeshift stage at half-court. Wearing a sharp jumpsuit and combat boots and mirrored aviators and a chunky watch. I remember getting choked up as he asked if we would stand for the future together or drown alone. The greatest war in history was at our doorstep. What would we tell our grandchildren when they asked what we did at the eleventh hour? The choice was up to me.

I say *me* because it felt like the recruiter was speaking to me directly. He was good. It helped that he had music booming behind him. And the arena screens projecting wildfires and screeching eagles and American flags. All orchestrated to create a strong effect on impressionable youth and as one such impressionable youth I can tell you it worked. Everything Dr. Alex had told me in the bleachers about fighting and joining a team and helping as the only way—here it was dropped into my lap. I signed up for a seven-month deployment on the spot.

———

You had to be eighteen to enlist but they were fast-tracking everything and I was so tall for my age. Nobody asked. As soon as you signed they made you choose a branch. I ran into Dr. Alex later. He had enlisted with the Maritime Corps—the Green Marines we would later call them—and assumed he would also see me on the water. I could imagine myself installing tidal turbines and floating seawalls and kelp farms. But with the recruiter hurrying me I had gone with the Forest Corps. He promised we would fight wildfires, and as you might imagine I had a stake in that.

Lucas enlisted in the Forest Corps with me. He was indifferent as long as we could stick together and the job came with a paycheck he could send to his folks. Osman joined us too.

In the end it did not matter which branch we chose. Not in that first scrappy year of the Transition. We signed our names and passed the physical and received our uniforms and marched around the arena to a farewell celebration. They deployed us north to the private timber farms. We spent two cold and uneventful months bulldozing fire lines and carbon-sinking treefall. Then new orders arrived: emergency redeployment. Every company of every branch in New England. They were shipping us all south. We were going to save New York City.

PART THREE

CHAPTER TEN

Hurtling through the hyperloop tube with my dad and a bunch of workers, I figure out a new fact about life: Every day can roll by in the same way—school, basketball, CareCorps, homework—and then in one flash everything can change. That's all it takes. Then life is suddenly a twenty-four-hour hyperloop ride, with each stop like a brand-new first.

First Day Zero parade.

First sip of liquor.

First sniper drone shots.

First stampede.

First jump in Nuuk Bay.

First Public Safety case managers at your door.

First missing parent.

First plane flight.

First step onto a sister city.

First hyperloop.

First hurricane.

But before the hurricane, we hear the hurricane siren, which is another first. We're riding the 2H from the airport. Lucas stayed behind to recharge the plane and—as he sarcastically put it—to make sure none of his friends hijack it a second time. So now it's just me and my dad shooting through New York with extraction workers in rain jackets and muddy boots and hardhats plastered in stickers.

My dad, from the moment we board the hyperloop, won't stop squeezing me against him, like I'm planning to follow my mom and disappear too. He keeps looking around, as if in a sister city of 200,000, he expects her to step onto our car. He's so jumpy that he makes me jumpy. I start imagining everyone on the hyperloop is staring at us. Or not staring, but quick glances before returning to their screens or closing their eyes. A worker sitting diagonally from us—bright blue nails, a Tundra hat, she's young, must've just turned eighteen—she meets my eyes then looks down like she's suddenly fascinated by the floor.

Dad?

Em?

I'm too afraid to ask. About my mom. If everyone on the hyperloop somehow knows something we don't.

How many stops left?

He nods to a map that has appeared above the door. Six stops until Greenwood Heights. From there, a water bus to Gowanus Outpost where we'll find my mom and fly back together to Nuuk, my dad says for the thousandth time. Unless of course I want to visit the Statue of Liberty first? The Big U Memorial? The Met?

Sure Dad, that sounds great, I say, to keep him from worrying that I'm worrying.

But of course I am. Worrying. I'm not dumb. There are two reasons my mom hasn't reached out to us: either she can't or doesn't want to. Hard to see a family museum trip following from either.

Then again, who knows? There could be a third reason. She could be so busy with work that she forgot about us. Or she hit her head on a turbine and lost her memory, so we'll take her back to Nuuk and she'll be a totally new mom. It isn't impossible.

We pull into a station called Rikers Island. When the doors open, I try again to catch my first true glimpse of New York, but all I get are wet crowds of workers on a wet platform, a slice of dark sky, rain. Heavy warm air pours into the car. Then the doors go *chunk* and seal off the view. *Hiss* and we're gone.

The map refreshes: five stops. A worker shuffles by, pushing a vacuum to suck rain off the floor. People move toolboxes for her. We lift our legs. She's listening to music loud enough that I can hear bass. I hug my knees to my chest. Ask my dad again to borrow his screen.

No, he says. Endlessly scrolling isn't healthy.

This is endlessly hypocritical coming from him, but I take a breath and ask again: I just want to check the news.

Try to be present, he says. You're in New York. Take in the sights.

Sights like that? I say, nodding to a guy across from us, his legs spread open.

My dad laughs quietly and points to the window down the car from Leg Spreader.

A hyperloop is different from a maglev because it travels through a raised tube instead of the open. The tube protects the train from weather like hurricanes. I knew this. What I didn't know is how the inside of the tube (at least on the 2H after Rikers Island) is lined with screens that burst into a sort of flipbook as you zoom by. If you synch your headphones—I learn—you get audio too. I catch the end of an announcement inviting workers to submit poems to a citywide contest. Then comes a reminder not to eat on the hyperloop. It stars an animated otter and makes my stomach lurch because I haven't eaten since Nuuk. But then I'm laughing because right across from us— next to Leg Spreader—are two workers gobbling messy sandwiches exactly like the otter says not to.

Next comes an ad telling extraction workers to vote Working Families Party for the New York Social Council—*Don't 'Nuuk' Our Rights!*—followed by a newscast on the Day Zero attacks, followed by weather, followed by a midseason Tundra highlight reel, followed by an announcement encouraging workers to spend their next extraction duty trapping invasive blue crabs, which are eating the oyster stock, which we need to filter pollutants from Jamaica Bay.

I see blue crabs and oysters. I see me, in three years, pulling traps from the glittering bay, banking my first extraction hours with smiling workers in kayaks. At the same time, I see the newscasts. Sirens. Lights. Drones. Running. Screaming.

Which brings up another fact about life: It's possible to see many things at once. You might have your eyes open to your future, and also open to a girl on a hyperloop with blue nails and rainwater dripping off the brim of her Tundra hat, and at the same time your vision is one hundred percent filled with the stampede, all of Nuuk trying to crush you and your dad alive.

But it's not like watching a movie, or even watching multiple movies at once. It's more like being split into versions of yourself. Like there's this one version of me who'd never in a million years climb the seawall and jump into Nuuk Bay—who physically could not—but then there's a version of me with scratches up and down my arms that prove I did.

And it's not just the Esplanade. It's everything. There's a version of me that wishes I was with my basketball team drinking hot chocolate in a ski lodge, but there's also a version of me that feels sort of important to be looking for my mom in New York instead of wasting my vacation with twelve girls who couldn't even pretend to be happy inviting me on their trip.

There's a version of me that agrees with my dad that assassinating people is one hundred percent wrong, and another version of me whose heart starts racing when I think about the Furies and the climate criminals who got one hundred percent of what they deserved.

There's the version of me that feels proud that Public Safety came to our door asking about my mom. Then there's the version of me that could throw up thinking that she might be in trouble, or hurt, or worse.

The most disturbing fact about life, however, is that none of these versions feels real. Not the me riding the 2H, not the me running from the Esplanade, not the me in three years pulling invasive blue crabs out of glittering Jamaica Bay.

It's like being in a warm winter fog. Like being dead. Like maybe I died on the Esplanade?

My dad promised me this isn't the case. He insists I'm alive.

But my question: How does he know? What if none of this is real? What if there was never a Transition, and this is one big quantum simulation to see what would've happened if the world had rallied together to overcome the worst of the Crisis?

He says it's normal after experiencing something like I did. What I saw.

To wonder if you're living in a simulation?

To feel disassociated. It's expected, Em. Flashbacks are normal.

Do you get them?

Sure. It's how we process. We have to relive things so many times.

How many times?

Depends, I guess.

On what?

On what happened.

We were on the Tundra plane when he told me all this. Crossing over a stormy Labrador Sea with brief openings in the clouds to whitecaps below. Endless kelp farms. Wind grids. Clipper ships like toy boats. I was trying to feel grateful for the view—I know nobody my age who's flown on a plane—but the same thing was happening: no matter how hard I stared at the world below me, I couldn't escape the world behind me.

So you just watch it over and over in your mind until the memory goes away?

Sometimes, Lucas cut in. Other times it doesn't go away.

My dad shot Lucas a look like *Not helpful*.

Aw, she can handle it, Lucas said. She's not a little kid anymore. Right, Em?

I nodded, but I was still seeing the Esplanade, and feeling that hot, tight taste in my throat that I get sometimes before falling off my wave. My dad knows the look. He jumped to get me a plastic vomit bag. Lucas handed me a soda.

Probably just altitude sickness, Lucas said. You'll get used to it.

The soda helped a little. What really helped, though, was my hunger. I hadn't eaten in twelve hours. I used the hunger to rebalance, grateful for something to focus on and stop the spinning of the Furies and my mom and Maru and the Esplanade. My dad encouraged me to do the shakes like he taught me. The shakes work. They really do. But I wasn't about to lie down in the plane and flop my legs in front of Lucas any more than I'm going to do so now, on a hyperloop full of strangers. Because even if I don't feel real, to everyone else apparently I am.

———

We glide into the next station: Jackson Heights. Workers leave. Workers enter. I'm breathing and blinking. Riding the wave. Settling into that flat calm. When the newscast appears again—shots of Nuuk, Moscow, Vancouver—people on the hyperloop barely look up. The attacks happened yesterday, and this is New York, my dad keeps telling me: spend one week in New York and you can get used to anything. The girl with the blue nails has her head back, Tundra hat low over her eyes. Short dark hair tucked behind her ears. Silver rings like a ladder up the rim of her left ear. I imagine myself as her: on my first extraction duty and what would I do if I learned about attacks somewhere else in the world?

The kids I look after in CareCorps—even the most tantrummy ones who're convinced their parents have abandoned them—they run out of tears eventually, fall asleep hot against your arm. Adults are the same—like what my dad said about the West Antarctic Ice Sheet collapse: Did everyone in the Great Northern Greens Arena pull out their hair and cry? No, they took in the news, and then got hungry for lunch.

Because you can only worry for so long.

I've felt this before and I'm feeling it now. You can't stay worried constantly. Even when you want to stay worried constantly. Even when you want to focus your energy on a specific worry because forgetting about that worry—even for a second—might cause it to come true.

I slip off my headphones and ask my dad again for his screen to see if my mom pinged us.

He shakes his head: She didn't.

Can you check again?

We're almost there, Em. Be patient.

I take an irritated breath and pop on my headphones. The next announcement, from the New York Social Council, reminds people that shifts over six hours should be flagged for overtime. The actors wear hardhats and wave welding torches like real workers, but they have such perfect noses and lips, they must be models. I take off my headphones to ask my dad if acting for an announcement counts toward extraction hours? Or would it be extra, like a favor?

A favor for who?

I don't know, your co-op?

The Tundra?

Not your co-op, any co-op, I say, but then I give up because he's not listening and the announcement is gone and the animated otter is back, demonstrating how we shouldn't set toolboxes on seats. I'm watching the otter but I'm also back on the Esplanade. I'm remembering to stay worried about my mom. Worried and angry and betrayed. Because she left us. But she also warned us, which is sort of the opposite of betrayal. And she could be hurt, I remember. Or worse. I see the case managers at our door, and it gives me that same mixture of worry and pride and embarrassment. The questions they asked, as if they knew her better than me. Which maybe they do. If not for my Great Transition project, what would I really know about my mom? And even then. She makes me ask all the questions. It's not fair. I remind myself again to feel angry. I pick the scratches on my arms and wonder if they'll scar to give me and her something in common. My headphones come off.

How do you know for sure that Mom's in Gowanus?

My dad looks around. She always goes there, he says quietly.

Why?

To catch up with old friends. Lots of Phoenix Company veterans do their duty in Gowanus.

Is that why the case managers asked about Phoenix Company?

I don't know, Em.

Does Phoenix Company run Gowanus Outpost?

They usually have a majority on the Outpost's Managing Council. So yes, in a way.

That's like the Leadership Council?

Managing Councils do the boring stuff, he says. Keep the turbines spinning, make sure batteries get loaded, keep everyone fed and safe. Every storm hub has one. Gowanus isn't even that large. Wait till you see Rockaway. Or Hunts Point. We'll visit the Point on the way back with Mom. You can see where Lucas and I were first stationed.

Sure, I say, then: What's the Social Council?

Oh, the Social Council represents all workers across the city— everyone on extraction duty at any given time. It makes sure the managing councils are treating workers fairly. And keeps workers informed. Helps with morale. That kind of stuff.

Have you served on it?

No. You have to volunteer for those seats.

What about a managing council?

He shakes his head.

Not even once? Why not?

I worked hard during the Transition, Em. I did my service.

I know, Dad. That's not what I'm saying.

We fall into silence as the train slides into the next station. The doors open to the hiss of rain. I hate arguing with my dad. Arguing is what I do with my mom. I focus on my hunger. I slip on my headphones and choose a song—"Dreams"—by the Cranberries, my second-favorite Irish band. When it's over, I turn back to my dad and ask about his flashbacks.

My flashbacks?

You said everyone has them.

I don't know about everyone.

But you do?

Sure.

Like what? When your mom and dad died?

He turns to me and says, Not all flashbacks are bad, Em. You can have happy ones too.

Like what?

He thinks for a second. Then he says, The first Day Zero. Winning a spot in the Nuuk housing lottery. You. When you were very young—you probably can't remember—we'd go downcity to the thermal baths after dinner, and then Mom would put you into your pajamas for the ride back and we'd get blackberries for dessert. You'd fall asleep in our laps.

My dad always does this, flipping something serious into something cheerful. The complete opposite of my mom. When I interviewed him for my project, he made the Great Transition sound like a fun adventure with friends. He thinks he's protecting me. But I think he's really protecting himself.

Did I cry when I was born?

Oh my god. Like a champ.

What was the first thing I did?

My dad and I have traded these questions back and forth before. I like hearing about myself from a time I can't remember. And my dad loves telling me.

You made a tiny fist.

Then what?

Mom held you.

Then what?

She gave you to me.

Did you cry?

Take a wild guess.

Did Mom?

Maybe because we're talking about crying I feel my eyes fill up. My dad's eyes do too. I try to lighten the mood, saying we should call over that worker with the vacuum in case my dad really starts bawling. We laugh. That's when the hurricane siren goes off.

Emi Vargas Brinkman
North American History
Mrs. Helmandi
Great Transition Project (First Draft)

Me: Mrs. Helmandi helped me brainstorm questions.
    Should I start at the top?
My Mom: The top sounds like a good place.
Me: Okay. Where were you born?
My Mom: San Pedro Tultepec.

Next draft, start here. ←

Me: What was it like growing up there during the Crisis?
My Mom: Hot.
Me: Like how hot?
My Mom: Well, we had a lake in town. My grandmother—
    your great-grandmother—she said she used to go
    swimming and fishing there as a girl. The entire town
    used to wade in to cool off during heat waves. She
    said they would catch fireflies and frogs and there was
    bougainvillea and jacaranda all around town. By the time
    I was a girl the lake was almost completely dried up. A
    smelly crater of mud and plastic bottles. The only animals
    were rats and mosquitoes, and all the pretty trees were
    gone. Does that give you an idea of how hot it was?
Me: But what did it feel like? You wouldn't just die if you
    stepped outside, right?
My Mom: Winter was tolerable. But summer . . . remember
    the saunas at the geofarms? How sweat beads from
    your pores?
Me: Yeah.
My Mom: At a certain temperature the human body can't
    cool down.
Me: Ninety-five degrees. We learned about it in science.
    That's the temperature.

My Mom: Well there you go. So yes, people died. Do you know how many funerals I attended as a girl? Growing up now, your generation can't imagine. Someone's grandparent was always dying. The heat was lethal. For the very young and the elderly. That was life.

Me: How did you cool off in heat waves if you couldn't go into the lake?

My Mom: We suffered. We had air-conditioning, but power came and went. Your great-grandparents all died of heatstroke. Did you know that?

Me: Yes. What would you do when the power went out?

My Mom: Ha. My grandmother used to occupy the bathroom for herself. She would lie on the floor in her underwear. That's what I remember from the Crisis. The floor was stone tile. The coolest place in the house. She would turn off the lights and put on the fan and listen to her shows from her screen. If we were good she might invite us in. Me and Yesi. She would drape wet bandanas on our necks. Any squirming though and she kicked us out. But you know kids—once they're ordered to be still, it's impossible. So we'd giggle. And she would too.

Me: What was she like?

My Mom: My grandmother? She was small. Shorter than my sister. But she had a deep laugh like a man. And all these silly faces and voices. She would do impersonations of us, our parents, our neighbors. She was a jokester. Like Yesenia. They were alike in that way. Trying to make the best of a terrible situation.

Me: Did you ever have your mom or dad as teachers?

My Mom: Yesenia did, I think. My father taught middle school math. Yesi might've been in his class. I can't remember. We left before I entered middle school. My mother taught high school history. Too bad you couldn't interview her for your project. She would have a lot to say.

Me: What was she like?

My Mom: She was serious. She had to be. Two girls and
an elderly mother to care for in the middle of the
Crisis. What immense responsibilities. She worked
very hard. At school and at home. She and my father
were active in the teachers' union. People were always
coming over for meetings. Sometimes Yesi and I were
forced to sit and listen. My mother didn't shelter us
like parents do today. She made sure we knew how
regular people were struggling and organizing and
fighting back. They took us to protests against Pemex.
Or we'd welcome a migrant caravan and distribute
supplies. But my mother was realistic, too. She was a
pragmatist. She never gave us a false sense of hope.
She never promised that everything would be fine. Life
is extremely hard and that is no excuse for giving up.
She taught us that too.

Me: Did you like school?

My Mom: I loved school! I loved reading. But we only
got three days a week, if that. It was always being
canceled because of a heat wave, a blackout, or teacher
shortages. Your generation is so fortunate. Stability is
one of those luxuries that people most often take for
granted.

Me: What would you do on days when school got
canceled?

My Mom: Play at home, I suppose. Read.

Me: Play what? Did you have friends?

My Mom: Families were constantly passing through on
their way north. There were always kids to play with. We
played in a rusted boxcar by the railroad tracks. We ran
around the lakebed. Built things out of trash. Yesenia
was good at corralling us. She was four years older.
She wanted to be a teacher. I remember her arranging
our tule dolls to teach them math. She would lead us

in games, like who could balance longer on the tracks. Capture the flag. Make-believe. She had us pick tule to braid into crowns and little homes. You work with kids. You know how they are. Give them an empty box. They'll make a game out of anything.

Me: What's tule?

My Mom: What's tule? Emiliana! Our ancestors are rolling in their graves.

Me: Sorry. I was just asking.

My Mom: Don't apologize. It's not your fault. Tule is a reed. People used it all over North America for twenty thousand years. You see—they didn't just murder entire biomes. They murdered our culture too. That is genocide. You know about genocide?

Me: Yes.

My Mom: What is genocide?

Me: It's what the Nazis did.

My Mom: Yes, and what happened to the Nazis?

Me: They committed genocide?

My Mom: No, afterward.

Me: They lost?

My Mom: They fled. Like cowards. And many were hunted down and brought to justice, to teach the world a lesson.

Me: Oh yeah. That's right. Um, what was the best part of growing up?

My Mom: The best part?

Me: Like your favorite memory.

My Mom: Have you heard a word of what I've said? I attended so many funerals. Funerals for babies. Death was a part of life. The best part of growing up during the Crisis was probably the ignorance of being a child. At ten years old, you don't think critically about what's happening. My parents never sheltered us. Even so, as a child, you have no idea how bad things are.

Me: What about later? During the Transition? What was the best part then?

My Mom: Off the top of my head? I don't know. It was hard work. Sacrifice. You know what happened to my sister. Look at my face. Does it look like I had fun? A revolution isn't a tea party.

Me: I wasn't asking about fun, just like a highlight. What about the day we won? The first Day Zero?

My Mom: We didn't win. You should know that by now. I was in line last week, at Trader Joe's, and there were two young women, not much older than you, their carts full of junk food and alcohol, talking with absolutely no shame about what they would wear on Day Zero and how drunk they would get. This is not what we sacrificed for. The holiday gets bigger every year.

Me: Isn't it good to celebrate a little?

My Mom: Not if nothing materially changes. Day Zero should not just be a holiday. We need justice, for what happened. We need to be working to make sure it doesn't happen again. Sixteen years ago, people would've laughed if you told them the Nuuk Financial and Mining Cooperatives would be minority-managed by the same people who nearly brought us to extinction. People say "Crisis" and want us to think emissions, pipelines, victory. But who do you think ran Pemex? Every decision that destroyed our planet was made by individuals who knew precisely what they were doing. We can never forget that, okay?

Me: Okay. What about meeting Dad? Wasn't that a good memory?

My Mom: We almost died when we met.

Me: I mean after. When you fell in love.

My Mom: I think this is called fishing for answers.

Me: I'm just trying to do my project, Mom. You said you'd help me.

My Mom: I am helping.
Me: Not if you don't answer any questions.
My Mom: Fine. Okay. I suppose you're right.
Me: About what?
My Mom: Your father. The period after we met. That was very nice.

Great first session, Emi!! You are a natural! You don't need to include all questions and answers in your transcript. Try to keep your subject focused on the past rather than the present . . . this is a "historical" informational assignment, after all. ☺
   —Mrs. H

CHAPTER ELEVEN

LARCH

That first spring of the Transition was the season they relocated the Statue of Liberty. Lucas and Osman and I wanted to see her while we could. We had just set boots on the ground with Maine Company and spent a demanding week deconstructing a row of Brooklyn brownstones. Our first day off the three of us hopped a ferry down the East River. Although the ferry turned out not to be a ferry but an architectural boat cruise packed with tourists—Saudis mostly—and the tour guide like a god directing our attention to which buildings would be spared and which would soon be home to harbor seals in the lobby. Other buildings she pointed out had already been deconstructed, leaving skyline gaps like missing teeth. We sailed under two bridges and around a bend and there she was. Rising from the water and cleaved almost perfectly at the torso.

Three cranes were lowering sections onto barges. Workers swarming all over her on scaffolding. Like sand fleas on a beached gull. Her top half was nothing but blue and cloud. Missing. Cut in two like Lucas and Osman and me and everyone. Probably the reason she was such a popular attraction then. I remember tourists pressing against the boat's railing, livecasting the scene. Fighting for views. Same scramble people were doing for elephants and the Amazon and natural sand beaches: get it while you can.

———

New York by this time was beyond saving. The signs of terminal decline were obvious even to those of us who had grown up in the Maine woods and considered Bangor serious urban living. Entrances to the subway had been sealed off from flooding. Trees dead from roots gorged on salt water. Beachfront neighborhoods where teachers and firefighters had lived were now reefs of rust and timber. And the trash: two blocks outside any mutual aid zone and you found yourself ankle-deep in garbage. Windows smashed. Graffiti on graffiti in every floral layer:

eat the rich for baby jesus

only rats jump ship

All Cops Are Still Bastards

under the pavement the beach

Visit Wall Street! Bring guillotine!

Mama Greta Save Our Souls

solidarity not charity

Occupy the Quantum Mind

Remember the Knicks

Something to do with gravity and New York's latitude meant that sea level rise was worse here than down south where the ice was collapsing. A difference of three or four feet. Lethal considering how closely the city had built to the edge. The work in the face of these facts was unending. Either we worked under the sun or under floodlights bright enough to leave white orbs floating in your vision.

The Department of Emergency Transition broadly divided the early effort into two campaigns: mitigation and deconstruction. Any given month Maine Company might be rotated through either. All the adaptation we now associate with the Transition—regenerative ag and hyperloops and algae farms—would follow on the heels of this initial push. First came survival.

Mitigation meant playing catchup to the Dutch. Flood barriers of riprap and fortified granite. Storm-capture parks. Catch basins. Living breakwaters and tide gates and artificial reefs and sponge jetties. Nobody believed we could stop the sea. The idea was to soften the surge. Lessen the punch. This meant trucking material or dumping material or operating excavators to move material. Monotonous but fulfilling. When they declared a job done—a new basin dug, a new tide gate installed—everyone would honk and cheer and then onto the next job often that very same day.

One job called the Blue Dunes was a forty-mile necklace of barrier islands from Staten Island to Long Island. The kind of project that sounded impossible. We did it in two months. Ten companies dumping sand and pouring concrete around the clock. We were kids—most of Maine Company was under twenty—nobody old enough to remember a time when big public projects outside China were built like this. We knew unemployment and food banks and suicide. The idea of forward progress was something from ancient American history when our ancestors built the Empire State Building and the Hoover Dam and the California bullet train and the Lunar Gateway station.

And now we were those people.

And it was no magic. It was one truckload of riprap after another. One spot-weld then the next. One concrete slab beside a second. Our bodies were the instruments that made it happen. Our hands. You couldn't not feel proud. Especially if the job was near a mutual aid zone. Families bringing handwarmers and coffee and enough pizza to make a flood barrier of its own. Kids running to tag our bumpers. Old folks leaning from windows cheering as our convoys rolled out.

People love comparing the Transition to war. Glorious combat with an invisible enemy. Humanity's last defense. Our final counterattack. The comparison felt a little uncomfortable because lots of

Transition workers had taken the military transfer offer. They had seen actual battle. But it did feel true in moments when the neighborhoods came out for us. I remember one study that got some attention after the Transition—it showed how suicides had dropped in direct relationship to enrollment numbers. Especially young people. Especially young men. I believe it. Sometimes heading back after pouring concrete all night by floodlight—the sky glowing red with dawn—the ferry captain would pull the horn for no good reason and we would all raise a fist and launch into "This Land Is Your Land" or some other song. Cheesy but it shot tears to my eyes. Partly from exhaustion. Partly from living through the end of the world together. As a family. And doing something about it. Trying.

————

That was mitigation. Deconstruction was another story.

Officially the DET referred to deconstruction as the Graceful Retreat. We would hear this on a streamcast after a day soaked in our sweat and picking drywall dust from our eyebrows and all you could do was laugh. Deconstruction was anything but graceful. It was the recycling of entire neighborhoods. Which meant homes. Which meant the heartbreaking wreckage that any family leaves behind. Our job was to take it apart right down to the studs. And then take the studs.

Maine Company might get assigned a block of single-family homes in Staten Island or a row of brownstones in Brooklyn or one tower within the massive complexes in Queens or the Bronx. We were further divided into work crews of six. Our crew was me and Lucas and Osman, plus Ezekiel from Portland and Ellen and Helen—island sisters who had evacuated from Matinicus. Ezekiel was army. They had sent him to Ethiopia. He had taken the Transition transfer offer to avoid going back. Whatever had happened in Ethiopia he did not talk about it. Just like Ellen and Helen and I did not talk about the ocean even though they had grown up working on the water too—lobstering with a Mid-Coast co-op. If you had asked us, we would have said there was no time to talk about the past. We were too busy saving the present.

Every work crew had a name. We called ourselves Done by Noon. We were that fast. We elected Osman our crew lead. He had construction experience and this work was similar if opposite: disassembling a home into its elemental parts.

First you would sort and chute the personals: pots and pans. Books and combs. Tweezers. Anything that could be recycled. Then you moved on to doorknobs and hinges and curtain rods. Sofas and dishwashers and ovens. You ripped up carpets. Pried out windows. Pulled off drywall. Unlaced wiring and plumbing. Knocked out bricks and finally the studs. Wood and iron and steel and porcelain and granite and wire and plastic. Huge mounds in the street for Material Recovery to ship out and turn into turbines and I-beams and rail and riprap. The rearguard would then roll in to dig up the street for the pavement and gas lines and fiber optics. An entire city block deconstructed into mud. Ready for the Green Marines to lay their turbine grids. Blades facing the ocean. Waiting for the water.

Done by Noon did not begin as Maine Company's fastest crew. We earned our name. It took trial and error. We learned to hydrate constantly to avoid heat exhaustion. Working deconstruction required respirators and polyethylene coveralls cinched with duct tape at the wrists and ankles to seal against black mold. But the seal worked both ways: soon as you suited up sweat started beading down your back and legs. Pooling at your feet sloshing around until break when we would stumble outside to gulp fresh air and dump our boots. Not uncommon to pour a quart of yourself into the thirsty earth. Sometimes we would compete: Who lost most? Other times we poured our boots out into a communal bucket to see how much we had given as a crew.

Something else we learned the hard way: Never open a refrigerator. Even dressed for outer space as we were, the smell would work its way in. You had to loop a fridge with duct tape before moving it. Whatever was inside had been mutating on the shelf for months or years. These were the abandoned neighborhoods. High tide lapping the foundations. Mold racing up the walls. Some blocks were within the new intertidal. Other buildings had just suffered one hurricane too many: windows blown out and nature moved in. Not unusual to find wildflowers rooting from couch pillows six stories high. Mushrooms sprouting from rolls of toilet paper. Pigeons roosting. At one complex in Queens we surprised an enormous bird nesting in the sink of a twentieth-story kitchen. Linoleum littered with feathers and bones of tiny animals. She squawked and flapped at us before flying out to leave two chicks behind—hungry little puffballs that would never survive the wrecking ball. We debated for all of five minutes before voting to adopt.

Maine Company had many mascots on account of all the abandoned pets. But these were our first with wings. We fed them crumbs of protein bars. Kept them warm under rigged floodlights. Huge arguments as to whether they were falcons or hawks or eagles. Then one of the crew leads—Mariah—declared they were turkey vultures and because Mariah had volunteered with the Audubon Society and was a Maine Company elder—almost forty—it was settled.

We let the neighborhood kids name them. We had been thinking vulture names like Styx or Roadkill or Wall Street. The kids had different ideas. They went with Pizza and Peck.

When Emi interviewed me for her Transition project one of the first stories I told her was about Pizza and Peck. I knew she would like to hear about the baby vultures. And she did. But in the same breath it was like she reminded herself not to be amused. She accused me of telling happy stories only. Leaving the bad stuff out.

I reminded her about the refrigerators. The smell. How Lucas once puked in his respirator.

She didn't mean like that, she said. She meant real stuff.

Like what? The weather? I told you, it was hot.

I knew what she was really asking. She wanted to hear about the squatters—the addicts and the mentally ill—begging us not to knock down their homes. The holdouts. The elderly who we would find mummified in their beds or a chair by a window. Committed to going down with the ship. Animal corpses too. So many pets. The three brothers from Rockland whose scaffolding collapsed into the hardening sludge of a surge gate we were building in Gowanus. The I-beam that slipped from its harness breaking Mariah's back. Emi was asking for this. Only the more she asked—pleading almost—the less I wanted to give. I don't know what age is the right age to open the book of your life to your child. But I do know it is not fifteen.

Emi however would not take no. Like her mother in this way. She said I had to tell her. For school. For her project. Unless I wanted her to fail?

I did not want her to fail. But.

She reminded me that her mother tells her everything.

Fine, if you really want to know I'll tell you. They died.

Who died?

The vultures. Pizza and Peck.

Well yeah, Dad. Baby animals never survive without their moms. I could've told you that.

———

The most important practice we learned working deconstruction was to remove photographs when starting a new unit. Graduations. Baptisms. Weddings. Everything. Otherwise the family was watching you ransack their life. They still followed you—race-car sheets or a Bible by the toilet or a dog dish on the porch—but without their eyes the job was a little easier. Every room contained ghosts. Not whole ghosts. Fragments. But fragments could assemble into something with power. It happened to us all. I would walk in on Lucas holding a basketball trophy in a kid's room. Helen touching the fabric of a dress in a closet. Osman with a graduation photo—parents sandwiching child—that he had not yet deconstructed into glass and particle board and wire hanger.

Need a break, boss?

Naw I'm good.

Take five. Hydrate. That's an order.

Every home we took apart was another family evacuated and scattered with nothing to return to. We could all relate. If I thought about my life before the fire—say I heard the gurgle of a tide pool or caught the herbal smell of my mother's kitchen—then I simply stopped thinking about it. We disassociated. You had to. Which was why we were so good at deconstruction: not just burying the past— bury something a mile deep and you can still dig it up—but taking it apart. Preventing reassembly. Deconstructing the past to build a fresh future.

We did this for weeks. Months. Over and over. Every home completely different yet exactly the same. Then we would ride back to Hunts Point to sleep and wake up and do it again.

———

Maine Company was fortunate to have our barracks in Hunts Point. We lived on the grounds of an old Metropolitan Transportation Authority lot. Four massive tentlike shelters with bunks for all one thousand of us. The shelters when we first erected them were bright white. Neighborhood kids took exactly one minute to name them the Marshmallows.

Hunts Point was one of the Bronx's most influential mutual aid zones. It had strategic importance on account of the food distribution terminal. Half of all food that came through New York went through the Point. The neighborhood had leverage. They had organized into a federation of unions and cooperatives and block associations and community land trusts. Confusing at first but then simple when you saw their Movement Assembly in action: Everyone in the neighborhood got a say. Which now included us. We were in this together.

We opened the Marshmallows for shelter during storms. After storms we helped rebuild. City services did not extend reliably outside Manhattan. A random sanitation sweep might pass through. NYPD drone flyovers were more common. And so the work fell to regular people. As it had for years now.

Not every work crew pitched in during their days off. But Osman was always out there. So we were too. I volunteered to help with breakfast shifts. Lucas started a youth basketball league. Osman did maintenance for a mutual aid preschool. He had fallen hard for a teacher and was working overtime to convince her to fall for him right back.

Life in Hunts Point was utterly different from what we had left behind. Which was exactly what we needed. We were too busy working to give an inch to past or future. But here is the thing about the future, I told Emi—the thing that previous generations did not realize until it was too late: The future is always waiting. Not just waiting but on its way.

CHAPTER TWELVE

EMI

The hurricane siren has this immediate effect: It causes all different versions of me to collapse into one dense point. Like what happens to a dying star before it goes supernova. Except it's not gravity or a black hole or whatever causing the collapse. It's the blare of the siren, and the red flashing screens, and my dad, who jumps out of his seat to squeeze me so hard that I'm back on the Esplanade unable to breathe.

Then the hyperloop hisses and, with a *kerchunk*, reduces speed. My dad loses his balance, almost bringing me to the floor with him. People leap over like they're competing to be the first to help.

Sorry about that, says my dad, laughing to everyone and no one. It's been a day.

The woman with the vacuum runs the nozzle over my dad's back. His clothes are gritty from the floor. Everyone's trying not to look like they're looking. It's embarrassing. The siren, I hear now, isn't even that loud. A voice comes over the speakers to report shifting storm patterns and the news that we'll be holding at the next station.

I pretend to resynch my headphones as my dad sits and puts his arm around me. I nudge him off. Not completely off, just a little. The siren wouldn't have surprised my mom. My mom wouldn't have everyone looking at her like they're looking at my dad: like he's some MineCo big shot who's never worked an hour in his life.

I want to stand on my seat and list all his Transition deployments. Tell people that he was here in New York at the Battle of the Big U and featured in season three of *Corps Power*. But, of course, I don't say any of these things. I do make eye contact with the girl wearing the Tundra hat. She's also staring at us, but not in an embarrassing way. More like a sympathetic way. Like the siren scared her too and she's glad she isn't alone.

I roll my eyes at my dad.

She rolls her eyes right back like, *Dads. I've been there.*

I smile.

She smiles in return. So wide and friendly it makes my cheeks go warm.

———

The hyperloop stops at Brooklyn Heights to wait for the storm to pass. We're only one stop from Greenwood Heights but the system doesn't like to take chances, my dad says. Better safe than sorry, and I agree one thousand percent.

We grab our bags and follow everyone out. I'm ready to finally see New York, but it's like the city's hiding from me: we walk from the platform through a tunnel into the station, and we might as well be at the bottom of the ocean.

Brooklyn Heights is a huge glass dish turned upside down. Similar to Nuuk's maglev stations, except less dome-like and more earthy-smelling and taller trees—because of the latitude, my dad says, more sunlight down here. It's an old station they deconstructed, moved across the river, and renovated. I try to be interested as he explains the history, but it's hard paying attention for two reasons. Reason one: the newscasts on the wall screens, flashing images of the attacks and the Furies' manifesto, reminding me that every minute we spend stuck here is another minute my mom could be in trouble, and how can my dad be talking history at a time like this? Reason two: the hurricane. It's insane. Sheets of rain cascading down the glass. More water than I've ever seen or heard outside of the ocean, and just like the ocean, the sight and song of it casts that same spell, drawing people over. Drawing me.

I pull my dad by the hand, hardly noticing the food booths or the pocket gardens. The station's rim is lined with reclining seats and rocking chairs. All occupied, but that's okay, I don't feel like sitting. I feel like walking to the edge and pressing my hands against the thick glass and staring into the storm.

If my dad had told me this wasn't actually glass but really a giant screen projecting rain, I would've believed him; this amount of rain just seems impossible. When I flatten my palms against the glass, however, I feel the thrum of the storm, and no screen can do that. The wind plasters leaves and twigs against the glass. The debris parts the rain briefly like an actor peeking from curtains before a play. I catch outlines of waves heaving, turbines going crazy, yellow seawalls inflating. And then the otter.

I shriek when I see it. My dad grabs me. Then he relaxes, seeing what I'm seeing: possibly—likely—the most adorable animal in North America, standing on hind legs, paws against glass, nose and whiskers twitching. The sheer cuteness hurts my chest in that nice, warm way I get at CareCorps when a kid runs over excited to see me.

The otter blinks. Its fur is a swirl of browns working to shed the water. It cocks its head. Looks me right in the eyes. Other than seagulls and lemmings, Nuuk has zero wild animals. I've seen orcas by the geothermal farms, and caribou herds from a blimp, but this is the closest I've come to a true wild animal.

Then it's gone. Tiny paw prints on the glass that the rain erases. I cup my hands trying to peer through the storm. Rain and more rain. My breath fogs the glass.

Will it be okay? Won't it drown?

Otters are made for water, my dad says.

But in a hurricane?

They've survived worse.

Like what?

Like us, says a man my dad's age, eyes closed, sitting next to us.

Another thing I've learned about New York: everyone's a stranger but nobody acts like it.

———

My dad switches his bag from shoulder to shoulder and says he needs the bathroom. I want to keep looking for the otter, but as soon as the words come out of my mouth, I'm glad my dad says no. I realize how badly I have to pee, for one, but also it rushes back to me again that my mom's missing. We're not here for wildlife sightings. We are in a crowded glass bowl in a hurricane, zero feet above sea level. I hustle to keep up with my dad.

What should I do if we get split up?

We won't.

But what if we do.

Em. We're not splitting—

But—

We'll meet by the stage. But it won't happen. Don't worry.

I pee first, then stand with our bags while he goes. A flock of six or so parrots chatter in the trees. A few fly off, winging over to a lattice where some workers shoo them away. The workers are harvesting veggies—cucumbers, I think. Next to the garden is a raised stage with a woman on drums and a man on violin. No lyrics, just a low beat with the strings in this watery, warbling back-and-forth. It's super calming under the roar of the hurricane, almost like a soundtrack for the storm, which I guess is the point. I feel a tap on my shoulder and catch the sharp whiff of coffee.

Hiya, I got this for you. Hope you like it sweet. I went hard on the sugar.

I spin around. It's the girl from the hyperloop, handing me a steaming cup.

Thanks, I say.

To layovers, she says, raising her cup. Cheers.

I touch my cup to hers, careful not to spill. Then I take a sip of coffee—another first—and almost choke with surprise: it's bitter but also delicious.

She pulls a croissant from a bag, tears off a bite, and gives me the rest. She hooks her arm with mine, linking our elbows. Her movements are so casual, like we know each other.

I'm Reena, she says, chewing.

Emi, I say. That's my name. Emi. Emiliana.

Put me with Maru or Lucas or ten kids at CareCorps, and I'm fine. But people closer to my age and sometimes I just freeze up. I can't find the right words to say.

Where's the big guy? Reena asks. He's your dad?

I nod.

Are you missionaries?

What?

Missionaries. Mormons?

She gnaws on a second croissant from her bag. The croissant she gave me is warm in my hand. The soft inside has rebounded from her bite. I break off a flake. My stomach swells, trying to spin me off my wave. I catch myself. Rebalance.

We're not missionaries.

You don't look old enough for extraction duty. No offense. Oh! Restorative justice hours? Is that why you're here? What'd you do?

I'm not in trouble. We're here to get my mom. She got hurt.

Oh. Girl. I'm sorry. Injuries were crazy yesterday. Everyone was on their screens, watching the uprising. I came *this* close to stepping off the roof. Algae harvesting if you're wondering, and no, it was not my first choice.

She makes a face and sticks out her tongue but I'm still seeing her eyes when she said *uprising*: big and shining in an almost dark blue way.

I was there with my dad, I say. In Nuuk. At the uprising.

Reena's eyes widen, getting even bigger and darker and prettier.

We had to jump into the bay to escape the stampede. It was so cold.

She throws up her arms: Pulling duty this week was the worst thing that has ever happened to me! I miss everything! Don't get me wrong—I don't love violence. Violence isn't my personal philosophy. But someone had to let the fuckers know we didn't forget they burned down our house. What else are we supposed to do? Put them in charge of the fire department? Invite them into our new home like it never happened? Ask them to sit down and help us redecorate?

I shake my head in agreement. It's a little surreal, hearing someone close to my age talk like my mom.

Of course not, she says. But they're trying. You heard about Duluth? How they're rechartering private corporations?

They are?

They're talking about it. Like hiya, ever heard of history?

She tucks a strand of hair behind her ear and touches the brim of her hat and tears off a hunk of croissant. I imagine myself at eighteen, on my first extraction shift: traveling solo around New York, talking politics with strangers, wolfing pastries, my nails a blue so luscious that people can't pull their eyes away.

Anyway, she says, swallowing loudly, I'm sorry about your mom. But I'm sure she's okay. Seriously. I have a good feeling about these things.

Okay. Thanks.

Hey, you two looping to the outpost?

A boy has drifted over to us. He's almost as tall as my dad, but wiry. The sleeves of his work uniform are rolled up above his elbows, his forearms ropey with veins. He has long black hair tied in a bun.

Excuse us, says Reena. We're in the middle of a private conversation.

Sorry, he mumbles, and turns to leave.

Wait, you mean Gowanus Outpost? I call out.

He stops. Yeah, you're going too?

You and us and half of New York, says Reena. It's getting *in* that's the hard part.

I got a connection, he says. My aunt rolled with Phoenix Company for a deployment. Says she can get me on the transfer list. I can put in a good word. If you want.

My heart does a double dribble at *Phoenix Company*.

I'm sure you could, says Reena flatly.

What list? I blurt.

The transfer list, he says. To join the revolution.

Reena rolls her eyes. Extraction duty transfer. To switch over to Gowanus. But there's a long waitlist. Everyone's trying to get in.

Why? I ask.

To be close to the action, Reena says. To help out.

The boy nods. Mutual aid. Like the old days.

My mom always does duty at Gowanus, I say.

Always? Reena says.

The boy asks: Does she know any Phoenix folk?

They're both staring. Their attention is a magnet that opens my mouth, almost pulling out the words to tell them *yes*, my mom knows Phoenix folk—she *is* Phoenix folk. But I swallow it back. I see the Public Safety case managers outside our door, asking similar questions.

Why's everyone care so much about Phoenix Company?

The moment I ask, I shrink back to a little kid in their eyes. I watch it happen.

What? I say.

Um, have you seen what's happening? the boy asks. The news?

She was there in Nuuk, Reena says, throwing an arm around my shoulders. She saw it go down.

What's that have to do with Phoenix Company? I say.

Reena and the boy throw each other a look that makes me feel even younger and smaller.

Phoenix and the Furies, the boy says, crossing his index and middle fingers: They're like this.

CHAPTER THIRTEEN

LARCH

In the bathroom I cup my hands beneath a faucet. I drink and slap water on my face and stare at the drain to avoid the mirror. I know what I will see. Exhaustion—no sleep last night at Maru's with her cat running around and Emi vocally researching which pet boarding center we should take her to and the whole time expecting another knock on the door. A relief to spend a few hours with Lucas on the plane but no rest, all talk. He had no more answers than MemeFeed. Agreed it made sense for me to feel crazy. Agreed these were crazy times. Exhaustion is causing my mind to misfire. On the hyperloop I saw Kristina stepping into the train car four or five times. I saw Rich and Min looking for us. Following us. Saw myself swinging wildly between two poles. One pole: thinking I made the correct move getting Emi away from Nuuk. Other pole: terrible mistake.

But the mistake is not mine. It is Kristina's. For leaving us. For involving me and Emi in whatever this is. For not telling me a god-damned thing.

I dry my face with a sleeve then lock myself in a stall and pull out my screen. I ping her for the hundredth or millionth time since she told me to take Emi and run. And for the hundredth or millionth time she does not respond. I put the screen to my face and cry a little and scream silently into the dark glass and it works: The screen lights up. I fumble, almost drop it.

But it's not her. It's Lucas.

Storm hit you down there yet? he asks.

Just landed, I say. They shut down the hyperloop.

That's what I was afraid of. Any idea when it will be up again?

No word yet. We're holding over in Brooklyn Heights.

I'm thinking we should head back to Nuuk sooner than planned, he says. I don't want to get stuck. Steal a plane for a day, it's a dumb mistake. Overnight and it's trouble.

I close my eyes and tell him we won't be ready soon.

Still haven't heard from her?

No, I say.

Well, how much time do you need? Are we talking hours?

You should just go. Head back while you still can.

I don't mind getting in a little trouble if I can help, he says.

You already helped getting us here, I tell him. We can blimp home. Anyway, we might stay a few days. See the sights. All of us together.

Love that optimism, he says.

Yeah, I say, my voice catching. I'm trying.

I hang up and cry and ping Kristina again. I ping her. I ping her. I am trying. Trying to hold it together. For Emi's sake. For my sake. But what is held together must eventually come apart. And here I go: Pinging her again. Telling her to answer. Yelling at her. Screaming. Throwing my screen against the floor where it skitters across the tiles.

The bathroom goes quiet. I step out of the stall and nod at two men who are watching from the urinals. I pick up my screen. Wash my hands. Look in the mirror. You come apart then you put yourself back together. That is life. I nod at myself. I head outside to protect my girl. To find my wife. To keep my family safe.

CHAPTER FOURTEEN

My dad walking out of the bathroom is both comforting and terminally embarrassing at once.

Hiya gang, he says, wiping his hands on his pants. Emi, who're your friends? He snaps his fingers and points at Reena's hat: Go Tundra!

Dad, I say.

He sniffs at my cup.

Coffee? You're drinking coffee?

Right then a small cheer erupts from a corner of the station, followed by another—little pockets of celebration as if the Tundra have just sunk a big three-pointer. But there's no Tundra game this holiday week. Reena's face turns blue in the glow of her screen. Same with the boy and others. Even the band goes quiet. I elbow my dad and tell him to check his screen.

Not now, he says, looking around.

Yes now, I say, reaching into his pocket. He grabs my wrist, but not before I pull out his screen. The glass is a jeweled web. A thousand little trapezoids.

I dropped it, he says when I look up at him.

Dropped it from where? I ask. Is it broken?

I think so.

But what if Mom's trying to reach us? Dad!

Calm down, Em. It's fine.

Reena and the boy are high-fiving.

We got another one! says Reena.

She holds up her screen: A livepic of an old man. A pop-up sticker identifies him as Ian Rios, a quantum investor and climate criminal. Assassinated by his physical therapist on a yacht in Lake Superior. The Furies are taking credit. I try to catch more but the screen is half-obscured in flying hearts from MemeFeed users. My dad swears under his breath and rubs his eyes. He swipes at his shattered screen.

Did it turn on? I ask. Is it working?

He clenches his jaw and shakes his head.

Did Mom ping you in the bathroom? Dad? Did you talk to her?

He pockets his screen and gives me that same infuriating shake of his head: *Not now. Not here.*

Around the station, people are cheering and whooping as the news spreads. The excitement leaves me feeling spinny and left out in that way I get with my basketball team. Like there's a secret team within the team and I'm alone in not knowing. I drink the rest of my coffee in a few big gulps, then turn back to my dad.

What did Mom tell you? I say. Did she know about this attack too?

He grabs my shoulders roughly and swings me around.

Quiet! he hisses. Everything's fine. We're going to find her and everything will be great. Until then you have to watch what you say. You can't just blurt whatever you feel like. Emiliana? Do you understand me? Tell me you understand the words coming out of my mouth.

He's angry—obviously—but also, I see that he's scared. We're not going to find my mom and take her home. There will be no museums. No Statue of Liberty. Which I knew. But knowing was easier when he was trying to pretend.

I twist away from his grip: Mom isn't perfect but at least she doesn't treat me like I'm five. You never tell me anything. You think I'm this helpless little kid. I'm not. I get what's happening.

Emi. My god. What's wrong with you? We can talk about this later. Now isn't the time.

Yes it is! Now is the time!

My vision sort of spins and this strange thing happens where the roar of the storm falls silent, and there's a high-pitched ringing in my ears, and the green birds in the station are squawking, and the band is picking up again, and a bone in my wrist is popping as I push my dad away and make a fist like I did first thing when I was born. That's when I see that my hand is empty. The croissant Reena gave me: It's gone. I swallowed every crumb. My throat didn't even notice. Which makes me feel the same way I feel about my mom and dad and everything right now: On one hand amazed, special, proud to be part of whatever this is. But on the other hand, completely and utterly betrayed.

Emi Vargas Brinkman
North American History
Mrs. Helmandi
Great Transition Project (First Draft)

Mom Session II: Refugees

Me: Where were you when the West Antarctic Ice Sheet
  collapsed?

My Mom: Arizona.

Me: At the refugee camp?

My Mom: Yes.

Great first question that grounds us in the historical moment. More like this!

Me: How did you hear about it?

My Mom: The collapse? A newscast probably. They always
  kept some screen blaring.

Me: What was your reaction?

My Mom: We cheered. We were excited.

Me: Excited?

My Mom: You have to understand, defeatism was
  rampant then. In the camp, obviously, but outside
  too. People were hopeless. Now here was one reason
  to celebrate—the guards and border agents and
  politicians and climate criminals would drown with the
  rest of us.

Me: How long had you lived at the camp when the ice
  sheet collapsed?

My Mom: Six, no—seven years. If it wasn't for the
  Transition, I might still be there. Or dead from some
  disease. Think about that. You wouldn't be here without
  the Transition.

Me: How old were you when you left Mexico?

My Mom: We didn't simply leave, Emi. We didn't wake up
  one morning and say, "You know what'd be fun, let's
  move to a place where everyone hates us."

Me: I didn't say it would be fun, Mom.

My Mom: But it's an important distinction. Nobody simply leaves a place they've called home for generations. Ask any refugee. We would've stayed if we weren't forced to leave.

Me: Why were you forced to leave? Because of the heat?

My Mom: I suspect so. The heat is so hard on the elderly. My grandmother was probably the reason my parents finally decided to go. All our neighbors had already left. Their homes had become shelters for migrants. There were no children left for my parents to teach. And the government was harassing everyone who stayed.

Me: Why?

My Mom: For making the most basic demands as human beings. Any place where people still had a shred of dignity, they were demonstrating. My parents took us to every Pemex protest.

Me: What's Pemex?

My Mom: What *was* Pemex.

Me: What was Pemex?

My Mom: The state oil company. They were still drilling and extracting. Even then. Squeezing every last peso. People would try to block the gas and oil trains. There were battles on the tracks.

Me: How would they block the trains?

My Mom: Old cars. Trees. Tractors. Sometimes standing on the tracks.

Me: You mean like people? People stood in front of trains?

My Mom: Sometimes. Yes. Everyone knew what had dried up our lake. And the rich getting richer as they killed us slowly. The cartels were angels compared to the destroying classes. But before people give up completely, if they have any dignity left, they get angry. There's nothing left to lose. I hope you'll never know that feeling.

Me: Did you ever stand in front of a train?

My Mom: I was ten. What kind of parents would let their ten-year-old girl stand in front of a train?

Me: Did the protests ever work?

My Mom: I remember one train they burned on the tracks.

Me: Did you ever see anyone get hit?

My Mom: People sometimes fell off. Migrants rode on top. We were fortunate enough to own a truck. That's how we were able to go north rather easily.

Me: I thought you sailed.

My Mom: We had to get to the ocean, didn't we? We drove to the Sea of Cortez. Took a ferry across then way up Baja to some bay in the middle of nowhere.

Me: How did you know where to meet the boat?

My Mom: I've wondered the same thing myself. My parents had arranged it somehow. Maybe with an American teachers' union? I don't know. There was a lot of cross-border solidarity then. So many regular people that you will never learn about in history books, all fighting together against impossible odds. Remember that. No matter how bad things get, there are always those who will risk personal comfort and freedom to help strangers. It's our true nature. The destroying classes tried to convince us that we are competitive. They persuaded us to compete against one another. And for what? To make them richer while destroying our planet. Well, we saw how that turned out. And now we see the opposite. Mutual aid. Participatory budgeting. Cooperative enterprise.

Me: What was it like on the sailboat?

My Mom: Oh, it was a dream. Everyone got seasick but me. I had a great time. The Americans had candy. Stickers. A little cooler with nothing but ice cream. Obviously they'd taken kids before, but in my mind it was all for me. We were so fortunate. Others migrating by sea had to pack onto rafts or rusty fishing boats that border drones could spot from miles away. Our boat was white and clean with gleaming silver fastenings, and the crew all white themselves, and dressed in sharp uniforms with collars and hats. Like they were our servants, and we were wealthy important people. Which I suppose was the illusion. And it worked. I remember one drone flew right over us without stopping. We sailed north with no problems.

Me: How long did it take?

My Mom: Two or three days? I don't remember. I remember anchoring one night off some islands that one of the Americans said were infested with rattlesnakes that had no rattles. Funny what you remember. I remember hearing sea lions. I don't even remember my family. Maybe because they were sick? To me it was ice cream and games and dolphins—

Me: Dolphins?

My Mom: Many. But a dream. Like I said. Because we had to land eventually.

Me: And that's when they arrested you.

My Mom: That happened later, the next day. There was a checkpoint. We were hidden in a truck. They pulled us out. Treated us like criminals. Two teachers, two girls, an old lady.

Me: Did they handcuff you?

My Mom: Not me or Yesi. We were tagged. Plastic bracelets you couldn't remove.

Me: Did they take your biometrics?

My Mom: I'm sure.

Me: When was the last time you saw your parents and your grandmother?

My Mom: We traveled together on a bus. They separated us after that. In Arizona.

Me: Were you sad?

My Mom: More numb than anything.

Me: You weren't sad?

My Mom: I was ten. I was in shock. When the most terrible
things are happening it's impossible to comprehend.
Even for adults. Now imagine you're ten. You think
you're sad when you have too much homework, or I
won't let you have your own screen, or you don't feel like
mulching for a few hours at the garden? Real tragedy
is different. Picture a bus filled with crying families
driving into the dark desert. The adults knew what was
happening. My mother knew. She wrote a number on
my arm in eye liner. Kids aren't dumb. We could hear
the adults crying. Praying. My grandmother smothering
us in kisses. You convince yourself it's not happening.
And my sister—when they did split us up—one bus for
adults, another for children—she took my hand and said
they'd be back. She was older. I believed her.

Me: What was the last thing your parents said?

My Mom: To me? I have no idea. It was chaos. People
screaming. Crying. Guards prying families off each other.

Me: What about your grandmother?

My Mom: I can't remember, Emi. Our memories block
those things for a reason.

Me: Do you think if you were hypnotized you could
remember?

My Mom: Ha. Maybe.

Me: I bet they said they loved you.

My Mom: Possibly. Or to be strong in case they never
made it back.

Great work, Emi. I'm seeing a lot of passion in these
transcripts. Not that the interviews of your father and your
neighbor are lacking, but I might suggest focusing on your
mother. Journalists will often return to the same topic
for repeated sessions to bring out more vivid memories and
reflections. Just a thought!   —Mrs. H

CHAPTER FIFTEEN

LARCH

I celebrated my eighteenth birthday on a Brooklyn rooftop. Done by Noon threw me a surprise party. They got me. I was surprised. I cried. Which was fine. This was in the middle of my third deployment with Maine Company. My crew was family. I felt comfortable crying in front of family. But we were not alone.

Culture Corps had launched a series of reality streamcasts and the producers of one—*Corps Power*—had decided to feature us over three episodes. The field producer, Joanna Lee, had supposedly walked off a big-time movie lot to join the Transition. By the time she embedded with us *Corps Power* was already streaming its second season. New episodes were events. Crowds gathered in the Marshmallows to watch. Season one followed an implausibly attractive crew laying high-speed rail across the Great Plains. Season two followed the Cajun Navy restoring wetlands in the Gulf. Not as attractive as season one but lots of daiquiris and venomous snakes to keep it exciting. And now with close to twenty million Transition workers across the continent *Corps Power* had selected New York for season three.

Day one shooting we were all nerves. We had been assigned a row of single-family homes in Queens. With Joanna's ring lights and camera drones buzzing around I doubt we spoke five words. We were sure they had made a mistake selecting us. Queens was not the bayou. No radioactive alligators were jumping out. And us. Were we special? We were not. The only reason *Corps Power* had selected our crew—I believed at the time—was because we had made a name working so hard. So that was what we did: We worked hard. Right up to the knife edge of heatstroke. When Emi pulled the first episode she could hardly recognize the human wrecking ball going berserk with his sledgehammer. Lobster-red face. Sweat pouring like tears. Forehead veins throbbing.

As she put it when we watched together: Dad, you were scary.

That first day shooting we smashed our crew best. Day two we picked up with the same breaking pace. Five minutes in Joanna called it quits. Grounded her drones and actually yelled the word *Cut!*

Are you trying to get me canceled? Act human. Be yourselves. Have some damn fun.

She reminded us that *Corps Power* was not a livecast. She would edit. That was her job. This was propaganda, she said. The good kind. Hearts and minds. She was not doing this for fame. She was doing this because the Transition had to succeed. Viewers needed to suffer a deep sense of missing out if they did *not* enlist or buy T-bonds or at the very least experience the itch to put an oil executive's head on a stake. In other words, she said, I need each of you to take a breath and loosen the fuck up.

We loosened up. I cracked jokes with Lucas as we gutted homes in the intertidal. I sang along with Ellen and Helen. We stomped our boots. Swung sledgehammers to the beat. I used my pry bar to gouge a smiley face in the drywall before crashing through to surprise Osman in the next room. I was myself. Not noticing the cameras. Hardly noticing the cameras. Just enough to push myself a little harder. Smile a little wider. Act a little extra.

Joanna filmed our downtime too. She caught us during breaks as we pried starfish off dumpsters. As we chanted dumb songs about the Carbon Capture Corps. As we hunted for a power source to spin a turntable we had found along with a vinyl set of Bruno Mars's greatest hits.

And Joanna's cameras kept rolling when we returned to the Point. She filmed us hunkered down during a superstorm to play cards in the Marshmallows. She filmed me in a mutual aid kitchen juggling jars of enchilada sauce. Judging a cake bakeoff. Learning from neighborhood ladies how to properly stuff and fold a tamale. She filmed me and Lucas short-sheeting Osman's bed. She filmed Osman attempting to climb into said short-sheeted bed with his girlfriend. She filmed them getting romantic. She filmed Ezekiel and Ellen getting romantic. She filmed Lucas and a guy from Vermont Company getting romantic. She interviewed us. She prompted. She pried. She had more luck if she caught us alone. Less luck in groups. No luck with me and Ellen and Helen in Staten Island after a day deconstructing: standing at the concrete shoreline with our coveralls unzipped and sleeves tied at our waists. Hair gray with drywall dust and the sun slipping into the water.

                              JOANNA
            Growing up you all worked on the ocean.
            That was the only life you knew. Will
            you go back after the Transition?

                              ELLEN
                        (whispering)
            Did she just say "after"?

                              HELEN
            Poor girl. Her parents probably never
            told her.

                              ELLEN
                      (clearing throat)
            Joanna. There's no after. The world's
            ending. The rich broke it.

                    JOANNA
                (laughing)
        Larch? What about you? Does the sight
        and smell of the ocean ever make you
        miss your family? Maine? Your home?

                    LARCH
        It's not the same ocean.

                    JOANNA
        Aren't all oceans one ocean? Aren't all
        waters connected?

                    LARCH
        You could say that about anything. The
        air. The earth.

                    JOANNA
        Okay. But do you?

   We were all balancing on the thin blade of the present and—in
the quest for entertaining emotional content—Joanna was trying to
push us off. She finally succeeded on my birthday. It was our third
deployment as a crew. For all the DET's promises of redeployment—
they had even sent forms for us to rank preferences—they kept every
company in New York. We would learn why later. At the time it was
just a lot of excitement stirred up for nothing.
   Personally I was ready to leave. Like much of Maine Company I
missed the wind in trees. I missed trees. I had enlisted with the Forest Corps for a reason. That reason did not include tall buildings and
concrete and nonstop noise. I wanted Done by Noon to apply to go
west. Colorado. Idaho. A landscape that resembled Maine but was
not. I wanted to fight fire.

Helen and Ellen were with me until the second Transition treaty. Now along with migration-visa, renewable-energy swaps with Canada and Greenland we were doing the same with Mexico and Belize. Helen and Ellen had their hearts set on La Paz. Supposedly there were beaches on the Sea of Cortez with almost no plastic.

As for Lucas and Ezekiel they believed we were supremely idiotic not to choose California. Sure there were mudslides and wildfire but what syllable of *Cal-i-for-nia* did we not understand?

                         JOANNA
            And you, Osman? As crew lead, where
            should Done by Noon go next?

                          OSMAN
            Nowhere, I hope. I'll miss them if they
            leave.

                         JOANNA
            You aren't applying for redeployment?

                          OSMAN
                   (smiling radiantly)
            I'm staying right here. I'm going to be
            a dad.

The teacher Osman had been seeing was three months pregnant. The news made an impact I did not expect. No one feeling that I could name. A tumbleweed of emotions that stayed tangled for weeks after he announced it. Lucas felt strongly too.

                         LUCAS
            True confessions, I am just deeply
            sorry for the dude.

> LARCH
>
> Osman or the baby?

> LUCAS
>
> Both.

> OSMAN
>
> You guys know I can hear you. I'm
> literally sitting right here.

We were taking our break on a rooftop. A partially deconstructed brownstone. As the camera pans you see work crews on rooftops all down the block. Emi and I watched the episode together. Three stories below the tide is coming in. Little rivulets against the curbs. You hear a dog barking. The background thrum of jackhammers. And me: resting against an air vent. Legs crossed. Head back. No idea that Ezekiel is on the fire escape trying frantically to light eighteen candles. No idea they know about my birthday. Joanna had told them.

> LUCAS
>
> I'm just saying I don't think it's a
> good idea.

> OSMAN
>
> What don't you think is a good idea?

> LUCAS
>
> Bringing a kid into this. Think about
> it. What the world's going to be like.

> OSMAN
>
> I think about it every day. That's why
> I'm out here. Why are you guys?

There was a pause after Osman said this. Everyone squinting at the horizon or adjusting a glove or following a V of cargo drones across the sky. But not me. To me it was an easy question.

                          LARCH
          We're here to save the planet.

                          HELEN
                (Scoffing)
          For who?

                          LARCH
          What do you mean "for who?"? For Osman's
          kid. For everyone.

                          ELLEN
          (pointing to the Manhattan skyline)
          For them.

                          LARCH
          That's not true.

                          ELLEN
          No? I've spent almost two years now
          building a three-mile storm moat across
          four boroughs with enough turbines to
          power their dumb quantum network for
          eternity. What have you been up to?

                          LARCH
          Fighting for the future. For the
          Transition.

                    HELEN
You're adorable, Larch.

                    LARCH
Fuck you, Helen.

                    OSMAN
Crew. Take a breath. If Larch wants to
hope, let him. Costs nothing to hope.

                    ELLEN
I love hope, boss! Give it to me.
Please. Name one Transition project
for regular working people and not the
motherfuckers who caused all this. Give
me that and I will hope all over your
face.

                    LUCAS
Umm . . . what?

                    LARCH
High-speed rail. Desalination.
Regenerative ag.

                    HELEN
You think your ass is ever riding one
of those trains? You think they'll pull
out a seat for us at the table later
when they won't even get us filters for
our respirators now?

> LARCH

We get a paycheck. Meals. A roof. Try
being grateful.

> ELLEN

I'll be grateful when they take our
safety seriously. When they let us have
a damn union.

> LARCH

Every second we spend fighting each
other the Crisis gains ground. We have
to stay united.

> HELEN

Someone has been memorizing his DET
streamcasts.

> LUCAS

(waving hands)
Can I please say something?

> ELLEN

The rich are coming off a two-hundred-
year rager that burned our planet to
the ground. We're the cleanup crew.
The moment we're done the party will
be back on. And if you think you're
getting an invite, Larch, I just feel
sorry for you.

> LUCAS

Hello? Can anybody hear me?

                    LARCH
Where would we be without the
Transition? Where would any of us be
right now? We could have it so much
worse.

                    HELEN
But Larch, we could have it so much
better.

                    LUCAS
I am feeling extremely unheard!

                    ELLEN
Oh my god Lucas, what?

                    LUCAS
Thank you. I just wanted to say that
as a crew that cares deeply about one
another I cannot in good faith allow
us to simply move past Ellen saying she
would hope all over Osman's face.

There was silence. Then laughter. Lucas's great talent. More so even than basketball. Osman came over to hug me. The others too. We ended up in a heap with me at the bottom. Crying and laughing. No word for it. Howling? Cawing? We would not be together forever. No family is. Obvious to me of all people. But just because something is obvious does not make it easy.

                    EZEKIEL
Surprise! Happy birthday, brother!
You're a man!

Ezekiel clanging up the fire escape. Cradling my cake like it was a baby.

                              EZEKIEL
              What happened? Did I miss it?

He put down the cake and fell on our pile. Watching that episode with Emi I wondered if Done by Noon had subconsciously learned to play it up for Joanna. Or if we used her cameras to unload our hope and fear. Either way I can testify that those are real howls coming from the bottom of the pile. Genuine laughter. True tears.

Joanna started singing "Happy Birthday" off-screen. Osman joined in. Lucas and Ellen and Helen and Ezekiel. Other work crews on neighboring rooftops. Standing and singing. If you have caught season three of *Corps Power* then you know how the episode ends. Cameras sweeping upward. Ocean on the horizon. Storm clouds gathering. And in the foreground Done by Noon singing "Happy Birthday." Screaming it. Holding each other. Holding me.

Emi Vargas Brinkman
North American History
Mrs. Helmandi
Great Transition Project (First Draft)

Mom Session III: Camp

Me: What happened after the border agents separated
you from your family?

My Mom: It was a blur. There were many buses. Many
adults asking questions, telling us to sit down, be quiet,
line up. They kept transferring us. Off one bus, onto
another. I got motion sickness. Yesi too. Kids were
throwing up. Crying from hunger. Then off into the cold
night, into a building—a warehouse, really—with pens,
like we were animals. Lining us up. Asking for birth
certificates. Checking our hair for lice. But not checking
very hard, let me tell you—I got lice right away and had
it on and off for years. Everyone did. We went half-mad
with it. You'd wake up scratching. We used to pick them
from each other's scalps, but without a lice kit you can't
get the eggs. Sometimes they would spray our bunks. I
remember Yesi breaking down one time. Crying on her
hands and knees, ready to pull out her hair. Every once
in a while a guard would take pity and bring in clippers
for anyone who wanted a clean shave.

Me: Shave your head? Did you?

My Mom: Once or twice. Yeah. I looked like a skinny
little boy.

Me: Did you live with boys?

My Mom: Near the end they split us by gender. But for
years we were all together. It was very embarrassing.
The toilets weren't far from the beds. There were no
walls. Yesi and I would hold a blanket for each other as
a screen.

Me: What was your first night like?

My Mom: I really can't remember, Emi. The nights all become one.

Me: Then what about that one night?

My Mom: Which one?

Me: The one night that all the other nights become. Like night in general.

My Mom: What was night like? Well, exhaustion. If you weren't waking up because of lice, then it was hunger. Your stomach would wake you at four a.m., it didn't care. And someone was always crying. People think of the desert as hot, but nights are cold. Before they gave us bunks we only had mats on the floor. We slept together for warmth. Yesi would put her hand on my foot. I couldn't sleep without it. Kids were up at all hours, crying, crawling around, stepping on your head, cuddling into you. It was very crowded. Some children were so young. Toddlers. Who was supposed to take care of them? We weren't parents. But we did it. We looked after each other. And even then, if everyone happened to fall asleep, the guards might burst in with flashlights to yell that we shouldn't have come to their country. To go home. For years there was one guard who'd wake us up to ask how many stripes on the American flag, name the founding fathers, recite the Pledge of Allegiance. If you failed, he would announce full count, which meant everyone had to stand and line up so they could make sure nobody escaped.

Me: Did anyone escape?

My Mom: In some ways.

Me: What do you mean?

My Mom: Suicide.

Me: Oh. What about like running away?

My Mom: One girl—I can't remember her name—she made a grappling hook with a water bottle and a bedsheet. It

got her over the inner perimeter fence during rec time—
we had one hour a day outside—and she made it all the
way to the outer fence. What was her name? It doesn't
matter. She could've climbed over. But she just straddled
the fence, waiting for the guards to notice her and pull
her down.

Me: Why didn't she escape?

My Mom: The camp was in the middle of the desert. Some
kids had family and knew where to find them. An uncle
in Toronto. A cousin in Ohio. But most of us had nobody.
Nowhere to escape to.

Me: What about the number on your arm that your mom
wrote down?

My Mom: I never got the chance to call it.

Me: Do you remember it?

My Mom: No.

My: You have no idea whose number it was?

My Mom: Yesi thought we had second or third cousins
in Texas, on our father's side. I don't remember ever
hearing about any cousins. Yesi could've been making
them up, to give us hope. That was Yesi. Wishful
thinking. Optimistic to a fault. Even if we did have
relatives in Texas, between the heat and hurricanes and
the nuclear plant, everyone was going north. No adults
were coming to take care of us. So we took care of each
other. You're so good with children. You would've been
extremely useful in the camp. There were kids with
younger siblings. Seven-year-olds caring for toddlers.
Holding them to their chests to keep them warm. We
would sleep on the mats all together with the youngest
in the center for warmth. Like penguins in a blizzard.
Can you imagine? That's how we survived. That's the
power of working collectively. That is solidarity.

Me: Did you have school?

My Mom: Ha. There were trailers they called classrooms.

Me: Were there teachers?

My Mom: Sometimes. Always very young. Nice and well-meaning, but they never stayed long. No sane person would remain in an environment like that if they didn't have to.

Me: So how did you learn?

My Mom: What do you mean?

Me: Like all about history and the Crisis? Everything you always talk about. You're so smart. How did you learn everything without going to school?

My Mom: School isn't the only place to learn, Emiliana. School can't teach you how to live with hunger, or go weeks without a shower. The greatest lessons come from life experience. That was how we learned to band together. Take care of ourselves. Solidarity. Where else do you learn how long you can last without sleep? Or how to really—truly—live with hunger? A few times we organized protests for the most basic things, like new underwear. Once, in retaliation, the guards made us go four days without food. Only water. Other times they fed us spoiled food like uncooked chicken—raw almost, you could see blood, but you'll eat anything if you're hungry. The body can't refuse, even when you know you'll be sick. That's why I get frustrated when you are so picky. You have no idea how fortunate you are. A professional chef for a father who will cook whatever you want—

Me: I'm not picky, Mom, I just can't help it.

My Mom: Of course you can. If I could swallow rotten chicken, you can eat your father's cooking without gagging.

Me: Can we get back to my project?

My Mom: Yes. What were you asking? How did I learn about the Crisis? I was living it.

Me: But how do you know so much about politics and economics and everything?

My Mom: We taught ourselves. Sometimes a load of
books would get donated. Lots of junk but I loved to
read. And in the junk were biographies and old college
textbooks. I read about the great mass movements.
The Zapatistas. Harriet Tubman and John Brown.
Toussaint Louverture. The African National Congress.
The First Nations. The Black Panthers. The Long March.
And economics, too. The Mondragon Cooperatives.
Smith. Marx. Keynes. We would learn and teach each
other. We had study clubs. Do they teach you political
economy at school?

Me: I don't know.

My Mom: Well you should know it.   *We do! Senior year!*

Me: How did you learn English?

My Mom: Out of necessity. There were lots of kids from
Haiti and Africa and the Pacific Island states that
had flooded. Also, kids who only spoke indigenous
languages. English was the common tongue. Spanish,
too, but guards only responded to English. Even the
ones that spoke Spanish, they would pretend not to.
I was sick once—there was always some flu going
around, colds and strep throat, fevers, malaria, West
Nile, dengue—and Yesi was pleading for the guards to
take me to the doctor. They pretended they couldn't
understand until Yesi asked in English. Then one guard
looked at me and said he'd seen sicker.

Me: Why were they so mean?

My Mom: They were sick themselves. The entire system
was. Everything back then, it was built to dehumanize.
From the top down. The borders. The economy. How
else could the destroying classes keep such immense
wealth to themselves? By convincing everyone below
them that there was someone yet further below—to
punch down instead of striking up to lop off the head.
Cruelty was the point. One year on Christmas a guard

woke us up for count just to explain that there was no such thing as Santa or Jesus or God.

Me: Did you ever see anyone die?

My Mom: I fought wildfires for ten years in the American West.

Me: I mean at the camp.

My Mom: Three girls hung themselves. I saw one, the morning after, before they got her down. And there was a boy. A toddler. He died overnight from a severe reaction. A scorpion, we suspected. You had to watch out for scorpions. Snakes too. Kids collected the skins. The camp was porous—the tents especially, but even the warehouses would shake from sandstorms. You'd wake up covered in dust, head to toe. The desert came right in. We were always filthy.

Me: There weren't showers?

My Mom: Yes, but no clean clothes to change into, so what was the point?

Me: What would happen if you asked for clean clothes?

My Mom: Ha, you sound like Yesenia.

Me: What do you mean?

My Mom: Buttering up the guards. Asking nicely for underwear. Seconds of dinner. Magazines, chocolates, tampons.

Me: Did it ever work?

My Mom: Sometimes. But it was charity. Charity comes with a price.

Me: Like what price?

My Mom: Do you really want to know?

Me: Yes.

My Mom: Yesi was sexually abused. Raped. The guards were sadistic. Not all. But some, and the rest would look the other way. What kind of grown man or woman would take a job like that? They were damaged individuals. There was no political education then.

Instead of directing their anger at the destroying classes, they focused it on us. You can't reason inside a power structure like that. You can't beg yourself out. You must fight. Yesi was a wonderful sister. So silly. So kind. Always looking out for the younger kids. But it was her weakness, too. She was too hopeful. She saw the best in everyone. She was always telling the little kids that everything would be okay.

Me: What's wrong with that?

My Mom: Well it was a lie. We know that now. We can't promise anything different. We shouldn't. That was Yesi's weakness—she asked. You can't ask. When has power ever given up anything? You never ask for it. We demand. We take what's rightfully ours.

Wow, Emi. Powerful. The child detention camps are such a shameful period in our history. Although it is extremely important, remember that this is technically a project on the Great Transition, so next session ask your mom about that time too.

Great work. —Mrs. H

CHAPTER SIXTEEN

EMI

They call this a layover, Reena tells me. When a storm amps up, or veers suddenly, and they close the hyperloop. Total roll of the dice where you land. This is her first layover in Brooklyn Heights, but it doesn't seem so bad, she points out: big reclining chairs, live music, hot drinks, food stalls. There are worse places to get stuck.

Like where? I ask.

Like Staten Island, she says.

Like Port Authority, says the boy at the same time.

They both laugh, then Reena explains how lost hours are still lost hours, no matter where you do a layover. If I was scheduled today, she says, at least I'd be getting credit for sitting on my ass.

You're not scheduled? I ask.

Nope. Six days on and here I go burning my one day off. Hiya.

Same same, says the boy.

The boy's name is Angel. He and Reena and I are sprawled in a loose circle on the floor, backpacks propping us up, relaxing along with everyone else in the station. People are either asleep or zoned out on their screens. My dad is in one of the comfy-looking chairs, his feet kicked up. I've positioned myself as far away from him as possible while still keeping him in sight, so he can see that I'm not done being angry. The hurricane has been lashing us for hours now. I let my eyes blur, watching the storm through the glass. Reena and Angel are quiet on their screens, long silences interrupted by whatever random thought the scrolling sparks.

Hey, says Angel, have you rented skateboards in Central Park?

No, Reena says. You?

I keep meaning to.

Did you catch the streamcast from Patagonia?

Just the highlights.

Kinda cold-blooded.

It's justice.

You think you could take out an old lady like that?

Was she a climate criminal?

Yeah. But still.

Well, that's why we have drones.

Have you been to that new club on the Point?

Golden Temple?

Yeah.

Not yet.

Me neither.

As for me with no screen, what can I do but be angry at my dad and try not to say anything stupid or laugh at the wrong thing? I'm working to piece together what I can about the Furies and Phoenix Company without sounding clueless. But every time I open my mouth I'm at the free-throw line: all eyes on me and one mere inch between a swish and an air ball.

So I watch. I listen. I learn that fourteen climate criminals have been killed in the past thirty-six hours. Almost all in their nineties or hundreds. Most by sniper drone. One or two bombs. The Patagonia woman, a stabbing. The Furies have taken credit but MemeFeed isn't sure. It could be a secret United Nations force. Or First Nations commandos. Or Mama Greta back from the grave. Or a corporate false-flag operation. Or some Transition veteran group—like Phoenix Company—fronting as the Furies.

But the assassinations happened all over the world, I risk pointing out. Phoenix Company is just in Gowanus.

Maybe, Reena says. Or maybe Gowanus is just their base. Maybe they're everywhere.

Maybe they're here with us right now, whispers Angel.

Reena laughs and punches his shoulder.

The two of them spend a lot of time reading MemeFeed comments and subthreads. I listen with one ear. In my other ear I hear Mrs. Helmandi lecturing us about reputable sources. Avoiding MemeFeed rumors. But rumors have to start somewhere, don't they? Because I can still hear my mom, talking exactly like the Furies' manifesto. I can hear her through my dad's screen on the Esplanade, telling us to run. How would she have known?

I lean back against the cool glass of the station. The croissant that Reena gave me is demanding company in my stomach, working with the news and my dad and the world to spin me off my wave. I rebalance, refocus. The musicians have returned to the stage. They make these long calming beats that warp one into the next as the hurricane continues raging two or three inches behind my head. I want the storm to end. Also, I don't want it to end. Because then the hyperloop will start up and I'll have to crawl back to my dad and Gowanus is just one hyperloop and one water bus stop away, and my mom will either be there or she won't.

———

A giant screen over the stage has this hypnotic fade, dissolving and reassembling:

Storm Gigawatt-Hours Captured: 140 . . . 141 . . . 141.8

Watching with my back against the glass, I keep my dad in the edge of my vision. He's in the same reclining chair, pretending to rest. His legs give him away. I can see him doing the shakes. Shaking off his worries. He feels bad for yelling at me. And grabbing me so roughly. And breaking his screen in a fit of anger.

He confessed once I got upset enough. Once he saw my tears. He pulled me in for a hug and kissed the side of my head and told me: He'd thrown his screen at the ground after pinging Mom for the thousandth time. He'd lost his temper. He regretted it. All of it. Everything. He was so sorry, he said. Sorry and frustrated and tired. He was crying silently as he said it.

I said it was fine. Even though it wasn't. My dad acts so calm and in control, but really he's the same person from *Corps Power*, season three: a very big man who, at any given time, might just as easily crash through a wall or burst into tears or tell a dumb joke or lose his temper. My mom can be harsh and not half as fun, but she's predictable. With my dad, he'll turn up his feelings to drown out yours. You want to cry? He'll cry harder. His emotions go bouncing all over the place. Dealing with him is like working with kids at CareCorps. Exhausting.

It's okay Dad, I said, patting his arm. I'm tired too.

Thanks, Emi. Sorry I yelled.

Me too, I said.

I suggested we get his screen fixed. There had to be a kiosk in the station.

But he said no. He said it was better this way.

Better what way?

I don't want people to know we're here, he said.

What people?

Anyone.

What about Lucas?

Lucas is family. We trust Lucas.

You said Mom didn't do anything wrong.

She didn't. I just don't want people to get the wrong idea.

What idea, Dad?

There's a lot of rumors going around.

Mom could be trying to find us. Dad. We need a screen.

Not right now.

We can borrow Reena's.

I said no! This is serious. We have to be careful.

That's why we have to find her! I'm doing it. I'm pinging Mom.

He touched my wrist and lowered his voice: Emiliana. Think about the consequences.

I shook free from his hand and told him I didn't care.

Yes you do, he said. I know you, Em. I know you care.

If he had outright forbidden me, I'm pretty confident I would've marched over to Reena and made a big show of borrowing her screen. But the way he was threatening to cry again and trusting me to do the right thing—it smothered my anger. Some of my anger. There was still enough to sling my bag over my shoulder and turn my back and walk across the station. To make sure my dad could see me sitting down with Reena and Angel. Laughing with them. Borrowing Reena's screen. Only to scroll MemeFeed until my eyes went blurry but I had to make him think that for once I might not care about him or anything at all.

———

Reena, it turns out, is also from Norsaq Plaza. The eastern ring, but still, we've probably crossed paths at some point. Angel grew up in Nuuk's Kalaallit Quarter, the Inuit zone. He pulled extraction duty at a gravity storage warehouse doing preventative maintenance on hydraulic cranes, he tells me. In Nuuk he's a poet. He has a soft voice that makes him sound even younger than he looks. I've never met a poet before. Realizing this makes me wonder what else I don't know I've been missing.

Aren't Indigenous exempt from extraction duty? I ask.

That doesn't mean we can't volunteer.

You volunteered to spend two weeks in a storage warehouse?

It's mindless work, he says with a wave. Gives me time to think and write. Anyway, someone has to do it. Everyone's gotta pull their weight.

Sexy, says Reena.

Angel blushes and looks at her.

Don't get weird, she says. I'm not into boys.

I'm eighteen, Angel says.

Aw honey, Reena says, patting his knee. I didn't mean it like that.

She winks at me. I smile back, feeling mature to be somewhat confident that I think I know what is maybe going on.

I can't tell if Reena and Angel are including me because they are nice or because they are bored or because of my mom. Everyone has an uncle or aunt or parent who served in the Transition, but Phoenix Company? That's superhero stuff they say, when I tell them my mom was a founding member.

If Phoenix hadn't lit the spark, we'd all be slaving for some corporation on a wasted planet.

Must be amazing, having a mom like that.

So amazing, I say.

Later, when Reena brings up the Tundra—tickets a cousin gifted her for her birthday—and she and Angel start talking playoffs, I don't dare mention that my dad works for the team. The games I've caught courtside. Growing up in the clubhouse kitchen. Eating with players. The privilege is embarrassing. And my parents—I decide—don't need to be any more popular than they already are.

———

Shortly after the big screen above the stage announces that New York has captured over two hundred gigawatt-hours of storm energy, Reena jumps up. Anyone hungry? I'm hungry.

I could eat, says Angel.

Emi?

No thanks, I say, looking at my dad. I don't want to give him the satisfaction of seeing me eat. When Angel says he'll stay to hold down our spot, I say, Me too.

But as soon as Reena leaves, I discover another fact about life: you might've spoken English your whole life, and pretty decent Spanish and even a little Danish and Kalaallisut, but suddenly you can find yourself with nothing to say in any language. Angel looks up from his screen like he feels me staring at him, which I am.

Hiya, he says, nodding at my headphones. What's on?

I run through my recents: Britney. Beyoncé. Cranberries. U2.

Old school, he smiles.

Yeah, I love oldies.

Music was how I got into poetry, he says, scooting closer. Have you heard of Kendrick Lamar? You have to read his lyrics. Great musicians are just great poets with a sense of rhythm. The New York Social Council has a poetry contest going on right now. Want to read my submission? It's garbage, but I always tell myself you can't win if you never try.

He hands me his screen.

The hours after Solstice scientists get creative.
They'll attach a quantum unit to a sunny day
that would otherwise go unused.

They'll see the earth from every possible angle.
They'll try to wrap their heads around the story.

The crags and alpine meadows
desert dunes
networked forests.
Beaches full of light.

Our bodies aren't meant to live inside.
New research suggests the sky.
The tides.
The rolling tundra that flattens
into a necklace of keys.

I hand back his screen and declare it not garbage.

Thanks, he laughs.

THE GREAT TRANSITION   151

You'll win for sure. What's first prize?

They put your poem in the hyperloops. Which would help me get into the U of G. That's my dream. They have an amazing poetry program.

When I graduate I'm going into CareCorps.

Hiya. I have tons of family in CareCorps. Juniors or Seniors?

Juniors.

Nice. Kids are way more fun than the elderly.

Yeah. I love kids.

I suddenly realize I've thrown a bunch of conversational air balls in a row, and all my language leaves me again. I look around for Reena. Instead I meet eyes with my dad. I glance away. The storm pounds the glass behind me. New York has captured 203 gigawatt-hours. I try to be like Maru and ask a question—any question—but my mind's seized. There's nothing to say except—again—that I really liked his poem. Especially all the nature stuff.

Thanks, he says. Have you gotten to experience nature?

My family volunteers at the geothermal farms. We saw orcas once.

If you like the geofarms you'll love the real thing. I did a semester in the Torngats.

The mountains?

Yeah. You should go sometime.

Aren't they in Half Earth?

So?

I'm not Indigenous.

I didn't say you had to live there. You could just visit. Volunteer. Do a bioblitz. Tag some plants for a weekend. You'll love it! Like the geofarms but a thousand times bigger. And wilder. And so quiet. Especially coming from Nuuk. But also not quiet? It's weird. That's why I use that word, *networked*. You feel sort of—quantumy. Like a hum. Like everything bleeds together. You close your eyes and it's ice, stone, cloud. Everything part of the same. It's hard to describe, he laughs. I guess that's why we invented poetry.

His description of nature reminds me of riding the wave of my hunger: arriving in that flat clean place where everything is clear and simple and still. I tell him that I know what he means.

Then you definitely have to go! he says. We're lucky there's any left. But that's the other thing—you get mad out there, learning what it used to be like. Walruses and glaciers and wolves . . . forests with trees five hundred fucking years old. You go from being super calm to super mad in a blink. That's why some people say real justice would be going after their families.

Whose families?

The climate criminals. Like real vengeance, you know? Pulling their family trees up by the roots. Extinction for extinction. Eye for an eye. This thing now? A few old people put down after long comfortable lives of destruction and profiteering? This is compromise. They should be grateful we aren't treating them like they treated us.

I lean a little closer and ask if he thinks it's really possible that Phoenix Company is the Furies?

I think we're living through a really important, exciting moment in history, he says. And I want to be a part of it. Do you?

I nod.

The way I see it is like this, he says. Everyone can't be the tip of the spear. We need the base of the spear too, you know? We need hands to hold the spear. Hands to support those hands. People to argue loudly and unapologetically that the spear must be used.

But isn't it terrorism?

No, he says. It's absolutely not. That's how they convince us to never demand anything. What they call terrorism I call solidarity with life. *They* are the terrorists. The destruction they caused? All that death? They could've made an attempt at restorative justice. They still could. Transfer your damn wealth, people. Commit your lives to extraction duty. Apologize. Would it undo the Crisis? No. But it would be a start. Anyway, it's a moot point. They'll never admit to doing anything wrong. So we have to bring the justice to them. Is it messy? Sure. A little bit.

A revolution isn't a tea party, I say.

Exactly!

We laugh and meet eyes again.

I ask what he'd do if the Furies wanted him to join.

I'd be honored.

Would you ever be able to go home?

Probably not for a while, he says. I hear they've been underground for years.

At this point I realize we've been talking for full minutes and I haven't even thought about it. Like I'm at the free-throw line sinking shot after shot and I can't miss. Which is exactly what you realize the moment before you toss an air ball. Before I jinx myself I take another shot: What about your family? If you joined the Furies, would you ever be able to talk to your family again?

That's tough, he says. I think a lot about my ancestors. Not even that far back. Like take our parents' generation, your mom and dad—they fought to stop the Crisis and win back power for regular people. So me, personally, I just want to help finish what they started. Do my part. We root out evil now, or the future gets stuck with it. It's on us. Like always. Regular people.

The words *we* and *us* are so little but they hold so much, and being included—*networked*—with so many people gives me this sort of low-voltage buzz that forces my throat to tighten, but not in a choking way. More like an excited way. I swallow so loudly that I'm sure Angel can hear. I rest my head against the glass. The thrum of the storm vibrates my skull. I let it fill my brain.

When I open my eyes, Angel is staring at me. I don't look away.

Emi, can I ask you a question?

I like that he says my name. I like that he asks my permission. I give it.

How old are you? he says.

Seventeen, I lie.

Okay, he says, smiling.

What's so funny?

Nothing.

Both of us are smile-blushing together.

I glance at my dad to make sure he's looking. I put a hand on Angel's ankle. I swallow and it's the loudest sound in all of Brooklyn Heights Station if not the world.

Riding the wave of my hunger has always rewarded me with a clean light-headedness. A spark to my fingertips. A momentary pause to the spinning of the world. These are the prizes for discipline. But this thing right now is something else. This is jumping off the Nuuk seawall. This is seeing people shot and killed. This is touching a boy's ankle at sea level as a hurricane tries to erase us from earth. This is me becoming a new person. Which must happen all the time. The way it happened to my parents and Maru and everyone. They called it the Great Transition for a reason. People change. Things change. Seasons turn. I'm not special. I get that. But nobody ever told me that you can observe yourself changing in real time, becoming the person you didn't even know you wanted to be.

Let the feast begin!

Reena returns with bags from McDonald's. I smell the greasy warmth. She sees my hand leaving Angel's ankle. I think I catch her frowning at him, but just as quickly she's smiling.

Anyone hungry?

You bet, says Angel.

They arrange the food on the floor like a picnic. Even though I said I wasn't hungry, Reena brought enough for three. I scoop a handful of fries, two nuggets. My dad is watching. I don't need to look up to know. I don't need to see him sitting alone and worried. I don't need to comfort him. Instead I pop a single fry into my mouth. I chew loudly using both rows of teeth. I relax my throat. I swallow. I smack my lips. I lick the salt off my fingertips. I eat.

CHAPTER SEVENTEEN

LARCH

Three months before Osman was going to be a father we got emergency redeployment orders: The Battery. Manhattan needed us after all.

The redeployment was unique in its magnitude. Not just Maine Company or Forest Corps but every Transition worker in New York and even some companies from Philly and Baltimore who erected temporary barracks in Central Park. Over 100,000 of us deployed to a single job: an integrated storm barrier to hug Manhattan from Forty-Sixth Street on the East River to Sixtieth Street on the Hudson. The Big U.

Many people think of the San Francisco BayGate or the Southwest Solar Authority as the largest projects of the early Transition, but the Big U was even more ambitious. Ambitious yet possible. After years of building mile-long barrier islands and artificial reefs we were trained up. We could operate cranes. Excavators. Bulldozers. We knew how to pour concrete and weld and set rebar and sink pilings. It was almost as if the DET had been prepping us to save Lower Manhattan.

Keep going, Larch, Helen said. You're so close to getting it. You're almost there.

Joanna Lee had finished filming us for *Corps Power*. Had she still been embedded in Hunts Point she would have captured hours of argument about the Big U. Because this was the other unique aspect of the project: it was divisive.

Either the Big U would channel water into other neighborhoods and cause apocalyptic flooding or it wouldn't. Either it was a conspiracy to save Wall Street or it wasn't. Huge arguments erupted at Hunts Point's Movement Assembly.

Isn't saving something better than saving nothing?

Not if it's Wall Street.

It's not Wall Street. It's our city.

How many times are we going to bail their asses out?

The Big U is worse than a bailout. They get saved, we drown.

Same as it's always been.

Not the same. Worse. They build the Big U, the next storm swamps us.

Didn't know you were a hydrologist.

Doesn't take a hydrologist to know which way the water flows.

Brooklyn'll get it worse. We'll be fine up here.

Point of clarification—regular people still live in Manhattan.

Vultures. Not people.

You sound just like them.

They broke our planet.

We all broke our planet.

I never worked no finance gig. I never funded no pipeline. I never flew no private jet.

We have to be practical. I'm the last one to defend them. But without Wall Street the economy could collapse.

And?

We need the economy.

What economy? Whose economy?

How you gonna live without money?

Same way I live without it now!

Money don't get up early to cook breakfast. Money don't raise my babies.

There's no such thing as money. It's just us. People. People making shit happen.

That's right—mutual aid, baby. All the way to the pearly gates.

So what do we do?

We stop the Big U.

How?

We call our reps. Named the People's Party for a reason.

Our reps are right here.

Hi y'all. We're working on it. We're trying.

You gotta try harder.

And if they can't?

Then we got no choice. We got to fuck shit up.

———

They fucked shit up. Not many but a committed few. Protested. Marched. Smashed store windows and lit some minor fires on the Upper East Side. NYPD and private security shut it down. Sealed off entry points to the island. Only residents were allowed through. Residents and essential workers. Which included us.

Crossing the Harlem River every morning now meant crossing the picket line. Not a huge picket line—not yet—but enough to ruin your day. People yelling and waving signs and rocking our bus. Kids pelting our windows with snowballs. Same crowds that used to bring us pizza and cheer as we rolled by. Now stomping their feet and freezing for the chance to call us traitors. Waiting to cross the bridge I would stare hard at my boots and zone out. Ellen and Helen bailed on day two.

Fuck this, they said when the bus stopped at the bridge.

Maybe half the bus followed them off. Same thing in buses all up and down the convoy. Huge cheers from the picket line.

Ezekiel stood over Osman in the aisle: Sorry boss.

You do you, Osman said. See you tonight.

Three days later they were all back. The DET had made it clear that anyone who refused orders would be stripped of pay, pension, education credits. And for the Ezekiels who had taken the military opt-out? They would be sent back into battle. Not the metaphoric kind we were waging. The real kind with smart bullets and cluster mines and drones.

So Done by Noon was back together. But it was different. A sense of defeat as we rode the bus each morning into Manhattan's southern tip.

Maine Company had been assigned a one-hundred-yard stretch of The Battery. We were not starting from scratch. The city in the old days had built what people now called the Mini U: an earthen berm that had woefully underestimated sea level rise. Buttressing the Mini U was our first big job. We would sit on it during lunch breaks. Overlooking the harbor you could hardly see water through all the floating cranes. Barges. Cruise ships housing Transition workers. Sometimes a gap would open and you might catch a flash of Liberty Island. Culture Corps had relocated the Statue of Liberty. But the pedestal remained.

Kinda symbolic, said Lucas, pointing with his half-eaten sandwich.

Like it's waiting for her to come back, I said.

Right. He nodded. Like all this is temporary.

You guys are so clueless, Helen said. It would be cute if it wasn't so pathetic.

Has anyone ever told you about the power of positive thinking? Lucas asked.

Helen rolled her eyes.

But for people like me and Lucas working the Big U was really like that: It made you hope. It made you want to hope. Crossing the picket line killed you a little each morning but the work itself—contributing to such a monumental project—was different. The people who still lived in Lower Manhattan were grateful. They hung green ribbons in support. Every window and lamppost and bumper. They stopped to thank us for our service. Ezekiel hated the phrase—he'd heard the same thing wearing his army uniform in public. If rich folk wanted to show their thanks they could grab a damn shovel, he said. But I enjoyed the gratitude. It made me proud. Which I was. Until we got assigned sixth shift.

Sixth shift started at one in the morning. Heading south after midnight our bus cruised through the black canyons of Lower Manhattan. So many buildings were dark. I wondered out loud if construction on the Big U had caused the grid to go down? Or was there some new initiative to save power?

Easy to save power when nobody lives here, said Ellen.

The buildings were empty. Not abandoned but vacant. Uninhabited luxury condos. I had heard about this. But it was different seeing it: block after block of black lifeless glass.

So I'm busting my ass to save a bunch of empty condos? Lucas said.

Not empty, said Helen. Filled with money.

Investment properties. Not even second or third homes but a place for the Saudis and quantum traders and speculators to dump profits. And once we finished the Big U and secured Lower Manhattan? Property values would soar.

I looked at Osman. He was resting his head on the window staring at the same buildings. Either not hearing our conversation or not caring. I thought of all the homes we had deconstructed. The families who had fled. Osman's family. Mine. I saw the refugee camps along I-95 in Maine. The Great Northern Greens Arena. Teaching Osman how to speed-chop carrots so we could cook dinner for a thousand hungry people. My father showing me how to re-square and level a tent platform in the woods behind our house in preparation for refugees. A flat surface was the least we could give these poor people, he had insisted. Doing what little we could. Compare that to Manhattan. And London and Sydney and Seattle and everywhere we later learned: enough empty investment units to house the world's climate refugees twice over.

They should let people live here, I whispered to Lucas as we crossed Canal Street.

Lucas nodded.

I was keeping my voice down to avoid Ellen and Helen. Whenever they criticized the Transition I had to argue back. It was a reflex. Even when I did not feel great about what I was defending. I found it easier to sort my thoughts without them cutting in.

Like why not let people live here temporarily? I whispered.

Or just me, Lucas said. Let me crash on your couch while I build your damn wall.

Sort of fucked up, I said.

Sort of super fucked up, Lucas agreed.

I glanced at Osman. He had closed his eyes.

I am no psychologist but it must be human nature to have such difficulty admitting when we are wrong. The Transition was my only family. Obviously I felt defensive. Even when I knew it was not perfect. And Osman: I looked up to him more than I realized. Not just because he was our crew lead. I wanted a family. A real one of my own. And his confidence in the future: I wanted that as well. So if Osman was committed to working hard on the Big U then I was too.

Transition's our only shot, he said when I asked him later. There's no Plan B.

But couldn't it be a better shot?

Osman smiled and said I sounded like Ellen and Helen.

It's not like that, I said. I'm not ungrateful.

We were on break. Another uncomfortably warm winter morning. Eating breakfast on the Mini U as dawn landed. All night we had been jackhammering. My hands still shook with ghost vibrations.

I'm just saying we could be more strategic, I said. You can't eat stocks. The Point is where all the food comes in. Why not build the Big U up there?

Wish we were, Osman said.

I just wish they'd give us new skull buckets, said Lucas, looking at us through a hole in his hard hat.

All I know is this, Osman said. If we do nothing, the future has no chance. And my kid. Even when he gets here. He can't make that choice. To do or not to do. So it's up to me. So that's what I'm doing.

I'm with you boss, I said.

Me too, Lucas said.

A whistle blew. We returned to work.

The hour after a break is the most dangerous on a construction site. Lethargic with a full belly. Relaxed from sitting. Less alert. Emi asked if I saw it happen. I am grateful that I did not. Helen and Lucas were less lucky. One of the electric bulldozers. So quiet. Osman's back turned. If he had just been one step to the left, Lucas said. If they had delivered our new reflective gear as promised. If the bulldozer's reverse alarm had not malfunctioned. Who knows. The machine pinned him against a battery wall. I heard yelling. Ran over as they got him down. He stood on his own. He waved us away. Said he was fine. Then he collapsed. An hour later he was dead. All I remember saying was no. No, no, no.

———

Five other workers died on the Big U that same day. Two on the East River. Two by Hudson Yards. One in The Battery not far from Osman's accident. Big meetings that night as you might imagine. Not just Hunts Point or even the Bronx but every Transition company and mutual aid assembly—the entire New York City federation all livecasting together.

People were very upset. There had been accidents before but on projects like the Blue Dunes that were engineered for the good of the entire city. For everyone. The Big U accidents felt pointless. Osman had died for what? To keep some luxury condos dry for the rich? What a waste. And Osman's girlfriend—Fern was her name—she was two weeks from her due date. The assembly pooled paychecks for families. T-bonds for the babies. And then we voted to act.

Some wanted to strike indefinitely. That vote failed. Instead we agreed on one day off. No work on the Big U for twenty-four hours.

People said this was the same as striking but the majority vote was more in the spirit of a day to mourn and make a formal request for our safety to be taken seriously: A delegation would march into

Manhattan to meet with Transition management. There was no meeting scheduled. Our requests had been ignored. We had not been invited. We were inviting ourselves.

The timing happened to overlap with the launch of *Corps Power* season three. No coincidence we later learned. Joanna Lee had been waging a small civil war within Culture Corps. They had originally chosen Done by Noon because of our reputation for hard work—that was true—but also because we were an example of multiracial solidarity, as she put it. Culture Corps was combatting allegations that white workers were being given easy jobs while everyone else was thrown into the trenches with the black mold and sewage. What Joanna had sculpted from her footage was all of us working and laughing and loving each other. Helen and Ellen and myself—the white half of the crew—working like maniacs for their Black crew lead while coming around to the important question that Joanna wanted her viewers to ask: For whom exactly were we saving the world? The quiet star of the season however was Osman. Confident. Tall. Handsome. Working hard for family and future. A loyal soldier of the Transition with a smile made for the cameras. Osman was a natural lead. And now he was dead. For the dumbest reason.

Some in Culture Corps had tried to shelve the season to avoid a spotlight on the Big U accidents. Others, like Joanna, saw it as a difficult conversation the Transition needed to have if we were going to succeed. Her side won. Season three dropped. Osman became a martyr, and we became famous because of it. Which did not feel great. I kept thinking he would be alive if we had all gotten off that first bus to join the picket line with Ellen and Helen and Ezekiel. If we had all held strong together. If we had refused orders to return to work. But we had missed our chance. I would not miss it again. When they asked the remaining members of Done by Noon to join the delegation to meet with Transition leadership my only question was whether or not we could march up front.

———

We never made it across the Harlem River.

The Manhattan side of the Third Avenue Bridge was a wall of private security. Behind them a phalanx of NYPD. Police and newscast drones swarming overhead. I remember thinking there had been a mistake—they thought we were another group here to torch Fifth Avenue. All we wanted was a meeting. We were maybe one hundred workers. Armed with nothing but a list of safety grievances. We repeated this as we stepped onto the bridge with our hands up.

A speaker drone blared: *Turn around. Failure to disperse will be cause for arrest.*

We come in peace! someone yelled.

Take us to your leader! said Lucas, to some nervous laughter.

But it did feel like that as we walked forward: aliens in our own land.

We were halfway across the bridge when they opened fire. Pepper balls. Tear gas. Heat to your eyes as bad as any wildfire. People screaming. Ellen doubled over dry heaving. I flung her over my shoulder and ran back across the bridge. Then returned for others. Found Helen slumped over the guardrail. Vomiting into the river. She had been struck in the knee with a tear gas canister. Lucas emerged like magic from the haze and grabbed her other arm. We hobbled back to safety where medics were flushing people's eyes. We learned later that the same attacks had happened to delegations on the Brooklyn Bridge, the Queensboro, and the Manhattan. People now call it the Battle of the Big U but it was no battle. It was a massacre. When the air finally cleared we saw we had left someone behind. A body. You could tell right away. Splayed near the middle of the bridge. Victoria Grove. I still remember her name. Yonkers Company. New York born and raised. A pepper ball through the eye. She was big news. A lot was big news then. Locally and nationally and globally. But it depended on which newscast you caught.

Rioter Felled by Stray Crowd-Control Projectile

Corporate Security Slays Solar Corps Lead, Mother of Three

———

The New York City Mutual Aid Federation recommended a general strike. Our vote in Maine Company was something like ninety-six percent in favor. I know people think of history as this clean arc of cause and effect but with everything happening then, good luck figuring out what had inspired what. People said there was something in the air. Around the same time was the farmers' revolt in China. The landless peasants in Brazil. Uprisings in Ethiopia and Palestine. France doing its usual yellow vest thing. Also First Nations in Canada. The IMF debt strike. It was contagious. I remember Joanna describing that moment after a movie wraps when the set comes down and you see how flimsy the backdrop was all along. That was the feeling: like our world was something we had all made up—so why not just make it differently? Who said things had to be the way they were?

Ezekiel claimed these challenges to power occurred once every century or so. I remember seeing graffiti to the same effect:

1789 = 1848 = 1968 = Now

People saw an opening. We had assumed for so long that the planet was doomed. But now we had a chance. If not to hold back the ocean then at least to drown with dignity. That was how I explained it to Emi: A last hope. And people lunged at it. The way we always do.

———

Transition companies around the country struck with us in sympathy. Sometimes only for a day but even those small gestures meant everything. Non-Transition workers too. The Teamsters. The Service Employees. United Food and Commercial Workers. They joined our picket lines. No more truckers bringing food into Manhattan from Hunts Point. No more grocery workers stocking shelves. The real tipping point however was when the Domestic Workers Alliance joined us. The folks who cleaned and cared for the wealthy. Manhattan had state-of-the-art buildings developed in Miami with elevated floors and pump systems that could withstand hurricane-level flooding. But even the best-designed palace cannot survive without its janitors and nannies.

All those green ribbons of support came right down. The wealthy fled Manhattan. Corporate newscasts streamed footage of empty Big U construction sites. Bulldozers asleep. All work stalled. They called us selfish. Greedy. The real climate villains. They tried to bus in temporary workers. Some made it through. Most refused. I walked the picket lines day and night. There were few moments more electrifying than a busload of workers from Buffalo or Albany realizing they had been lied to and coming over to join us.

Solidarity. The team of teams. The high of highs.

And we needed the highs. Because the lows were low. The DET refused to consider our demands. They would only negotiate if we returned to work. Until then they made good on threats to freeze pay. Suspend benefits. Which was scary at first. But life on the Point limped along: Trash got bagged. Kids got taught. Gardens got weeded. Basketball got played. Every morning I woke early with a small army of cooks to defrost hashbrowns and hydrate powdered eggs and search madly for some thyme or tarragon to give breakfast a little flair. People had been on their own for so many years now. Mutual aid was the new normal. Money was losing its shine. How were almost three years of savings in my Transition account going to help me on an uninhabitable planet? Or take Lucas—he'd been sending paychecks to his family from day one. How were they? Fine. A little better fed. But still living in the Great Northern Greens Arena. Either you had enough money for an eco-bunker in Duluth or you did not. The gap was bigger than ever. Untraversable.

The real low of course was the Crisis which did not care about picket lines. Newscasts of the last Greenland glacier. Another dolphin species declared extinct. Heat waves killing thousands. Migrant flotillas sinking in every sea. And closer to home: the Pine Barrens went up in New Jersey—eighty-five miles south and smoke clouding New York's sun in that way I remembered all too well.

Moments like these—on strike while the Crisis advanced—felt like we had made a tactical error. Winning the battle but losing the war. There were big arguments. A growing faction wanted to finish the Big U. I considered it. What else were we doing? You started to believe the newscasts. Maybe we were demanding too much. I could hear Osman saying that the future had no choice to do or not do. There was no Plan B.

But then there was.

It happened in Arizona. Not the Solar Authority but a single company within Forest Corps. They had been deployed to fight a wildfire threatening a Scottsdale suburb. A gated community known as Billionaires' Row. The company refused orders. They were not risking their lives to protect mansions and country clubs. Not anymore. This kind of wildcat strike was not unheard of since our work stoppage on the Big U. People said the Transition was fraying. Coming apart. In retrospect we were reorganizing from the bottom up.

The company refused to protect Billionaires' Row but they did not stop there. They packed up their hoses and chainsaws. They drove their bulldozers and flew their slurry bombers twenty miles south to the Salt River reservation where they supported tribal crews in digging fire lines and wetting roofs and extinguishing firebrands. They did not save everything—you never do—but they saved a lot: Community farms. A grocery store. Two schools. A pharmacy.

As for Billionaires' Row?

Burn baby burn.

That was their message. Culture Corps was livecasting from the scene. I remember getting back from the picket line to watch at the Marshmallows. Hollering and cheering along with everyone else. The firefighters on-screen were filthy with sweat and soot. Exhausted but in that joyful way. They were Phoenix Company. Comprised entirely of refugees and felons. And Kristina—in the center of the screen—jostling and celebrating with her crew. Helmet under one arm. Ash like war paint beneath her eyes. Face not yet scarred. Staring into the camera—nineteen years old and telling all of us watching in New York and Paris and Mumbai and Johannesburg to do what Phoenix Company had done: Seize the Transition. Make it our own. Join us. We are the workers, Kristina was telling the world, thumping her chest. We do the work! The time has come for us to save the future that we want. For us.

Watching the archived footage with Emi she asked if I had fallen in love with her mother the first time I saw her on-screen. Yes, me and everyone else, I told her. I remember taking in the newscast the same as those around me: completely enraptured. Did I linger on Kristina's face? Think of her individually among all of Phoenix Company? Yes and no. It wasn't like that, I told Emi. It was bigger than any one person. A bolt of hope when we needed it most. After Osman. After all our terrible losses.

So did you or didn't you? Emi wanted to know.

Did I or didn't I what?

Fall in love with Mom at first sight?

Oh. Yes. Very much so.

Emi Vargas Brinkman
North American History
Mrs. Helmandi
Great Transition Project (First Draft)

Mom Session IV: Phoenix Company

Me: Would you have joined the Transition if they didn't
give you citizenship?

My Mom: The deal was for residency, not citizenship.

Me: But that's how they let you out of the camp?

My Mom: Yes. I would've done anything to get out.

Me: Were you excited to join the Transition?

My Mom: I didn't believe all the hype. None of us did.
There had always been some delegation visiting
the camp from the UN or the Democrats. So many
promises. You learned not to get your hopes up.
Otherwise, you were like Yesenia, expecting the best,
and reality crushing you every time. Even when the
Transition started and we were released, we knew there
had to be a catch.

Me: But there wasn't a catch, was there?

My Mom: Ha. We were free prison labor for some well-
connected people. That was the catch. It was a racket.
They marched us parade-style in our fancy new
uniforms. Called us heroes—

Me: But you *were* a hero, Mom. You *are.*

My Mom: Thanks to us. Not them.

Me: Who?

My Mom: The Department of Emergency Transition. The
people put in charge of Forest Corps, Phoenix Company.
Many were former oil and gas workers, sent over as
part of the "Just Transition" to keep them employed.
They didn't care about the Crisis. Soon as the newscasts
left, you should've seen them. They took us straight to

Phoenix where they had two tents. Tent one, we had
to remove our uniforms. Our packs and boots. All our
brand-new gear. Tent two, they issued used uniforms,
surplus from the third Iraq war. Boots with holes. Packs
chewed by mice.

Me: Why?

My Mom: To sell. For profit. Why else? The same with
our trucks and slurry bombers. Anything that wasn't
guarded, they'd strip for parts. Nowadays the
newscasts show us with our electric chainsaws and
flame-resistant jackets. That wasn't until we seized
the Transition. My first deployments they gave us
hand saws and pruning shears! Make sure you include
this part in your report—my very first Forest Corps
deployment I spent in a warehouse, loading trucks
with the same supplies they had taken from us. What
a glorious start to the Great Transition. Loading stolen
gear to make some gas and oil men wealthy on the
black market.

Me: So when did you fight your first fire?

My Mom: Sooner than I expected. Within a month or
two. We hadn't been trained. No orientation. Nothing.
They woke us up one night and suddenly we were back
to being "soldiers in the war to save the planet," and
"doing our duty for future generations." As it turned
out, we were being rushed out to save *their* homes, the
same people profiteering from our gear. We didn't find
this out until later, of course. Still, it beat working in a
warehouse. It was very exciting.

Me: What was exciting?

My Mom: Everything. Embers flying around. People yelling.
Propane tanks exploding. Talk about baptism by fire.
Your eyes won't stop watering. You can't take a full
breath. Everything slows down. Sometimes we worked
from three in the morning until three in the afternoon,

stopping only then to eat. The air was terrible. We
didn't have respirators at the beginning. Nothing but
a wet bandana. And no gloves. They gave us white
bread sandwiches sometimes. You would leave bloody
fingerprints on the bread. Then right back into action.
"Wet that roof. Dig this ditch. Clear that brush. Roll
that car." I was glad for the orders. Something to do is
always better than nothing. You go calm. Reason takes
over.

Me: Were you scared?

My Mom: Abstractly, I suppose. I knew it was dangerous.
We would find bodies in swimming pools. In basements.
In car seats. Pets too. I remember one long line of
cars all burned to their frames. They'd been caught
in traffic trying to escape a narrow mountain road.
Things you can never unsee. So yes, I was scared—for
Yesi. My friends. But not for myself. I suppose it's some
self-preservation mechanism. The way soldiers will
charge into hopeless battles. But we had our share of
casualties. Especially at the beginning. You asked about
the catch? That was the catch: the danger. Our freedom
in exchange for fighting wildfires with no training or
gear. Look what happened to Yesi. To me. I know I was
never beautiful, but I liked my face. Look at me now. This
was the catch.

Me: I think you're pretty, Mom.

My Mom: That's nice of you to say.

Me: What is it like when someone dies in a fire?

My Mom: You really want to know? I'll tell you. It's horrible.
The skin blisters and glistens. Pockets of fluid if the fire
happened recently. Or the body is charred with patches
of white. Globs of tar. Smell of burnt meat. What else
do you want to know? Sometimes the face is gone. The
body a husk with a sort of yellow crust—lymphatic liquid,
one nurse told me—or the skin sheds. Oh, and tendons

tighten in extreme heat. We found lots of bodies curled in the fetal position.

Me: Did Yesi die like that?

My Mom: Not like that. Thankfully.

Me: What happened?

My Mom: We had dug a fire trench. But the flame front curled right over. We were in New Mexico. The Gila Wilderness. We ran. Yesi must've fallen. I don't know. I circled back as soon as I could. A medic was already there. She gave me scissors to cut Yesi's clothes. Her burns were bad, but what killed her was smoke inhalation. Her airway had filled with tar. The medic wanted to intubate but had no endotracheal tubes. We were short on medical supplies along with everything else. Some nights the medical team would have us wash old gauze pads. Can you imagine? They had us clean off pus and blood, boil and dry the bandages to be reused. Everything had been siphoned off and sold. Look—you see this, Emiliana, how my hands are shaking? It's not because of Yesi. I've done my grieving. It's the people who killed her and destroyed our planet and got away with it. The Leadership Council trots out veterans who grew up in the refugee camps and claim no bitterness. We hear about people from deconstructed towns who lost everything to the Crisis and say it was just one big adventure. As if forgiveness is some godly virtue. Forgiveness is not a virtue. It's cowardice. A way to avoid the unpleasantness of justice. People should be *outraged*. Yesenia never should've been out there. She wanted to be a teacher. Well, we don't get to choose our paths. History comes knocking. Either you answer the call or you cower. Yesi was so scared of dying. But she answered the call. The night before she died, she woke me up. We were sharing a tent. In the Gila. She'd had a terrible nightmare. I told her not to tell me but—

Me: Why didn't you want her to tell you?

My Mom: We never talked about death. It was an unwritten rule. No talk about death or the future. It was bad luck to discuss either.

Me: What was her nightmare?

My Mom: I wouldn't hear it. I told her to go back to bed. She held my foot. Like when we were children in the camp. The next day, well—the saving grace of a severe burn is that it destroys all nerves. There's no sensation. She couldn't feel a thing.

Me: She just fell unconscious?

My Mom: I had propped her up on my lap. She was naming everything she could see. Tree. Bird. Cloud. Leaf. Sister. Sun. I got to be with her. I was grateful for that. I still am.

Often it can be emotionally challenging to interview those closest to us. (I know I would've had a hard time interviewing my mom when I was your age!) You are doing a great job. Let me know if you want any advice or even just to chat. I'm here. Keep up the good work.

   —Mrs. H

PART FOUR

CHAPTER EIGHTEEN

LARCH

Emi shakes me awake from a dream. My first day as a smokejumper. Day one on the job—about to parachute into a burning forest—and like an idiot I have lost my rig. Desperately trying to find it before we get orders to step out the door of the plane.

Dad. Storm's over. Everybody's getting ready to go.

Morning sunlight slants through the curved glass of the station. Seagulls and clouds. Shadows of blimps. Takes me a moment to re-adjust. I am not a rookie who has lost his rig. I have lost something far more important. I jolt up. Look around. As if the dream was not a dream but a sign. The station is packed with workers lacing boots zipping bags sipping coffee. No sight of Kristina. Only a shock of pain from turning my neck too quickly. There is an age for sleeping in a car or the forest floor or a chair in the Brooklyn Heights Station. I have long graduated from that age. Sudden rush of shame for getting old. Falling asleep while I should have been watching Emi. Breaking my screen. For Kristina. I have lost Kristina.

You okay, Dad?

I'm fine. I just slept wrong, I tell her, rubbing my neck.

Want me to get you coffee?

You don't have to get me coffee, Em. Let me get you something. Are you hungry?

Station loudspeakers announce that the hyperloop platforms are reopening. Following the announcement I hear Emi's name. The young woman with the Tundra hat. Waving to Emi. The young man too.

They're going to Gowanus, Emi says. Can we ride with them?

Sure we can.

Watching Emi last night after she sulked off—I knew she was punishing me but it was still good to see. Good and not good. Never has she yelled at me like that. A chord of anger usually reserved for her mother. She is growing up. Becoming independent. These are positive developments. Maybe Kristina was right. Maybe I have made her life too easy.

Sure you're okay, Dad? You look super tired.

I'm fine. I'm glad you're getting along with your new friends.

They're not my friends. Just some people I met.

Nice of them to get you dinner.

I guess, she says. Then she adds: Angel's a poet.

Is that Angel?

Dad! Don't point.

Who's the Tundra fan?

That's Reena.

What did you tell them, sweetie?

Nothing. Just that Mom got hurt. And that we're here to get her.

I saw you with Reena's screen. Did you reach out to Mom? Em? Did you ping her?

I feel the air charge between us. That ozone smell before a storm.

We have to be careful, Emi. People might not be friendly for the right reasons. You don't know them. We don't know what's going on.

I do.

Do you? I say. I open my mouth to remind her that she is fifteen. That this is her first time off Greenland. That the Public Safety case managers at our door were not exactly who they said they were. But I stop myself. There is nothing to be gained from adding to her worries.

The others call her name again. She waves then blurts to me: I didn't ping her. You have to trust me.

I do, Em. I just want to keep you safe until we find Mom.

So let's find her. Come on. And I don't care what you say, I'm getting you coffee. You look insane.

————

One stop to Greenwood Heights then everyone transfers to the water bus. Emi and I follow Reena and Angel to the top deck. Steps and railings are beaded with rain from last night's storm. The deck is slippery and overcrowded. We squeeze in as the bus pushes off. Water rushing by below. I point out to Emi where the life jackets are kept beneath the benches. Always good to take a mental note when you're on the water, I say.

Emi nods absently then turns to Reena and Angel.

I put my hand over hers so that we are holding the wet railing together.

I'm serious, Em. It's a good habit. Could mean life versus death in an emergency.

Got it, Dad. Relax.

I try. I really do. The rest of the bus is excitement and laughter and music. I am the oldest passenger by many years. I try to see everything fresh like those around me: Sunlight shattering off the water. Pelicans dive-bombing the surface. Harbor seals barking on oyster reefs. A four-masted cargo ship streams by. Black photovoltaic sails rising against the bright sky. We rock a little in the wake then Emi gasps with delight and points out two jumping dolphins.

I laugh with her. I tell her that she cannot begin to imagine how it used to be. Waterfront dead. Garbage everywhere. Look, I say—if you had told me and Lucas thirty years ago that we would live to see the bottom of the bay, we would've laughed in your face. It's a miracle—

Sorry to interrupt, but it wasn't a miracle, says Reena, holding her hat against the wind. It was the product of hard work. The reward for collective action against the destroying classes.

I take a calming breath. Before I can tell this very young woman that I do not need the reminder, Emi jumps to my defense.

He knows it was hard work, she says. He was here at the beginning of the Transition. He was at the Battle of the Big U.

Respect, says Angel.

Yes, says Reena, thankyouforyourservice. Obviously. But I'm talking about now. Corporate charters, public-private partnerships, everybody skipping extraction duty and saying we should just let the climate criminals get away with it like nothing happened. People need to be reminded how hard you all worked to get us here. And how easily we could lose it all.

Emi throws me a quick look.

Hiya, says Angel. How many times does history need to repeat? We need to wake up and rise up. A revolution's not a tea party. Right, Emi?

Right, she says.

It is like they are reading from a script that Kristina wrote. Which is possible, I remind myself. Exhaustion seeps back into my bones as we round a jetty that is absolutely radiant with bird shit and the Gowanus Canal comes into view. Flanking either side of the canal are the surge gates draped in Day Zero banners with Phoenix Company's emblem. The water bus erupts in cheers. Has any group ever been so excited to report for extraction duty? I see them cheering in the station at news of the assassinations. Every generation feels distant from the ones below. I know that. But this distance feels different.

Emi whispers under the cheering: When was the last time you were here?

I nod at the closest of the two open surge gates. Maine Company dug that berm.

No, I mean after the Transition. When was the last time you did extraction duty?

With Mom, I guess.

When?

The exact date? I don't know. Before your time.

Before I was born? Not since?

It's not easy for me to get away.

Why not? Mom does.

That's why, I think but do not say. Someone had to make you breakfast. Get you dressed. Help with homework. Wash your clothes. Volunteer in your class. One of us had to raise you.

You've seen the Tundra kitchen, I say. You've seen how crazy it gets. You skip extraction duty because you're too busy?

We grab each other for balance as we hit some choppy water.

I don't skip, Em. I apply for exemption. I follow the rules like everyone else.

She frowns as we turn up the canal. Then without looking at me she declares it isn't fair that cooking for the Tundra should exempt me from duty.

I take another breath. I know where she is going with this. Kristina goes there often. I grip the railing hard enough to press raindrops between my knuckles and remind Emi that I do my part. The geo-thermal farms we volunteer at every summer, I say. What would you call that?

Vacation?

I don't know what to tell you, Em. I don't make the rules.

Mom volunteers for extra duty, she says softly, almost—but not quite—to herself.

Yes, your mother does whatever she wants, whenever she wants.

I watch something struggling behind Emi's face—the hint of an eye roll—and it triggers me along with my utter lack of sleep and the throbbing pain in my neck and the burning opinions of these young people who have enjoyed safe lives of bliss and comfort. As we are slipping through the shadow of the southern surge gate I point to the hulking wedge of steel and concrete and—in a voice meant for an audience larger than Emi—I remind her who rebuilt New York.

There was no two weeks on and fifty weeks off. There was no man-datory duty. We worked because we wanted to. We saved the world. Talk is easy. Criticism is easy. Murdering senior citizens by drone is easy. Tearing down is simple. Building is what takes work. I did twenty-one deployments. Try building a new world from the bottom up. That's the real work.

Okay Dad. Got it.

Her eyes are pleading with me to stop. But she is getting it wrong. I am not trying to embarrass her. I am merely articulating what must be said.

———

Workers greet us at the pier. They anchor the bus and help unload bags. They order passengers to disembark and line up.

This line for new transfers.

That line for preapproved transfers.

Hurry—*let's go!*—another bus is coming in fast.

Emi and I shuffle down the gangway. The sky is thick with cargo blimps and the buzz of drones. The canal is a two-lane highway: tugboats pulling empty clipper ships toward the energy docks or pushing loaded ships out to sea. Flanking the canal are the buffer parks and Gowanus's turbine plants and battery factories. And people everywhere at work: raking hurricane debris. Coiling lines. Hauling algae on rooftop farms. Washing solar arrays. The place is humming with purpose. I understand why these young people are so eager to journey here. I can feel it. Kristina warns often that Emi's generation has a gaping void to fill without the purpose and solidarity of the Transition. Well here it is. Two steps onto the pier and the drug rushes my veins. For a breath I am back at Hunts Point. And this is before I take a good look across the canal. The sight stabs me in a way I would not have expected: the cluster of buildings are retrofitted with some sort of rooftop carbon capture but otherwise they look exactly as I remember.

Look Em, that's Gowanus Green. Maine Company stayed there. It hasn't changed a bit.

Emi nods, overwhelmed.

Excuse me, sir, are you with Phoenix Company?

A kid steps in front of us. Cannot be much older than Emi.

Do you know where to transfer? To get sent into the field?

We just got here, I say.

Someone yells at us: You all—get in line!

The kid heads to the back of a long line snaking down the pier. I grab Emi's hand and barrel in the opposite direction. At the front is a row of security turnstiles and workers with screens. One looks up and shakes her head: Turn around, you have to wait like everyone else.

We're not here for duty, I say. We—

Do you have preapproval from your managing council?

No—

Then you're in the wrong line.

She has an inland accent. An embroidered black phoenix on her rainbreaker.

You hear me? Move it. You and your friends.

I look over my shoulder. Angel and Reena are directly behind us. They grin.

Please, I say to the woman. We're looking for my wife. Her mother. She's—

Her face is scarred, Emi says, touching her cheek. A big burn scar. You couldn't miss it. And her ear. It looks sort of shrunken. You'd remember.

I don't, says the woman.

You didn't even try! Emi blurts.

The woman looks at the line behind us. Listen, she says, I can't remember everyone I process. And I can't process anyone without a transfer.

How can we have a transfer if we aren't transferring? I say as firmly and calmly as possible.

I'm just doing my duty, the woman says. Don't ask me. I process transfers and assign rooms. Come back with preapproval, and I'll assign you all a family room—

We don't need a room! Emi cries. We need to find my mom!

I put an arm around Emi's shoulders. A few short days ago she would have been thrilled to have some space from her mother. Was extremely thrilled. Now she is about to start a war with this woman if she won't help us.

What if you talk to the Managing Council? I ask. They'll know her. She's—

She's with Phoenix Company! Emi interrupts, grabbing the woman's arm.

We're all Phoenix, hon. Welcome to Gowanus.

Hiya, brother, a lot of us been waiting a long time here.

A voice behind me. I turn around to a guy twenty pounds heavier and twenty years younger.

You need to wait like the rest of us, he says. He goes to put a hand on my shoulder but Angel appears at my side and in a flash has the man's arm wedged behind his back. Angel shoves him, causing a ripple down the line with lots of yelling and colorful language. The man catches his balance and rebounds. Comes back at me only to find Reena and Angel have stepped up together.

Reena points to Emi: Her mom's missing. Be a fucking gentleman. Show some patience.

I'm pinging security, says the woman at the turnstile.

No! I say. I turn to the man. Please, friend. We aren't skipping the line.

Sure looks like you are, he says.

We're not here to transfer, I say. We have an emergency to deal with. Please.

Right then a shriek rips through the sky. A plume rising from the Gowanus Green complex like a rocket. It is a rocket. The plume ends in a small explosion that sends sparks to die in the canal. Not more than a second has elapsed but in this short time Emi has disappeared beneath Angel and Reena. They are crouching over her. Shielding her.

Relax, says the woman with the hint of a smile. It's just the drone dome.

I help Emi to her feet. Brush some grit off her back. The machinery on Gowanus Green across the canal is not carbon capture as I had assumed. Some kind of missile battery. Noticing this sets off a domino reaction: The workers on the rooftops—I see—are not farming algae or servicing solar. They are security. Surveillance. And the drones and blimps are not ferrying cargo but hovering. A dispersed sky-dome.

Angel sees me craning my neck to take it all in.

Third-busiest energy port in North America, he says. Can't take any chances.

Chances from what? I say.

People who want to roll back the Transition.

If storm hubs in New York have been arming themselves then either the news has not made it to Nuuk or I have simply missed it. Seeing what I want to see. Like we all do. Like I have been doing since we stepped off the water bus: I wanted to see Hunts Point. That mutual aid rush. Wanted Emi to feel that high. But Gowanus has a different taste. More severe. Lines and retina scans. Weaponry. A metallic flavor.

Reena is talking to the woman in charge. There is some heavy gesturing. Nodding. The woman speaks into her screen. Waves to me a moment later.

All set, you two. I just need your eyes. Then go directly to the Managing Council. They're in Central. You know how to get to Central?

I nod vaguely up the canal as she scans my retinas.

He hasn't been here in like a hundred years, Emi says. We don't know anything.

The woman gives directions then scans Emi. She taps a key fob against her screen. Drops it into my hand. A family room, she says. In case you decide to spend the night.

I thank her. We pick up our bags and pass through the turnstile. Emi stops.

What about them? she says, pointing to Reena and Angel.

What about them? the woman says.

Emi looks to me. I am too frayed to put up a fight.

They're with us, I say. They're helping search for my wife.

Lucky woman, she says, scanning and waving them through. Wish I had this many people who cared about me.

She hardly has the words out of her mouth when Emi ducks back through the turnstile to wrap her arms around the woman's waist.

Thank you thank you thank you.

———

The Managing Council offices happen to be in the Gowanus Green complex. To get there we ride a tram to a pedestrian bridge. Over the bridge to a second set of security turnstiles and then the park on the far side. The greenery is dotted with trees and carbon capture and funnel windmills that start to spin lazily as the sky begins to mist. The canal's edge is marshy with reeds and ducks and frog calls—a spongy buffer zone that Emi hardly seems to notice. Neither does she give more than a glance at the posters plastered on the windmills. Some are Wanted posters in Wild West style. Others have the Furies' manifesto. Many feature the Phoenix emblem in negative or neon or Gothic or Transition art deco. Emi speed-walks past all of them. Pausing only to swivel her head at me. Her face beaded in mist and a look of annoyance, like why can't I walk any faster?

———

Twenty-seven years ago—when Maine Company helped to build the Gowanus surge gates—we bunked in what had once been a public school at the edge of Gowanus Green. Now the school has been re-purposed again into the offices of Gowanus's Managing Council. Two steps inside and it reminds me of Tundra headquarters in the days leading up to the annual draft: Everyone talking loudly to be heard. Screens blinking and beeping. Aroma of coffee and overworked electronics. No quantum network in North America powerful enough to code a sense of calm.

It takes a while to get anyone's attention. Even longer for them to send someone to the little reception area and hear me out.

Slow down, who sent you? a man asks.

Registration. At the pier. She pinged you. She said we were all set.

Who said that?

The man is late-twentyish. Glasses on a thin nose. He might not be attempting to act like an asshole but he is certainly auditioning for the role. Splitting his attention between three screens—one in each hand and one on his wrist. Which leaves little attention for us.

Try Public Safety, he says. Or medical. We are sort of busy coordinating energy exports to half the hemisphere.

He scoffs slightly. Which helps me decide that he has earned the role of asshole. I reward him by removing the screen from his left hand and in one smooth motion breaking it over my knee.

How about with your workload cut in half? I say, handing back the shattered screen. Can you help us now?

He looks around to see if anyone else has noticed. Many have. The volume of the office steps off a cliff. Emi is staring at me with huge liquid eyes.

My wife's missing, I announce. Her mother. Last we heard she was here for duty. We just want to know if she checked in. If she's hurt or—

Please! Emi cuts in, her voice breaking. Her name's Kristina Vargas.

Emi's words cast a spell across the office. At first I think they feel sorry for her or perhaps they recognize Kristina's name from her campaign for Leadership Council. But then I sense it is something more. The man whose screen I shattered. He is gesturing to a woman in a back doorway. The woman nods. Walks forward briskly with hand extended and introduces herself as deputy assistant to the Managing Council. Avery Jackson. She has a spray of moles across her face. Thick braids shot through with gray. She invites us to sit in a row of hard white chairs. I decline.

Where's my wife?

She frowns. Puffs her cheeks. Twists a braid. She clearly has something to say that she does not want to say. Which says it all.

The blood leaves my head in one violent rush. Emi staggers as I lean against her. Two steps like a drunken dancer to the white chairs where I sit so heavily that I am met with a loud crack. I cannot say it. Cannot ask it. Cannot form even the first syllable of the first word of the question.

Emi has no hesitation: Is she dead?

Jackson puts a hand to her mouth. No. Sweetheart. No! Who told you that?

To be led to the very edge only to be yanked back—you might feel relief. Which I do. But it is relief eclipsed by anger.

Nobody told us, I say. Nobody will tell us anything. That's the problem. Where is she?

You're Larch? And you must be Emiliana?

How do you know us? I say, standing up. Where the fuck is Kristina?

Mr. Brinkman. Please calm down.

I am calm. This is me being calm.

She forces a smile and looks behind her as if pleading for assistance. The entire office is watching. Screens beep. That background hum. Jackson's eyes dart between me and Emi.

Have you tried pinging her?

Obviously. Yes. Of course.

And?

We haven't heard anything since Day Zero.

Jackson twists two of her braids into a helix. If it was pity behind her eyes that would be one thing. But it is not pity. More like puzzlement.

Do you think she knows that you're here? she asks.

I don't know. How could I know that? Why?

Well, the Managing Council's in a meeting. I can't help you until they adjourn. I'm sorry.

Is she in the meeting? Emi says. She turns to me: Is Mom on the Managing Council?

No, I say, rubbing my face. I groan loudly. What a nightmare, I say.

Mr. Brinkman, please try to be patient while we figure things out.

What's there to figure out? What the hell are you people talking about?

This would be easier if you just calmed down. Believe me.

I told you, I say, brushing by her to cross from the reception area into the office. I am so calm.

Kristina! I shout.

Mom! yells Emi at my side. It's me! We're here, Mom! We're here!

Jackson sighs. She nods to the man whose screen I broke over my knee.

He speaks into his wrist. I hear the word *security*.

If I were here solo I could imagine deconstructing the Managing Council into its elemental parts. But if Public Safety detains me then Emi will be truly alone. Orphaned on the ledge.

Fine, I say, putting my hands up. Okay. Forget it. We're leaving.

Mom! Emi yells as I grab her and pull her back through the reception area and out the front doors.

Mist has turned to rain. Reena and Angel are taking cover on either side of the entrance. They jump to attention as we come barging out.

No luck? Reena says.

Nope. I rip my rainbreaker out of my bag and pull it over Emi. Her shoulders are shaking.

We have to go back, she says flatly. We have to find Mom.

We will, Em. But first we need to get dry. Eat some food. Regroup.

Angel pulls out his screen and leads us to a nearby food court where we join workers taking shelter from the rain. The shortest line ends at Pizza Hut so Pizza Hut it is. We order. I force two slices. I am running on empty. My neck aches. My hands vibrate with exhaustion. Emi wolfs a slice then stares at her plate and stands to go to the bathroom. Angel pulls up a weathercast: Another big storm's coming. What're you going to do? Want help finding your room?

I thank them. For helping us get into Gowanus. For backing me up on the pier.

No problem, Reena smiles. This is a million times better than farming algae.

And thanks for being nice to Emi, I say. She's had a tough year. She's a good kid.

Suddenly I am aware of how much time has passed. I knock back my chair and run to the bathroom. Two women at the mirror jump as the door bangs open.

Emi! Emiliana!

I kick open the stalls. She is not here.

I run into the hallway. The nearest door leads to a back patio where tables have been pushed aside for storm season. I barrel outside sick with panic. Squinting through the rain. Emi. She is standing at the patio's edge. Her back to me. A pool of chunky vomit at her feet.

Em!

She turns slowly to reveal a drone hovering at eye level. Black. Not small. Cat-sized. Red light blinking. The lens perhaps eight inches from her face.

Four quick steps get me across the patio. The drone veers but not fast enough. Someone who has known me for only the past twenty-four hours might believe I regularly travel around smashing electronics. I am getting good at it.

A rotor bites into my hand as I grab it. I bring the machine down onto the patio railing. Again. Again. Until the red light dies. There was a feeling in the early days of the Transition when we were working hard while the ocean continued rising making it clear we could never do enough. It is a similar feeling I often find as a father. A general helplessness. Those rare chances when you can make even a small difference? I try not to let them slip away. I rip the drone in half with a grunt. Drop the carcass at my feet. A flash of lightning brings me back. Emi is yelling at me. Her shoulders heaving. Pounding my chest with her fists.

Are you hurt? Em! What's wrong?

I run my hands over her. I see the glint of blood. My blood. My hand cut from the rotor. Emi is uninjured. But not okay. She is sobbing. Wailing. Punching my chest.

We have to find Mom! Why aren't we looking for her?

We are, I tell her.

We're not! We're sitting around eating pizza. We should be out there! She could be in trouble. We have to go back to the offices. We have to find her!

I pin her arms to her sides.

Stop it, Em. Calm down. Listen to me. We're going to find her but you can't run away like that. Understand? You're not allowed to leave my sight. I need to hear you say it. Look at me.

I am squeezing her shoulders. A little too roughly perhaps but she must understand how badly I need her to allow me to protect her. I am trying to explain this to her when Reena and Angel step outside. They see us standing in the rain shouting at each other. Crying. Blood and vomit and a broken drone at our feet. Not our finest father-daughter moment.

I hold Emi's hand. Feel her heat. Her pulse. She is shaking. Moisture like droplets of mercury in her eyebrows.

Say it, Em. Please. Promise you won't leave me like that again.

I won't leave you like that again, she says, monotone.

Good, I say, blinking away the rain. Now let's get out of here. I toss Reena the key fob: You all lead the way.

Emi Vargas Brinkman
North American History
Mrs. Helmandi
Great Transition Project (First Draft)

Mom Session V: The Great Transition

Me: Did you seize the Transition right after Yesi died?

My Mom: Not right away. It took months of establishing workers' committees. Identifying leaders. Educating. Organizing takes time. Especially when people have been denied basic dignity for so long. They have to rediscover the courage to demand it. But then we had more fatalities, which helped motivate the urgency for change.

Me: Why did you enlist with Forest Corps if it was so dangerous?

My Mom: It wasn't like your father, where he got to choose what interested him. They chose for us. Protecting property was the priority. America had a long history of sending prisoners to fight wildfires. We were following tradition.

Me: But why did you follow orders? Why didn't you just refuse from the beginning?

My Mom: And have them send us back to the camp?

Me: You could've run away. I would've run away the first chance I got.

My Mom: Really. Run where? The world is burning and everyone you know is either dead or enlisted. You would abandon your sister? Your friends? Phoenix Company was my only family. There was no *me* or *you*. Just *us*. Why did I follow orders? That was why: for those around me. Not for the corrupt managers, not even for the Transition. We had grown up together, many of us. We'd survived all those years in the camp looking after one another. What it came down to was saving each other's butts.

Me: You could've run away all together.

My Mom: I suppose. Sure. But even with all the corruption and lack of training and equipment, we were still Phoenix Company fighting for the fate of the planet. It may have felt hopeless, but even then—there's nothing better than being a part of a cause larger than yourself. Nothing comes close. Maybe you've felt it with basketball?

Me: I think so.

My Mom: I hope so. Sharing in a struggle with others, working for a common goal—it's the most powerful emotional force. Capable of pushing us to extraordinary acts. Things that no individual could ever dream of accomplishing alone.

Compliments on your questioning, you led your interviewee to a really fundamental idea that was key to the Transition. Focus on those ideas: What exactly did we accomplish together that we could not alone? Was individualism responsible for the Crisis? The Transition? These are deep questions you are exploring!

   —Mrs. H

CHAPTER NINETEEN

EMI

My dad is a snorer. My whole life I've heard him from my room. But those were bleacher seats. Now I'm courtside—sharing a bed—and realizing that his snoring must be the true reason my parents hate each other. Nothing to do with politics, or me, or the Tundra, but because my mom likely hasn't slept an hour in years.

His pattern, once I decode it, goes like this: Three long snores, short pause, loud snore—more like a snort—that almost wakes him up, followed by some pillow readjusting followed by a minute or two of silence. The silence is when I have to focus to stay awake. I ride the wave of my hunger. I listen to my stomach complaining. I haven't kept anything down since the Brooklyn Heights station. I slip on my headphones. I listen to Prince, the same song—"Purple Rain"—over and over, which some people might find annoying, but in my opinion it gets better each time. Then my dad's breathing deepens and his cycle resets with a snore that nobody could sleep through but him.

The family unit they assigned us has a private bathroom and two bedrooms. My dad and I have the room with the big bed. The other room has bunks: Reena on bottom, Angel up top. They were grateful my dad let them stay with us for the night. A million times quieter than the dorms, Angel said when I slipped into their room to apologize for my dad's snoring. According to Angel, the dorms have dozens of bunks. Snoring, farting. Talk about night terrors, he said. Sleep is impossible without earbuds, and did I want to borrow his? He held them out for me. Reena stuck a finger down her throat: Gross. Thanks but no thanks, I said.

Now the glow from their screens leaks under their door. I hear whispering. No specific words, just a ribbon of soft sounds that makes it hard to stay awake. I know I'm drifting off when I see the red blinking light of the drone that came to me on my knees as I was barfing up Pizza Hut.

No drone I've ever seen has behaved like that one outside the food court. It first got my attention circling slowly. Not jerky, the way they usually zip around, but more like an animal, approaching on the sly, almost daring me to touch it. Rotors purring softly. Like Alice, Maru's cat. It even dodged playfully like Alice when I reached out. More alive than machine. Especially how it hovered, looking me in the eyes. Logically—I know—it could've been anyone piloting it. Or AI. But it didn't feel like a machine. It didn't feel like just anyone.

I realize I've fallen asleep again when my dad wakes me with a loud snort.

I yank off my headphones. I'm awake. But the red blinking light remains, the way the sun burns a disc into your eyes at a glance. Red, red, red. My mom is here, in Gowanus. I just know it. I feel it. She is looking for us, or she's waiting for us to find her. Either way we need to be out there—*doing something*—instead of snoring in bed, wasting precious time. Which is why I'm wearing my clothes under the sheets. And why I've been fighting to stay awake. And why I've been waiting for my dad to enter a long stretch of deep sleep that has—finally—now arrived.

All the times I snuck into the kitchen late at night? I think of those as practice. Except I'm not feeling for the refrigerator in the dark. I'm feeling my way around the bed. Feeling my feet into my boots. Arms into my rainbreaker. Hand for the door.

The hallway is empty. So is the elevator and the downstairs lobby. At the entrance, I take a half step outside and my face is instantly damp. The rain has softened into a misty fog. Fifteen feet in any direction and Gowanus dissolves into white. Like a Greenland blizzard except snow doesn't have this salty seaweed tang. I catch a faint background hum, but otherwise the outpost is so quiet that I can hear my heart with each thump in my throat. I take another half step into the white, as far as I can go while still holding open the door.

There was that moment at the Managing Council offices when my dad lost his temper and broke the man's screen. And when he lost his temper again, charging into the office. There was a line, and he crossed it. And I crossed it with him. Running into the office, calling for my mom. I was surprised how easy it was to cross the line. Doing what we weren't supposed to. I didn't even think about it. Like my body was ready and just waiting for my mind to follow. Like how animals must feel. Guided by instinct. Like me right now. Taking a breath to fill my lungs with mist. Crossing the line. Doing what needs to be done. Stepping onto the street and releasing the door to shut behind me with a click.

———

Gowanus Outpost is one giant horseshoe. The main canal shoots up the middle with docks like bristles on the inside curve. The legs of the horseshoe have the factories, warehouses, airfields, residential blocks. Pretty simple, but there are all these smaller canals threaded throughout, which—I'm finding—makes retracing my steps to the Managing Council more confusing than I anticipated. Still, as the mist swallows me, I remember Gowanus is an island, and not that large. Keep walking and eventually I'll end up where I started.

Two right turns bring me to a wider walkway. The background hum is louder. Streetlamps cast cones of orange light like rafts in the fog. At each streetlamp I stop to make a mental note of how many I've passed. The lamps are identical—plastered in the same posters, mounted with the same funnel windmills—but as long as I keep count, I can retrace my path like a breadcrumb trail back to my dad. The plan works great until I'm between streetlamps, cutting through the dampness, when I hear bootsteps behind me.

I panic. Sprint to the next streetlamp. Holding my breath, I wipe the moisture off my face. Whine of an electric engine. Headlights. A truck turning down a side street. Voices warble through the mist. The buzz of a drone somewhere above. The truck disappears. Silence again.

I count to ten, then run to the next streetlamp. The humming is louder here to my left. Two steps from the light brings me to a guard-rail and the water's edge. The tide, going out, is spinning turbines. Thousands of them. All through the outpost. The background hum. Like cells in our bodies. Powering us. I listen to the hum and watch the tidal turbines spin, and this is when I realize I've totally lost count of the streetlamps. Which isn't great—obviously—but also weirdly freeing: because even if I could retrace my steps and sneak in without waking up my dad, I don't want to turn back. Not without my mom. Not without trying.

My dad would never say it, but privately I know he agrees with my mom: I'm a privileged post-Crisis kid with no clue about real struggle. But how can you overcome struggle if you're never given the chance? I'm the youngest person, possibly ever, to be out here alone in the Gowanus Outpost. Not on a school field trip. Not with my parents. Just me, in the mist and the damp and the dark, and younger even than my mom or dad when they enlisted with the Transition to become heroes and save the world. But they couldn't save their own parents. They never even got the chance.

Suddenly I hear steps again. Much closer.

Hello?

The sound of my voice makes the hair stand on the back of my neck. I turn and run.

I try to stay light on my feet like warm-ups before basketball, but fear makes my legs unwieldly. I stumble and lean against the next streetlamp to catch my breath. The lamp is plastered with peeling copies of the Furies' manifesto. One line in particular sticks out, the words almost luminous in the mist: *We all know loved ones that should be with us but are not.*

I hear it again: bootsteps. Someone is following me.

A moan escapes my throat. But then another drone zips by overhead. Faint lights through the mist. Blinking red. And I get that same instinct as before. Like she's near.

Mom?

My voice dies in the mist.

I try louder: Mom?

A figure steps out of the white. A woman. My body is an ocean of turbines all humming, millions of blades spinning together in one dizzying blur.

Hiya, girl, you're fast! Thought we'd never find you.

It's Reena. And Angel right behind her. Hands on hips as they catch their breath.

I let out a gasping exhale that turns into extremely embarrassing tears that turns into my shoulders shaking. Shaking partly for release like my dad taught me. Shaking also because sometimes you can't stop your body from doing what it wants.

———

Reena and Angel apologize for scaring me.

It's fine, I tell them. It's okay.

Then Reena suggests we head back.

Back? No. I can't go back.

Why not?

I'm looking for my mom.

Oh.

We are all whispering. I don't know why, but it feels right out here in the mist and the dark.

Reena squints. So what's the plan? Hope to bump into her?

As soon as Reena asks it, I realize how ridiculous it sounds. But she's right: I was hoping to run into my mom. Maybe even counting on it. Maybe even counting on her to be out here also, looking for me.

I'm going back to the Managing Council, I say. I'm sure she's there.

Reena and Angel look at each other. The mist has turned into light rain. A funnel windmill starts rotating on the streetlamp closest to us. I pull up my hood.

I think we better head back, Reena says, bumping my shoulder with hers. We'll go to the Council first thing in the morning.

You go back if you want, I say.

Angel holds a palm to the rain: Another storm's coming.

I don't care.

You will if it catches you outside.

Reena takes my hand. Let's head back, get a full night's rest, wait for the storm to pass, then start fresh with your dad. All of us together. Strength in numbers. Right?

That's right, says Angel, reaching for my other hand.

I step back.

Reena grabs my shoulder.

What are you doing? I cry out, twisting away.

Emi, says Reena. You have to trust us.

Trust you about what?

Right then we hear voices. Footsteps. Almost on top of us. Angel and Reena move fast, practically carrying me into the dark entryway of a warehouse. Three figures walk by, talking as they cross beneath a streetlamp. Workers on their way to a late shift, maybe, or returning.

We crouch silently as they pass. Rain falls harder. Slanting into the warehouse entryway. The funnel windmills on the streetlamps spin faster. Reena and Angel let go of my arms. Which makes me realize how tightly they were holding me. I have an urge to call out for help. But then they are helping me to my feet, readjusting my rain hood, and agreeing a little too cheerfully that I'm right: better to search now than tomorrow when the storm could shut everything down.

You don't have to come with me, I say.

We're here, Reena says, holding out her arms. We're already soaked. So why not?

Hiya, Angel says.

So which way? Reena asks.

I look around and admit that I got a little mixed up.

Angel pulls out his screen, illuminating his face in blue.

Central Canal's this way, he says. We can follow it from there.

We take one step from the entryway and two bright lights snap on, blinding us.

Don't move.

Hands where we can see them.

Two voices. Male and female. Angel and Reena move quickly, stepping in front of me. I hold my hand to block the light.

Emiliana Vargas?

Hearing my name is like jumping into Nuuk Bay. That cold shock.

Here, I say. Like I'm in class. Like an idiot.

Thank goodness. Are you okay, love? Are you injured? Did they hurt you?

She's fine, says Angel. Who are you?

Nuuk Public Safety, says the man. They tilt their lights to show their faces. They are the case managers from Nuuk.

Your mother sent us, love, says the woman, smiling. She's been so worried.

I'm falling again into Nuuk Bay. The water ten times colder. Shock stealing my breath. Relief upon relief.

You found her? I say.

She knew you were out here. She'll be so relieved. She was looking for you.

Reena leans back and whispers: *Your mom sent us, Emi. She sent me and Angel to keep you safe. We're with the Furies.*

Step away from her right now! barks the man.

Emiliana, says the woman. Emi. I don't know who these people are, or what they told you. But you know me. You know who we are. We're Public Safety. We're here to help.

Reena whispers again: *Run when I say to.* She reaches to squeeze my arm.

Hands where we can see them! yells the man.

Run!

Everything happens so fast. Angel lunges at the case managers while Reena knocks into me hard, pushing me back but catching me before I fall. She pulls me by the arm, throwing open the doors to the warehouse. We're inside and running. It's a gravity storage warehouse. Dimly illuminated. The *hiss-whir-whomp* of cranes and hydraulics raising huge blocks into the rafters. The woman yells behind us. I take maybe ten panicked steps, then stop, yanking against Reena. I look back. In the doorway I see Angel wrestling the male case manager. They're rolling. Grunting. Hitting. Their screens have fallen to the ground, one casting a blue beam straight into the rain, the other brightening the pavement. I hear a wet snap. A growl of pain.

Emi! Reena yells. Come on!

No Emiliana! says the woman. Stop! Both of you. Stop right there.

I watch in slow motion as Reena whips a small black object from her rainbreaker. A crackle of blue electricity arcs from her hand. She leaps at the case manager, but the woman sidesteps and swings her fist, punching Reena in the ribs. I run.

I duck beneath a block the size of a maglev being raised off the warehouse floor. Hurdle a spool of cable. Crash through a door where the rain meets me hard. Left through a pocket park. Right down an alley. Aimless, panicked turns until I hit a dead end, railing on three sides, water below. I turn around just as a blinking red light comes down to meet me. A drone the exact same size and shape as the one my dad destroyed. I wipe rain from my eyes. I stare into the lens. The red blinking light.

Mom? I whisper.

Then footsteps and the two case managers come jogging through the rain.

Emiliana, love, are you okay? Are you hurt?

I stutter. I shake my head. I don't know what to say.

The man is cradling his arm, wincing. The woman has her flashlight in one hand and Reena's stun gun in the other. I peer past them.

Don't worry, says the woman. You're safe. They won't hurt you.

A wave of heat washes across my face. I step back. The guardrail presses against me. The drone remains hovering between me and the case managers. Rain spinning from its rotors. Then the man uses his good hand to swipe at a wrist screen and the drone pivots, zooming off.

Leave me alone! I cry.

It's okay love, says the woman. You're safe. We found you just in time.

Where's my mom?

Emiliana, listen to me, she says, her voice calm but firm. Your mother sent us. She's expecting you. We're lucky we found you, but a hurricane is about to land. We don't have time to stand around talking. You must come with us. Please. Right now.

I look past them, into the darkness. Rain streams into my eyes. I blink it back. I blink and I blink and I blink. The water, though, it just keeps coming.

We seriously need to move, the man says. Storm's here.

The woman extends a hand. I watch myself take it.

It's going to be okay, she says, giving me a squeeze. We have you now.

CHAPTER TWENTY

LARCH

Sequoias are made for fire. The giant trees can lose ninety-five percent of their crowns to the flames and still come back to add another hundred rings to their trunks. And sequoias need fire. Their cones will not—cannot—release seed without that heat. Like atoms forged in the furnace of a sun. But nothing can withstand unending trauma. Always there comes a breaking point. Same for the sequoias as it was with us.

Forest Corps leadership was well aware of the strain. Fire season in the American West had become a twelve-month event. Preventing entire biomes from turning into atmospheric carbon required year-round work. To pace us, leadership cautioned smokejumper crews against more than eight jumps per month. But eight jumps were a recommendation. You could volunteer for more. You could volunteer every chance you got.

Lucas and I were seconds away from making our tenth jump of June. Triple-checking our harnesses and water. Our saws and battery bags. We were a mile above the burning Sierra Nevada. Our plane dipping and rattling in the thermals. This was our eighth deployment with Forest Corps' Western Division. The first seven had been grunt work. Digging trenches. Clearing brush. Uprooting stumps. Dragging hose. Dousing flames. Running for our lives. *Extreme wilderness landscaping*, Lucas called it. Now we were halfway through our first deployment as smokejumpers. Three intensive training months in Idaho's Sawtooth Range—here's how you jump with a chainsaw, here's how you splint a broken ankle, here's how you fold a heap of nylon into a rig that will deploy evenly at five thousand feet and handle in the fire winds—then they dropped us into the field—remote places where few roads reach.

Sometimes we set controlled burns following the Karuk Traditional Method. Sometimes we dug fire lines. Extinguished spot fires. Prevented bad situations from getting worse. But this jump was different. This was a rescue mission into one of three remaining stands of giant sequoias on the planet. A ground crew—hotshots we called them—had established a defensive ring around the trees. But the fire had spawned in a reversing backwind and cut them off. Two days now and counting. We were jumping with supplies. Rescuing the rescuers. That was the plan.

Nearly five years had passed since Lucas and I redeployed out of New York. Five years since the Battle of Big U. Five years since Osman. Five years since Phoenix Company had seized the Transition. Difficult explaining to Emi how fast things moved after that. Five years may not seem like a long time. But so much can happen. Ask any parent.

In those early days after Phoenix Company led the charge to remake the Transition, I remember this exciting period of what felt like nonstop wildcat strikes. Huge union drives. Rank-and-file sailors even organized the navy for a short time. Money was being redirected from the military into the Southwest Solar Authority and carbon capture and grants for worker cooperatives. McDonald's—I remember—was the first big corporation to go worker-owned. Free Happy Meals to mark the day. All of Hunts Point smelling like fries. Lots of happy kids. Lots of big changes very fast. Which we needed. The planet needed. But it was just a start. Still so much to do. We had to deconstruct the Big U to rebuild it around Hunts Point where it could protect people instead of real estate. We had to send our own delegates to steer Transition leadership. We had to repurpose Wall Street's quantum computing networks for something more useful than gambling on stocks.

The financial firms had hired private security to sneak their quantum systems out by barge. They might have succeeded if a Wind Corps crew with Syracuse Company had not been transporting turbines down the Hudson. They accidentally rammed the barge carrying the entire Goldman Sachs network. Computers and cooling towers and all. Made all the newscasts. Wall Street lost what little popularity it had. The DET seized the networks. Borrowed them indefinitely.

Efficiency. Logistics. That was the quantum difference. Subtle at first. Fewer supply shortages. Fresher food. Nothing as flashy as promised by those who believed technology would save us. But important all the same. We first felt the difference during the months we spent slapping PV panels on warehouses across Queens. Suddenly we were getting all the safety gear and equipment we required—often before we knew we needed it. Ellen and Helen found themselves with almost nothing to complain about.

Time to retire, they said. Joking. But then not.

A startup DET program was offering grants for Transition veterans to form carbon sequestration cooperatives. Ellen and Helen wanted to start a kelp farm. Ezekiel was all in. I thought hard about it. Returning to the ocean could feel good. But also not. Like going backward. My father on the granite ledge. My mother as the heat shattered our windows. I had enlisted with Forest Corps to fight fire and had yet to see a flame. But even more so—I had enlisted for the same reason we do anything to escape: to find something larger than ourselves. And New York was feeling small. Done by Noon had not been the same since Osman. I needed something else.

As for Lucas it was either kelp farming or redeployment west. Given the choice between water and fire he followed me into the heat. In no time we could hardly remember the sight of blue sky. Could not tell you how fresh air used to taste. Could not believe there was a tree standing in America that had not yet turned to silver ash.

———

The flaming cross of a utility pole in the Dakota night. Melted golf balls like marshmallows in the smoking woods by an Oregon country club. Half-burned garden hoses leading into cellar holes. A bobcat kitten with singed paws in Utah. A manure pile erupting into flames. A safe in the ruins of a Washington farmhouse containing a single raindrop of melted gold. A silver bell melted in the steeple of a church in Colorado. Rabbits escaping fire darting between our boots. A weather vane spinning then stopping then spinning the other way. Fire appearing seconds later to crest the hillside and eat the sky. Burnt pines in Montana with root balls exploding the moment we knocked them over to meet the thirsty air. Another safe in another smoldering farmhouse—this one in Wyoming—so hot that bundles of dollars burst into flame when we opened the safe door. Looters loading a full-size pool table onto the roof of a two-door sedan. Helping them push the car up the driveway. The *bang-bang-bang* of cellar oil tanks exploding. The beep of bulldozers in reverse. A Grand Canyon souvenir spoon embedded in a slag of melted window glass. The sky raining embers like falling stars. Sweet nighttime relief when the wind dies and the fire mulls buttery along the ground, almost inviting. Digging a furious foxhole with Lucas. Holding each other as the flames pass over. Around us. Sparing us. Racing on.

Seven deployments like this. Four full years. And then I'm falling.

Ten eleven twelve glorious seconds. Five thousand feet. Four thousand. Three thousand. A *whoosh* as I pull the drogue, jerking me upright with a snap. The thermals ruffling the canopy. The creak of my harness. That was always my favorite part: the sudden quiet compared to the racket of the plane above or the fire waiting below. Flames flickering in creek beds. Legions of charred trees emerging from the haze. Land streaked pink with fire retardant. All coming to meet me. To find my boots. But until then: silence. The land so far below that the distance played tricks on the eyes. Made you feel as if you were not in fact falling. As if the earth was not getting closer. As if you were somehow pinned to the sky.

———

Three trees made up the ancient sequoia stand. Blackened scars up the trunks as high as the neckline but still green at the crowns where it mattered. The sequoias had been pushing roots for two thousand years into this steep slope. Not an ideal landing zone but the hotshot crew had cleared brush and were there to help us land and gather our rigs. We arrived with minimal acrobatics. No busted ankles. Immediately started snapping batteries into saws and handing out water.

Their crew lead debriefed us. His beard and face so blackened that his teeth seemed to glow. His crew was exhausted. Depleted. No fatalities, thank God. The injured were resting under the sequoias. Our medic ran over to attend to them. But even the uninjured looked terrible. Black with ash. Pink with fire retardant. They had deployed with bulldozers and water tankers and hundreds of yards of hose and sprinkler. Then came the reverse wind. Bulldozers now charred husks. Hoses burned. The hotshots had been reduced to shovels and axes. Putting out spot fires. Praying for the wind to die. Listening for the next slurry bomber drop. Waiting for us.

Our division chief was from Los Angeles. Sadie was her name. She had won an Olympic bronze medal for skateboarding in her teens and had fought fires for the Transition since. She gave orders: Some of us would run downhill to set a defensive blaze in the dry creek bed. The rest would work with the hotshots to extinguish spot fires. The defensive blaze would split the larger fire chewing up the far hillside. This would give us time to attack the smaller fire uphill and reconnect with the road.

Ready set break.

Sadie jogged into the creek bed with three others. White smoke soon followed. The rest of us scattered along the containment line like outfielders. Watching for firebrands in the wind. There were maybe thirty of us. Lucas had a glittery Puerto Rican flag sticker on his helmet that helped tell him apart. He was a hundred feet to my left. I watched him stamp out a firebrand. The ground was scattered with sequoia seed. Impossibly small when you considered the trees towering above. Two thousand years to climb those heights. They could not fathom the world their descendants were going to inherit. Few of us can.

Spot! We got a spot!

The fire erupted uphill from our containment line. I turned in time to see the flames grow from campfire to bonfire in two seconds, maybe less. If everyone was fresh we might have raced uphill in time to attack. But the hotshots were exhausted. They moved as if underwater. Then another spot fire erupted downhill and the situation turned deadly just like that.

Area ignition happens when vegetation is so dry and the air so hot that the grass spontaneously combusts beneath your boots. I had seen it happen on two occasions. But not like this. This was like the slope had been laced with land mines. It exploded.

Shelter up!

The order came squawking over the radio. Last words we heard from Sadie. I dropped my saw. Unclipped my pack. Ripped out my emergency shelter. Deploying an emergency fire shelter can take thirty seconds if you are as fast and focused and experienced as Sadie. I was not. And I did not have thirty seconds. I had ten. Maybe less. I dropped the shelter. I pivoted uphill and ran. And right away tripped over something. Someone. I picked myself up. It wasn't Lucas. No flag on the helmet. It was a hotshot. Covered in ash and filth. Hands and knees. Coughing. Moaning. Retching. Trying to stand. I threw their arm over my shoulders and ran. One boot in front of the other. Ignoring the blast of heat behind me. Ignoring the sear in my lungs. Pushing away the roar that had come for my parents and had now found me.

We made it past the sequoia stand and met the wall of the upper fire. And just then the flames parted. Opened for us. Cannot explain it. A small two-foot gap as if the fire was offering me one more chance. So I took it. We stumbled through. Heat like nobody should know. Sharp smell of burning hair and plastic and flesh. Screaming. Both of us. We collapsed in a dry streambed that intersected a wide strip of gravel. Got to my hands and knees and took a moment to realize what I was looking at: the road. We had made it. But the fire was still coming.

The streambed ran through a steel culvert beneath the road. Fast as I could I burned back a stretch of dry vegetation at either end. Then dragged us in. A skunk was inside the culvert. Some rabbits too. They moved to the far end but did not leave. All of us sheltering together. Waiting. The hotshot I had dragged in was moaning. Head lolling. Face and hands totally blackened with ash.

Hold on, I said. Here it comes.

The sound was the same freight train I remembered from the granite ledge offshore from my childhood home. Knife in one hand. Ribbon of kelp in the other. Same exact roar. The fire had been following me all these years. Seconds dilating into hours. Air too hot to breathe. And then it was over. Gone.

I stumbled from the culvert. Heard screaming from all directions. Crackling. The low drone of a slurry bomber arriving too late. The canopy of one sequoia was totally engulfed. Blooms of fire dancing between its branches. The other two trees were decapitated. Two thousand years. I tried to yell—Medic!—and fell to my knees in pain. Clutched my throat. Smoke and heat damage. I whispered into my radio: Medic.

Someone heard me. Radioed back. I told them where we were. A moan came from the culvert. I scrambled in. The hotshot was in bad shape. Sunglasses shattered. The frames melted—partially fused to her cheek. Uniform in tatters. Hair burnt. I extended the hose from my hydration bladder. Water touched her blistered lips and her eyes snapped open like floodlights—the whites iridescent against the soot of her face. We locked eyes and then she slumped. Her head fell to the side. She had a bird drawn on her helmet in black marker. A firebird. A phoenix.

Help's coming, I rasped. Hang on. We're going to make it. You'll be all right.

Footsteps. Radios squawking at the mouth of the culvert. Voices. Hands reaching in to pull us from the ashes.

And that's it, I told Emi. That's how I met Mom.

CHAPTER TWENTY-ONE

LARCH

Emi is standing with her back to me. Her hair dripping. Water pooling loudly on stone. Not our bathroom in Nuuk but one just like it.

Em? Sweetie? You okay?

I put a hand on her bony shoulder. She turns. She has no face. I want to scream. My throat has closed up. Heat. Smoke damage. I cannot speak a word. Emi cannot swallow. She is too thin for her age. She needs more calcium. Born too early. So good with children and animals. We should have pushed her more. We pushed her too hard. From the place where her mouth should be gushes a stream of water. *We all know what happened.* We are in our bathroom in Nuuk. Emi is a toddler modeling Kristina's extraction gear—mud boots to her hips. Jacket sleeves brushing the floor. We are in newborn intensive care. We are in the culvert. There is the skunk. There are the rabbits. We are in a residential dorm in Gowanus Outpost. Knocking. Banging. A bright light. Kristina over me. Water dripping from her hair onto my face. She is shaking me. Yelling. Light so strong I have to squint and blink to see her. I see her. Kristina. Haloed over me. Her face. I am not dreaming.

My love.

———

I bolt from bed. My hands go to her hips. Her neck. Her face. I kiss her smooth right cheek. The silver scrubland of her left. Feel her strong back. Her arms. Her hands on my chest. It is really her. Her exact smell of sweat and soap and moisturizer.

Kristina. Oh my god. Kristina.

Lucas asked me on the plane while Emi was absorbed in the view: What was my plan when I found Kristina? Assuming she was safe. What would I say?

No planned speech, I told Lucas. No words. Tired of arguing and being angry. Yet I was. Angry. Kristina had abandoned me and Emi both.

Now that she is here before me however there is no trace of anger. Caught like this between dream and waking time I do not care if she has become involved in events beyond her control. Even if we have wasted years fighting. Even if we have done and said things we wish to take back. Remember the forest mere months after a fire—green shoots emerging from ash. Wildflowers. Sequoia seed sprouting. I guess those are the words I would have wished for: A plea for new beginnings. A chance to reset in the heat of disaster. For Emi. For us.

But none of this makes it out of my mouth. Kristina does not give me time. She puts her hands cold and wet on my chest. Shakes me. Tells me to wake the fuck up. She has gotten so beautiful with life. I am a lucky man. She slaps me.

Larch! Where is she? Where's Emi?

I see the empty bed and I am suddenly more awake—more alert—than any time in my life. People in the hallway are coming into the room. All wearing the same black rainbreakers as Kristina. Dripping water. Radios squawking. Screens illuminated. None of them Emi. The feeling of teetering on the lip of the plane door about to jump.

Larch? Where is she?

Kristina shakes me. Her eyes enormous. Unblinking. Like when we first saw each other in the culvert. Pleading with me to answer the most important question. But I cannot.

Her face goes white when she realizes it too: our girl is gone.

Emi Vargas Brinkman
North American History
Mrs. Helmandi
Great Transition Project (First Draft)

Mom Session VI: The Great Transition, Part 2

Me: Was individualism partly responsible for the Crisis?

My Mom: Yes. Of course.

I might suggest a "How?" or "Why?" follow-up question.

Me: When did you find out your parents and grandmother died?

My Mom: I was thirteen.

Me: How did you find out?

My Mom: Someone told us. A social worker maybe? I can't remember.

Me: They died from West Nile virus.

My Mom: That was my mother. My father got hepatitis. My grandmother died from heatstroke. That's what I was told.

Me: Don't we have vaccines for West Nile now?

My Mom: We had vaccines then. Just like we had respirators and PPE and all the technology needed for a clean transition. We'd had it for decades. The Crisis never needed to happen. So why didn't we transition when we had time? There's your individualism for you. Follow the money. Who profited from the delay? From the destruction? Too bad you can't interview them. Many are still alive today.

Me: What did you do when you found out your parents died?

My Mom: We were prisoners. What could I do?

Me: I would've cried.

My Mom: Oh I cried.

Me: Really?

My Mom: Of course. Do you think I'm a monster?

Me: No. But you never cry.

My Mom: Well maybe I used up all my tears. I'm not going to cry right now for your report if that's what you're hoping.

Me: Don't get mad, Mom. I was just asking.

My Mom: Who's mad? These are uncomfortable conversations. It's wonderful that your teachers have you studying the Transition. But don't think for a second that it was all parts per million and wind turbines and solar panels. History isn't facts and dates. It's people. It's suffering. It's war between the powerful few and the powerless many. And it never ends. We celebrate Day Zero like we won, but we lost and we're still losing.

Me: How are we losing?

My Mom: People used to be proud to fulfill extraction duty. But the new generation? If they aren't skipping, they're complaining that it's a chore. Yesterday on the maglev I overheard a woman on her screen, moaning about Transition veterans, how we're spoiled and privileged with the best housing with the best views—as if we did nothing! These are the same people who say we should cancel the Half Earth Accords already and redevelop the land. The people who say the climate criminals were only business leaders who didn't know what they were doing. Or worse, that we should invite them to lead our industries. And it's happening! Just look at the Financial and Mining Cooperatives. It could've been so different. We came back from the Transition so strong. We had power. But we weren't given the chance to complete the victory. You never are. We should've taken it. That was our mistake. Victory cannot last without struggle. That's life. Struggle and sacrifice. And pain.

Me: Okay Mom.

My Mom: I'm sorry, Emi, but this is the hard truth. I'm not trying to scare you. I'm telling you because I love you. I would die before allowing anything to happen to you like what happened to me or my sister. That's why we can never forget what they did. To us. To our only planet. People talk now as if the Crisis was an inevitable act of nature. As if it wasn't preventable. But in every corporate boardroom, in every central bank—they knew precisely what they were doing. They hope history will forget. They hope young people will learn about Day Zero and emissions and victory. But we can never forget. We can never forget what we lost. The moment we forget is the moment we guarantee it will happen again. There was a French delegation on the goodwill tour I did in the Americas, they had a phrase: *Run comrade, the old world is behind you!* That's why I tell you these things, Emi. Progress is fragile. Revolution is a delicate bird. We think we have fixed everything, but the old world—the destroying classes—they will roll it back the instant they can. They are trying. Are you listening to me? Emiliana?

Me: Yes, Mom. I'm listening.

My Mom: I know you're listening. But are you hearing me?

Me: Yes. I hear you. I do.

Your mom is right, Emi: these are uncomfortable, difficult conversations. Remember what I said—if you ever want to talk about anything just say the word. I'm always happy to chat. I recommend cycling back to this topic again. The period when workers "seized" the Transition is so crucial to our history. Good luck.

   —Mrs. H

PART FIVE

CHAPTER TWENTY-TWO

EMI

The female case manager pulls me by the hand, pleading with me to hustle.

Please, love. It's not safe here. We have to go. We don't have much time.

And then we have zero time. A blare in the distance that I recognize as a hurricane siren.

The male case manager swears—Oh fuck—and a wave of warm wind slams us, knocking me into the woman and sending the funnel windmills screaming into blurs of white. The storm is here. A flash of lightning and we're off—the woman pulling me by the hand. We run through flooded side streets. Make sudden turns. Cross bridges. Pass beneath overhangs and scarves of rain. The case managers don't say a word. No flashlights. They move like they know exactly where they're going. Like we're in danger. From the storm or from something else.

A branch of lightning freezes the windmills for a blink, suspending individual blades in midair. Then everything returns to black until the next flash and the windmills are shutting down, folding back into the streetlamps like they've decided the storm is too fierce. Something metal whips by, clanging along the ground. I slip. The woman catches me. I lean into the wind with her. I can't think. The storm won't let me. Nothing has ever existed except wind and lightning and the wet scrapes of thunder that fill my chest like bass from a speaker tower when you're dancing close. Rain in my eyes. Down my back and my butt crack and my boots. My feet slosh as I run. If there was a way to drown on land this would be it.

Then we are single file. The case managers pushing me so I'm between them. Cable railings. A metal bridge sloping upward. Water below. A heavy door banging shut behind us and it's like they flipped a switch to turn off the storm. No more rain. No more wind. The only sounds are the drip of water on the floor, and the heave and wheeze of us catching our breath.

Good job, love, says the woman, smiling, squeezing rain from her hair.

We're in a wide dim space. A warehouse. Not gravity storage, just shipping containers stacked in towers. The high ceiling dissolves into darkness like the Tundra arena before they introduce the team. The woman brushes rain off my shoulders. Never, not even during basketball, have my legs felt so heavy. The man cradles his injured right arm. He sees me staring and does like my dad: Forces a smile. Pretends everything's fine.

Think you stepped in a poodle out there, he says, nodding at my boots.

I look down, then back at him.

Because it's raining cats and dogs, he says.

The woman groans. I laugh. Not because it's funny but out of relief.

I'm safe from the storm. Alive. One step closer to my mom.

———

The first year my family traveled to the geofarms for vacation my dad got us a super nice place. We had a balcony with views of the ocean and the ice floes. We had a sauna and a thermal jet tub big enough for us to soak together after our hours. I had my own room with my very own screen and pillows covering half the bed. I remember breakfasts in the lobby with blueberry crepes and lemon custard buns. I re-member carpet like thick cream. But mostly I remember my parents fighting. My mom saying the whole thing was embarrassing. My dad saying there's nothing wrong with treating ourselves one week a year. We never stayed there again. It was the nicest place I'd ever seen in my life. Until now.

The case managers lead me through a tight maze of shipping con-tainers, down some stairs, through another maze of narrow hallways, then a metal door, and suddenly I'm stepping into the warmest golden light. Soft wood paneling. Shelves with books. One huge window. A pink and gray canopy bed almost as large as my room in Nuuk. Globe lamps. A wall screen. The carpet so thick my feet actually sink. The room has everything. Almost.

Where's my mom?

I take a step back. The male case manager fills the door.

She got held up in the storm, he says.

You said she was waiting for me.

Let's get you dried off, says the woman. You're shivering, poor thing.

I have to talk to my dad. I have to let him know where I am. That I'm okay.

Of course, she says, turning to her partner: Byron, go ping Mr. Brinkman.

You can't, I interrupt. His screen's broken.

That's okay, the man says. We know where he is.

He smiles and leaves.

No point freezing while we wait, the woman says. The shower here is magic. Follow me.

I don't follow her. I stand rooted, dripping into the thick carpet.

What is this place?

This is a safe house.

But where are we?

You're safe here. That's all that matters.

She reintroduces herself as Case Manager Min. She tells me to call her Rachel. And her partner, I should call him Byron. She knows I'm upset. She thinks it'll calm me to use their first names. As if we're going to be friends. As if I should suddenly trust them.

You followed me and my dad from Nuuk, I say.

She nods: Luckily for you.

How did you know where we were?

It's our job, she says.

I see the drone outside the food court. The blinking red light I wanted so badly to be my mom.

Case Manager Min takes my hand. Let's get you out of these wet clothes.

I let her lead me to the bathroom, a palace of polished metal and white tile and glass. She steps outside while I peel off my clammy clothes. I turn the water as hot as I can bear while listening for the front door. For my mom. Press my hands against the shower wall. Inhale the steam. The shower is every bit as magical as promised. The nozzle the size of a frying pan. The water as strong as the hurricane, which in my mind I'm still running through. I'm also jumping into Nuuk Bay. Flying over the Labrador Sea. Running with Reena. All the versions of me at once and none are real. Like when they separated my mom and her sister from their parents: You can't comprehend it, my mom said. You convince yourself it's not really happening.

I let the hot water run in and out of my mouth. The glass has steamed over. With a finger I draw a spiral. Starting in the middle and going around and around.

———

Case Manager Min has dried off and changed by the time I'm out. She's wearing jeans. A black shirt. She's younger than my mom. Taller. A large mole on her hairline near her temple. She hands me a cloud of soft white towels. She gives me a face lotion that smells like mint. A different lotion for my body. Have a seat, she says, pointing to a red stool. I'll brush your hair.

I can brush my own hair.

Someone's offering to do something nice for you, she says kindly. Don't mess it up.

I sit and let her comb then brush my hair. She rubs yet another lotion into her hands and massages it into my scalp. I close my eyes. I smell tea tree oil. My scalp tingles. She says I have such healthy hair. I say thanks. The situation is a little awkward, but then I give in and relax and honestly it feels nice. Not just the tea tree oil. Her hands too. My mom has not done anything like this since I was so little. I feel my entire body relax.

Then my eyes snap open as she touches my neck. She needs to inspect me for injuries, she explains. She examines my underarms, my back. Inputs notes into her screen. Takes pictures of the scratches on my forearms. Embarrassing when she asks if I'm comfortable removing my towel, but just as quickly it's like I'm at the doctor's—one second you're clothed with a stranger, the next you're not. One second you're packed to go skiing with your basketball team, the next you're jumping into Nuuk Bay. Flying to New York. Running through a storm in Gowanus. Searching for your mom.

Emi, can you do me a favor? says Min, bringing me back.

What?

I need your help. The young man and woman who were with you—I know you're tired, love, but it's better to discuss events while they're fresh. Could you answer a few questions?

I guess so.

Did they give you their names?

I don't think so.

How did they first approach you?

Um. I can't really remember.

She looks at me in the mirror and says that the instinct to protect others is natural. A sign of a caring, empathetic person. I'm guessing they were nice to you? she says. Maybe did a favor or two? Complimented you? Maybe flirted a little?

I see Reena bringing me coffee, a croissant, McDonald's. Angel sharing his poetry, asking me about music, nature, life. How unusually easy it was, talking to them. How they just happened to approach me the second my dad left me alone in the station. Recalling it all now sends a surge of heat up my neck, into my cheeks. I watch it happen in the mirror.

Don't be embarrassed, says Min. They're professionals. It's what they do. That's why I need your help. Whatever you can tell me. Information might not seem important to you, but it could quite literally save lives. Can you do that for me?

What do you mean *save lives*?

What were their names, love?

Reena, I say. And Angel.

I explain how Reena was on the hyperloop. How Angel came up to us in the Brooklyn Heights station. How they seemed to know each other, now that I really thought about it.

Min inputs notes on her screen. She asks if they gave last names.

No.

Was anyone else with them?

No. I don't think so. Who were they?

She glances at the doorway: We can't talk about ongoing investigations. But I'll tell you this: those were dangerous people following you.

Like they were going to hurt me?

Possibly. That's why I need to know: Were there others?

I don't think so.

This is important, Emi. Try to remember.

It was just them. I'm pretty sure.

Describe again when they first made contact. What they said.

I tell her everything a second time. Then a third. When she says they were trying to win my trust, my question is: For what? Why me?

She looks out the big window into the storm and rubs her eyes with her thumb and index finger. You're mature for your age, Emi. I feel like I can trust you. Am I right?

Trust me with what?

They were following you because of your mom.

What about my mom?

Your mother's upset a lot of powerful people, love.

Her words are a weight on every cell in my body. My eyelids want to slide closed and lock. I want to ask if she means upset because of my mom's campaign for Leadership Council. But I know she doesn't mean that. I'm back on my bed in Nuuk reading the Furies' manifesto. My dad is saying my mom had nothing to do with it. Everybody talks like that when they're angry, he says. A gut feeling. Intuition. He was trying to make me feel better. But now I'm thinking he knew too. Like Angel. Like Reena. Like Public Safety. Everyone but me. I feel even heavier. I'm pretty sure I've never been more alone in my life.

Did you kill them? I ask.

She meets my eyes again in the mirror.

No. But don't worry. They can't hurt you here.

She finishes her examination, then gives me a white cotton jump-suit that fits perfectly. She shows me around the safe house. The kitchen has an induction burner, blender, microwave. A refrigerator stocked with soda water and premade meals. A vase by the bed with soft pink flowers. Next to the flowers, an antique telephone, white with gold around the earpiece.

Have you ever used one of these? she asks.

You just pick it up and talk.

That's right. Don't hesitate to call. Anything you need.

Can I call my mom and dad?

No, love. It's a direct line between you and us.

You said if I need anything. Well, I need to talk to them.

Not now. Trust us. Please. This is for your safety.

Why should I trust you? I say flatly. You could be lying too.

She holds her palms out and asks if she's ever claimed to be any-thing she's not. You know who I am, she says. Want to see my identi-fication? I'm an open book. Ask me anything.

How'd you find my mom?

She found us. As soon as you and your father went missing. She contacted us.

We didn't go missing! We came to rescue her.

She didn't know that.

She would have known if she just pinged us back.

Case Manager Min sits on the bed and crosses her legs and asks how old I am: Fifteen, right?

I nod.

I have a daughter your age, she says. That's why I joined Public Safety. To keep her and my family safe. My daughter's a wonderful girl. You two would get along. But between us, Emi, she isn't half as brave as you. You're such a special young woman. Any mother would be grateful to have you as a daughter. I know I would. Your mom must be so proud.

Okay, I say, turning to look out the window and blink back some unwelcomed tears.

Min rubs my back.

I know it's hard, love, but we have to sit tight and wait for the storm to pass. Rest. Relax. Eat a snack. Watch something. Call if you need me. Enjoy the room. You've earned it.

I continue staring out the window at the rain, the dark clouds, the lightning. I blink and blink. Focus on summoning the wave in my belly, not moving a muscle until I hear the door shut with a heavy thud.

I let out a breath. I look under the bed and behind doors to make sure nobody is hiding. I open and close the fridge. I flop on the lake of the bed. Knead my toes and fingers into the comforter. Let my vision blur into the gauze of the canopy. Swallow. Shake. Breathe the sweet dampness of my hair. Think how one second you can hate your mom and the next you would do basically anything to make her walk through the door.

CHAPTER TWENTY-THREE

LARCH

The ocean took the Everglades. Fire got the Great Smokies. Big Bend went to drought. Many coastal cities by this point had fully or partially drowned, but it stung worse somehow each time we lost another park. We had set the parks aside. Promised protection. From us. Our worst impulses. And yet.

With Yosemite however we had not given up.

Yosemite got the full Forest Corps treatment. Fire trenches like castle moats. Acre upon webbed acre of hose and sprinkler. Endless buzz of slurry bombers. Much of the Sierras had burned or been ceded to beetle kill. But Yosemite Valley was still forest and meadow. Slab rock and river. An island of life in a sea of death. That was one way to view it. A fortress under siege was another. Kristina and I saw it yet another way: our first date.

For the six months of Kristina's recovery we got Yosemite practically to ourselves. No tourists. No crowds. Nobody but Forest Corps and Miwok tribal members. The park had been converted into a forward operating base in the battle for the American West. Medical had taken over a wing of the Ahwahnee Hotel at the foot of a glacial cliff. The hospital had a burn ward that had become very experienced at what they did. Kristina graduated from walker to cane. I was off oxygen. We had escaped death. We were going to get married and win a spot in the Nuuk housing lottery and have a baby girl with ten fingers and ten toes. We had no idea how lucky we were. You never do. First though we had to fall in love.

———

Kristina made love easy. Smart. Confident. Her reluctant smile that came like a geyser: out of nowhere and all at once. I loved her passion—so dedicated to the cause that she would ignore her pain in order to get out of bed and empty catheter bags so the orderlies could take a break. Limp outside to sharpen chainsaws for the smokejumpers. I remember arriving for a kitchen shift to find her slicing zucchinis. Unable to stop herself from helping despite doctors' orders to rest. They had grafted a patch of donor tissue from her left thigh to her left cheek. Later when we had arrived at that fun place of open flirtation, I could say how blessed I felt that they had not scraped the graft from her butt: You don't destroy a Picasso to repair a Bob Ross.

Is that a compliment? she asked.

Yes. You have a masterpiece of an ass.

You only want me for my body.

Not true. I want you for your body and your fame.

There it was: that smile.

———

Kristina was famous. People recognized her every time she walked the Valley Loop Trail. She was the face of Phoenix Company, and Phoenix Company—to many—was the heart of the new Transition. Kristina had risen from the ashes just like the mythological bird, and she had the scars to prove it. Everyone wanted time with her. She never refused a photo. She would stop to smile and shake hands and hug and listen. Culture Corps producers flew into Yosemite to lob softballs on the Ahwahnee patio where cameras could capture Half Dome over her shoulder.

Kristina Vargas, many would say you've sacrificed more than any one person should. You could retire with full disability. Yet you've already requested redeployment. Why?

The Transition isn't over. The fight's still on. I'm needed. All of us are.

But emissions are dropping. Atmospheric carbon has fallen back below five hundred parts per million. Isn't it time to let others carry the torch?

The enemy's in retreat. Retreat isn't victory.

What will you do on the day we reach zero emissions?

Ha. Ask me when we get there.

She handled fame like a pro. In private however she was relieved not to be the only celebrity in Yosemite. The other celebrity was me. Because now—in addition to *Corps Power* and the Battle of the Big U—I was the guy who had saved Kristina Vargas.

A shared near-death moment would bring any two people together. And of course we were both orphans. And refugees. There was a buyback program for the new Half Earth biomes to acquire land for rewilding and carbon capture. Theoretically I could have been compensated for the spit of Maine where my mother and father had died. But that would have required a deed. Paperwork. Lawyers. Digging up all I had buried. Easier almost to forget it. Easier to let the ocean and forest reclaim it. Easier to stay here in Yosemite with Kristina for days weeks months while Culture Corps producers packaged our story into a survival adventure-romance.

From Destruction Arises Love
Transition Heroes Find Romance in Fiery Hell

From there it was easy. All we had to do was lean in.

———

I left Kristina bouquets of wildflowers I collected from the meadows.

She wrote me a love note on a roll of fresh gauze.

I froze a spoon in a pudding cup to help her prank her favorite orderly.

She drew me a flip-book featuring two firefighting dinosaurs falling in love.

She had asked me in passing what food I missed most. Then somehow coordinated for the mess hall to surprise me with my mother's potato-leek soup.

We read to each other from a novel I found in the Ahwahnee library: *Slaughterhouse-Five.* About war and death and one big fire. But funny. Which made it okay. Looking back it was probably therapeutic to laugh about fire. Sometimes we laughed so hard it hurt. Kristina holding a hand to her bandaged face. Me bent over coughing. A pain that felt good.

———

When walking around Yosemite in public we felt pressure to always be on—acting like the people others needed us to be. Strangers would stop us to introduce themselves. Thank us for keeping the Transition alive. Share their own losses and tragedies. Tears were not uncommon. The Crisis had stolen from everybody. What could we do but listen and sympathize and promise to fight on? In private though we could talk about the weight of carrying hope for so many. In private we could be ourselves.

Kristina was expected to be the young and fearless and battle-hardened face of Phoenix Company. She always removed her bandages for the cameras. She wanted viewers to see her scars. Her medals, she called them. No time for vanity when battling for the future of the planet. So many had suffered worse. She spoke openly about her parents. Her sister. Her home. Her belief that we could not give an inch to self-pity or it would all be for nothing. The only way to honor our losses was to see the Transition through. Which meant collective sacrifice. Work. A victory dependent on every one of us.

Off camera she was different. She had the mirror removed from her bathroom. Her wounds itched so badly she would cry. Lash out. Tell me to stop looking at her. Stop visiting. Let her die. I respected her anger. Her healing. I was healing too. Smoke inhalation. Second-degree burns. Not a fraction as bad as her but enough to ground me while Lucas and the other smokejumpers continued deploying. Before meeting Kristina I would have been anxious to suit up and rejoin them. Now I was dreading the day when they cleared me to return. There was exactly one place I wanted to be.

———

You've visited me every day since they brought us here?
  Correct.
  Even when they induced my coma.
  Correct.
  Meaning you've spent hours watching me sleep.
  Would it be creepy if I said yes?
  Creepy and sweet.
  I'll take it.
  Me too.

———

The daily schedule for burn victims is hell. Regular dressing changes and physical therapy and a horror called debridement in the scrub room where they brush your burnt flesh. Even on morphine the pain cut through. I would hear Kristina through the door. Moaning. Crying. A tear trail afterward down the unbandaged side of her face. If not passed out from morphine she would be loopy with it.
  Why do you keep visiting?
  Because everyone else in the ward is sick of me.
  You're sick, man.
  Me?
  You've got savior complex. I don't need a hero. I don't need a white knight.
  I'm no hero. I'm just a guy who likes spending time with you.
  I guess.
  You guess what?
  I guess I like spending time with you too.

———

Neither of us followed sports closely but when the WNBA went player-owned everyone became a fan. The shift didn't happen like most co-ops with workers taking grants and loans to purchase majority shares. The WNBA made it a spectacle: The players' association quit en masse and re-formed. The Women's New Basketball Association. We gathered in the Ahwahnee lobby to watch games. The league had partnered with Culture Corps for recruitment and morale—like the military used to do with musicians and comedians overseas. Lucas got tapped as a Forest Corps liaison. His duties included much of what he had loved doing for years—setting up exhibition games, tournaments, practice sessions for kids. His new responsibilities had him flying around to organize publicity days so players could dig fire trenches and plant oak saplings. He had never seemed so happy and fulfilled in the nine years I had known him. He said the same of me. He visited when he could between travel. Which usually meant visiting me as I visited Kristina and giving us both a hard time.

What? I would say. What's so funny?

Nothing. Just look at you two. Fire-crossed lovers. Freaking adorable.

Shut up, Kristina would tell him. Smiling as she said it.

We were taking things slowly. Partially because burn victims have weakened immune systems. Partially because we were both so inexperienced at love. This was as surprising to me as it was to Kristina. I had assumed the face of Phoenix Company would have her pick. And she thought the same for a *Corps Power* reality show star.

I don't know about *star*, I said. Does three episodes make you a star?

You were so funny.

Lucas was funny.

You were the most loyal. And inspirational. And most handsome. You know how many people probably enlisted because of you? Mmm. Could've watched you swing a hammer forever.

Uh-huh.

Do you miss those days?
I miss Osman.
I miss so much, Larch.
I miss so much too.

———

Then the day came. The doctors cleared me to resume jumping. Or—if I was gun-shy about leaping back into the flames—I could enlist in reforestation. I had options. I did not tell Kristina. I wanted our slow days to go on forever. Thankfully the Yosemite kitchen was shorthanded. I got a culinary transfer. They needed help with camp-wide meal planning. Thanks to my experience at the Great Northern Greens Arena and Hunts Point I knew how to cook for big hungry crowds. How to time hashbrowns to emerge from the oven crispy just as the eggs were done and the fruit cups were approaching room temperature. Between meals I made comfort food for Kristina and the burn ward. Sometimes I would be walking from the kitchen—balancing warm containers of soba noodles or lasagna or fresh Dutch babies—when a plane would take off low overhead. My old crew heading out. The sight and sound always left me with a double-sided lump: On one side guilt for not going with them. On the other an intense, almost radiant relief to be exactly where I was.

———

Larch?
I'm here.
You saved my life.
It was a rescue mission. You would've done the same.
I should be dead.
But you're not.
Someday.
Yeah. Me too.
That's the problem.
With what?

With us. We'll have to let each other down eventually.

She fell back asleep. When she woke again I admitted that I deeply cared about her. I used the word *love*. She was quiet so long that I thought I had miscalculated. As close as I came to passing out as ever. But she was just nervous too. She beckoned me. I went for her cheek. She shook her head. She wanted me in bed with her. To hold her. To hold me.

———

The next day after her scrub room debridement she woke suddenly from her morphine rest and declared that just because we had sex once didn't mean it would keep happening.

True, I said.

Just because you saved my life doesn't mean I have to fall in love with you.

Okay.

I'm not getting married.

What's the point?

Or having a baby.

Who would bring a kid into this world?

I loved Kristina's morphine ultimatums. It meant she was thinking about these things too.

———

We finished *Slaughterhouse-Five* on the Valley Loop Trail. Sitting on a flat rock by the Merced River. Kristina read the final page which ends with a bird singing—and right then a bird tweeted from a branch directly above us. We looked at each other and laughed. Human beings have been carving meaning from coincidences as long as we have walked the earth. How else to make sense of the few decades we are given? Kristina and I were fated to survive in a culvert with a skunk and rabbits as the fire passed us. We were fated to fall in love as two heroes of the Transition recovering from our injuries. Everything that was. It was all meant to be.

Slaughterhouse-Five dealt with a lot of time travel. The main character had survived a terrible fire and become unstuck in time. He could not change the past or future but he could visit different periods in his life.

Where would you want to go if you got unstuck? Kristina asked.

We were walking our usual trail. Holding hands. Gurgle of water over rocks. A sound not unlike the tide flowing into pools. Could almost catch the kelpy scent of my mother's kitchen. Feel my father's strong arms helping me into the boat. That was where I would go, I told Kristina. What about you?

Not the past. The future.

What's in the future?

You. And me.

Later she suffered through the scrub room and her morphine dreams. I sat by her bed. Watching her breathe. Twitching a little. I put a hand on her arm to let her know she was not alone. I had a new answer to her question. I would not wish to become unstuck in time. There was nowhere else I wanted to be but now.

Now ended abruptly when Kristina's doctors cleared her for discharge. Culture Corps had recruited her for a goodwill deployment. Twelve months of travel. Cuba. Bolivia. Venezuela. Chile. Mexico. Giving talks. Organizing. Building bridges between worker cooperatives. Sharing best practices. She had been counting down the days. Which meant weaning off morphine. She asked for space during withdrawal. She did not want me to see her in that condition. She had to go cold turkey. From the drugs and me. She was teary-eyed as she told me this. But it was not one of her morphine ultimatums. She meant it. Our days were numbered. As they always are.

Falling in love was easy, Larch, she said, a hand on my face. We'll do it again.

I had requested reenlistment to Mexicali. A yearlong reforestation deployment in the Colorado River delta. By then Kristina would be back in North America, she said. We could coordinate our leaves. We would pick a place and time. She promised. She would make it happen.

Years later—when we had moved to Nuuk and had Emi and become luckier than we could have imagined—Kristina would end up being right: falling in love was easy.

Staying in love however. That was the tricky part.

CHAPTER TWENTY-FOUR

LARCH

More than one thing may be true at once. Everyone knows this. I know this. Yet it bears repeating.

The planet is healing. Also it remains very sick.

We won the battle against the Crisis. Also we lost.

Emi is a young woman. Also a missing girl.

I am weak with joy to see my wife of sixteen years. Also nauseous with anger.

So many questions for Kristina but only one matters right now. Where is Emi? We search the residential building. Level by level. Bathrooms. Storage closets. A dozen of us, including the woman Jackson and others I recognize from the central office. Shouting Emi's name. Knocking. Doors have never been thrown open with such force. I wake people entire dorms at a time. Sorry, I announce. But I am not sorry. Just tell me: Have you seen my girl? We search the adjoining food court. The kitchen. Emi cannot be gone. She is gone. Both things true at once.

We reconvene back at the bedroom. Take stock. Also missing are Emi's rainbreaker and boots. But the most glaring absence is Reena and Angel. Their room is empty. Obvious to me that they took Emi. Kristina however only nods robotically as I fill her in. How they appeared at the Brooklyn Heights station and tagged along with us.

Are you listening? I ask.

Kristina is staring at the bed where Emi is supposed to be sleeping right now. Where she would be sleeping if Kristina had pinged us even once.

Where have you been? I ask. What the fuck is going on?

Larch. Quiet. Let me think. None of that is important right now.

I swipe at a pillow in disagreement—throwing it across the room—and in doing so reveal Emi's blue headphones wedged between the head of the mattress and the wall. A bubble of dread rises in my throat. I pick up the headphones. Cradle them to my chest.

Emi would never leave these behind, I say. Reena and Angel. They took her.

No. You would've heard a struggle, Kristina says. You're sure you didn't hear anything?

I already told you. No.

She is not overtly accusing me of sleeping through Emi's disappearance but that is the subtext. I know because I am accusing myself of the same. Hating myself. I am sorry. So sorry. I want Kristina to know that. I want to tell her. As soon as she says how sorry she is first.

You should've let her have a screen, I say.

Kristina's eyes snap up. Do you honestly want to have this argument right now?

I consider it. Decide no. But I do need to state one simple fact: Emi would not be missing if Kristina had let her have a damn screen. If she'd treated her like a regular kid.

Regular like sending her north to go skiing for a week? That's where she's supposed to be right now, Larch. None of this would have happened if you hadn't brought her—

No, I say. Stop it. You cannot possibly be blaming this on me.

Um, Kris? says Jackson. She and the others are standing in the hall. What should we do?

Kristina blinks back to attention. Wake up the Council, she says. Prep a hub alert. Any word from the surge gate?

Jackson swipes her screen: Closed fifteen minutes ago.

Kristina breathes a sigh of relief: Thank God.

What? I say. Why does that matter?

Nothing can fly in this wind, she says. Only way out of Gowanus is by sea. As long as the gate's closed, nobody can leave.

Why would Emi leave?

The words are out of my mouth when I answer my own question. A feeling again like leaning out the door of a plane. Emi would not leave. But someone might take her.

Kristina's eyes moisten like she is thinking the same. She shakes her head once like a shudder and tells me to pack.

Where are we going?

To wake up Gowanus and find our daughter.

I have possibly never been so angry with Kristina. Have also never been more grateful to have her by my side. Two more things that are true at once.

I throw everything into my bag. I am about to toss in Emi's headphones when I hear a faint tinny sound. Music. I hold the headphones to my ear. Someone is singing that he never meant to cause any sorrow or pain. "Purple Rain."

CHAPTER TWENTY-FIVE

EMI

Waiting for a hurricane to end is like what my dad says about water boiling: the longer you watch, the longer it takes. I do everything to avoid standing at the window. I walk to the refrigerator. Blast my face with cold. Pass my eyes over the food. Let the wave of my hunger swell. Close the fridge. Open the fridge. Ride the wave. Return to the window. Stand with my nose pressed hard against the glass. Rain and rain. Lightning and lightning. My room must be at the very back of the warehouse. The view is dark water and a squat row of dark buildings. Dark clouds. To make the time pass I count the seconds of darkness between lightning flashes.

Four seconds. Two. Three. Four.

I should pull myself away. I should enjoy this fancy room. I should be grateful for the freezer filled with mint chip ice cream and mush-room pizzas. Grateful for the blue chair with super comfy arms. Grateful for the six shelves of books, the spines all perfectly flush, to run my fingers over. Grateful for the giant screen with every reality streamcast including one channel dedicated solely to the *Bachelor* universe. Grateful to be born after the Crisis. Grateful to have not grown up in a refugee camp. Grateful to not know real hunger. Grate-ful to have both of my parents alive.

So I try to be grateful. I microwave a pizza. I choose a book, *White*

Teeth. Nothing works. You can't make yourself feel. One bite of pizza and my throat says no. My eyes skim *White Teeth* without reading a word. I can't even enjoy *Bachelor in Paradise*. It's the season on Mackinac Island and I've gotten all the Laurens and Ashleys confused and no idea who Trevor is, or why he's crying, and people love to make fun of contestants for being miserable in paradise, but I get it.

The problem is the storm: I can't take my eyes away. The window has gray and pink curtains. The same fabric and pattern as the canopy over the bed. I pull the curtains closed. I wander back to the kitchen. I blend a smoothie just to watch it go warm. I dump it. Pizza goes in the trash. I collapse back into the blue chair. I sigh and the sound makes me jump. That's when I realize how completely quiet the safe house is. The window is so thick I can't hear the storm. I reach for my headphones around my neck and it's like my hand passes through a missing limb. I search the room on my hands and knees, looking in the bathroom, under heaped towels, when the antique phone rings with the sound of a real bell.

Hello?

Case Manager Min asks if everything is okay. Do I need something?

Um. Actually I do. I can't find my headphones. Did I have them?

Try the screen, she suggests. You can stream whatever you want.

Thanks, I say.

Music pumped directly from headphones into my brain is always ideal, but a screen is better than nothing. Anything but silence. I go immediately for Taylor Swift just because. Ten seconds later it's the Rolling Stones. Then Pink. Adele. Janis Joplin. Cher. The Doors. Rihanna. Then Valerie June. Then back to the Stones. Sometimes when faced with all music in human history it freezes me. I turn off the screen and walk to the window and slide open the curtains.

Four seconds between flashes of lightning. Two seconds. Three. Four.

The storm over Brooklyn Heights took a long time to pass, I remind myself. Half a day and a night. Only then I had Reena and

Angel for company. Thinking of them makes my stomach flip. My dad warned me about people acting nice for the wrong reasons. I didn't listen to him. And then I ran away. Like my mom ran away. I see my dad snoring himself awake and everyone he loves is gone. When this is over I'm going to make things easier. For him. For my mom. For me. Easier in every way. A new version of myself. Better. I press my nose harder against the window until the pain pushes tears to my eyes.

Everything okay? How're we doing, love?

The door swings open. Case Manager Min has my clothes, dried and folded.

Fine, I say, wiping my eyes with the back of my hand.

There is a moment where she gives me a look like she doesn't believe I'm fine, but instead of saying anything, she hangs my rainbreaker on a hook by the door. My boots go underneath. She hands me my clothes in a warm stack. Heat radiates from the fibers.

Thanks, I say.

She touches my hand. She says that she knows this is hard. She says I'm being brave. If I want to talk, well that would be pretty convenient, she says, because she's here to listen.

I run a finger over a rivet on my folded pants, the metal hot to the touch.

I just want this storm to end, I say.

You and me both, love. You'll be happy to know that we spoke to your dad.

I almost drop my clothes. You did? Can I talk to him?

She winces, almost apologetically: Not yet.

Why not? Is he mad?

Mad? No! He's relieved that you're safe. As soon as the storm passes, we'll bring him here with your mom.

They're together?

They are.

I have to wipe my eyes again but this time I don't hide it.

She squeezes my arm tenderly and points to the phone and reminds me to call if I need anything. Even if it's just company. Even if you're bored. You're a wonderful young woman, Emi. I'm more than happy to keep you company.

Thanks, I say. Then I stop her when she has one foot out the door. Case Manager Min?

Yes?

Um. Do you like music?

She smiles and says, Everything but soft jazz. She tells me to call her Rachel. Please. She steps back in the room and wonders if we should make tea.

I say, Sure Rachel. Tea sounds nice.

CHAPTER TWENTY-SIX

A truck gets us to Gowanus Green more or less dry. But the ten steps to the Managing Council offices are uncovered and the storm makes a joke of my rainbreaker. Inside are lots of faces as tired and wet as mine. Strong smell of coffee. I see the guy whose screen I broke yesterday. I give him a look that says sorry but also says I have far bigger things to care about now.

Kristina uses a chair to climb onto a desk. She orders one group to focus on the airfields. Another on the docks. Another to wake up recent transfers and begin coordinating the greater search. She needs lists of every ship that departed before the gates shut. Every blimp that lifted off before they grounded the airfields. She wants storm updates every five minutes. People rush off. I extend a hand to help her down from the desk.

What can I do? I say.

Come with me, she says.

I follow her to a back room with a table and three chairs. A phoenix mural covers one wall. She tells me to sit. Brings me coffee black which she knows I like. I blow to cool it. She puts a hand in my hair. I rest my head against her hip.

So you're in charge here, I say.

I'm on the Managing Council.

I didn't know that, I say. I blow on the coffee. Then ask bluntly: Are you with the Furies?

Yes, she answers.

I sip the coffee surprised at myself. For not feeling more. Anger. Hurt. Disgust. Anything. Because Emi is missing—the void made by this fact is so deep and impossible that Kristina could tell me anything. I would not care.

Did you kill any of those people?

We can talk more later, she says. Right now, Larch, you need to focus. These first hours are our best chance to find her. What do you remember? Tell me everything.

I take a breath. Explain that it is quite rich—hypocritical some might say—that she is asking me the questions when she has been withholding so many secrets for how long?

I understand you might feel that way—

Oh I do feel that way.

Maybe this would be easier if others led the questioning?

Maybe, I say.

Kristina nods at a lens I had not noticed until now. A moment later the door opens. Two men enter. One my height with a long black braid. The other with a wide forehead and shorter than Kristina. She introduces them as Rishi and Ravi and says they will help me remember.

She leans against the door with arms crossed and watches as the men ask me in polite yet excruciating detail about the past few days. I start with Reena and Angel. Rishi and Ravi are far more interested however in Rich, and especially Min. They do not seem surprised when I explain how I checked with Public Safety and discovered that she was not listed. They ask me: What exactly did she want to know?

Where Kristina was, I say. When we'd last heard from her. I didn't tell them anything. We spent the night at Maru's—our neighbor—her place was empty. Then straight to the airport in the morning. Nobody followed us. I made sure. There's no way they could've known we're here.

You did the right thing, Kristina says from the doorway.

Good to know, I say with a bite. But what if I hadn't? You couldn't ping me back even once?

I wanted to. We were compromised. I couldn't trust our communications.

Compromised by who? Public Safety?

Possibly, says Kristina. That's what we're trying to figure out. She nods at Rishi and Ravi to continue.

They pick back up. We go over the same conversation four five six times. I give them a physical description of Min as best I can remember.

Who else knew you were coming here?

Lucas Caro. My friend.

Did he tell anyone?

No. Kristina, you know Lucas. He wouldn't do that.

Unlikely, she agrees.

Rishi and Ravi present me with two cloth bags. One bag has fresh socks and underwear and a gray sweatsuit. The other bag, they explain, is for my wet clothes.

I change. They take my clothes and leave. Kristina moves to follow them.

Wait, I say. Where are you going?

I had not recognized the comfort of being with her until she is stepping away. Cannot imagine how alone Emi must feel right now.

Next door, she says. I'll be right back.

I am exhausted. Also completely wired. Two more things that can be true at once.

A minute later the door bursts open. Kristina strides in holding a pair of tweezers. A peppercorn between the tips.

This was embedded in a card in your pocket.

She holds the tweezers to my face.

The peppercorn is not a peppercorn. Some microchip. A tracking device.

The man, Rich, I stammer. He gave me his business card . . .

You weren't the least bit suspicious?

I—

I try to explain. Cannot. My body buckles with the terrible shame of leading them here. Also with incredulity that Kristina would blame this on me.

Of course I was suspicious, I say. That's why we came here. Because I wanted to keep our daughter safe. Because I was there for her. Me. Someone had to be the parent.

Larch.

I point to the phoenix mural on the wall and remind her that she is the reason Public Safety knocked on our door. Not me. You, Kristina. This is your fault.

Stop it, she says. Stop. Blame does nothing right now. We need to focus.

Who are they? I yell. What the fuck have you done?

The door opens. Jackson enters at a clip and whispers something that turns Kristina white.

What? I say. What is it?

Kristina brings a hand to her mouth.

I am suddenly so done with knowing nothing. All the secrets. She is my daughter too, I announce while batting the coffee off the table and throwing a chair against the wall. Jackson jumps out of the way as the chair bounces off the phoenix mural.

We sent two of ours, Kristina explains. To keep an eye on Emi. And you. For safety.

You sent who?

Reena. Angel.

The kids? They're with you? How did they find us so fast?

We were tracking your screen. As soon as I knew you took Emi to the Esplanade. They were waiting for you at the airport. They volunteered. They were trained. They wanted to help.

Kristina is talking to me but really she is talking to herself. She tells me in a flat voice that they were found in a gravity storage warehouse. Dead.

There is a vent in the ceiling. A fan has been whirring softly. I do not hear the noise until it is gone. Sucked from the room along with Kristina's voice and the blood from my head. I can barely hear myself say Emi's name.

Kristina shakes her head: No. She wasn't there. No sign of her.

You can be gutted that your daughter is missing. Also relieved that she was not found. Two more things that can be true at once.

Kristina and I fall into each other.

I'm sorry, I cry into her hair. I'm so sorry.

I know, my love. I'm so sorry too.

Emi Vargas Brinkman
North American History
Mrs. Helmandi
Great Transition Project (First Draft)

Mom Session VII: The Great Transition, Part 3

Me: What was your favorite deployment?

My Mom: My favorite? The most rewarding was probably my last, with the Cajun Navy. But if you mean the most important, that would be the goodwill deployment.

Me: Why?

My Mom: We learned so much, from the Bolivians, the Chavistas, the Zapatistas. Working alongside one another. Building solidarity. And I made some of my closest relationships. You remember my friend, Charlie Little Crow? We first met on the goodwill tour. Talk about a natural leader. Charlie visited Nuuk when you were young. Do you remember? He had a boy your age.

Me: I don't remember.

My Mom: Well you kids got along great.

Me: Why was the Cajun Navy so rewarding?

My Mom: Because it was the most difficult. Snapping turtles, alligators, snakes, you name it. We all had trench foot. And intestinal bacteria that gave everyone diarrhea. It was the complete opposite of those Forest Corps posters you see now, with smiling young people planting saplings on hillsides popping with wildflowers. We were knee-deep in swamp. Pumping sediment to rebuild barrier islands. Digging channels to restore the mangroves.

Me: Like Dad's deployment to Mexicali.

My Mom: Ha. He didn't have nearly as many mosquitoes.

Me: What about in Yosemite? With Dad?

My Mom: What about it?

Me: Wasn't that one of your favorite times?

My Mom: I don't think anyone would call six months in a burn ward a "favorite" time.

Me: What does it feel like being burned?

My Mom: Good question. I was barely conscious when it happened. I remember a sort of warm feeling. Almost pleasant. That's the body's magic. It floods you with chemicals. The same happens at childbirth. So you can't remember the pain.

Me: What do you remember about first meeting Dad?

My Mom: I remember exhaustion. We had been working that sequoia grove for days. People were literally vomiting with fatigue. My legs were lead. Shaking uncontrollably. And we were out of water. The air was so dry. Thirst—real thirst—is magnitudes worse than hunger. My tongue was swollen. Hanging out of my mouth. I remember resting against the trunk of a sequoia, closing my eyes to conserve moisture. At some point we finally heard the plane. I helped the smokejumpers land. Helped them collect their rigs. They passed out water. Like gifts from heaven.

Me: Did you help Dad land?

My Mom: It's possible. I didn't know him then.

Me: You didn't recognize him from *Corps Power*?

My Mom: Everyone had on helmets and respirators and sunglasses. We all looked the same. And I was practically hallucinating with exhaustion. But when the smokejumpers landed, it did give us a second wind. That's the power of solidarity; we can support one another through the lowest of lows.

Me: And then the fire happened.

My Mom: Yes.

Me: Do you remember Dad rescuing you?

My Mom: I remember him risking his life to save mine. We both should've died. He carried me up that steep hill.

I could hardly move my legs. My hair was burning. My face was melting. He threw my arm over his shoulder without a second thought. That was the essence of the Transition: risking your well-being for total strangers. For generations not yet born. Remember that for your report. What's important isn't me or you or our family. It's all of us. All life. Together. That's what matters.

Me: Do you remember being in the culvert with Dad?

My Mom: There was a skunk sheltering with us. That was surprising.

Me: And rabbits. Dad said there were rabbits too.

My Mom: That's right. I've heard your father's version so many times, it's hard to separate our memories. I remember the tunnel. And a bright light at the end. Ha. Go figure. At some point I lost consciousness. I was hallucinating. I thought my sister was the one holding me. Dripping water into my mouth. Saying I'd be all right.

Me: Maybe she was there too.

My Mom: Maybe.

CHAPTER TWENTY-SEVEN

Case Manager Rachel Min has never heard of Jennifer Lopez or Bon Jovi or Otis Redding. She knows Michael Jackson and Madonna, but she doesn't *know* them. I have her pick any year, any place on earth, and I recite the top song at that time. She says I have an amazing memory. I play her my favorite Valerie June and ask her to be honest: What do you think?

Honestly, she says, I'm pretty sure I'm in love with Valerie June.

Right? I say. I'm sitting cross-legged on the bed. She's on the carpet with her back against the blue chair. Tea steeping in a white pot on a cutting board by her hip. She's barefoot. Her toenails are a shiny red.

Quiz me again, I say.

She closes her eyes: Nineteen seventy-nine. United States.

I think for a moment, stumped. I ask the screen: What was the number one song in nineteen seventy-nine in the United States?

The screen doesn't respond. I tell it to pull up MemeFeed.

We don't have MemeFeed, says Rachel.

Can you install it?

You don't need that garbage.

She pulls her screen from the back pocket of her jeans and repeats my question.

My Sharona? she reads.

Oh yeah! Either you'll love this one or you'll hate it.

We play "My Sharona" on the wall screen. Rachel declares herself a lover. She pours two cups of tea. Chamomile. Supposedly calming, but it has zero effect on me. My mom is okay. My parents are together. I can't stop repeating these facts in my mind.

I sit on the carpet next to Rachel. Our knees almost touch. I ask her to quiz me again. I nail every year and place she throws my way. Jimi Hendrix. Elvis Presley. Alanis Morissette. I have to pee. When I come back she's in the kitchen inspecting the trash. She opens the fridge.

You've hardly eaten.

I'm not hungry.

Not yet, she says, unwrapping a burrito. But have you ever met a true microwave black belt?

She zaps a burrito and slices it like sushi on a plate. Not pressuring me. Not watching me. Not caring if I eat or don't. I bite from the smallest slice. Nothing fancy. Beans and cheese. I lick a single grain of salt. Let myself relax on the wave of my hunger.

This is nice, she says. Listening to music. Talking. My daughter—Rose is her name—if Rose and I are together usually we're watching something. Not exactly quality time. Do you and your mom do this a lot?

I try not to laugh. Um. No? Mostly we fight.

She flashes a smile and says, Like daughters and mothers since the beginning of time.

I nod. Then I blurt that my dad and I never meant to lie to her back in Nuuk.

Of course not, she says.

Are we in trouble?

Not at all.

Not even my mom?

Emi, she says. We're here to make sure everyone stays safe. That's our job. We're Public Safety. It's what we do.

There's a pause. We both stare at the screen. It's streaming Chuck Berry. Nineteen seventy-two.

Though I'm curious, she says, why might you think your mom would be in trouble?

I shrug. I don't know.

Has she ever mentioned the Furies?

No.

Does she talk about climate criminals?

Not a lot.

So sometimes?

Everyone does sometimes. I mean they caused the Crisis.

Has she ever mentioned the name Matthias Barrack?

I don't think so. Who's that?

What about Ian Rios?

No. I can't remember.

Where was your mom on Day Zero?

She had extraction duty.

Was she here in Gowanus?

There's an awkward silence that not even Chuck Berry can fill. Rachel is questioning me like a case manager, I realize. Which she is. I don't know where to look, or what to do with my hands. I feel suspicious just existing. Like every second of silence makes my mom more guilty.

She didn't have anything to do with what happened on Day Zero, I say.

Rachel lets out a breath. Well that's a relief.

Yeah.

Did she talk to you on Day Zero?

I look at her and then back into my tea so quickly that I know she knows I know.

Just to say hi, I say.

She shifts her legs and says that sometimes, when we try to protect people, we end up hurting them. The more you tell me now, Emi, the better for you and your mom and your dad.

Okay.

So let's try again: Where was your mom on Day Zero?

I feel my face turn red. I try to hide behind my teacup. Why don't you ask her?

We did, she says cheerfully. I'm just corroborating what she said. Double-checking.

You said she wasn't in trouble.

Does she bring friends home often?

I don't know. What's often?

Do you know Charlie Little Crow?

Not really.

Not really?

I think he's a friend of my mom's? Why?

She frowns, as if concerned for me, and asks how well I'd say I know my mom.

I hate the question. I hate the lilt in her voice, and the pity in her frown, and that she's obviously being nice so she can learn about my mom. She thinks I'm hiding something. What she can't understand is that even though our moms are the people we should know better than anyone—the first people we ever meet—some of us hardly know them at all.

My mom has the most volunteer hours in our plaza, I say. She's a hero of the Transition.

Yes. She certainly is.

She takes a careful sip then balances her teacup on her knee. Chuck Berry becomes Justin Bieber, but he might as well be white noise. I have that hot taste in my throat that means I'm one careless step from falling off my wave.

I don't feel good, I tell her. I think I want to be alone. I need to rest.

She stands and brushes off her jeans. The carpet keeps a faint imprint of her butt. I thank her for the tea. The burrito. She thanks me for the music. We're acting nice but it's fake nice—like the girls on my basketball team. The moment she leaves and shuts the door behind her, I feel guilty, like I've offended her. She was just keeping me company. She was only being nice. I was the one who asked her to stay. I was the one who started asking her questions and talking about my mom.

I jump up to apologize. But when I get to the door and turn the handle, it's stuck. I try again. I push. Pull. Lean my full weight on the handle. Make a fist. About to start banging and yelling when the phone rings. I run across the carpet to pick it up.

Everything okay? says Case Manager Rich.

Um yeah, I say, glancing into the corners of the room. I don't see any cameras, but I feel that prickle on the back of my neck like I'm being watched.

You sure? he says.

Actually, I think the door's stuck?

It's locked.

Oh, I say.

For safety, he says. Did you need something?

No. I guess not.

Have a nice rest then.

Okay. Thanks. I will.

CHAPTER TWENTY-EIGHT

LARCH

News like the tides. High and low. Good and bad.

Good news is the hurricane. Grounding air cargo. Keeping the surge gates closed. Gifting us precious time.

Bad news is no storm can last forever.

Good news is lightning has tapered.

Bad news is high winds have not. The surveillance drones are inoperable.

Good news is Gowanus Outpost has meteorological drones capable of withstanding hurricane winds. And they are equipped with thermals which allow for searching larger areas.

Bad news is that there are less than ten such drones. Not nearly enough to scan every warehouse and residential building and mess hall and turbine factory and battery plant and quantum hub and hangar and dry dock and the endless stacks of shipping containers.

Good news is that there are other ways to search. As we discovered during the Crisis: Technology was never going to save us. Always it fell on people. And we have many: All the young people swarming into Gowanus desperate to help. They are rousted from dorms and asked to run around in a hurricane and find a missing fifteen-year-old girl and they jump at the chance. The Managing Council organizes search crews of four to five. I throw in with one group heading out. They slap me on the back: Don't worry sir, we'll find her.

We are assigned a row of battery warehouses. One of our crew unpacks a suitcase drone. Sends it buzzing into the rafters. The rest of us go by foot. Calling out. Opening shipping containers. Yelling into the darkness. Once cleared we ping the Managing Council for our next assignment. The search works outward like ripples in a pond. The epicenter is the gravity storage warehouse where Reena and Angel were found. Which is the worst bad news of all: The people who took Emi. They are willing to kill.

Good news is they haven't hurt Emi. Kristina promises that she is okay.

What do you mean? I ask. How do you know?

Because this has happened before.

We are sitting across from each other in a food court nearest the epicenter. Jamba Juice. Subway. Panda Express. Transformed now into a command center. People registering. Heading out. Eating. Taking a break from the rain. I do not want to take a break but at some point the body forces you. Soaked and tired and doing the shakes at a table when Kristina appears. Hand on my shoulder. Coffee in a mug. Four chairs at the table like points on a compass. She takes the north to my south. Curls her hands around mine around the mug. She is dry. Which makes sense. She is leadership. Organizing the search. But also seems wrong.

What do you mean it's happened before?

Remember Charlie Little Crow?

Charlie? Of course. What about him?

They took his son.

Who did?

Ian Rios.

Who's Ian Rios?

Kristina gives me a look I know all too well. She says she is almost jealous of my ability to remain so utterly detached from what is happening in the world. Especially now of all times.

A week ago this type of comment would have shot us into the kind of loud and spiraling fight that would feel luxurious—joyous—right now. But at this moment I am too wrung out to fight.

Just tell me, I say. Who is he?

A climate criminal, she says. Made a fortune in natural gas trading. Fought the Transition. Made another fortune profiteering from it.

And he kidnapped Charlie's son.

Not him. These people don't do anything themselves. Contractors. Private security. They took Charlie's boy.

Took him for what?

Collateral.

Collateral for what?

For safety. For Rios's life.

Because the Furies were going to assassinate him, I say, putting the pieces together. And Charlie is with the Furies.

Kristina nods.

Then the name comes back to me. The newscast in the Brooklyn Heights station. The kids celebrating. Rios was the one assassinated on his yacht, I say. Killed by his masseuse.

Physical therapist, Kristina corrects me. But yes.

So you killed him anyway. Even though he took Charlie's boy as collateral.

The Furies killed him, she says.

You said you were with them.

Kristina shakes her head: It doesn't work like that.

Like what?

We operate together but independently. Horizontally. There's no head.

I take a breath. I am bouncing between two planes of concern. On one plane I want every detail about the stranger sitting across from me. On the other plane I could not care less about the organizational flowchart of her secret army. I do not care about anything except Emi. If the mug between my hands were not carbon composite it would have shattered by now.

So they killed Charlie's boy, I say.

Kristina looks down. Gives the smallest of nods.

They killed Charlie's boy, I repeat.

My hand comes down hard on the table. Coffee splashes over the lip of my mug. Heads turn.

You said they wouldn't hurt Emi, I say. You just promised.

Instead of rising to my level as usual, Kristina grows quiet. Pushes a bead of spilled coffee around with a finger. I said they *haven't* hurt her, she says. And they won't, as long as their client stays safe.

Who's their client?

They'll let us know soon.

And then?

She uses the back of her hand to wipe her eyes.

Then you'll cross that person off your kill list, I say. You'll leave them the fuck alone.

I can't give those orders, she says in a hush.

Bullshit. I see the way people look at you around here.

Here. But we aren't centralized. I told you. The physical therapist who got Rios—she was underground for ten years. We have people embedded everywhere. I can't tell them what to do. That's how we designed it. So no one person calls the shots.

Whoever took our daughter obviously disagrees.

They're wrong, she says. They're desperate.

So am I! I yell, my voice breaking. Do something, Kristina!

We don't negotiate with terrorists, she says.

How can you say that? How can you even think that?

My hand comes down on the table again. Kristina flinches. I yell. No words. Just an animal sound of pain and anger and loss.

We have the storm on our side, she says. We have time. We can find her. She's here.

Her voice is soft however and her eyes red. Like she does not believe herself. Like she is scared. Which makes her more of a stranger to me than this secret life she has been living. I need her to be herself now. Fighting. Fighting me. Fighting anything. Throw something. Hit something. Yell. Fix this one problem that you created. Make it right. Find our girl.

She puts her head on her arms on the table. Her back heaving.

I stand and shift the chairs so we are no longer sitting across from each other but hip to hip. I put a hand on her back. I rub either side of her vertebrae.

The good news is that I am almost too empty with panic and fear to be angry.

The bad news is that there is still so much to be angry about.

CHAPTER TWENTY-NINE

My door is locked.

My door is locked from the outside.

My door is locked from the outside and I'm being watched.

I walk the safe house, searching casually for cameras. I don't find any. What I do find is a million times worse. First I notice that none of the books have creases in their spines except for *White Teeth*, which I opened. And the bathroom mirror is warped. And a row of tiles by the toilet are spaced unevenly. Little things but they add up until the safe house begins tilting into something that resembles what it was before yet is also totally different.

I sit on the bed and try to ride the swell of panic. I go to turn on the screen. I realize it must be the only screen in all of North America without MemeFeed or newscasts or any connection to the outside world. Then my eyes go to the outlet below the screen: it's crooked. Then I notice how the curtains on either side of the window are creased like they were just removed from the packaging. Then I notice something that stops my heart with a heavy liquid squeeze.

I stand. I shuffle over to the window. I count seconds between flashes of lightning. I count and count. There's a pattern. It repeats. And repeats. I tap my leg between flashes to triple-check I'm not imagining it.

Four seconds.

Two seconds.

Three seconds.

The pattern never changes. I'm not imagining it. And not only the lightning: After the two-second pause a leaf sticks to the window in the lower left corner. The leaf flutters there until the four-second pause, then blows off. And it happens again. And again. Same leaf. Same spot.

The ground sways beneath me like the safe house is moving. I bend my knees for balance until the swell passes. I put my palms flat against the glass like I did at the Brooklyn Heights station. At the station I could feel the thrum of the storm from the other side. Here there's nothing. Because it's not a window. It's a screen. A screen set in a wall projecting a storm on a loop. Hung with curtains that have recently been removed from the packaging. What looked before like a fancy room was clearly just made to appear fancy. And made in a hurry. And just for me.

A scream tries to escape my chest. I remind myself that they are watching me. There are cameras. I ride out the wave.

Okay.

I chug a glass of water at the kitchen sink. Any trace of chamomile has taken an emergency exit from my veins. I turn on the screen. Anything to fill the silence. Michael Jackson pops into my mind so Michael Jackson it is. "Smooth Criminal." I am being held prisoner. Why? Because of my mom. She'll come to save me, and they'll take her. I'm bait. It's a trap.

Everything comes out of the fridge. The freezer empties. Kitchen therapy, my dad calls it. I blend a smoothie. I microwave a pizza. I pour an immense bowl of cereal. Michael Jackson jumps into "Wanna Be Startin' Somethin,'" which is normally my favorite but now only reminds me of my room in Nuuk. I microwave a glass of oat milk. I add cinnamon. Honey. Like my mom would do for me if she was here. I lay out my feast. I eat. I drink. My throat wants to close but I say no, no, no. I swallow. I gulp. I chug. And then I jump.

Jumping is different from falling. When I fall off my wave it's loss of control. When I jump it's because I want to. And I do want to. I run to the bathroom, drop to my knees, find that hot relief. I'm lying on the cold tile floor, just like my mom and her sister and grandmother used to do to escape the heat of their dying world, when Rachel comes running in.

Emi! Love. Are you okay? You poor thing.

If I didn't think they were watching me before, I'm certain now. It brings a new set of waves that knock me around. I scramble to kneel again at the toilet.

She holds my hair. I say I ate too fast. She murmurs that it's okay.

She helps me into the shower. I wash and dry off and rinse my mouth. She says I must be exhausted. I mumble weakly that I am. I give her my full weight as she helps me into my fresh clothes and from there into bed. I nod yes to a glass of water. Yes to a cool wash-cloth on my forehead. Yes to turning off the music and the lights.

Call if you need me, love. We're right here. Anything. I mean that. I'll run right over.

Thanks, I whisper.

She sits on the bed, rubbing my arm softly. I close my eyes but don't sleep. I drift in and out. Like my mom in the culvert. Except I don't have my dad to save me. Nobody to save me but myself. I crack an eye when she leaves. The door opens outward. I know what I have to do.

CHAPTER THIRTY

LARCH

I join another search crew. Three blimp hangars. Workers busy loading turbines for shipment to go out as soon as the storm ends. They take a break so we can open containers and inspect the holds. The workers are polite if annoyed. They want to complete their hours and finish their duty. Return to Nuuk and their families. I get that. But also feels wrong they are not helping us search. Feels wrong that everyone does not know what is happening to Emi. To me. The entire world should be shutting down until we find my girl.

———

The dawn of Emi's life was not easy. Born six weeks early with complications. Strange infections. Autoimmune issues. The doctors unsure what or why. We would be home from the hospital for a day. Delirious happiness. A new family with a new baby in a new city in a new world. Propped up on either side of her in bed. Smiling with her. Making faces. Our go bag by the door in case her temperature spiked again. Which it would. One hundred one. One hundred two. Rushing downcity to Seaport General. Passing her off to nurses we had come to know by first name. Sensors and thermometers and IVs. Gauges in every orifice of Emi's tiny body. Our baby in good hands that were not our hands. Nothing we could do but be with her. The longest stretch at the hospital was eight days. Rubbing her little feet. Kristina singing in Spanish. We slept when Emi slept. Held each other in a most uncomfortable trundle bed. Deeply in love. And saying it. Stating our love. Claiming it. Similar to the Crisis in that way: Catastrophe bringing out the best. Bringing us together. I want to be like that again. But Emi's infections as an infant could have been caused by anything. This thing now? It is squarely our fault.

———

We clear the blimp hangars. Ping Command. Return to the food court where I choke down a slice of cold pizza and find a quiet corner to slip on Emi's headphones. "Purple Rain." Her last song. No. God. Her last song for now.

My eyes open to the sharp crinkle of an emergency blanket. Kristina kneeling over me. Tucking me in. I shuck off the blanket. Roll away. Tell her I need to rest so I can go out again.

She sits next to me. Hand on my knee. Back against the wall. She is wet. She has been outside to join the search. Not good. Once the generals are fighting in the trenches the war is lost.

She points to Emi's headphones. Asks what she was listening to.

Music, I say—a very Emi answer—and slip the headphones onto my neck. I do not feel like sharing. I sit up against the wall so that we are side by side. Not saying anything. Like when Emi was in newborn intensive care. Holding space. The moment is interrupted when a woman I recognize from the Managing Council offices comes over to put a hand on Kristina's forearm and tell her to hang in there.

Thanks, Ruby.

After her comes Jackson with an update and a shoulder squeeze. Then a man with bushy gray eyebrows. His knees pop as he squats to hug Kristina. He calls her Kris. He is crying. Like our pain is his pain.

Kris? I say when he leaves.

Paul and I go way back.

Have I met Paul?

I don't think so. He was on the Goodwill tour.

How long has this been going on? I say, knowing I will explode if she says How long has what been going on?

But she knows what I mean. This other life of hers. Phoenix. The Furies. This other family who calls her Kris.

One year? I ask. Two?

The woman who killed Rios, Kristina says, she went to school for physical therapy. Just to get close to someone like him. We didn't build this overnight.

So more than two years?

Kristina sighs. Yes. More than two years.

Five?

More than five.

Ten? I am ready to scream. The number should not matter. Yet it matters.

Sixteen, she says.

Jesus. Kristina.

We started organizing at the end of the Transition. Laying the groundwork. Just in case.

In case what?

In case people forgot. In case the world was going to let the fuckers get away with it.

Jesus, I say again. I see her the day before she left Nuuk. Cooking breakfast tacos. Walking Emi to school. Begging me to skip work so we could dance and laugh and make love. All that time she was with the Furies. And before. Long before. Visiting Emi's classroom for Parents' Day. Summers at the geofarms. Rubbing Emi's little feet in intensive care. Every memory as a family.

This whole time I thought you were just having an affair.

I told you I wasn't.

I would've preferred it.

We both laugh a little. Which feels immediately wrong. Like we have forgotten Emi.

You lied to me, I say. Our whole marriage. And Emi. God. Her entire life.

I didn't lie. I just kept it separate. We all had to. To keep our families safe.

So much for that.

My comment hurts her. She sobs quietly into the well of her crossed legs. It does not make me happy to watch her in pain. But I am glad she feels bad. Because she should.

I didn't want this to happen, she says. I ran for office. We tried other paths. So many. You have no idea. We gave them options. This was always the last resort.

Murder, I say. The last resort was murdering people.

Criminals, she says. Monsters. You know what they did.

And killing them accomplishes what? You can't change the past.

Nobody's trying to change the past.

So what, then?

Justice. A wound festers if ignored. Infection sets in. We can't truly move forward without healing. We must acknowledge the loss. We must hold people responsible. This isn't for the past. It's for the future.

Killing is wrong, I say. I can't believe I even need to say this! Everyone knows it, Kristina. Little kids know it.

She whips her head around to look at me with fierce eyes: Say I put you in a room with the people who took Emiliana? You let them walk? Or what about the people who hired them? Knowing no court will ever convict them. No authority will jail them. Seriously. What do you do?

That's different.

How?

It's personal. It's family.

These people would've destroyed our planet if we'd let them. God knows they tried. And they will again. They already are. It's only been sixteen years. Sixteen years is nothing. This is our one planet. Our only child's only home. How does it get any more personal?

It hurts me to hear Kristina talk in these circles. She has had sixteen years to develop every logic and rationalization. I am not going to convince her otherwise in five minutes in the corner of a food court. And it does not matter. Only Emi matters. I know this. I know that arguing will accomplish nothing. But that has always been our problem. We keep circling back for more.

You almost got us killed on the Esplanade, I say. Emi could've died.

Why do you think she was supposed to go north for the week? You think that was a coincidence, her teammates inviting her? You think those girls are her friends? I made sure she would be as far away as possible. *You're* the one who took her down there! How many times did I warn you? How many times did I tell you not to go? How could I have been any clearer?

By telling me that you were organizing a mass assassination.

I did tell you Larch! I took an enormous risk warning you and Emi to run.

At the last second, I say. Emi was almost crushed to death. She had to jump into freezing water. She swam for her life. She could've died.

But she didn't. Because we raised her to be strong and resilient.

I raised her! Me! I did everything for her!

You travel around North America on a plane with a professional basketball team, Larch. You spend more time perfecting sourdough than you do volunteering for our plaza. The most basic asks. When did you last pitch in? You're totally unengaged politically. You have no idea what's going on. You care more about the protein needs of twelve athletes than you do about the state of the world your daughter will inherit. That is not doing everything. That is giving up. Selling out.

I gave thirteen goddamned years to the Transition. Twenty-one deployments.

Yes, and you've skipped extraction duty practically ever since.

Someone had to stay with Em. Someone had to be the parent. I'm a good dad.

You're a great dad. But parenting your child alone—that's the bare minimum. That's the mentality that led to the Crisis. Everyone caring so deeply for their own children. What about other children? What about the rest of the world?

Did you ever really love us? Or are we just part of the act too?

I ask the question to hurt her as much as she has hurt me. But between the crack in my voice and the snot running from my nose it is clear I am also asking the question to hurt myself.

She takes my face in her hands. You and Emi are my family. I love you. Of course I do.

Then what happened? I whisper. If you had put a fraction of the effort into us as you did into all this—

You have no idea how hard I've tried. The pressure. You have no idea.

I admit that she is right: I have no idea. No idea who she really is.

As if to prove my point a group approaches. Two women and a man. They express condolences. Their outrage. They hug Kristina. This time Kristina introduces me. I nod my hellos. Accept their sympathies. Immediately forget their names. I do not care. I am not angry. Would I murder the people who took Emi? I would. And whoever hired them. Kristina is right about that. I am a good father. I am getting up to join another search crew. I am giving Emi's headphones to Kristina. Placing them gently around her head so she can live with the music.

CHAPTER THIRTY-ONE

EMI

Watching the same fake storm loop in the same fake window. I have no idea how long it's been playing. No idea how long I've been here. No way to warn my mom. No way to contact my dad. No escape. Which is how people must have felt during the Crisis: helpless. It's the worst—to know exactly what's happening with no way to stop it. My mom's parents took her to protest Pemex. My dad's parents installed solar. Deep down, I bet they knew these little acts wouldn't help. But I wonder if they felt better doing something rather than nothing. Or maybe people really did believe that small things would make a difference? Like if everyone did enough small things together, they could prevent the Crisis?

Which they could have, I remind myself.

That's the thing about working together. Mutual aid. You can build the Big U. The Southwest Solar Authority. You can save the world.

But it's also the problem—getting everyone to work together. You have to make it happen.

The advantage of being alone is you don't have to convince anyone.

The disadvantage is you have to convince yourself.

———

I stream a song, "Every Breath You Take," by this band called the Police, and I try to imagine life back in 1983 when people basically had no idea that the Crisis was coming. But trying to imagine that world feels just as impossible as imagining the world from one short week ago, when my biggest problem was my Great Transition project, or packing for a ski trip I didn't want to go on, or fighting with my mom over dinner. People my age have crossed borders. Survived slavery. Fought wars. Saved families. Died for strangers. Joan of Arc. Harriet Tubman. Anne Frank. Mama Greta. My mom. Compared to them, what I am doing? I'm doing nothing. I'm lying in a pink-and-gray canopy bed listening to the Police.

———

Every year in the lead-up to Day Zero, my parents have the same argument. My mom makes fun of the banners and decorations, declaring it a fantastic waste of time and resources, while my dad says the holiday is important so people can have hope and believe that things will work out.

I agree with them both. Things might hopefully work out. But nothing will work out on its own. You have to make things happen. Imagine if Phoenix Company had never disobeyed orders? If the New York City Mutual Aid Federation had never voted for a general strike? If my dad had never carried my mom into the culvert? If everyone in human history had stayed in bed during the most hopeless times, waiting for someone else to save them?

You have to do something instead of doing nothing. You just have to.

I reach over and pick up the phone before I can change my mind. Rachel answers immediately.

Hi, love.

I ask her to come right away. There's something I need to tell her. Something important I remembered.

Okay, she says. Be right over.

CHAPTER THIRTY-TWO

LARCH

They called it reforestation—and there was some planting involved—but mostly I dug. The Mexicali Valley Forest Corps camp had been established at the beginning of the Transition. The project was symbolically important as an early mission centered on a shared biome rather than national borders. I was proud to be part of it.

The goal was twofold: rehabilitate the Colorado River delta and re-connect the river to the estuary at the Sea of Cortez. We planted cottonwoods and willows and mesquite. Dogwoods and and ironwoods. Globemallow and salt grasses. There was an enormous nursery. Tens of thousands of saplings in the neatest rows you could imagine. Some days you got watering duty and nothing else. Other days I worked irrigation. Laying pipe. Stretching mist-collection membrane. Repairing faulty valves. Much of the actual reforestation had already happened by this time. You could travel upriver to the cottonwood groves planted in the first year of the Transition. Trees now fifteen feet tall. The air cooler. Birds diving into the glass of the river. Wind rustling leaves. Beaver and deer.

Downstream was a different story. The river narrowed to a trickle. Flanked on either side by fields of dust. Desert shrubs. The delta before European colonization had been home to thousands of emerald lagoons. To restore the biome we had to reconnect the river to the tides. This required digging out sandbars so the seawater could reach upstream. Because of access issues most digging was done by hand. If Forest Corps had deployed me here at the beginning of the Transition, I might have gone insane with boredom. Lucas certainly would have. But I was older now. Five hours shoveling was nothing. I knew hard work. I knew loss. I knew love.

Kristina kept in touch via old-fashioned postcard. Her first arrived from La Paz. She was meeting with a youth corps. Installing PV panels on impossible terra-cotta rooftops. But she was also still with me in Yosemite on the Loop Trail. And wherever it was that we would meet next.

> I'm unstuck in time, my love. Past, present, future, there you are. There we are. That is the future I want. The one we are building together. Let's make it.
>   In solidarity — K

We sent postcards for months. Mail arrived at the Mexicali camp before dinner. Either the best or worst part of my day. I read about her travels through South America. Speaking to worker cooperatives. Organizing future collaborations. Pitching in with projects. She wrote about her deployment with an ease—as if lucky to be working so hard.

> Mangrove restoration in Venezuela. Organized new volunteer corps of 3000, mostly fishermen and students. Mud up to our knees. 14-hour days. Sunsets so gorgeous you could cry.

Every postcard she sent was a physical object she had touched. I could feel her. Her dedication. Her passion for a better world. Everything that had made me fall for her so hard. What I wanted even more than descriptions of her work however was the mushy stuff. She could be so tender over mail. She wrote how much she missed me. How much she loved me. How desperately she needed our deployments to end. How about somewhere wintery over New Year's? She had never seen snow. She wanted hot chocolate. She wanted me.

———

Michigan's Upper Peninsula was both wintery and convenient: a straight shot on the bullet train from Tucson to Chicago, with only one short transfer through Milwaukee to Marquette. I headed out the day my deployment ended—settling into my seat and resting my head against the window at four hundred miles per hour. The train shot through the black photovoltaic ocean of the Southwest Solar Authority. Then in a blink from sun to wind: the hypnotic fields of the Great Plains—turbines spinning to the horizon. Herds of bison grazing below. I could hear Helen and Ellen saying that regular people like us would never get to ride the trains we were building. So much had changed in what felt like a very long time and also no time at all.

The ride from Tucson to Marquette felt similar: only four hours—both too long and far too quick. What if distance and time had built me and Kristina into something we were not? I was nervous to see her. Everything with the fire and Yosemite had seemed fated. This trip on the other hand was premeditated. She had reserved a cabin at a Transition camp on the shore of Lake Superior. Seven days. Far more time than we'd ever spent together alone. In the weeks leading up I casually suggested we could invite friends for the first few days. Kristina admitted that she was thinking the same thing. That was how Lucas ended up meeting us at the cabin with twelve bottles of champagne and his boyfriend, Rafi, who also worked as a liaison with the WNBA.

Kristina had invited a couple too: Charlie and Katya. Friends of hers from the international goodwill tour. Charlie Little Crow was a young Lakota leader. Katya was Swedish royalty—a literal princess—

but had absconded in her teens to live in a cohousing community where Greta Thunberg had briefly stayed, she told us. She was a huge fan of *Corps Power*.

Mama Greta was a fan? I asked.

No, I was, said Katya. I saw every episode. I remember you fondly.

Hey, what about me? Lucas said.

You were cute too, Katya said. But Larch swung such a large hammer.

Careful girl, teased Kristina. He's my reality star. Go find your own.

I had been nervous that my reunion with Kristina after nine long months would be awkward. But we had nothing to worry about. We could not leave each other alone. She could not get out of my lap. I could not take my hands from her legs. We could not wait for our good dear friends to shout "Happy New Year!" and pack up and leave.

Until then the six of us drank champagne. We sledded behind the cabin. We slid around on the ice of Lake Superior. We soaked in the camp's communal hot tub. The Ojibwe used the camp in the nonwinter months as a regenerative agriculture Transition training center. Now all the cabins were occupied by Transition workers on leave. We had one big communal bonfire but otherwise groups mostly stuck to themselves. The six of us stayed up late talking. Drinking. I told them about Mexicali and the cottonwood groves—a real sense of hope not only for the Colorado but for the Transition. Ontario had just signed another energy-visa swap with the Southwest Solar Authority. So many visas floating around now that the old borders felt ornamental. And emissions significantly dropping. The Amazon showing signs of tilting back into the great carbon sink. The navy had hooked up their nuclear fleet for offshore power. Korean engineers had developed a more efficient fusion reactor. And new worker-planned cities like Nuuk were well under construction. So much hopeful news.

It's a fair start, Kristina said.

But decades too late, Charlie added.

And it holds none of the climate criminals responsible, said Katya.

No no no. It's New Year's Eve, people! said Lucas, waving a bottle. Tonight we celebrate. No doom and gloom, thank you very much.

Celebrate this please, said Rafi, holding his cup for Lucas to refill.

Kristina and her friends looked at each other. We were all sitting on the carpet. Woodstove raging. Snow ticking the windows.

Let's eat, I said. Come sit down. Dinner's almost ready.

I had spent nearly a month procuring and coordinating ingredients to impress Kristina this one week. For New Year's Eve dinner I had made a miso soup of softened kelp with dried and smoked shiitakes and cubed tofu and sliced scallion rings. I had whisked eggs with sugar and rice vinegar and seasonings that I cooked in these very thin layers to roll and fold together Japanese style over sushi rice. Warm fingerling potatoes with caramelized onions and fried capers and arugula. Blueberry pie. The table was set. I encouraged everyone to their seats. Reminded them I had been cooking all day. Promised they would not be disappointed.

Nobody moved.

What's wrong with celebrating? Lucas asked Katya. Please. Tell me. I want to know.

We cannot become complacent, Katya said. This is no time to relax. Soon people will be saying the Transition has gone too far. Just wait.

Well, what is far enough? said Lucas. It's a fair question.

That's just it, said Charlie. The moment we stop is when the destroying classes win. We must always be on alert. The Transition can never end.

Sort of ruptures the definition of a transition, doesn't it? mumbled Rafi.

I think it's fine to celebrate but we have to keep fighting, said Kristina, shifting in my lap. The push for everything to go back to normal is about to become relentless.

I like normal, said Lucas. I miss normal. What's wrong with normal?

Normal brought us to the brink, said Charlie.

So we need a better normal, I said. That's what we're working for, right? Come on. We can cheers to that.

We drank to a new and better normal. I served dinner. We ate then left dishes to soak in the sink so we could bundle up and walk the woods. Kristina and Katya tugged low branches to sock Charlie and Rafi with snow. Lucas and I fell behind. He was not allowed to tell a soul that the Hawks were planning to relocate to Nuuk as the Tundra, he said, but he *had* to tell me. He said he could put in a good word. I could be a team chef or nutritionist. But first I would have to enter the Nuuk housing lottery. I would have a better chance applying with Kristina. Two Transition heroes. Wounded in action. And you'd get your pick of units if you apply as a family, he said. You two need to get married and have a kid, like, yesterday.

Do we? I said, smiling so widely that my teeth ached in the cold air.

We all got back to the cabin with seconds to spare. We counted down. We popped more champagne. We kissed. We rang in the New Year. The next morning Kristina and I hugged everyone goodbye and shut the door and for three days hardly opened it again.

———

Kristina loved running her hands over my arms. My cartoon muscles, she called them. All that shoveling in Mexicali. And she thought my tan was hilarious. Elbows down I was as brown as her. But she needed a welding visor if I was going to take off my shirt, she would laugh. And forget about your ass, man. Like staring into the sun.

The worst of her scars disappeared into her laugh lines when she smiled. Her wounds had healed into raised silvery channels. She applied vitamin lotions. Moisturizers. She didn't care, she said. And maybe she didn't. She was so selfless. So brave and beautiful. Her passion for the Transition made me dizzy with love. Even during the limited time of our New Year's leave I had to beg her from volunteering. She felt bad for the maintenance staff who'd pulled such shitty deployments during the holiday season. Couldn't we give them a break? We did a few shoveling shifts but otherwise I tried to keep her happy with the most elaborate meals I could prepare.

Breakfast popovers with a compound butter of mint and grapefruit zest.

Marinated and toasted nuts.

Herb and flower salad.

Tamales folded in the method I had learned from the ladies of Hunts Point.

Outside the cabin I built us a quinzee in the way my father had taught me: A huge mound of snow hollowed out. A steep upward-sloping entryway to trap warm air. I dragged in every blanket from the cabin. I carved candle shelves into the walls. Our body heat warmed the space quickly. We were careful. We held each other afterward. I told her what Lucas had said about the Tundra. Putting in a good word.

She frowned. I watched the candlelight make shadows against her face and the snow. You want to work for a basketball team? she said. What about the Transition?

I meant after, I said.

After what? We have to keep the Transition alive.

Right. I know that. It's just a thought. In case we wanted a temporary base. A place to call home between battles.

I told her about the Nuuk housing lottery. How Transition veterans got seeded higher and we would have a good chance if we applied as a family. Meaning more than two of us.

Kristina did not respond. She was quiet for a long time. Her head on my shoulder.

I think I'd like that, she finally said.

Her face was radiant. Her breath warm. That smile.

I think I would really like that a lot.

CHAPTER THIRTY-THREE
LARCH

Yet another search. Yet another maintenance garage. But the others in my crew not hustling with the same step. Not yelling Emi's name with the same urgency. Nobody slapping my back assuring me she will be okay. And my heart no longer leaping with hope at every door I open. I had counted on being the one to find her. Then accepted the possibility that another search crew might. Now doubting even that.

We clear the garage. Head back. The storm is winding down. The sky opening to patches of blue. Funnel windmills reemerging from streetlamps to catch the wind. Rain letting up. No ships yet in the canal or blimps above but for how much longer?

Back at the food court we enter to an audible buzz. Everyone gathered at the far end. I muscle my way through to Kristina where she informs me with a sob that Emi is alive. Alive and seemingly well. And—in the best-case scenario—we will never see her again.

———

The video is short. Twelve seconds. Filmed straight-on. I had been expecting the worst but Emi seems fine. Dry. Her hair shiny and healthy. Wearing her navy blue sweatshirt and jeans and standing in a luxurious room. A large canopy bed behind her. Bookshelves shining with the glint of genuine wood. Emi looks straight ahead as if she knows she is being filmed. No sign of being harmed. She chews her lip. Touches her throat. Taps her hand against her thigh as if counting a beat. Squints as if trying to stare through the screen to tell us where she is.

Kristina holds my arm like I am a post.

I am using her for the same purpose. Keeping each other upright.

The video ends. Starts over. We watch the loop. Again and again. I wipe my eyes with a sleeve. Someone is busy authenticating it, Kristina tells me, but we know the video is no deepfake. No code could replicate our girl in such detail. Unharmed except for her arms which are still scratched from climbing the seawall and jumping into Nuuk Bay. But then she had her mother to warn her. She had me and Lucas to help her. Now she has only herself.

A simple encrypted message accompanies the video: any further targeted assassinations will result in reciprocal punitive action.

Fuck them reciprocal, snorts someone behind us. A teenage girl.

A fifteen-year-old girl who knows every hit song in modern history. Who works so hard at school. Who has the best free-throw percentage off the bench. Who can corral twelve toddlers into cleaning up and washing hands. Who only ever asked for a cat and a screen and smoothies and why did we ever say no? What were we thinking? I'm not. Thinking. My head is ringing with the high whine of rage. Suddenly I understand the Furies with a clarity as pure as crystal. Vengeance. Revenge. Justice. Call it whatever. A need that can be as immediately urgent as water or air. The only thing I want more than hurting the people who took Emi is to save Emi. To rescue my girl. But that is the problem—the message informs us—we cannot have both.

They do not give us a specific name. They have learned the lesson of Ian Rios. They have learned that nowhere is safe. They cannot trust their physical therapists or cleaners or gardeners. They have learned the mistake of identifying themselves. Instead they have formed a consortium. That is what they are calling it. They are not interested in being shot on yachts offshore. They are interested in nonviolence. And to ensure nonviolence they will be holding Emi indefinitely.

The sound drains from the food court. I am trying to process. Cannot process.

The timeline is what makes it impossible: There is no deadline. If the assassinations do not stop they will kill Emi as they killed Charlie Little Crow's boy. That part I understand. But if the assassinations do stop? Then Emi is kept to ensure they never resume.

Either way we never see her again. Which is the most implausible timeline of all. A future without Emi is no future. It is a cliff. The abrupt end of time.

———

How many are there? I ask.

How many what?

People that could've done this. Hundreds? Thousands?

Not thousands.

Kristina and I are back in the food court. Numb. Freshly empty-handed from another search. A row of cargo hangars at the airfields. Searching together this time. Our throats raw with Emi's name. Eyes blurry from watching the video as if each loop might be the last.

I want to help, I say. Let me work with you. Phoenix. Furies. Whatever. I want to kill them.

Don't say that. Don't talk like that.

I know what she means. I am behaving like we have already lost her. Which we have. I brought Emi into a war that Kristina started. I slept while they took our girl.

We're her parents, I say. We were supposed to protect her.

We'll find her. It's not too late.

I want to believe Kristina. Want to believe she is in supreme command of every inch of this outpost. But even she has her limits. She cannot control the weather. Cannot interrupt the global energy supply chain. This is made painfully clear when Jackson shuffles over with a nervous urgency and tilts her screen to inform Kristina that we are out of time.

The shipping cooperative is demanding we open the surge gate, she explains. Pilots are pissed too. Asking why we won't green-light liftoff.

Tell them we got nailed by the storm, Kristina says. Tell them the gate's broken.

What about the airfields?

Keep them grounded.

How?

Say the satellites are down. I don't care. Just do it.

Jackson grimaces at a group that seems to have been waiting for this very sign. They shuffle over with her same nervous energy. There is Paul who came by to hug Kristina earlier. Rishi and Ravi who interviewed me. Others too. Kristina's secret family. Phoenix leadership. Furies. I cannot keep it all straight.

Nuuk is pinging us like crazy, Paul explains. The Council wants to know what's going on. We have to tell them something. They're not happy.

Neither is the Social Council, someone adds. A delegation is on the way.

Tell them we need time, Kristina says. Another day.

Kris, you know that's not possible. We've gone over this. I'm sorry. We always knew this could happen. To any one of us. I can't even begin to tell you how sorry I am.

Kristina shakes her head. We're not giving up until we find her.

She might not be on a blimp, Jackson says. She might not be on a ship. We won't stop searching. We'll clear every building. That's a promise.

The group murmurs in agreement.

No, Kristina says. They'll get her out of here as soon as they can. Nothing leaves Gowanus until we okay it.

Paul runs a hand over his face and explains in the gentlest tone that three hundred blimps are loaded and waiting. And almost as many clippers in the canal. It's too many, Kris. All those containers. It would take a week to search. We can't hold them. You know we can't. Nuuk will step in. They won't risk shortages. We'll lose Gowanus. We'll have to start over from scratch. Think of the big picture. It could jeopardize everything we've built. All these years.

We have people on the Leadership Council, Kristina blurts.

Not enough, Paul says.

Nothing leaves! Kristina yells. That's an order.

Paul's voice falls to a hush. I'm sorry Kris. We already voted. I'm so sorry.

The wail from Kristina is high and thick and unlike anything I have heard from her. Not during the fire that almost took us both. Not from the scrub room in the Yosemite burn ward. Not with the final push that invited Emi into our new, new world.

Rachel says she's on her way. I tell her thanks and return the phone to its cradle and start counting down.

At twelve seconds I'm sitting upright on the edge of the bed.

Eleven seconds, I'm running across the creamy carpet to pull on my boots by the door.

Nine seconds, I can't get my left foot in. I'm swearing. Fuck it fuck it fuck it. Jamming it. Deciding to go barefoot. Deciding one boot is better than none. Deciding to bail on my plan.

Seven seconds, my left heel slips in. My boots are on.

Six seconds, I pull on my rainbreaker.

At five seconds it occurs to me that Case Manager Rich is surely watching me and alerting Rachel. I realize I could just quit right now. I haven't done anything wrong. It's not too late. I run back to the bed. I could just slide under the sheets. There's time. But then there's not.

I hear the click of the door. Everything in the room narrows. The handle turns. My insides go liquid. My heart is hammering in my ears. It's time to be a person who does nothing or it's time to be a person who does something.

I launch from the bed. The last stretch to Summit Park and this is the morning I'm going to beat my mom. By running through the finish line. By leading with my shoulder. By giving my all.

I meet the door with a hard crack just as it opens. It whips back a few inches then stops with a dull thud, and two things happen at once. One of those things is the most astonishing pain that radiates from my shoulder to my elbow and rings my ears. So hot and explosive it's like I've discovered a sixth sense. I can't move my right arm. I look at it sort of amazed. The other thing that happens is a low scream of pain. But not from me.

I squeeze through the opening, using my good arm to push. Behind the door, Rachel is kneeling on the floor, holding her nose, blood pooling scarlet in her hands. She looks up. We meet eyes. I run.

I have an incomplete mental map from when they brought me here. In my head, the map leads up to the warehouse and ultimately to a door outside. A direct line of escape. But now with my arm limp at my side and pain ringing my ears, nothing looks the same until I reach a set of stairs. I remember stairs. Two flights, I think. Maybe three.

I climb the first flight, turn the corner. A door bangs open on the landing above. Case Manager Rich. His arm in a sling. He sees me and speaks something into his screen. I hear Rachel shouting from below. I'm trapped. Maybe I can take it all back. I'll apologize. But it's too late now. No escape but one: the first-floor landing. Either the door is locked or it isn't. Only two options. Which is comforting in a weird way. Like it's up to this door to decide instead of me.

The door decides to be unlocked.

I'm through. Running faster. A mechanical room. Pipes and valves and screens. Another room with circuitry, the smell of electronics and batteries. Narrow hallways. Turn left, turn right. Searching for stairs. Elevation. I need up. Meanwhile the pain in my shoulder does fascinating things. A nauseous rolling like a blossoming almost. But the pain also sharpens my senses. Widens my eyes. I feel electric. Like I'm leaving sparks behind me with each step.

Another metal door. Another narrow hallway. A steady vibration through the floor. A buzzing. Wondering if they are deploying drones, I start shutting doors behind me. Careful not to slam. Cringing at the squeal of hinges. Finally, another flight of stairs. I take the steps two at a time. The top door is unlocked. It swings open, and although the sight of shipping containers stacked to rafters is not the kind of thing that would ordinarily fill someone with a choking joy, that's what the sight does to me. I'm in the warehouse. I'm close. Then I hear voices. A door slamming. The mosquito whine of a drone.

I duck into the maze of shipping containers. Impossible to tell where the voices are coming from, sounds bouncing and echoing off all the metal. I lean against a container the color of mud to catch my breath. My shoulder is a hot pulsing beacon, so bright I worry it will lead them to me. And it does.

Directly above, over the lip of a container, appears a drone. A red blinking light. I hold my breath. Remain still. Willing it to keep going. But it stops. A spotlight blinks on, casting me in light. I take off, juking around the containers, my boots squeaking on the metal floor. But it's hopeless outrunning a drone. I can't shake the spotlight. A high moan starts in my throat.

Rachel's voice comes amplified from somewhere in the warehouse:

Emi. It's okay. We're not angry. We don't want you to hurt yourself. Come back.

How nice to believe her. To return and reset. Reset all the way to Day Zero, only this time my dad and I don't go downcity. Or deeper back, my mom asking me to skip school and walk with her to Summit Park, and I say, Sure Mom, I'd love to. Or further still, to before my parents met. Before their parents died. Before the Crisis.

I take another turn. Another. Anything to escape. And then I do.

I'm out of the maze. In front of me, a large metal door with a round portal window. A real window. Scuffed glass. Daylight leaking through.

Relief sweeps me up. Floods me with adrenaline, which I need because the door has a thick wheel that requires two good hands to turn. I wince against the wheel, using the sharp edge of pain to cry out and lean and push. The wheel groans. Turns. Then opens and fills my world with light.

My eyes water in the brightness. I blink and stagger out onto the deck of an enormous clipper ship. There was no warehouse. The swaying I sensed beneath my feet—it was real. I'm at sea. Above me, a long line of cargo blimps. The storm's over. Has been over for a while, judging by the patches of blue between the dark clouds. I smell salt. Seaweed. The wind against my face. The heavy snap of sails. The xylophone clang of guy-wires against masts. In one direction is the gray of the ocean meeting the gray of the sky. In the other direction, land. Gowanus. The surge gates wide open and growing smaller. I'm free. But not.

Stop! Stop right where you are!

Case Manager Rich is in the doorway. Holding a stun gun with his good hand. Chest heaving as he catches his breath. The drone slips over his shoulder to hover above me.

I'm shaking. Crying. It's the sight of the stun gun. It's the pulsing in my shoulder. It's the whine of the drone. It's the comedown after a second wind. It's the snap of the ship's sails taking me farther out to sea. It's my mom who is not coming to save me and probably never was.

Calm down, he says. Calm down. It's okay. Just step away from the railing.

Rich moves toward me. I back up. My butt touches metal. A guardrail, waist high, runs the length of the ship. I put a hand on the cold metal.

Stop! he shouts. Step away. Don't move. I fucking swear to God.

He raises the stun gun just as Rachel appears in the doorway, a rusty triangle of blood running from the neck of her shirt. She puts a hand on Rich's arm and steps between us.

It's okay. Take a breath. Come back inside, love.

Stop calling me that! I yell over the wind.

Emi. You don't know what you're doing. You're scared. Come inside before you hurt yourself. We're not mad. We want to keep you safe. Please.

She says something to Rich that I can't hear, her words taken by the wind. He lowers the gun a few degrees. They exchange a look. It might be my only chance. I bolt.

Emi!

The guardrail leads around the top deck in a long oval. There's no escape in an oval. But fixed on the railings every fifty feet or so are life buoys. I sprint for one at the very back. I hear yelling. The enormous sails snapping above me. The ocean hissing and rushing far below. I hear my mom telling me I'm brave when I want to be. I hear my dad on the seawall reminding to breathe and keep swimming. I wrench the buoy from its hook. Sling it over my good shoulder. Throw a leg over the guardrail.

No! yells Rachel. You'll drown! Emi! Stop!

The genuine concern in her voice freezes me just long enough for Rich to catch me as I swing my other leg over the rail.

With his good arm he grabs the hood of my rainbreaker. If Angel hadn't injured his other arm, he would easily be pulling me back. If Reena hadn't punched Min so hard in the ribs, she might be here too. If my mom hadn't woken me to run upcity all those mornings. The things we do for a future that we might never get to enjoy ourselves. With a scream, I shuck off the rainbreaker, slipping out of Rich's grasp, and just like that I'm free.

I'm falling.

There's the churn of the ship's propellers. The snap of the sails. Wind in my ears.

Then a shock of deep cold and silence.

CHAPTER THIRTY-FIVE

LARCH

Kristina and I had a long and emotional goodbye at the Marquette bullet train station. Outside the world was white with fresh snow. The new year was here. We were a new couple. We had staked out a future that included both of us and the Nuuk housing lottery and a family. But not just yet, Kristina decided. There was still too much work to do.

Her deployment with the goodwill tour was behind her. She had already applied to the Gulf Coast for mangrove restoration. The Gulf Coast crews called themselves the Cajun Navy, which sounded adventurous but mangrove restoration was widely considered one of the most miserable deployments. They had mosquitos. Alligators. Disease. Rot. But to Kristina it was an easy choice. She felt compelled to work the most understaffed and high-need deployments. Why? Because the work had to be done. Someone had to do it. The future we wanted with a home and a family? We could not allow ourselves that future until everyone could have that future. And that future was not going to build itself.

I could not agree more. The Transition was everything to me. My only family. The reason I had met Kristina. I would do anything for it. I applied to the Gulf Coast with her. We would sacrifice together. Side by side. And perhaps the staffing algorithms would have approved our request if we had been married. But the match did not go through. Kristina got sent to the bayou and I got sent to Nevada for twelve of the loneliest months of my life.

––––

The lithium mines were set in the desert amid bubbling mud pools and not a tree for a hundred miles. No escape from the sun. The mines were hybrid operations paired with geothermal plants. The geothermal plants produced a slurry by-product rich with trace lithium. Our job was to pass the slurry through delicate beaded modules. Once the beads were saturated we used an acid solution to flush the lithium. A filthy monotonous process with nothing in the shimmery distance to look at but the glint of solar fields and the saltywhite basins of ancient oceans.

The camp was small. Less than one hundred of us. All sunburnt. All depressed. Someone always sick or coughing. The nearest crossroads resembling a town was twelve miles away. The road had a single overhead electrical track for trucks. You had to stand by the track and stick out your thumb. Autonomous trucks never stopped. You had to hope for a human driver who would slow long enough for you to jump on. I tried every chance I got.

In town I dropped off postcards for Kristina and picked up hers. Our notes had become painful but in a good way. A shared yearning for a future together. A family. Plans to meet after our deployments in nine months. Five months. Three months. Then one day I received a letter. Until now we had sent only postcards. Her letter worried me. I stuck the envelope in my pocket and waited with a group to ride back to camp. A truck slowed. We jumped into the bed. I took out the envelope. My hands were shaking. I tore open the flap.

Kristina had been pregnant. Ten weeks. Then miscarried. It had happened months ago. It was sad, she wrote, but sad things happened. Such was life. She had kept up her spirits by getting back to work and trusted I would do the same. She loved me. She could not wait to see me. She was proud of us. We were two loyal soldiers of

290 NICK FULLER GOOGINS

the Transition. We were doing the hard loving work for generations to come—whether they included our children or not.

I folded the letter into fourths and stared over the dead land as the truck bounced along. I had not realized how deeply I wanted a family of my own. It had never felt so close or so far away. An ache grew in my throat. Behind my eyes. I thought of Osman. I blinked in the dry desert air.

Seaweed Guy? No freakin' way.

I looked up. On the bench across from me sat the fake therapist from the Great Northern Greens Arena. Dr. Alex. Impossible. Yet here he was. A decade older and wearing the light blue uniform of the CareCorps but I recognized him right away.

We laughed and jumped up and hugged. Holding each other to keep our balance as the truck bounced along. He had done five deployments with the Green Marines mooring kelp beds off Newfoundland. Then came the call for mental health professionals. The Transition trained him and sent him out. He had been to every corner of the continent.

What about you, my man? he asked. How'd you get stuck way the hell out here?

I opened my mouth. Touched the letter in my pocket. Everything came out. Over the noise of the road I told him about New York and Osman. The Battle of the Big U. Bodies I had come across fighting fires. The fire that almost killed me and the woman I loved. I told him about Kristina. How I was scared of dying and lonelier even than after my parents died.

Because you got hope! You got something to live for! This is great, man! Ya'll hear this? He's got hope! Yeeha! He whooped and slapped my back. The other men in the truck smiled.

Dr. Alex stayed at the mine for two days and one night. I wanted to spend more time catching up but I had my work and he had his. He walked and talked with whoever needed him to listen. Everyone did. Anyway, he wasn't worried about me anymore, he said. Remember what I asked you back in the bleachers?

In fact, I did: What am I going to do with my freedom?

Well now you know, he said. And that's scary stuff. Means you got something to lose. But it's a million times better than having nothing. You're going to be all right kid. I can tell.

I was unconvinced. The bayou was dangerous. Kristina could be injured. She had almost died once. I was not there to protect her. Or the Transition could fail. The oceans were still rising. Extinctions were mounting. Disaster loomed. Everywhere.

I want to show you a trick, Dr. Alex said. We call it the shakes.

He taught me the series of poses. The keys to release.

Does magic, he said. Stress or trauma or anxiety. You name it you can shake it. You ever seen a dog during a thunderstorm?

Sure.

Same thing. We're animals too. We forget that. Now go ahead. Shake it out. Yep. That's the idea. Good. Now try it again.

CHAPTER THIRTY-SIX

Don't panic. Keep breathing. Even when you feel like you can't. Keep your head above water. Sweetie. Kick. Swim. Swim where? Waves like mountains. From the peaks all I see is sky. Then down into the valleys and quiet numbing cold. Up and down. Shaking. Not trying to shake. Shaking like my body knows what's best. Shaking and blinking and coughing. Red and red. Riding the biggest swells down into that quiet stillness. Letting it suck me in. Close my eyes. Sink my legs. Underwater everything is quiet. Calm. Still. But then it's not. I hear a whine. A buzzing that grows louder. I stroke to the surface. Lift my head. Open my eyes to the barnacled hull of a boat and arms reaching down.

I moan. I kick and try to swim away. Hands hook my armpits. Pulling me backward over the lip of a rubber raft. I kick and bite and scream. It's not Rich. Not Rachel. A man with long black hair, and slick like a seal in his wetsuit. Gently removing the buoy from my arm. Slipping me into a life jacket. I scream when he turns my shoulder. I cry. My eyes burn. I cry that I'm sorry. I can't stop shaking. I'm sorry. I'm crying and screaming. The ring buoy is on the floor of the raft. The buoy is a foam donut affixed with a bright light. A rescue beacon. It blinks red and red and red.

—

A blur of boats and hands and thermal blankets. Voices telling me I'm safe. Which I've heard before. The man in the wetsuit brings me onto a ship where a woman cuts off my clothes and wraps me in blankets. I guess I pass out because at some point the light has changed and a medic has appeared with two other women. I scramble back at the sight of the weapons on their hips. Guns of some kind. I scream and cry and shake. I just can't stop. They say it's okay. They're here to keep me safe. Which I've heard before too. They are going to transfer me to their boat and the mainland. No. I won't go. I won't. I want my dad. Where's my dad? I want my mom.

'We're bringing you to them, they say. They're on their way.

But I've heard that before too.

They pass me like cargo. Ship to ship. Then land. I try to stand. I can't. They roll me in a wheelchair to an ambulance to a medical ward. Maybe they give me something for sleep. Maybe I'm just more tired than I've ever been. I close my eyes. I'm visiting Maru and Alice. Alice's fur has this brilliant blue that runs in electric streaks from her ears to beneath her chin. I ask if I can rub the blue and she—Alice—says, Go ahead girl, be my guest. She is purring. Her tail flicking in pleasure. What does it feel like? I ask. Like this, she says, and with a paw does the same to me.

I wake to my mom's hand on my face. She's lying next to me. Standing on my other side is my dad. His face is stubble, almost a full beard. My mom is crying quiet tears that run in little streams through the channels of her scars.

Hi sweetie, she says.

Hi Mom. Hi Dad.

PART SIX

CHAPTER THIRTY-SEVEN

LARCH

It is the longest and most brutal fight of our marriage. Also the quietest. We must whisper to avoid waking Emi. She has been discharged from surgery. She has a new right shoulder. Carbon composite. She is sleeping. We have brought her from the Gowanus medical center to this room: Kristina's secret home where she has lived her double life apart from us.

Her room is small. Sparse. A twin bed where Emi now sleeps. A desk. A chair. A screen on the wall. A trunk. A sink with a mirror plastered in photos. Kristina sits on the trunk. I take the chair. We face each other. We square off. We fight.

We fight in rounds. A round begins when Emi's breath slows and she drifts to sleep. A round ends the moment she rustles her sheets or moans or calls for us.

Twenty-four short hours ago I believed I would never see her again. We were in the food court when Kristina's screen pinged with the news. Her hand went to her mouth. She could not speak. She gave me her screen: An adolescent girl had been pulled from the ocean a mile from the surge gate. Disoriented. Hypothermic. Badly injured. But safe. And demanding to see her mom and dad.

The only thing I can compare it to is the first Day Zero. When we learned that the future we had fought and sacrificed for was here.

News like this brings an odd tangle of disbelief and grief and joy. I experience it fresh every time Emi wakes now in Kristina's secret room and calls to us. I am back in newborn intensive care rubbing her impossibly small feet. She is really here. She is alive. Then she drifts to sleep and Kristina and I resume our fight. We say terrible things. We shake with anger. We cry. We hate each other. We love each other. We make a plan.

———

Our first round begins over the photos on Kristina's mirror. A stupid place to start but all fights must begin somewhere. Every picture on the mirror is Emi. Emi ready for school. Emi on the basketball court. Birthdays. Christmases. Halloweens. What angers me is that the pictures are not simple digital displays but actual physical photographs. Meaning Kristina took time to choose them. Have them printed. Tack them to the mirror. Small efforts that should not be surprising in a mother. But coming from Kristina they are. Could've fooled me, I say.

Fooled you?

Never would've guessed you cared enough to go to all that trouble.

Are you trying to fight?

I'm making an observation. You never do anything like that at home.

Why would I have photos of Emi at home when I can see her in person?

You know that's not what I mean.

It sounds to me like you want to fight.

I want to understand why you couldn't be bothered to give any day-to-day sign that you care. Why is it so hard for you to show a little love?

She looks at me with her fiercest eyes and says I'm being cruel.

I say I am sorry—I am sorry to make her feel guilty for being a bad mother.

She stands and lets out a shaky breath and balls her fists. She whispers that it is so easy to give your child whatever it is they think they want. So easy to be the good guy. She tells me how lucky I am. How much she wishes she could have been the fun and easy parent.

Nobody told you how to be, I say. I never made you.

Someone had to teach her resilience, she says. Someone had to keep her from becoming so fragile like kids these days. Spending life on a screen. Waiting for other people to solve their problems. Someone had to teach her that life is hard. That bad things happen. *That* is love, Larch. What would you have done? Raised her to live for the next Tundra game? If it had been up to you, Emi wouldn't know anything about the Transition. She'd have no idea of how hard we fought. How cruel life can be. She wouldn't have known what it takes to fight back. She wouldn't have survived this. You know that. If it had been up to you, she would not be here with us right now.

I have to bite my hand to keep from yelling. I put my head between my knees. I sputter and spit through my hands to remind Kristina that she was the one who nearly got Emi killed. I remind her that we almost died on the Esplanade. I remind her that *I* saved Emi while she was two thousand miles away.

I was not two thousand miles away.

What?

I was in Nuuk. While you were getting drunk and encouraging our daughter to be as close to the Esplanade as possible despite my warnings. I was there.

I open my mouth. Then say I do not want to know. I do not care. She is trying to make this about her. This is about Emi. It is about our daughter who could've *died*—

Emi jerks in bed as if she senses we could use a break.

Kristina walks over to tuck her in although none of her blankets need tucking. She returns to sit on the trunk. Crosses and uncrosses her legs.

We could've coddled her to death, she says. She was born so small. Other parents would've. I'm hard on her. I know that. But hard is what she needed. Look at her, Larch.

I look. Together we follow the rise and fall of our daughter's breath.

I told her you'd be proud, I whisper.

I am.

We're pretty lucky I think.

I think we're the luckiest, she says.

———

The next round comes back again to the photos. I cannot help it. Emi wakes up and I feed her a few spoons of potato soup. My mother's recipe. Kristina rubs her legs and asks if she wants music. Emi nods but falls asleep before we synch her headphones. Kristina leaves to use the bathroom. My eyes drift back to the photos on the mirror. I feel so petty. Still. I confront her as soon as she steps back in the room to wash her hands at the sink.

Why don't you have any photos of me?

Here, she says.

She pulls one from the mirror and flicks it through the air. I pick it off the floor. A photo of us at the geofarms. Emi is nine. Maybe ten. Kristina and I flanking her. Posing as a family on the cliffs above the sea. Frozen smiles.

I meant just me and you.

She throws up her arms and says I caught her.

I'm not trying to catch you.

Then what do you want me to say?

She is looking at herself in the small square of mirror that she made bare by removing our one and only family picture. The glass reflects her face alone.

I want you to tell me what happened to us.

She sits on the trunk and leans forward, bracing her arms with her hands on her knees. We have not been in a good place for a very long time, she says. Surely you've realized this.

I nod my head yes. Why? I ask. What happened?

What do you think happened?

People change.

That's right. People do change.

And they give up. People stop trying.

Exactly, she says. Nodding. Agreeing. A softness in her eyes.

But when?

When what?

When did you give up on us?

Her eyes harden like slate. She shakes her head and says she cannot imagine what it must be like to go through life so self-centered and unaware.

Me? I blurt. I am self-centered. Me? How am I the selfish one here? Besides yelling at me for not having enough photos of you?

That was about *us*. Not me. *You're* the one who ran away. You're the one who's lived a secret life all these years. I've done everything for this family.

Quiet. You'll wake her up.

I've done everything for this family! I whisper. I cook every meal—

You're a professional chef.

—I clean. I go to Emi's games. I help with homework. I talk with her teachers. I do everything!

That sounds lovely, Larch. I wish I could've enjoyed such luxury. You have no idea what I've given up. What I've sacrificed. I've worked so hard for Emi's future. For everyone's future. Don't tell me for a second that I haven't done anything.

I never said you don't do anything. You do exactly what you want and nothing else.

She tells me to shut up and listen. She tells me that sixteen years ago she was preparing to go underground. They knew Day Zero was near. They knew the Transition's days were numbered. She reminds me again about the physical therapist who earned her degree and moved to Duluth to build a reputation among the old and wealthy. Years and years and years. Just to get alone with Ian Rios on a yacht on Lake Superior.

I was supposed to become a nurse, says Kristina. A personal health aide. I was going to move to Alberta and work my way into the gated compounds and wait.

What happened?

You did, Larch. You happened. And then you changed. Why can't you see that? You're the one who gave up. Not me.

———

At some point in a long fight you lose track of the rounds. You circle back. Same footsteps. Same feints. Same combinations. You take the same punches. Start looking for them. Start needing the sharp jolts of pain. Kristina and I go on like this. Dragging each other. Kristina says she does not want credit for making a family with me instead of going underground. But I know she does. Only I will not give it to her. Just as she will not give me credit for raising Emi. Or my work with the Tundra. She can admit there is a place for entertainment and sports. But that's Lucas, she says. Not you. She asks a pointed question: What happened to the man I married?

He's here, I say, thumping my chest. He's right here.

You were a soldier of the Transition. You inspired thousands. Maybe millions. You led by example. The best kind of leader. You were strong. You were proud.

I was a kid.

You were willing to take up slack to help others. You sacrificed. You fought to save the world. And I fell in love with you for it. The man I met would not accept what he has become. He was not interested in comforts or status or flying around in a private plane.

Her words hit hard. I flounder. I argue that she is wrong: The plane is not private. It belongs to the Tundra. A cooperative. Meaning all of us.

Listen to yourself, she says. You promised we would never stop fighting.

We won, Kristina. It's over. It's been over for years.

She shakes her head. Ask my parents if we won. My sister. Your parents. Everyone who lost their families and fled their homes so a few wealthy people could get wealthier. We did not win. We prevented total collapse. That's not victory.

What are we supposed to do? You can't keep fighting forever.

Why not?

Because you have to enjoy life.

I enjoy life.

Bullshit.

I enjoyed the Transition. I loved those years.

And what about the sixteen years since?

Kristina looks at Emi then back to me and admits flatly that she has been lonely.

No, I spit. *I've* been lonely!

I am angry because it feels so senseless. If I had known that Kristina was half as lonely as me. If we had fought this openly. Before it felt too late.

I ask Kristina if she feels that too: Are we too late?

She looks at her boots: I don't know.

We watch Emi for a long time without speaking. We were not always like this. I remember Emi's baths—Kristina sitting afterward on one side of the bathroom as the hug station. Me at the other side as the kiss station. Emi running between us naked and shrieking like there was nothing better on earth and she was right. I ask Kristina whether any of it was real. Any moment of the past sixteen years. I'm not trying to be cruel, I tell her. I just need to know. Was any of it real?

Of course, she says. I love you. I love Emi.

Why was it so hard to show it?

She walks to the sink. Runs the water over her hands. Holds a cool palm to her scars. Turns and whispers that she never knew if the Furies would really go through with it. If any of this would happen. At any moment I could've been pulled away. Knowing that, it creates—a shield. It makes it hard. Emi would be alone. Without a mother. Like me. Like you. I had to prepare her for this. And now she is ready.

What do you mean *is*?

She looks at me, her eyes deep and filled with hurt.

You're not coming back to Nuuk, I say.

She shakes her head: I can't.

My vision goes narrowdark. We are quiet until someone knocks on the door. A nurse to check on Emi. He announces himself from the hallway.

We were in love, I whisper, as Kristina stands to let him in.

Yes, she says. And it was the best thing that ever happened in my life.

———

The nurse checks Emi's temperature and blood pressure without waking her. Changing her shoulder bandages however cannot be done as gently. Emi awakes in pain. She winces. She asks for water. Asks for us. The nurse switches out her IV bag. He gives a thumbs-up and closes the door silently behind him. The little bed groans as Kristina and I gently climb on either side. One small family can make so much warmth. Emi closes her eyes and asks in a whisper if they were going to kill her.

You're safe now, sweetie, Kristina says. You couldn't be safer anywhere on the planet.

What about Reena and Angel?

I shake my head at Kristina but—as always—she insists on giving Emi the truth.

They didn't make it. I'm sorry.

They're dead?

Kristina nods.

Emi starts hiccupping and crying. I feel her heart beating. I rub her good arm. She says between sobs that she didn't know she was supposed to trust them. She didn't know.

It's not your fault, I say. None of this is.

When can we go home? she asks.

As soon as the doctors say you're ready, I say. As soon as you want to.

I feel Emi's heart beat faster. Harder. Trying to escape the thin cage of her chest. She pinches my elbow skin. Kneads it like dough. We tilt Kristina's wall screen and synch Emi's headphones and invite her to choose whatever she wants. She picks some VR show. Kristina and I stay in bed watching with no audio. Kristina massages Emi's scalp. Once we are sure she is asleep we crawl gently out of bed and make a plan for the future of our family.

———

The problem with the future is that it cannot happen the way I need it to happen. In two days I must be back in the Tundra kitchen prepping for the second half of the season. And Emi—she must return to school. We must return home. But Kristina says we cannot.

For how long? I ask. Months?

Longer.

Years?

Maybe never.

I cannot accept that answer. I make her repeat it.

You can't go back to Nuuk, she says. They know where we live. They'll be waiting. If not now, then in a year. Two years. Ten. I'm sorry Larch. It wasn't supposed to happen like this.

I tell her that sorry isn't good enough. I tell her that sorry is not the least bit helpful. Anger cannot change anything—I know—but I must allow it to lap through my veins. I tell Kristina that I don't care if they're waiting for us. I'll kill them before I let them near Emi again.

These people are trained, she says. They're professionals.

A fifteen-year-old girl escaped from them. How professional can they be?

She was extremely lucky. We can't protect her forever.

What about your people? Aren't you embedded everywhere?

I couldn't guarantee her safety. It's not a risk I'm willing to take.

I shake my head. Rub my eyes.

So, what? Emi stays here with you?

That's one option, she says.

I laugh and tell her that she is out of her mind if she thinks Emi is spending the rest of her high school years in some bleak industrial hurricane hot spot.

We grew up in far worse, Kristina says.

What about school? What about her friends?

She doesn't have any friends.

I have to stand and walk around I am so furious. I have to put my forehead against the wall. I have to say no: Absolutely not. Emi isn't living here. She'd be the only kid. I won't force her to do that. Out of the question.

I said this was one option, says Kristina.

What's the other? I ask.

You two could come with me.

I laugh so hard with such a loud bark that Emi briefly wakes and removes her headphones to ask if everything is all right. Everything's great, we tell her. We soothe her back to sleep. Then in whispers—practically mouthing the words—we fight on.

Kristina elaborates: Emi and I could join her. We would travel and live by Kristina's side. We would be safer with the Furies than anywhere.

You want Emi to live underground? Hiding in the shadows? Fighting in the trenches?

It's not like that. We call it a moving front. The Half Earth biomes. Indigenous lands. Emi would see more of North America in a year than most people see in a lifetime.

She's not a soldier, Kristina! She's fifteen.

And she has proven herself more capable than most adults.

You're serious. I can't believe you're serious. What about school?

She'd receive a real-life education like nowhere else. And the chance to make genuine friendships based on a common cause. More and more young people are joining us every day.

Yes, like Reena and Angel.

I would never send her into danger. She would stay by our side.

Our side. You think I'm going to come with you.

If you want.

I'm not helping you murder people.

It's justice, not murder. Don't be so reductive. Thirty-six hours ago, you were begging me to let you kill them all.

That was when they had Emi.

The same people are still out there. They'll hurt others. Think of Charlie's boy. Think of what they did to the planet. They'll never stop. Why not help us? We could use you. You've traveled with the Tundra. You know people all over.

Are you trying to recruit me?

I'm trying to keep our family together. I'm trying to make this work.

Oh my God, Kristina. It's out of the goddamn question. We're not going with you.

We should let Emi decide.

She already decided. She wants to go home. You heard her. As soon as she's ready I'm taking her back to Nuuk.

I can't let you do that.

You're going to stop me?

Not me personally.

I would never hit Kristina in a moment of anger but the urge is so powerful that I must holster my fists in my armpits. I must turn to face Emi and cry the most silent frustrated rage.

You did this to us, I say.

I did not, she says. I simply decided to fight back. And you can too. We can be together. As a family. It's not too late.

She puts a hand on my shoulder that I do not shake off. I try to see that future for us. I sincerely do. I let it play out. I see us falling in love again. But no. After Emi coming so close to death? I cannot seal her future like that. I cannot risk it. Cannot steal her youth the way the Crisis stole ours. There must be another way. If only we could start over like the forest after a wildfire. Sequoia sprouting from a single fire-burst seed.

Then it comes to me. Maybe we can.

There's another way, I say. And you're right—we should let Emi decide.

Emi Vargas Brinkman
North American History
Mrs. Helmandi
Great Transition Project (First Draft)

Mom Session VIII: The Great Transition, Part 4

Me: In Yosemite, did you fall in love with Dad at first sight?

My Mom: Love in a burn ward? Ha. No.

Me: So when did you fall in love with him?

My Mom: You have to realize—your father saved my life, but friends of mine had not been so lucky. Some I had known since the camp. You've heard of survivor's guilt? It's real. It felt like burying my sister all over again. I was in so much pain. Mentally and physically. I was very depressed. I overheard the nurses talking about my face. They thought I was asleep. I was on great quantities of morphine. But I could hear them. I thought I'd never be able to see again. All I wanted to do was reenlist to go back out. For years I remembered the face of each guard from the camp. God I hated them. And the border agents who took my parents. And our first Transition managers—the profiteers who sold our gear. But at some point I realized the people at the very top were the ones to blame. The ones who pulled the strings in luxury and comfort while the rest of us fought each other and suffered. I couldn't let them win. My sister, my friends—they couldn't die for nothing. What did you ask me? What was I talking about?

Me: How you fell in love with Dad.

My Mom: Right. Well he saved my life. And he was very handsome. And famous because of *Corps Power*. But he wasn't one of those Transition stars where fame went to their heads. He was humble. And tender. And funny. And persistent. And a talented chef, as you know. He would cook meals that sent me back to my childhood. Tamales. Mole. Chiles. And not just for me. The entire burn ward. Patients, orderlies, nurses. I don't know how he found the time. He was recovering too.

Me: When did you know for sure that you loved him?

My Mom: The exact moment? I can't remember. It sort of sneaks up on you, I guess.

Me: Love sneaks up on you?

My Mom: You don't notice it until it's already there.

Me: But how do you know?

My Mom: You just do. But there's a difference between falling in love and being in love.

Me: What's the difference?

My Mom: Falling in love is easy. It's all chemicals. Dopamine, serotonin. Biology. The same way we're wired for cooperation. We're a social species. Like almost all mammals. Once, in Colorado, a dog came running into our camp, barking its head off until I followed it to a clearing where there was another dog on the ground, burnt and unconscious. I remember one farm in California, the barn filled with smoke, and inside so many animals—pigs and geese and goats—all crowded around an open window in the back. Not fighting each other for fresh air but sharing. Cooperation. That's life's great success story. Not competition. Our biology pushes us to be with others. To help and to care. That's why it is so easy to fall in love. You'll see. It'll happen to you. But *being in love* requires something deeper.

Me: Like what?

My Mom: Shared joy. Shared loss. Shared desire in life. Your father and I . . . during the Transition, we had a shared goal. Everyone did. But then, after—people began to change.

Me: Change how?

My Mom: We only went halfway. You've heard me say all
this. The criminals who caused the Crisis—many are
still alive, living in luxury, actively working to claw back
our progress. We didn't finish the job. Which we knew,
sixteen years ago. But some people thought we'd gone
far enough. They thought the war was over. Like your
father—he's happy to make concessions for comfort.
Which is the very mentality that brought us to the brink.
No . . . take out this part about Dad. Okay? Forget what
I said. He's a good man. He is a wonderful father. Just
write about him as a hero of the Transition. Because he
was. He is. That's the man I fell in love with.

*Great job, Emi. You have juggled so many difficult
topics. As your last step, I would start thinking about
how to synthesize everything you have learned. What
conclusions can you draw?*

   —Mrs. H

CHAPTER THIRTY-EIGHT

EMI

Our bus docks at Forty-Second Street at high tide, so everything south is basically water. There are some shallow islands where seagulls perch and seals slide over each other, wrestling and barking and glistening in the sun. My mom helps me step from bus to dock. She points out how the islands are in a neat grid. Do I see it? Do I see the grid?

I see it, I tell her.

Foundations of old buildings, she explains. The city kept them as reefs. At low tide we can walk around if you want. There's a whole tour. You can tour the old sidewalks and see the old sewer grates. If the weather holds, we can take the boat tour through Grand Central Station.

It's a pretty epic tour, my dad adds.

Truthfully, I'm not so interested in old sewer grates and sidewalks. The ruins and Grand Central Station are all part of the junior-year field trip. I'll see it next year. But my mom's excited to make this a special day for me. She's trying. My dad too. So I smile and say it sounds like fun. But first can we go to the park like we talked about?

Of course, sweetie. Whatever you want.

She hails two pedicabs. One for us, and a second for Rishi and Ravi, who are with us for security. My mom steps up to the pedicab and nods for my dad to climb in.

312 NICK FULLER GOOGINS

Ladies first, he says. He holds my mom's hand to help her up.

Thank you, kind sir.

My pleasure.

I almost say that they can stop pretending to be nice to each other, but the sun's so warm on my face, and the drugs for my shoulder are like a soft weighted blanket, and I'm about to see Central Park for the first time. My dad helps me into the pedicab. I lean against my mom. My dad sits to my right. The driver starts pedaling. I can already see trees in the distance. The driver asks if we want some music. My parents look to me.

Can you play any oldies? I ask.

He swipes at his screen and asks if I've heard of Queen.

Queen's great, I say.

He chooses a song called "Another One Bites the Dust," which has this amazing bassline. Rishi and Ravi hear and whoop behind us. I ask the driver to please turn it up.

———

At first while recovering from my broken shoulder and hypothermia and nearly drowning, I only want to stay in my mom's room. I don't want to leave, and nobody makes me. My parents are always there. Both of them. Which ordinarily would be a nightmare, but they've clearly agreed to some peace treaty. It's super weird and unnatural. And also really nice. The three of us watch reality streamcasts until our eyes burn. We listen to music: Marvin Gaye and Aretha Franklin and Cher. One Adele song is so pretty that all of us are crying just like that, even my mom. We play cards in bed. War and gin rummy. At night my mom sleeps with me like she did the night before she left: holding me against her in the best kind of melting. My dad sleeps on a mattress by the door. He won't say he's guarding me, but I know. I'm glad he's there.

My mom puts my socks on for me. Brushes my hair. Hugs me at random times. She's being so gentle. When I panic—I'm missing school and basketball—she tells me not to worry. When I'm scared to go outside for Reena and Angel's memorial, she says I don't have to. When I decide to go anyway, she tells me I'm brave. It's like she's a totally new person. Part of me keeps expecting her to turn around with fangs and evil cat eyes and explain that I actually died jumping off the ship and she is a demon pretending to be my mom and—by the way—welcome to hell. The closest she comes to snapping is when I'm supposed to be interviewed about what happened. I don't want to talk about it. She says it isn't an option. She almost ignites.

Emiliana. You're not a child. We all have to do things we dislike. That is life.

So okay. Fine. Her friends interview me. Rishi and Ravi. They are super nice. At first I can't remember much, but the more we talk, the more comes back. The mole on Min's hairline. Rich's dumb jokes. Which arm he injured. I describe the safe house. The ship. What they said. I try to remember every word. The only time I hesitate—I choke up, start crying—is when they ask about Angel and Reena. I didn't know to trust them. Rishi and Ravi, however, only want to know the cold details of what happened. I try my best. I'm a good interviewee, they say. They are especially interested in names. They run a list by me. No names are familiar. Until one is.

That one. Him.

Matthias Barrack, they repeat. You're sure?

Yes, I say. She wanted to know if my mom had ever mentioned him.

Later, I ask my mom: Who is he?

She doesn't need her screen to look up his crimes: Financing oil and tar sands and pipelines right through the heart of the Crisis. First via the Bank of Canada. Then his own firm, lobbying against the Transition. All that time squandered. All those profits reaped.

I ask if the Furies will kill him.

My mom does what Mrs. Helmandi does in class, and turns the question on me: What would you do?

I don't want people to die, I say.

I don't want people to die either, she says.

But he can't just get away with it.

Why not?

I like that she asks my opinion. I like that we are talking like two adults.

It sends a message if you let him get away with it, I say.

Hmm. What kind of message?

Like we don't care what happened. Like anyone else can get away with it too.

———

Central Park is forest and meadow and ponds and fountains. It's beautiful for everything you see, and even more so for everything you don't. No funnel windmills. No solar. No carbon capture. No overhead EV tracks. No quantum hubs. No vertical farms. That's why people call the park a living museum. Like the Crisis never happened. At first it seems wasteful—all that sunlight and soil—but then it seems special. Like something holy.

The one big change is the Statue of Liberty. She stands watch at the park's northern boundary. The statue is also part of the junior-year field trip, but next year I'll be sharing it with my entire class. Today we get the place almost to ourselves, just me and my parents and Rishi and Ravi, plus a tour guide and four or five extraction workers enjoying their day off.

The guide has a brown uniform and a wide hat. She explains how Culture Corps relocated the statue in year one of the Transition.

My dad saw them deconstructing it, I say. Right Dad?

You were here? the guide asks him. Me too. Which company were you?

She and my dad jump into a nostalgia hole while the rest of us climb the spiral staircase that leads behind the statue's face, where the metal folds like fabric to form her lips and nose and eyes. From there we take an elevator, two people at a time. I go with my mom. The doors open to the outside. A platform circling the torch. Three hundred feet off the ground, the guide says when she arrives behind us. One look down flips my stomach. The railing is like the one I climbed to jump off the ship. Except this one is thinner, and the drop bigger. I hold it tight with my good arm. My other arm is pinned to my side in a blue sling. My mom puts her hand gently on the back of my neck. My dad steps out of the elevator. And behind him Rishi and Ravi. All here to protect me. I take a breath. I ride the wave. I can see for miles. Not a storm cloud in sight.

———

We spend maybe a half hour at the torch. The guide tells us to look as far as we can see. All this was home to the Lenape people for twelve thousand years, she says. Today their descendants are leading the most successful regenerative and rehabilitative efforts. If you're lucky enough to see an otter here, thank the Lenape. I look at my dad. He's staring out but has this sort of glazed expression like he's not actually seeing anything. He notices me noticing him and smiles.

The guide takes us around the platform, pointing out the Hudson River cliffs. The bridges. The raised hyperloop tubes. The Big U. The algae farms and oyster fields and offshore wind. And if you'll direct your gaze south, she says, you can *just* make out the foundation of the Empire State Building, which tells us the tide is going out. A fun fact for all you Transition buffs: ninety-seven percent of the Empire State Building's core materials were recycled directly into the Big U.

Circle of life, says Ravi, which for some reason makes us all laugh.

We take in the sights. Then my dad unpacks sandwiches he made that morning. The plan was to have a picnic in the park but up here it's all sun and views so why not? He passes the sandwiches around, including a simple one just for me: bread and butter and brown sugar. I rip off pieces. Try to relax my throat. My mom doesn't say a word. My dad doesn't even look my way.

After lunch, people head back down until my parents and I stand alone on the platform. My dad nods at my mom. She nods back.

What? I say.

Emiliana, says my mom. I'd like to talk with you.

Okay.

See you back on earth, says my dad.

He shoots me a double thumbs-up from the elevator as the doors close, leaving me and my mom together three hundred feet above ground. The day before she disappeared, I refused to walk to Summit Park with her because I was mad and wanted to punish her for reasons that seem so stupid looking back. But also I refused because I was nervous. Like I'm nervous now.

What do you want to talk about? I ask.

In Spanish, she explains that she knows she's been very hard on me. I know how much I have pushed you, she says. I know I am demanding.

Okay.

A mother's job is to prepare her child for life. And life is hard. As you have now seen. All I ever wanted was to make sure you were strong enough to overcome any hardships. And you have been strong. You are so strong. I'm proud of you, Emiliana.

Thanks, Mom.

I turn my head to watch two blackbirds flying by. They pass so close I can hear their wings brush the air. If I don't keep watching them I know I'll start crying. On the ground my dad and the guide are talking. I'm holding the railing so hard my hand aches.

Is that it? I ask.

No, says my mom quietly. That's not it.

She takes a breath and does something that makes her seem more unfamiliar to me than anything she has done this past week: she apologizes.

I'm sorry, Emi. For what I had to do. For what I must do. For making things difficult. I don't like to argue. I don't like to fight. I love you. So much. I'm so sorry.

Her apology is a key that unlocks all my tensed muscles. Tears come to my eyes and I lean into her chest and say that I'm sorry too. I tell her about being kidnapped, how I promised myself I'd make things easier. Some of this I say in Spanish. Some in English. I don't plan which language to use, the words come out however they want.

I won't complain so much, I say. I'll eat whatever. I won't try to make you so mad all the time.

You don't make me mad all the time, she says.

I don't?

She pauses. Smiles. Bumps her shoulder against mine and says maybe on rare occasions she gets the tiniest bit upset.

We laugh. I wave to my dad on the ground.

I don't like to fight either, I tell her. So let's just stop, okay? We'll start over. We'll be nice to each other. You and dad too. All of us.

That sounds nice, she says. I wish it was that simple.

She points down to Rishi and Ravi on the ground, here for my security. She points up and says she has three surveillance drones that have followed us from Gowanus.

I can keep you safe here, she says. In Nuuk, I can't.

What do you mean?

You can't go home, sweetie.

Yes I can.

No. Your father and I have decided. I'm sorry. You can't.

I hold the metal railing. The view extends for miles, but all I see is Maru and Alice and my room. The kids at CareCorps. The basketball court. School. Mrs. Helmandi. My life.

School already started, I say. My Great Transition draft is already late. I'm going to fail.

Your grades don't matter, my mom says.

I can't drop out of school! I didn't do anything wrong. This isn't fair!

Three words that can most easily make my mom ignite. But she only nods and says she understands why I might feel this way. We want to respect your agency, she says. That's why your father and I have talked about it. And we want to let you decide.

Decide what?

Where you'd like to live.

Anywhere in North America, she explains. New home. New school. New neighbors. New everything. The only way to be safe. The destroying classes are desperate, she says. They know there's nowhere to hide. Nothing is more dangerous than a desperate animal.

What about you? I say, pointing to her scars. Everyone will recognize you. They'll find us.

She turns and holds me to face her so there is nowhere else I can look.

You're right, Emi. You didn't do anything wrong. None of us did. We didn't start this. But I have to see it through. I'm not coming with you and Dad.

I don't mean to cry so hard and so quickly but the tears, they just leap out.

What're you going to do? Where will you go?

Underground, she says.

With the Furies?

She nods once.

I'm coming with you, I say, wiping my nose. I'm joining the Furies. You can't stop me. If you don't let me I'll just run away. I'll find you.

Great.

Great?

Once you've finished school, you can do whatever you want. It's your life. Until then it's up to me and your father. And we've decided.

I don't want you to go! You could get hurt. You could die! Mom. You have to stay. You're my mom. Please! You have to!

She pulls me into her so that our heads are pressed together.

We don't get to choose which battles we're born into, she says. The only choice we get to make is what we'll do. Will we join the fight or will we turn our backs?

I want to join the fight! I say, pushing away from her so she can see how serious I am. That's what I'm saying! I want to fight!

No, she says softly. But her eyes are a little misty. Like she wishes she could tell me yes.

You said it was my choice. You literally just said that.

After you finish school. First you have to be a teenager. You have to enjoy life a little.

Dad made you say that.

Your father and I are in agreement. We're your parents. We're trying to be fair about this. You can decide where you want to live while you finish school. It's completely up to you.

I look over the land that was home to the Lenape for thousands of years. Compared to thousands of years, two-and-a-half years of high school should feel like nothing. But it's everything.

Where does dad want to go?

He doesn't care. It's up to you.

Anywhere in North America?

Anywhere but Nuuk.

Windsor-Detroit, I say.

You don't have to decide this moment, she says. Take your time.

I don't need time. Windsor-Detroit has Cleveland as a sister city.

Oh?

The Rock and Roll Hall of Fame, I say, as if it should be obvious.

She smiles. Of course.

CHAPTER THIRTY-NINE

LARCH

An empty water bus down the canal at dawn. Then a tram to the Gowanus airfields. Finally into a hangar. A pilot clubhouse where we wait for a crew to ready the blimp. Our last moment together as a family. Kristina and Emi and myself. Except Emi is no longer Emi. I am no longer me. There was a kidnapping. A botched rescue. We have watched the newscasts. We have scrolled MemeFeed. We are dead. And in a few short minutes we will board a cargo blimp for our new lives in Windsor-Detroit.

It takes three days for Kristina's people to kill us and bring us back. Emi and I receive new names. New housing. New stories. The retinal re-ID is the most difficult. The procedure takes skill. But the Furies have been shuffling people underground for years. They can get themselves into the walled lake compounds of Duluth. Private yachts on Lake Superior. Compared to that? Disappearing me and Emi into a city of nine million is easy.

They have secured us a unit overlooking the Detroit River. A co-housing community. We are moving because of a death in the family. My wife. Emi's mother. An extraction duty accident. Where? What happened? If Emi and I are inconsistent with the details it will be because we are so foggy with grief. We are in mourning. We need a change in scenery. We need to start over. This will be our story.

In some ways the pretending will be difficult. In others it will not. I have said goodbye to Kristina so many times. Throughout the Transition. All her extraction duties. After our biggest fights. Sometimes silently to myself. Other times out loud. This goodbye feels different however. Like it could be the last.

Kristina's screen glows.

Ten minutes, she says.

She has come to send us off but the feeling is more like we are sending her off. Kristina and I have explained to Emi that families have said goodbyes like this for thousands of years. Pick any soldier in history. Any war. Statistically speaking, almost every soldier comes home. And we are lucky to be able to say goodbye. And the time will pass quickly. Three years until we can return to Nuuk. Three years until I can laugh about this with Lucas over a beer. Beg his forgiveness for making him believe I was dead.

Three years, I tell Emi. But of course I am also telling myself.

Three years is a myth. A myth I have created for the reason all myths are created: Something to hang the present on. To fill the void. In truth it could be far more than three years. Over which time we may have changed dramatically. As a family. As husband. As wife.

Kristina agrees with me when I share this specific concern. We get a rare moment in private while Emi is taking a bath. I tell Kristina that it is probably unreasonable to expect us to remain strictly monogamous during this separation.

You're probably right, she says.

We shouldn't make promises for the sake of it, I say.

I agree.

You do?

It sounds reasonable. It makes sense.

All of which I wanted her to say. But maybe I was also hoping she would fight. Maybe I wanted her to tell me to remain faithful. To wait for her. To keep the flame alive. If not the flame at least an ember. Some faint glimmer of our fire that had burned so bright.

Something I have felt but cannot say: Our new life without Kristina might be easier. For me. For Emi. For Kristina. Not all separations are bad. I get the feeling that Emi senses this too. When she wonders out loud what kids at her new school will be like. If she will be able to try out for varsity basketball. She asks when we will visit Cleveland. She is scared and angry just like I am scared and angry. I know she is. But also—like me—she is shimmering with something like excitement. A restlessness to die already. To taste new life. To be reborn.

Kristina gets pinged again. Five minutes, she says.

Sometimes there is so much to say that it is too much to say. Words cannot do the job. Instead we say it by being together. Holding space. Sharing warmth. The pilot clubhouse in the hangar has posters of old planes and famous blimps. There are comfortable-looking sofas that none of us use. We remain standing at the window. Looking over the airfields. Blimps tethered. Others lifting off. Emi between us. Kristina and I have our arms around her so that we are holding each other too. In the faint reflection of the window is a happy family. Over the past week we have been that family. We visited every museum and landmark on Emi's list. We saw the Big U Memorial. We looked at family photos. We played cards. Listened to music. Spent time together. Good time. We made it work. Which hurts. Because it required such little effort. So easy once we tried.

Kristina's screen glows. They're ready, she says.

Time to go.

Time to bend down and curl my hand around the strap of my bag.

Time to say goodbye.

Simple impossible steps.

I am dizzy with doubt. What are we doing? I stumble. My vision goes.

Dad?

Kristina and I had promised not to make a scene. For Emi's sake. Impossible. Life will not be easier without Kristina. We could have made it work. We still can.

Dad? Emi says again.

I'm fine, sweetie. I'm just a little emotional. I'm going to miss Mom.

Me too! she cries, and we are all falling into each other's arms, Kristina saying, Come here my loves. Come here. Come to me.

My father left me on the granite ledge. He ran into the flames for my mother. I am doing the opposite. I am staying with Emi. Keeping her safe. I am making that choice.

Time to go, Kristina says, still hugging me.

I guess this is it, I say, not moving.

No, my love. This is something. Next comes something else. As it always does.

We are holding each other. Me and Kristina and Emi. My family. I am a husband. A father. A son. I am standing in my wetsuit on a granite ledge as my world burns. I am an orphan in the Great Northern Greens Arena. I am whispering Osman's name at the Big U Memorial. I am falling through the sky to meet Kristina. I am rubbing Emi's feet in newborn intensive care. Life is a razor-straight path except when it is not. Suddenly you are walking with your daughter onto a Gowanus airfield. You are staggering into the sunrise. Filing up a gangway. Nodding hello to the air crew. Buckling into a seat. You are waving goodbye to the love of your life. You are floating off into the morning light with your daughter. You are starting anew.

CHAPTER FORTY

LARCH

The final years of the Transition were my most difficult. I worked the lithium mines for a second deployment. I joined a crew grading windmill access roads across sunblasted Utah ridgelines. Two deployments carbon-sinking dead pine forests in Wyoming. Reforesting in Colorado. Kristina continued suffering her own grim deployments along the Gulf Coast: whatever the Transition algorithms deemed most understaffed and highest priority. But the hard labor was not what made these final years so difficult. The work needed to be done. We were glad to do it. What made the time so painful was the distance. I was lovesick. Kristina and I were communicating daily via screen. Postcards no longer cut it. We had to hear each other's voices. I needed her face prior to sleep and after waking and before returning to the work of saving a planet we might never get to enjoy. Some days I wondered if we were punishing ourselves: if we could not be happy together then we would be as unhappy and exhausted as possible.

The one upside to the difficult labor was that it made our time together that much sweeter. We coordinated every possible minute between deployments. In the weeks leading up to one such gap Kristina proposed a trip to the Dakotas. Charlie Little Crow had invited her to a ceremony. We could stay with him and Katya. We didn't have to go, she said, but it was an honor to be invited, and we would probably regret not going for the rest of our lives.

I don't need convincing, I told her. You had me at *we*.

———

We arrived the day before the ceremony. Bullet train to Bismarck. EV track south to Standing Rock. The bus crested a final hill and there—spread out on an ancient floodplain of the Missouri River—stretched acres of tents and teepees and domes. Flags fluttering from poles. Kites high in the sky. Strings of lights from tethered blimps. Horses and bikes and trucks. I had been expecting a crowd. But here was a small city.

Getting to Charlie and Katya took half a happy day of winding through the encampment. Everyone was in a joyful mood. You could not walk five feet without someone inviting you to share a meal or help with a task. We stacked chopped wood. We washed dishes. We ate wild rice with six older women who invited Kristina to a sweat lodge while I waited outside. We dunked afterward in the Missouri so she could cool down. There we lucked upon a kid on horseback who knew Charlie. He led us to a tent near a central dome used for meetings. We brushed back the flap and there was Charlie Little Crow and Katya her royal highness. Five years had passed since our New Year's Eve party but Charlie's face had aged beyond those years. The same I knew was true of me. Katya however was glowing. She was very pregnant.

I'm getting strong male vibes, she said, taking my hands and Kristina's to make sure we could feel a kick. Don't you think so?

When are you two starting a family? asked Charlie. He was enraptured by Katya. He could not take his eyes off her.

We're taking our time, Kristina said.

Moment to moment, I said, nodding in agreement.

Don't take too long, Charlie said. We need the next generation of warriors. Who else will train the water protectors and healers and solar installers? Plus, it's extremely fun.

Says the man who's not seven months pregnant, Katya said.

Charlie laughed. The man could not stop smiling. He had been in the Dakotas all these years overseeing prairie rewilding. The program was an international success. The grasses and animals were returning. And now he was going to be a father. And—on top of all this good news—there was tomorrow, when he would be giving an important speech, Katya told us.

What exactly is happening tomorrow? I asked.

Charlie smiled widely and put an arm around my shoulders: Tomorrow we party.

———

The ceremony took place on the banks of the Missouri. Crowds so thick that Kristina and I could not see the speakers, only hear them. Everything came in Lakota first then translated to English. After a number of prayers we heard Charlie. He started with an old Lakota prophecy: A black snake would bring sickness to our communities, he said. The snake would poison the land and the water. Our hearts and spirits. But from this evil would spring a resurgence. The Lakota would band together. We would rally. We would kill the snake and emerge as a new people to heal the earth.

Well we all know what happened, Charlie said. We all know the black snake arrived. Not as one snake, but a nest. Not one sickness in our community, but a sickness of all society. Oil and gas pipelines pumping poison through our land. Killing our earth, our water, our air. The world as we knew it ended. It did. We all know that now. We all know that the old world is gone.

But the other part of the prophecy held true as well, Charlie said, his voice booming over the speakers. For almost a century now, Lakota have fought the destroying classes. We banded together. Grew strong. Among the people who have seized the Transition, we have led the way. We have ripped the black snakes from our land. Piece by piece. We have forged them into turbines and solar farms and school roofs and irrigation pipes. We remade the world. And today another snake is dead.

A wave of cheering and applause and drums and horns started at the river and rolled back over us. For ceremonial purposes they had kept a final segment of pipeline underground. Before the cranes and excavators could remove it from the earth however a group of Lakota elders requested a prayer circle. Not among themselves but everyone. They wanted to join hands—all of us—and give thanks to our ancestors for ensuring we would be strong enough to rise together and fight in this moment when the earth most needed our courage.

We took a long time to form a circle of thousands of people. Everyone was wondering out loud if the prayers had begun or were we waiting for some signal? Then—just when we seemed ready— some new group would ride up and need space or the chain would shift, causing a break. But we were in no rush. The day was gorgeous. Just enough cloud cover to stay cool. The Missouri running gently. I held Kristina in my right hand. To my left was a young man in a red bandana. We made small talk. It turned out he was Penobscot. He had traveled here from Maine as a representative of the Wabanaki Alliance.

I grew up in Maine too, I told him. I had to leave. After the fires.

I was a kid then, he said. Shitty times.

How is it now? I haven't been back.

We're healing. Same as everywhere.

That was when it happened. A low murmuring. Rolling over the crowd in ripples. Then waves. At first I thought the prayer circle had started. But it was something else: news. Someone yelled it. Someone else said no—don't believe rumors—it couldn't possibly be true. Then people were shouting. Crying. The circle fell apart. People needed their arms to hug strangers or cover their mouths in shocked silence or do like the Penobscot man who lifted me off the ground then Kristina. We formed a group hug. Cheering and crying with joy.

The planet had reached net-zero emissions.

Technically the target had been hit a week ago but the scientific cooperative in Hawaii that tracked the numbers had certified it just now. Years and years of battle. And we had won. If you have survived to see the end of war you know that confusing joy. Joy laced with sorrow. You think of those who never made it to celebrate. All that was lost. We exhausted ourselves in celebration and mourning and disbelief. From morning to afternoon. Into the night. Bells and horns and drums. We danced. Huge drum circles. Kaleidoscoping spirals of bodies. Arm over arm. Singing and crying and dancing. Nobody slept. You did not want to miss a moment.

At some point though, Kristina and I were delirious with celebration. She was practically asleep on my shoulder. I borrowed a blanket and mattress from Charlie's tent. With the mattress balanced on my head and Kristina on my arm we strolled upriver past the shadowy mounds of other couples with the same idea. I found a flat spot near the river. We lay on our backs. A sky of stars and satellites. Drumming and shouting drifted on the warm air. The happy yelp of a coyote pack in the distance. The river gurgled. I thought Kristina was asleep but then without turning to me she said: I was talking to Katya.

About what?

Well, I want us to have a baby.

Me too, I said, smiling in the dark.

And I think we should move to Nuuk.

Me too.

And start a family.

Me too.

She took my hand and put it on her chest so I could feel the beating muscle of her heart.

And I think we should have a happy life, she said. We should be in love. And never stop fighting to make the world a better place.

Yes. Yes. Yes.

You promise, my love?

I promise.

We made love. Kristina fell asleep with her head on my chest. I massaged her scalp and looked as far as I could into the heart of the universe and decided there was nothing up there or down here in the past or the future that could stop me from being happy.

Then Kristina startled awake. She jerked up.

Did it happen?

She thought she had dreamt the news. I reassured her it was true: we had won.

She rode the ups and downs of it all over again: the joy and sorrow. She was crying. It was so big. And us lying so small beneath the cosmos. She settled back under the blanket.

We won, I whispered. To her. To myself. To my parents and Osman and the universe. It's over. It's really over.

She reached through the dark to put a finger to my lips.

Don't say that, my love, she said in a sleepy voice. It's not over. It's only just begun.

Emi Vargas Brinkman
North American History
Mrs. Helmandi
Great Transition Project (First Draft)

Conclusion

I asked my mom what she would've done if there had never been a climate crisis and she could've lived a totally normal life. She told me she would've liked to be a veterinarian. This was surprising because I've never seen her especially love animals. She won't let me have a pet— not even a cat—no matter how many times I ask. But the more I thought about it, the more I realized how the Great Transition didn't just save people. It saved biomes and prevented entire branches of life from going extinct. So, in some ways, my mom and dad and everyone who fought for the Transition were like the most important veterinarians, caring for the entire planet.

With the big Day Zero celebrations, and parades, and projects like this one, and Transition heroes who come to speak at school every year, it's easy to think the Great Transition was the best thing that ever happened. And in lots of ways, it was. Thanks to the Transition we have cooperatives and cities like Nuuk and more equality than any time in history. And of course, a planet we can live on.

To compare and contrast, however, what if the Great Transition had never happened? What if it had never needed to happen? What if our ancestors had stopped the climate criminals so that we didn't have to hold them responsible now, after the damage has been done? What if people before us had been willing to be a little less comfortable and a little braver so that future generations and animals and biomes wouldn't need to suffer?

In conclusion, without the Climate Crisis and the Great

Transition, my parents never would've fallen in love or even met. My mom might be a veterinarian living happily in San Pedro Tultepec with her sister, Yesenia. My dad would be cutting seaweed in Maine with his family. For sure, I wouldn't be here to write this. But I'd be okay with that. Really. If it meant the Crisis never needed to happen? I'd take that trade. I bet almost anyone would.

AFTER

EMI

Three ways that Nuuk and Windsor-Detroit are total opposites:

Nuuk air is so dry that you can never stop moisturizing; Windsor-Detroit air is warm and humid so you never stop sweating.

Nuuk is one steep hillside; Windsor-Detroit is a pancake.

Nuuk has landscrapers that go underground; Windsor-Detroit has supertowers like spikes puncturing the clouds.

The tallest supertowers are across the Detroit River. The tower my dad and I move into is Fordson Tower, in a neighborhood called Dearborn. Our cohousing community is floors seventy through ninety. My bedroom is on floor eighty-two, which Nika says is lucky because floor eighty-three is CareCorps Juniors, meaning nobody is up there stomping around all night long like the family above her loves to do.

Nika is the only girl my age in our community. They held a big welcome circle when my dad and I arrived. They passed around a talking stick for everyone to say hi. When the stick got to Nika, she looked across the circle at my arm in a sling and said, Well I guess we have to be friends now, so I hope you busted your wing skating and you better like Nirvana.

The rules for a community circle are pretty strict. You're only supposed to talk when you have the stick. But I was new. I didn't know the rules.

I *love* Nirvana! I blurted.

───

Cohousing is so different from how we lived in Nuuk. Here each family gets its own unit, but everyone cooks and eats and makes big decisions as a group. We share day-to-day chores like washing windows and sweeping common spaces. Everyone has hours to fulfill. I do mine at CareCorps. My dad does his in the kitchen. Nika completes hers on the roof farm. She likes the smell of tomato plants on her fingers. And the farm is the only place to get away. To Nika cohousing is hell. Everyone's in each other's business all the time, she says. Don't you hate it?

Actually I kind of like it, I tell her. I like having people around. It feels safe.

Safe? Are you mental? Safe from what? Having a single thought to yourself?

Nika has a big family. A grandmother, both parents, and two cute sisters—Tara and Leela—who I see afternoons in CareCorps. Their mom is insanely kind, always hugging me, trying to feed me, begging me to stay longer. Their home is a hurricane of shoes and screens and toys and Disney songs. I love it. Nika can't wait to leave. Cohousing. Fordson Tower. Windsor-Detroit. Get me out of here, she says.

In spring we get to go to Cleveland, I say.

I don't mean some dumb field trip. I mean for good.

Where would you go?

Anywhere but here.

She comes over most nights after cohousing dinner. Sometimes we do homework on my bed. Sometimes we only pretend to. One wall of my room is solid glass with a view of the supertowers across the river. We lie on the carpet and kick our feet up on the glass and listen to Nirvana and Lauryn Hill. A Tribe Called Quest. No Doubt. Salt-N-Pepa. Nika loves oldies too. She agrees that today's music is bland and forgettable. She's jealous of my recall abilities but says I could be more discerning. According to her, the 1990s are IGAM: the Indisputable Golden Age of Music. Why would anybody listen to anything else when there's the Smashing Pumpkins and TLC and Destiny's Child and the Fugees? Nika is convinced she was born in the wrong era. Imagine seeing Wu-Tang live? Imagine moshing to Rage?

Rage Against the Machine is Nika's favorite when she's angry at her mom. Also Hole and Metallica and Nine Inch Nails. IGAM has something for every occasion, she says.

Why are you angry at your mom? I ask her one night after dinner.

You must *apply* yourself, Nika says in her mother's crisp voice. You must earn better grades. Wear something other than black for once. Be a role model for your sisters. Put on a helmet. Make your bed. No music at the table. What's wrong with you? What will you do with your life?

Hearing Nika complain about her mom makes me remember how easily I could ignite mine. And vice versa: how easily she could set me off. Now I think Nika's problems would be wonderful problems to have. But nobody wants to be told that their problems are small. Instead, I hear myself telling her that my mom died in an extraction duty accident.

I'm so sorry, Selena, Nika says, reaching over to hold my hand.

Thanks, I say.

She doesn't ask anything else. Not then, not since. The extraction duty accident is a great cover story because people feel uncomfortable talking about death. So they say nothing. But sometimes I want them to. I want Nika to ask while we're lying on my soft carpet with the soles of our feet against the cool window glass, Hey Selena, what was your mom like? What do you miss about her? What would you tell her if you could see her again?

Nika calls me Selena because Selena's my name. My dad also calls me Selena. It felt weird at first but even weirder how quickly I got used to it. My dad has the more difficult job. I still get to call him Dad. His name is Andrew. Andy. Andy Grant. Selena Grant. I keep expecting us to slip up in front of people, but we don't. It's surprisingly easy—a relief almost—to pretend.

Just because Nika and I are friends doesn't mean we share everything in common. Nika hates sports, for example, while I try out for basketball. I train hard, running the riverwalk paths. My shoulder is healed but the carbon composite throws off my shot. I only make junior varsity. It's a little embarrassing. I don't join. But my dad insists that I do something after school. He says I have to keep myself busy. Fine. There are other sports. Other clubs. One club is the Global Justice Project. That's the official name. Unofficially people call them the Young Furies. Nika warns me it's all boring, popular girls, but I can't stay away. The club is as close to my mom as I can get.

I show up early for a meeting after last period. Everyone who comes in is very pretty. They all know each other. They're nice to me but in that fake way, like my old basketball team. They cast a huge portrait of Mama Greta on the wall, alongside Wanted posters of climate criminals. Some of the criminals are crossed out. Matthias Barrack is crossed out. He was assassinated the day after Thanksgiving break. I was sitting in English class when it happened. We were discussing a novel called *The Left Hand of Darkness*. You aren't supposed to have screens in class, but everyone does. The news bubbled up until Mr. Andrade finally gave in. We watched a newscast as a class. We discussed morality and revenge. When Mr. Andrade called on me, I shrugged twice, then burst into tears. Everyone stared with their mouths open until Mr. Andrade suggested I visit Ms. Washington, the school counselor. I knocked over my chair on my way out. That was two weeks ago. Now, at the Global Justice Project meeting, the sight of Matthias Barrack isn't such a big deal. I've spent a lot of time on my screen, learning about him and his crimes. I stare at his crossed-out face as the girls go around doing introductions. When it's my turn I say I just moved here and want to get involved.

Great! they say. The big agenda item is a winter dance they're planning in support of the Furies. I'm slightly confused. Support how? Like recruiting people to join?

They smile. Um. More like a demonstration of support. Solidarity. You know?

The rest of the meeting is dedicated to what they'll wear. Who they'll invite. Decorations. Food. Music. I suggest oldies. They say they'll definitely take my suggestion into consideration.

The meeting ends. I don't go back for another. Nika is kind enough not to say she told me so. When my dad keeps asking what I'm going to do to keep busy, I finally tell him that I've joined the after-school RPG club.

RPG? he asks.

Role-playing games. You make up a character and go on quests.

On a VR platform?

No. There's no screens. It's just dice and your imagination. It's complicated. You wouldn't understand.

Really it's more of a friend group than an official after-school club. The group is me and Nika, plus two of her skateboarding friends from another school—Marcos and Maya—and two of their friends— Giacomo and Esme. We meet at the library near the river, where we take over a basement room to blast the Indisputable Golden Age of Music and play this game called Dungeons & Dragons. We're on a quest to save a village from an ice dragon and in the process become filthy rich with treasure. We fight goblins. We slay giant spiders. We're a crew. We have each other's backs. After playing we bag our dice and then we skate.

Nika is a million times more patient teaching me how to skate than she is giving a fair listen to Dolly Parton or Led Zeppelin or The Doors. We start slow, me holding her elbow for balance, then we build up to me pumping solo. She teaches me to never hold my skateboard by the trucks unless I want to become a meme for every skater in the city to ridicule. She teaches me to sneer at battery-

powered decks. She teaches me that the only way to truly learn is
with a nasty first fall, and she hugs me with the widest smile the
afternoon I finally get it over with.

I come home with my forearm dripping blood through my sleeve.
I try to sneak in but my dad catches me wiping up a few stray drops
outside my room.

It looks worse than it is, I say.

He won't hear me. He overreacts like I knew he would. He makes
me tell him what happened, then overreacts even more when it
comes out that I'm not in a real after-school club. He yells at me for
lying. For being reckless. He says Nika is a bad influence.

I yell back at him that I guess he'd rather I start smoking ghost and
having tons of unprotected sex like every other kid at school.

We slam doors. He forbids me from hanging out with Nika or
skateboarding. Which obviously makes me committed to doubling
down on both. He must realize this too, because the next afternoon
he comes home from his cooking shift with a present: a helmet and
elbow pads and wrist guards. His way of saying sorry. And be careful.
And have fun.

———

The best place to skate is the riverwalk, because of the piezoelectric
paths. The same material that generates energy when people walk
also makes the paths the smoothest in all of Windsor-Detroit. Thus
the signs every ten feet:

SKATEBOARDING PROHIBITED

Which is why we must! Nika says in her Dungeons & Dragons
voice. 'Tis the sworn duty among the race of skaters: Thou Must
Shred!

One afternoon we're fulfilling our solemn duty when someone
shouts.

You two! Stop! Right now!

Scatter! says Nika.

I pump as fast as I can to keep up. I hear footsteps behind me and the sound almost knocks me off balance, but I bend my knees and correct the wobble. My heart rams the back of my eyes. My throat. We make some distance, then duck behind a windbelt. Peeking through the coils we watch two Public Safety officers lumber by.

Hiya! says Nika, her breath hot against my neck. That was fun!

Then she sees me shaking. Crying. This time she does not stare at me like she did along with everyone else in English class when I burst into tears at news of Matthias Barrack's assassination. Instead she throws her arms around me. It's just Public Safety, Selena! You saw them. They sit around all day eating donuts. They're old and fat. You're okay. Come here.

She walks me home. I don't leave my room all weekend. I skip school on Monday. And Tuesday and Wednesday. No dungeons. No dragons. No CareCorps. No Nika. I tell my dad I'm sick. Since moving here, I'd gotten better with eating, but now it's like I'm back in Nuuk, gagging on anything solid. I can't help it. My dad makes smoothies that turn warm and watery on my bedstand. He asks over and over, What's wrong? Talk to me, sweetie. Please. He asks me through the door if something happened at school. Or with Nika. Or am I worried about Mom—

Stop! I plead.

Nobody can hear us, he says. It's safe here. It's just us. We can talk if you want to.

I don't, I say. I don't want to.

He says, Okay, sweetie. Just know I'm all ears. I love you so much, Em—

That's not my name, Dad. You can't call me that!

Thursday morning, I refuse again to go to school. I listen to music. I watch clipper ships sail the Detroit River. I ride the wave of my hunger. I hear my dad singing to himself and chopping veggies in our little kitchen. By skipping school all week, I've discovered how my dad spends his days. I hadn't realized he'd become so active. He has his cohousing kitchen shifts and he's also joined the IHOP cooperative; he can't stop telling me how excited they are to get his breakfast nachos on the trial menu. He's always singing or whistling along to something and every day I'm home he invites me to lunch with his new friends at the Forest Corps Veterans' Club. I know I should be happy to see him happy, but I'm not. Instead, I watch myself trying to ignite him. Searching for the right spark. Arguing for the sake of arguing—like Friday morning, when he comes barging in to throw open my curtains and tell me I don't have to go to school but I do have to either help him in the kitchen or invite Nika over after dinner, or else talk to him about whatever's on my mind, whether it's Mom or school, or drugs or sex or whatever—he doesn't care, he says, he's just worried.

Although I would in fact like to talk about my mom, I can't. We can't. It's not safe. Why can't he understand this most simple fact? I'm asking him this question, rather loudly, causing both of us to raise our voices, when there comes a knock at our door.

We look at each other.

Another knock. The sound gives me that feeling of stepping right up to my window and staring down eighty-two stories to the ground. Someone heard us talking. Public Safety. Min. Rich.

Selena? Hello? Mr. Grant?

It's Ms. Washington. Our school counselor. Visiting because I've missed all week, she explains when my dad lets her in. I show her my room. She props open my door and sits on my bed, says that Nika came to her office and told her about my mom.

I'm so sorry, Selena. Grief is incredibly difficult. We can't simply pick it up and put it down. We have to carry it. Sometimes for years. Often for life.

Okay, I say. So how?

———

The bereavement group isn't mandatory, but I keep going. I like Ms. Washington. I like the other kids. They're nice and good at listening and some like to flirt, which is weird because it's bereavement, but also not weird because we know so much about each other. This one boy, Emmanuel, whose dad died from cancer, keeps making eye contact with me. At first I think he's figured out I'm an imposter whose mother isn't really dead. But then it becomes clear that he just likes me. And I stop feeling like an imposter when I realize I share the same issues as him and everyone else. Like them, I get to talk about someone I loved who's no longer in my life. What I wished I'd said. What I wish I hadn't. What I miss most. What annoyed me most. What I'm doing to carry the grief. Everyone nods when I talk about skateboarding and music and Dungeons & Dragons and friends.

One day, after Ms. Washington dismisses us, Emmanuel walks straight up to me.

Um, hey, he says.

Hey.

Got a second?

Sure.

Nika's waiting for me outside like she always does after bereavement. We have a tradition. We go skating and blast music and no talking allowed. We just ride and see where we end up. But today also happens to be the Global Justice Project's winter dance. I'm both hoping and dreading that Emmanuel is about to ask me.

I'm a dragonborn warlock, he says.

Huh?

Dungeons and Dragons. I play too. I'm Dark Blade. I breathe lightning.

Hiya, I say.

There's an uncomfortable pause. We walk into the hallway. Nika's leaning by the elevator with her skateboard as usual. She looks up from her screen and sees Emmanuel by my side. She and I make eyes at each other as we step onto the elevator. Doors close.

Nika, this is Emmanuel. He plays too. He's a warlock named Dark Knife.

Dark Blade, he corrects. Ninth level.

I'm tenth level, Nika says. My name's Alludra. I'm a half-elf ranger.

What about you? Emmanuel asks me.

Oh, I'm only third level. I just started. I'm just a halfling rogue.

Just a halfling rogue? Nika scoffs. People think she's this quiet little hobbit but then *blink* and they're dead. She's stealthy and hilarious and she earned a feat called Second Chance so she can force a reroll and change the course of history. She rescues our asses every single day.

We could use you on our campaign, Emmanuel says. We don't have a rogue.

The elevator doors open to a blast of cold wind. We step onto the street under gray skies.

So you want to play sometime? he asks.

Okay.

Okay. Bye.

Nika and I are all giggles as we jump on our boards and kick off, our hair blowing behind us. No set destination. Nika blasts Nirvana so loud that we almost miss Emmanuel yelling.

Wait! Hold up!

Someone's getting invited to a dance, Nika teases me as we skid to a stop.

Shut up, I say.

What's your name? Emmanuel yells from the corner.

Selena! I yell back.

No! Your character! The halfling rogue!

I cup my hands around my mouth for maximum volume.

Emi, I shout. My name is Emi!

ACKNOWLEDGMENTS

The Great Transition—like every book, like everything we build as humans—is a project of the collective. The novel would not be here without an enormous number of supporters, editors, mentors, friends, family, and collaborators—a group too large to name, but here's my best shot:

Big thanks to literary-agent-superhero Danielle Bukowski, for handling everything with such calm and confidence while working ever-diligently behind the scenes. Thank you Orly Greenberg for launching the novel beyond the page. Thanks to Will Wolfslau, Samantha Fingerhut, Emily Nemens, and especially Jillian Buckley. This book would still be fifty pages on my desktop if not for your selfless help in nudging it along.

Thanks to Sean deLone and the team at Atria Books. You took the novel into your care and made it shine. Sean, thanks for believing from day one. Thank you, Dominick Montalto and Liz Byer, for poring over every word. Thank you, Kyoko Watanabe, James Iacobelli, and Danielle Mazzella di Bosco, for your taste and artistic eye. Thanks, Holly Rice-Baturin, Maudee Genao, Morgan Hoit, Nicole Bond, and every single person on the all-star marketing team, for bringing the novel into the greater world. And thank you, Libby McGuire, Dana Trocker, Lindsay Sagnette, Peter Borland, and

Paige Lytle, for captaining the ship that is Atria. I'm grateful to be aboard.

Thanks to the teachers! Irwin Fischer, for second and fifth grade; Chris Dubose, for high school. Hasanthika Sirisena, Thaïs Miller, and Calvin Hennick, for Gotham Writers' Workshop and Grub Street. Thanks to Jayne Anne Phillips and Alice Elliott Dark, who took a chance on my writing (and my civil disobedience arrest record) to gift me the two best years a writer could ask for. Thanks also to Rigoberto Gonzales, Tayari Jones, and Akhil Sharma for that most stellar education.

Thanks to the first readers: Nienke Schuler, Will Urmston, and Far Urmston. Your early encouragement and feedback went all the way. Thanks to Chef Seth for help with Larch's culinary skills, and to the Kalwani brothers for their burn-ward and ER experiences. So many thanks to the friend-consultancy-cheerleading crew, for the love, the advice, the jokes: Ben, Geoff, Madelaine, Will, Greg, Kat, Sophia, Katrina, Joe, Eric, Kelly H., Sarah, Kelly D., Christine, Tom, Allison, and Matt.

Thanks most of all to those who made me: my brother, Ben, my first and oldest friend, for teaching me early how to live a life of wild imagination, laughs, and creativity. My mother and father, for filling our home with books and warmth and love, and always steering us on the path toward happiness. And to Lizzy, my partner in art and joy, thank you for everything. You kept the ember glowing at the darkest moments. You are my fire. I love you.